PROLOGUE

Château de Montségur, France, 16 March 1244

In the castle's main hall, Knight Jean de Combel, his once proud frame thinned and bent by months of starvation, knelt hesitantly before The Perfect One and swore the consolamentum, the Cathar's final oath. Besieged and without hope, the Cathars were about to surrender their fortress to Hugues des Arcis and his 6,000 Catholics. Defeat and death lurked patiently, their aura already permeating the thick stone walls of the castle's rooms. De Combel crossed himself then rose, looking anxiously across the room for his young son Pierre.

After a moment de Combel spotted him standing next to two older boys, the sons of The Perfect One. He signaled Pierre to join him, took his son by the arm and ushered him into an empty room. De Combel locked the door, then turned and faced the boy. 'Pierre, you must escape, flee this madness.'

His son stared at him in bewilderment. 'I, I want to be with you, Father,' he said, wrapping his emaciated arms around his father's waist.

The knight looked upwards, fighting back tears of pain and sorrow. Images of the massacres at Béziers, Lavaur and Minerve flew briefly before him. Bloodied ground everywhere, raped women screaming for mercy, heads of children . . . children for God's sake . . . on soldiers' spikes. He steeled himself. No, not Pierre, not my son. He bent down, took the young boy's head between his hands and kissed it. 'Pierre, you are small. You can get through. You can avoid the sentries. They're—'

'No, no. I want to stay,' pleaded the boy as he gripped his father's waist with all his might.

De Combel tore himself free and dropped to his knees. Holding his son's thin shoulders, he looked fixedly into the frightened eyes. 'Listen to me, Pierre. Tomorrow we surrender. You must escape. You must carry on our faith.'

The boy's shoulders convulsed and he began to cry.

'None of that. You're a man now. You must go. You must survive. Do you understand?'

'Yes, Father,' he answered meekly between sobs.

'That's better. Now promise me, Pierre, never, never recant your faith.'

'I promise.'

De Combel hugged his son for a long moment, then handed him a small leather pouch. 'Take this, go to the village and give one écu to Godefroi. Keep the rest for food and shelter. Tell Godefroi to take you to Genoa, to your aunt Jordane. You'll be safe there. Now go,' he said and thrust him away.

In the moonless night, the boy, crying softly, squeezed through the small hidden opening in the castle's outer wall, careful to avoid the Catholic sentries' scrutiny. He made his way cautiously down the steep trail from the mountain peak to the safety of the dense woods below, the woods he loved and knew so well. Finding an old rotted trunk, he lay on the soft moss beside it and fell into a restless sleep. Throughout the night, fits of fear mixed with the hurt of separation prodded him awake.

THE CHIMERA SANCTION

A fast-paced, action-packed international thriller

ANDRÉ K. BABY

JOFFE BOOKS

Revised edition 2021
Joffe Books, London
www.joffebooks.com

First published by Robert Hale in Great Britain in 2014

This book is a work of fiction. Names, characters, businesses, organizations, places and events are either the product of the author's imagination or are used fictitiously. Any resemblance to actual persons, living or dead, events or locales is entirely coincidental. The spelling used is British English except where fidelity to the author's rendering of accent or dialect supersedes this.

Cover art by Jarmila Takač

ISBN: 978-1-78931-958-3

Now it was dawn. The crackling of a fire and the smell of burning wood roused him from his tormented sleep. Dizzy with hunger, the boy crept to the edge of a small clearing on the outskirts of the woods. In the middle of the clearing, the Catholics had built a huge pyre.

Alongside stood a staircase, its timbers glazed with mud to prevent it from burning. Purification by fire, thought Pierre. His father had warned of the Catholics' horrific punishment that awaited any unrepentant Cathar. Dread overtook the boy. Peering from behind a large oak, he watched the soldiers as they fed the fire with large branches of pine.

The fire reawakened his thirst. He stared at the Catholics, hatred in his heart, when suddenly the memory of that day resurfaced: soft singing, peals of laughter while she played in the courtyard with her doll. Then, without warning, the dull thud of the stone, hurled by the Catholics' catapult. The singing stopped. He'd rushed outside to see her small body, lifeless, lying in a pool of blood. His little sister Anne . . .

He pushed away the horrible vision. The flames rose higher, their orange hue licking the sides and top of the wooden pyre. Around its base, the Cathars sat on the damp grass in small groups, their hands tied, praying quietly. As Pierre searched in vain for his father among the groups of seated Cathars, a ray of hope began to form, lifting his spirit. Had the knight escaped?

The crackling of burning branches suddenly broke the spell and even from where he stood at the edge of the clearing, Pierre began to feel the pyre's increasing heat. To his left, a hundred yards away, a row of knights on horseback sat waiting while their squires, bridles in hand, tried to control their nervous steeds. A movement, a jostle within the column and suddenly a knight broke rank, advanced and pointed his sword at a Cathar sitting close to the pyre. The Cathar rose, and the soldier beside him led him to the base of the staircase. As he started upwards, the Cathar appeared calm, resigned, purposeful, as if transported by his faith. As he reached the top, a gust of wind sent flames swirling around his tunic and it caught fire. The man looked upwards briefly, hesitated for a moment then fell into the blaze.

A collective gasp, then silence interrupted the Cathars' praying below. The knight on horseback signaled again, and soldiers began prodding the Cathars up the staircase, into the raging inferno.

The boy stared in horror as moments later, his Uncle Robert de Sasseville fell into the pyre and hung, impaled on the half-burnt trunk of a large pine until the fiery timber broke and his body dropped to the embers below. Pierre choked back a cry and started to shake.

The smoke's color changed from gray to brown and the fire abated slightly, now fueled by human flesh. Gradually, a nauseating sweet stench filled the air. The boy turned away, bent over behind the tree and vomited until finally, his stomach empty of bile, his retching stopped. He got up weakly and peered from behind the tree, mesmerized by the horrific scene. He watched transfixed as the Cathars, as though in a trance, kept ascending the massive staircase. Women followed their husbands, pulling their children up, up the steps of death. Suddenly Pierre saw the knight point his sword to a Cathar, seated alone. 'Father,' the boy uttered, and his shoulders started to convulse again.

A soldier grabbed de Combel's arm, but he shrugged free. De Combel got up, his gaze taking in the remaining Cathars. 'Courage my friends,' he shouted. 'Today we meet again in Heaven.' He walked up the staircase, stood defiantly on the last step and yelled, 'Long live Montségur! Long live the Cathars!'

De Combel turned and plunged headfirst into the holocaust.

CHAPTER 1

Mount Assiniboine, Canadian Rockies

Inside the alpine shelter, nestled in the warmth of his duvet sleeping bag, Thierry Dulac looked at his watch: 6:25 a.m. He noticed the rain had finally stopped its relentless pounding on the Hind Hut's aluminum roof. Beside him Karen was still fast asleep, snoring peacefully. Dulac rose from the uncomfortable wood cot, stretched his tall, thin frame, and dressed quickly. They would have to start their ascent soon if they were to summit and get back down before dark. He rummaged in his backpack for the small Icom VHF radio and went to the hut's door, opening it discreetly. Outside, the air was damp, windless. A thin gauze of mist hung precariously over the valley below, its veil beginning to evaporate under the heat of the morning light. Behind the hut, Mount Assiniboine's daunting pyramid rose imperially, its outline etched into the mauve sky. 'The Matterhorn of the Rockies', boasted the lodge's brochure. And just as dangerous, Dulac thought. He inhaled deeply, savoring the purity of the thin atmosphere, then glanced at the thermometer on the side of the hut. It read -3°C. Perfect for summiting.

Dulac turned on his VHF radio and pressed the small WX button, the weather channel. The electronic voice droned in a monotone, interspersed with static: 'This is the 6 a.m . . . forecast for the greater . . . which includes Mount Magog, Mount Assiniboine, The Marshall and . . . A hazardous weather warning is in effect from 11 a.m. to 4 p.m. today. A strong cold front is moving . . . Winds of . . . to 60 km an hour, with gusts to 80. Expect heavy snowfall, up to 25 cm in higher elevations. Repeat, a hazardous . . . warning is . . .'

Damn. A spring blizzard. Just our luck. He stood looking at the mountain, its peak clear, inviting. A cool chill ran up his spine at the thought of how quickly mountain weather could change, how deadly it could become. The memory of Mount Mercedario started to resurface. He willed himself not to dwell on it, pushing it back into the recesses of his subconscious. After a moment Dulac, despondent, returned to the warmth of the prefabricated hut, went to the cot, and gently shook Karen's shoulder.

'Karen, wake up.'

'What time is it?' she said drowsily.

'It's get-off-the-mountain time.'

'What?' Karen sat up abruptly, pushing aside wisps of hair from her face. 'What do you mean?'

'The weather just went south. There's a blizzard coming in. We've got to get back down.'

'But last night's forecast was fantastic.'

'This morning's is downright ugly.'

'Shit! Just once I'd like to get a hold of one of those meteorologists and . . .'

'There's plenty of time if we leave now. It's five hours to the lodge. We'll be down and off Gmoser's Highway before the storm hits.'

'And then what?'

'We wait it out at the lodge and try again later. We still have a full week.'

'But we're so close to summiting. Why not wait here?'

'And risk being trapped? No thanks. That storm could last a day, maybe a week. I . . . I . . .' Mercedario flashed before Dulac's eyes. His younger brother Eric . . .

'What is it, Thierry?'

'Nothing. It's just a . . . Nothing. We must go.'

After a breakfast of tepid, glue-like oatmeal downed with cups of rancid coffee, they finished packing their gear. While Dulac adjusted the scope of their walking poles for the descent, Karen tidied up the inside of the hut. Moments later, they started their downward trek to Assiniboine Lodge, the clanging of their poles against the path's stones marking their brisk, steady pace.

An hour later, the path had widened. On either side, the dull green lichen had given way to buds of yellow cinquefoils and pods of white avens, piercing through a luxuriant bed of purple saxifrage. Dulac was admiring nature's rich bounty when something far ahead on the horizon caught his attention. He stopped short. Karen, following a few steps behind, smacked into his backpack.

'Hey, careful,' she said, annoyance in her voice.

'Look.' Dulac pointed to the speck in the distance.

The speck grew quickly, until Dulac could see the distinct bubble and skids of a helicopter and hear the rhythmic whirring of its blades. The helicopter approached, slowed, then began to hover, a hundred yards away. Dulac recognized the red Canadian maple leaf insignia on the helicopter's yellow tail, surmounted by large red letters: SAR. Search and Rescue. That's odd. Why . . . ? Suddenly, Dulac's satellite phone started ringing in his backpack. He threw the pack off his shoulders and grabbed the phone.

'Dulac.'

'This is Search and Rescue chopper Bravo Juliet Uniform. Are you Inspector Thurley Doolake?'

'Thierry Dulac, yes?'

'We're coming down.'

'Why? We're fine.' Dulac threw an inquisitive glance at Karen and hunched his shoulders in bafflement.

The pilot didn't answer and the helicopter landed, coming to rest slightly off-kilter to the right of the path. The chopper's blades were still rotating slowly when a helmeted man jumped from the open side-door and made his way towards the couple.

'We have orders to pick you up, you and Ms Dawson,' said the man, lifting his helmet's visor.

Dulac looked quizzically at Karen, then back to the man, busy rubbing his left eye. 'From whom?'

'From our base colonel in Edmonton. It's urgent.'

'What's this about?'

'Don't know. I just execute. Something to do with a secretary general or something?'

'You mean the General Secretary of Interpol?'

'That's it.'

'We'll see about that,' said Dulac, fuming that Harris had interrupted his first vacation in three years. He punched Harris' number into the sat phone. After three rings, the all too familiar voice came on.

'Harris.'

'Dulac. We're being told to get into an SAR 'copter, supposedly on your orders?'

'Don't talk. Your phone is corrupt. They've hacked our lines. See you back here in a few hours.'

'But why . . . ?'

'Just get on the damn chopper.'

The line went dead.

CHAPTER 2

'Where are we headed?' yelled Karen to Dulac, seeking reassurance in the Frenchman's deep-set brown eyes.

'I'll ask the pilot,' said Dulac. After a moment, he turned to Karen. 'Canadian Forces Base, Edmonton.'

'But our things are at Assiniboine Lodge.'

'They picked them up earlier,' he said and pointed to the suitcases behind them. Karen looked at Dulac in stupefaction. As the Griffon banked steeply left, she caught a last glimpse of the arched-shaped Hind Hut, their love nest for a night. Behind it, Mt Assiniboine surged suddenly into view, its sharp summit piercing the cloudless azure sky. Karen felt the pang of yet another foreshortened vacation coming rapidly to an end. And it was going so well.

Dulac's resentment was growing by the minute. See you back in Europe in a few hours? Is he drunk? It's at least thirteen hours from Edmonton to Paris by the polar route. Even more if we fly east. Harris was not in the habit of being inaccurate. At least not when sober.

Just as Dulac strapped himself into the narrow seat, the rotor's vibrations shook the helicopter, awakening his old demons again. He nervously ran his fingers through his thick locks. He hated flying. 'Flying is strictly for the birds,' he'd proclaimed during a dinner with Rebecca, the humorless airline pilot, after enduring her endless lecture on landing an Airbus 360 with only one engine. She'd ended their relationship that night.

He was beginning to feel nauseous when Karen pointed out the window. 'Look down there. Mount Magog. Beautiful, isn't it?'

'I suppose.'

An hour later, the fog wrapped itself around the low-flying Griffon and the pilot, adjusting the main rotor's pitch, signaled their impending arrival. As they landed and the din subsided, Dulac could hear Karen mumbling something to the co-pilot. He nudged her.

'Just asking him why we're going to Edmonton,' she said. 'He doesn't know.'

It was raining hard, and as they followed the pilot and co-pilot towards the small, gray building, Dulac shot a side-glance at Karen. Despondency and reproach were sketched all over her face.

'Inspector Dulac, Ms Dawson, I presume,' said a mustachioed, bald-headed man standing in the open doorway of the building, clad in a beige and maroon uniform one size too small for his bulging gut. 'I'm Colonel John Pettigrew, senior officer, CFB Edmonton. I—'

'What the hell is this all about, Colonel?' interrupted Dulac. 'Why all this cloak and dagger crap?'

'I haven't the foggiest. I was told to pick you up, you and Ms Dawson.'

'Why are we at your base, Colonel?' Dulac said, glaring at Pettigrew.

'You'll see. It should be coming in any minute,' said Pettigrew, almost nonchalant. He went behind the small counter and reached underneath it, pulling out a clipboard and pen. 'We need you both to sign here. Government formalities. By the way, Mr Dulac, have you had a medical recently?'

'What bloody business is that of yours?'

'Just a precaution,' said Pettigrew, holding up his right hand defensively.

At that moment, the unmistakable wail of a jet engine on final approach pierced the opaque fog. Not knowing exactly why, Dulac felt his stomach lurch.

'That will be your limo, sir,' said Pettigrew, pointing to the tarmac and bending over slightly like an obsequious bell-hop.

The F-16 Viper attack fighter emerged menacingly from the fog. Dulac watched, incredulous, as its gray, lithe shape taxied slowly down the runway onto the tarmac. A hundred feet from the terminal, the Viper turned its missile-like nose toward the building and came to a stop.

'Merde,' said Dulac, butting his cigarette on the edge of the water fountain.

'We've arranged for Ms Dawson to take the next commercial flight to Paris,' said Pettigrew.

Dulac watched as the yellow and white fuel truck pulled up alongside the Viper and a man stepped out and went to the rolled-up hose at the back of the truck. The pilot signaled to him. After affixing the hose to the jet's fuselage, the man began quenching the gray bird's thirst for JP-8 kerosene. The canopy opened, the pilot alighted nimbly from the aircraft and walked towards the building, carrying an extra flight suit and helmet.

'Buongiorno. I'm Captain Emilio Zegna, Royal Italian Air Force, Roma base,' said the short, black haired man with a hooked nose, as he entered the doorway. He looked about the room. 'I am here to pick up inspector Thierry Dulac. Is—?'

'I'm Dulac,' Dulac said, turning away from the window.

'Yes, hello inspector, these are for you,' said the pilot, handing Dulac the suit and helmet. 'We leave as soon as they finish refueling.'

Dulac shook his head in disbelief. 'You want me to get into that?' he said, pointing at the F-16.

'We're due back in five hours.'

Pettigrew looked askance at Zegna. 'Captain, Italy is at least three thousand miles from here over the Arctic. You refueled at—'

'In midair,' interrupted the pilot in a condescending tone, as if stating the obvious.

'Resolute could have handled it,' said Pettigrew. He eyed Dulac. 'They must want you there in a helluva hurry.'

'Think so?' Dulac said, grudgingly tugging the flight suit over his damp fleece shirt. He glared at Karen. 'Don't you dare comment.'

'I didn't say a word,' she said, unable to suppress a smile. 'See you in Paris, Thierry.' She tossed her hair back, leaned forward and kissed him.

'Want to trade places?' said Dulac.

'No thanks.'

Dulac followed the Italian toward the door, when Zegna pointed to the building's restroom sign.

'Better use the facilities here. It's a bit tight in the cockpit.'

'I'm fine.'

As they walked to the plane, Dulac felt his level of discomfort rising, fueled by something more than the imminent plane trip. What could possibly justify Interpol commandeering an F-16? It has to be catastrophic. 'Anything terrible happen in the world recently?' he asked Zegna.

'The usual,' he said with an indifferent shrug. 'Yesterday two car bombings in Baghdad, one in Afghanistan.'

'In Italy?'

'The bus drivers. Always the bus drivers. Their third strike in two years.'

They reached the F-16 and Zegna helped Dulac up the ladder into the tiny rear seat. Dulac squeezed himself in and fumbled with the helmet.

'Here, let me help you,' said Zegna, as he adjusted and tightened the helmet's strap under Dulac's chin.

'Thanks. Now what do I do?'

'Nothing. Do not touch anything. Just sit back and enjoy.'

'Yeah, sure. Where are we headed?'

'Roma.'

Dulac felt the voltage increase within his central nervous system in anticipation of takeoff. Meanwhile Zegna went through his lengthy cockpit check, flipping the occasional toggle-switch and lever. Seemingly content with the result, he flipped a final switch and the big GE engine rumbled to life, its low pitch slowly increasing to a hissing whine. Zegna released the brakes and the jet slowly taxied off the tarmac and onto the main runway.

Hands sweating, Dulac inhaled and exhaled deeply as Zegna lined up the F-16 on the runway's white line and waited for the green light from the control tower. Suddenly, the GE engine burst into a deafening roar, its 32,000 pounds of thrust compressing Dulac helplessly into the seat-back. His head snapped back like a rag doll, as he felt the skin of his face tighten against his jaw and cheekbones. His eyes watered, blurring his vision.

The Viper screamed, and in an instant the runway had disappeared from underneath it. Dulac felt the gray, shapeless sky envelop him, as he hurtled into it at close to the speed of sound. His spine tingled not so much with fear, but with sheer amazement. Despite his phobia, he couldn't help but marvel at man's invention of such a compact, efficient, awesome weapon.

Moments later, the Viper pierced through the clouds and broke into the calm of a cobalt sky. As Zegna throttled back to cruising speed, the angry wail of the jet engine became a dull drone.

'Bellissimo, eh?' said Zegna over his helmet's intercom.

'I suppose,' said Dulac. 'When do we get to Rome?'

'Not so soon. First we have to refuel.'

'I don't see any gas stations.'

'Very funny. We have better: they come to us.'

Dulac looked down inside the cramped cockpit and rubbed the numbness from his long legs, squeezed by the

Kevlar sides of his unpadded seat. 'Not much room here. How do the Americans get into these?'

'Only the short, skinny ones. Not many qualify.'

As opposed to all Italians, Dulac thought.

Two and a half hours into their flight, Dulac was still trying to decipher the intricacies of the instrument panel's dials, switches and toggles, when Zegna signaled him to look ahead.

The F-16 slowed and the silhouette of a Boeing 707 appeared through the front of the canopy, slightly overhead. Dulac could see a long, fixed appendage extending from the underbelly of the Boeing.

'Now it's getting tricky,' said Zegna over the intercom. 'We get three tries.'

'Why only three?'

'We run out of fuel,' said Zegna.

'You've got to be kidding.'

'Not kidding.'

'Don't we have parachutes?'

'We're over the Arctic Ocean. It's -80°C outside. We are very dead before we hit the water.'

'Great. Just pissing great,' mumbled Dulac.

As Zegna aimed the F-16 towards the funnel at the end of the tube, the F-16 bolted up suddenly. 'Air pocket,' said Zegna, narrowly missing the Boeing's fueling funnel with the F-16's nose. Dulac gasped, frozen rigid in his seat. Goddamn Italian cowboy. Probably drives a taxi in Rome in his spare time.

Zegna waited until the F-16 steadied, and approached again. Dulac watched him making minute corrections with the joystick and throttle, when suddenly the Boeing suddenly lurched sideways and Dulac saw the funnel alongside his head, inches away from the F-16's canopy.

'Jesus, can't you—?'

Suddenly, a loud beeping interrupted the hissing sound of the jet's motor. 'What's that?' Dulac said.

'Low fuel, first warning.'

'Great, just pissing great.' Dulac instinctively grabbed his knees in a vice-like grip, as the funnel slowly eased forward. Zegna was silent. He steadied the Viper and again approached the funnel with the Viper's antenna-like fueling pod.

'Contact,' Zegna shouted to the Boeing's crew.

'Synchronize autopilots,' a voice replied over the intercom.

'OK,' said Zegna.

'Beginning fueling,' said the voice.

Zegna turned his head back towards Dulac. 'No swimming today.'

Two hours later, the clouds thinned for a moment and Dulac could see the glitter of Rome's lights below. He heard Zegna obtain landing clearance from Guidonia Air Base's control tower and moments later, the Viper swung onto final approach and lined up between the blue lights of the runway's narrow corridor. Dulac read the clock repeater inside the cockpit and adjusted his watch: 9.02 p.m., local time. He sensed Zegna throttling back and the plane begin to decelerate when, to his horror, Zegna nonchalantly raised both hands and clasped them behind his head.

Dulac went ballistic. 'Jesus! What the hell are you doing?'

The runway was coming up to greet the F-16 with alarming rapidity, the soft blue lights a continuous blur. Zegna calmly pointed to the label under the switch: Computer Landing Program.

'Below 220 km per hour, the F-16 has negative stability,' he said. 'The computer compensates quickly. Some pilots have very fast reflexes. They land without it. Me, I don't take any chances.'

'Great. Just pissing great.'

The Viper bounced on touchdown, and Dulac sucked in air and drew back. As the jet's speed slowed, his moist hands gradually unclasped the armrests of his seat, the end of his suffering finally in sight.

As they walked towards Guidonia Airbase's limestone buildings, Zegna turned to Dulac and said, 'Great trip, yes?'

'I hate, hate fucking flying. Capisci?' replied Dulac, reaching for his pack of Gitanes. Zegna gave him a disconcerted look and shrugged. 'Too bad for you.'

'By the way, you were joking when you said "Only three tries", right?'

'Of course,' said Zegna, a sardonic smile forming from the right corner of his thin-lipped mouth.

'Asshole,' Dulac whispered.

They approached the building and Dulac saw Harris, clad in a beige overcoat, step out of a black limo and wave him over.

'Enjoy the ride?' Harris shouted as Dulac walked towards the limo.

Son of a bitch knows I hate flying. 'Great fun,' Dulac replied, bent on robbing his boss, the General Secretary, of his perverted satisfaction. 'What the hell's all this about?'

Harris didn't answer, standing in front of the limo, hands in his pockets.

Dulac reached the limo and could see a small flag on the front fender, but in the darkness, couldn't make out the flag's insignia.

'Get in,' said Harris.

Dulac butted his cigarette. He stooped to enter, saw the man seated inside and froze. He recognized the sad, heavy-lidded blue eyes, the large Roman nose: 'Cardinal Legnano, what are you doing here?' Dulac stared in disbelief at the Secretary of State of the Vatican, the most influential man in the Catholic Church after the Pope.

'Good evening, Mr Dulac. Please be seated.'

He sat down and the cardinal, his face haggard and drawn in the dim reading lights of the limo, said in a barely audible voice, 'It happened this morning. It's the Pope.'

CHAPTER 3

The Vatican, 2.37 a.m., Monday, 22 May

The increasing pain was pulling him from the quiet of sleep. His chest was being crushed by a huge invisible hand that pressed relentlessly. Pope Clement XXI sat up in his bed and the pain eased slightly. Sweating profusely, he turned on the reading light and peered at the bedside clock: 2:37 a.m. He tried to calm himself as his mind raced in a thousand directions. Was it something I ate? Must be the Polish sausages and pierogis. He tried to feel his pulse but couldn't. Then the pain spread to his left arm. He grabbed the buzzer beside his bed and pressed. Moments later, he heard a subdued knock on the door.

'Come in, sister.'

Sister Vincenza opened the door and walked in hesitantly. 'Your Holiness called?'

'Yes sister, I, I don't feel well . . . I—'

'I'll call Dr Bruscetti,' said the small, gray-haired nun.

'No it's all right. Probably just indigestion. Just give me a glass of water, will you sister?'

'Of course, your Holiness.' She went to the bedside table, opened the bottle and poured its contents into the glass. 'Here you are.'

He sat up in his bed, drank slowly and handed the empty glass to the nun. 'Feeling better, your Holiness?'

The pontiff winced, and brought his right hand up to his chest. 'Perhaps you should call Cardinal Legnano. I, I—'

'Right away, your Holiness.'

As Secretary of State of the Vatican, Cardinal Legnano was an extremely busy man. He worked long hours and needed every minute of his precious sleep. After the third ring, he reached for the bedside phone.

'Yes?'

'Your Eminence, it's Sister Vincenza. I'm sorry to disturb you. I know it's—'

'What is it, Sister?' said Legnano.

'It's His Holiness. He's not well. I didn't know what—'

'Did you call Dr Bruscetti?'

'His Holiness said he didn't want me to disturb him.'

'I'll be right over.'

Legnano called the Pope's personal physician, Dr Flavio Bruscetti, then grabbed his nightgown and rushed down the hall and along the dimly-lit corridor leading to the papal apartments. He nodded to the two Swiss Guards on sentry duty on either side of the door, knocked and entered. Across the room, Pope Clement XXI was sitting in bed, propped up against the pillows, his hair disheveled, his face a deathly gray. Sister Vincenza, a look of worry on her face, rose quickly from the bedside chair and offered it to the cardinal.

'What is it, your Holiness?' said Legnano as he sat down.

'It's nothing. It must be the pierogis. I don't know. I—' The pontiff put a hand to his chest and grimaced.

Legnano heard voices behind him and turned. The short, rotund doctor Bruscetti, his bluish gray mane accentuating the tan of his oval face, rushed past the Swiss Guards to the pontiff's bedside. 'Your Holiness, cardinal, sister.'

'Hello doctor,' said the Pope, 'it's really nothing. Please sister, give me my handkerchief.'

'Let's take a look, shall we?' said Bruscetti.

Legnano got up, watching anxiously as Bruscetti proceeded to check the pontiff's pulse and blood pressure.

'What is it, doctor?' asked the Holy Father.

'Nothing serious, but I want you to take some tests. We'll go to the hospital for an electrocardiogram. Right now, just try to relax, your Holiness. Are you feeling any pain?'

'It's my chest. It feels like it's in a vice.'

'I'll give you a sedative,' said the doctor, reaching into his medical bag. He took out a small bottle of morphine, filled a syringe and pressed the needle into the Pope's arm.

Cardinal Legnano was standing slightly behind and to the side of Bruscetti when Bruscetti turned and motioned Legnano to the doorway. The doctor rose from the bedside and, his face ashen, walked over to Legnano. 'He's had a heart attack,' Legnano whispered. 'We must get him to the hospital. Every minute counts.'

'*Mio Dio*,' exclaimed Legnano. 'I'll call for the ambulance.'

'I'll get the guards to bring the stretcher,' said Bruscetti. Legnano paced to and fro, as the phone kept ringing.

'Come on, come on . . .'

'Emergency.'

'Legnano here. Get the ambulance over here immediately. The Pope—'

'It's not here, your Eminence,' replied the voice. 'It's being serviced.'

'Good God.' Legnano hung up and shouted to the Swiss Guard. 'Get me the papal helicopter pilot's number.'

The guard snapped into action, opened his cell and scrolled down.

'Here, your Eminence,' he said, as he rushed towards Legnano and showed him the number. Legnano dialed.

'Yes?'

'Cardinal Legnano here. The Pope has had a heart attack. We must get him to the hospital. Get the helicopter ready. We'll meet you there.'

'Yes, your Eminence.'

Legnano thought for a moment. The helipad was at the northern extremity of the Vatican. It would take forever to carry the Pope through the corridors and streets of the Vatican to reach it. He phoned the pilot again. 'It will be faster if you meet us in St Peter's Square. Hurry.'

'Understood, your Eminence.'

Legnano called the Agostino Gemelli Clinic, its tenth floor reserved exclusively for the Pope on a 24-7 basis. 'Cardinal Legnano. Get me the emergency doctor.'

A high-pitched voice came on the line. 'Donatello.'

'Doctor, I'm Cardinal Legnano, calling from the Vatican. I'm here with Dr Bruscetti. His Holiness has had a heart attack. We're flying him over by helicopter now.'

'*Mio Dio*. We . . . we'll be waiting.'

Legnano watched, fear in his heart as the two Swiss Guards entered the Pope's apartment with the wheeled stretcher and gently eased the pontiff, now barely conscious, onto it. Legnano leaned towards the stricken Pope. 'How do you feel, your Holiness?'

'I've felt better. It's my heart, isn't it?'

Legnano nodded silently. They hurried down the corridor to the elevator, and Legnano heard Bruscetti instruct one of the Swiss Guards: 'Have the defibrillator brought on the helicopter. Bring the oxygen tank also.'

The cortege rushed outside the building, down the dark passageway and through the eastern colonnade of St Peter's just as the Huey appeared and landed in the middle of the square. Legnano breathed heavily, the cool damp air filling his lungs, as he tried to keep up to the Swiss Guards while they wheeled the stretcher alongside the awaiting chopper. The guards crouched and carefully transferred the stretcher inside the helicopter, then helped the pilot and co-pilot secure it to the chopper's floor.

'I'm coming with him. I'm his doctor,' yelled Bruscetti to the pilot over the din of the rotor. The pilot took him by the arm and helped him aboard, then closed the helicopter's door.

The motor's whine became strident, as Legnano stood shivering in the cold of the night, sick with worry and impatient for the helicopter to take off. Through the canopy, he could see the reflection of the dimly-lit cockpit shining on the pilot's opaque visor. The pilot turned and nodded to him before easing the chopper up into the moonless night.

Legnano hurried back to his office, determination and purpose over-riding the maelstrom of his anxiety. I must hope for the best, but prepare for the worst. He called the members of the inner Curia, the Pope's most trusted advisors, to an emergency meeting in his office.

Five minutes later, the four cardinals started arriving in Legnano's office, each query the same: 'How bad is it?'

'I don't know,' said Legnano, pacing by the window. 'I'm awaiting news from the hospital.'

'A heart attack? He's never shown any signs of a weak heart,' said the portly cardinal Paolo Signorelli, the Pope's personal secretary, sinking deeply into the leather sofa.

'Perhaps Bruscetti was wrong. Maybe it's only indigestion,' interjected Cardinal Eugenio Brentano, head of The Congregation for the Doctrine of the Faith and keeper of the Church's sacred doctrine.

'The pierogis, I've told him many times,' chimed in the head of Investments and Information, the diminutive and bespectacled Cardinal Andrea Sforza. He wagged a remonstrative hand. 'Too many pierogis.'

'He's strong. He'll pull through,' said the tall, thin Camerlengo, Cardinal Jean Fouquet.

'Let's pray he does,' said Legnano, turning towards Fouquet. 'Are you ready to—?'

'To take over the papal functions if he dies? Yes. I'll begin advising the staff of the situation immediately.'

'A bit hasty, Cardinal. A bit hasty,' said Legnano. 'Besides, we should be getting news from the hospital at any moment.'

While they waited in Legnano's Venetian-style office — the light of the large Murano chandelier sending its soft rays onto the gold and red striped walls — the cardinals attempted to break the mood of anxiety with assorted conjecture. From time to time, each would throw a surreptitious glance across the room at the bronze-gilded mantelpiece clock, slowly ticking away the endless minutes. Half an hour passed. Exasperated, Legnano grabbed the phone and dialed the clinic's number. 'Get me Dr Donatello.' After a brief pause, the doctor's familiar voice came on line.

'Donatello.'

'Legnano speaking. How is His Holiness?'

An awkward silence made him fear the worst as Legnano waited, looking at Brentano, then at Signorelli.

'Ah, he hasn't come in yet.'

'What? What do you mean? He left half an hour ago. The clinic is only ten minutes away.'

'We have a team waiting on the roof. They called a moment ago. They haven't seen the helicopter. We thought it was delayed.'

'Good God!' Legnano bolted up from his desk. 'Get me the pilot's number again,' shouted Legnano to the Swiss Guard standing at the door.

'Yes, your Eminence.'

Legnano dialed, but the pilot didn't answer. Instead, every ring announced impending fatality. He hung up and dialed again. Nothing. 'Get Colonel Romer,' Legnano said to the guard.

'Yes, your Eminence.'

Legnano walked towards the cardinals, now standing expectantly next to the sofa, 'Something has happened to the papal helicopter. It hasn't arrived at the hospital.'

'*Mio Dio*,' exclaimed Sforza and Brentano in unison.

Legnano rushed back to his desk, picked up the phone and called the Questura Centrale, Rome's main police station. He anxiously eyed the cardinals, phone in hand. 'They've either crashed or . . . Yes, Cardinal Legnano here. Get me Inspector Guadagni. It's urgent. No, I'll wait.'

'Or what?' said Signorelli.

'Or the Pope has been kidnapped.'

CHAPTER 4

The Vatican, 4.05 a.m.

Cardinals Legnano, Brentano, Fouquet, Sforza and Signorelli, now joined by Colonel Romer, sat in stunned silence. A short while later, Inspector Guadagni burst into Legnano's office, one of his shirttails sticking out of his trousers.

'Ah, good, finally you've come, inspector,' said Legnano, not bothering to extend a welcoming hand. 'You know Colonel Romer of course.' Romer, head of the Swiss Guards, and Guadagni exchanged nods. Legnano continued. 'Meet Cardinals Fouquet, Sforza, Brentano and Signorelli.'

'Your Eminences,' said Guadagni, visibly out of breath.

'Inspector, I asked you on the phone if you'd had a report of a helicopter accident?' queried Legnano.

'We checked all precincts before I left. No accidents have been reported in the Rome perimeter or its vicinity.'

'My God. Just as I thought.' said Legnano, wringing his hands nervously. 'Perhaps they went to another hospital,' said Sforza.

'Then why isn't the pilot answering?' said Legnano. Sforza didn't reply.

'There must be some other explanation,' said Romer.

'Like what?' Legnano said angrily.

'I . . . I was just—'

'Gentlemen, gentlemen, please try to stay calm,' interrupted Guadagni. 'Cardinal Legnano, let's start from the beginning. Tell me what happened.'

Legnano walked towards the window and started pacing back and forth. 'At approximately 2.30 a.m., the Pope was taken ill and rang for Sister Vincenza. She phoned me and I immediately called Dr Bruscetti. He's the Pope's personal physician. I then went to the papal apartments, to the Pope's bedside. He looked ill. The doctor came, oh, it must have been just before 3 a.m., and took his pulse and told me the Pope had had a heart attack. I called the Agostino Gemelli Clinic, then phoned for the ambulance and was told it was out of service. So I phoned for the helicopter. At about 3.25 a.m., having no news from the clinic, I phoned to find out how the Pope was.' Legnano paused, gathering his thoughts. 'Dr Donatello told me the helicopter never arrived. I immediately phoned you both,' said Legnano, eyeing Guadagni and Romer.

'Did you try to reach the pilot?' asked Romer.

'Yes, I tried repeatedly. No answer.'

'And the ambulance attendant?'

'I verified with administration. The ambulance is out of service every two months, for a full one-day servicing. The attendant hadn't picked it up yet.'

Inspector Guadagni telephoned the Questura Centrale and was put through to the Rome Airport traffic control center in an instant. 'Did you have any contact with a helicopter flying over Rome in the last half-hour?'

'Just a minute, I'll check.' After a moment, the air traffic controller said, 'Negative. One of our men saw one on radar and tried to get a flight plan, but no answer.'

'And now?'

'He's off our radar screen. He'll be out of our range.'

'Or on the ground,' muttered Guadagni.

'Could be,' answered the controller.

'Call me immediately if you get a contact,' said Guadagni. Turning to Legnano, 'I'm calling the Air Ministry.'

'Oh, I forgot to tell you,' said Legnano, 'they also have Dr Bruscetti.'

'With your permission, your Eminence, I'll have forensics come over immediately and go over the papal apartments. It's important we gather all information and evidence as quickly as possible.'

'Of course,' said Legnano. 'By the way, I've called Interpol. I've asked that they send that Inspector Dulac, the one who helped solve the Archbishops Salvador and Conti murders.'

'But why? This is purely an Italian, a Vatican matter,' said Guadagni, offended.

'You know that for a fact, inspector?' said Legnano.

'Well, no, but we have—'

'As Secretary of State of the Vatican, it's my decision,' said Legnano glaring at Guadagni.

Somewhere over the Italian countryside, 3.20 a.m., same day

For a moment, Bruscetti looked away from his barely conscious patient and glanced outside the helicopter's window. Below, the lights of buildings were strangely sparse. He looked at his watch. It's been over fifteen minutes. That's odd. We should have arrived by now. He leaned forward and tapped the co-pilot's shoulder. 'Where are we going? The clinic—'

The co-pilot turned quickly, pointing a pistol inches from Bruscetti's face. 'Shut up. Be quiet and you won't get hurt.'

Bruscetti recoiled and sat back, speechless. For an instant, the realization didn't register, but then, it all became terribly clear: they'd been kidnapped. Tired, dazed and confused, Bruscetti sat back and stared blankly at the opposite side of the Huey. He bent down beside the Pope and saw that his breathing was shallow, but regular.

An hour later, Bruscetti felt the Huey slowing, then land in the darkness.

He watched as the pilot and co-pilot transferred the stretcher bearing the Pope out of the chopper onto the ground. Bruscetti could make out a van, parked alongside the helicopter. Suddenly the gate of the van opened and four men bearing Uzis in bandolero style jumped out, took over and carried the burdened stretcher into the van. A hooded, stocky man grabbed Bruscetti's arm, pulled him out of the helicopter and shoved him onto the van's middle seat. Bruscetti, his nerves raw, his hands trembling, looked beside him: the Pope lay inert on the stretcher, his breathing barely discernible. The stocky, hooded man clambered into the front beside the driver and ordered, 'Go.'

The driver floored the accelerator and Bruscetti was pushed back in his seat.

'Give me my bag. I must check his vital signs,' said Bruscetti to the hooded man, visibly in charge.

The man signaled to one of the men in the rear to hand Bruscetti his bag. 'Make it fast.' After a cursory check, the doctor, for the first time, felt relief. The Pope's pulse had dropped to normal, and his pressure was up. As Bruscetti removed the Velcro strap from the pontiff's arm, the pontiff awakened and smiled faintly.

'Where are we, doctor?'

'Your Holiness, I wish I knew.'

A while later, Bruscetti heard the engine whine as the van struggled up a steep, tortuous incline, the driver muscling the vehicle through a set of narrow switchbacks.

Eventually, the van slowed in front of a large villa and stopped in front of one of the doors of its three car garage. The door swung silently upwards underneath the wide, cantilevered veranda and the van entered into the gaping hole. The stocky man led Bruscetti out of the van, through a doorway into the house, then along a narrow corridor. The man stopped before a small room, its door ajar.

'You stay here,' he said, shoving Bruscetti into the windowless room.

'For God's sake, the Pope's had a heart attack. We must get him to a hospital immediately. Otherwise you'll kill him.'

The stocky man gave a raucous, sinister laugh then closed the door.

The Vatican, 5.15 a.m.

Colonel Romer and Guadagni had remained in Legnano's office with the five Cardinals, trying to instill calmness to the anxious prelates.

'What can we do?' asked Cardinal Signorelli to Guadagni.

Before he could reply, Sforza interjected. 'We don't even know who's behind this and where they've taken them.'

'With that heart attack, he could be dead by now,' said Brentano.

'Gentlemen, please. Panic is our worst enemy,' said Guadagni. 'We must—'

Suddenly, one of the Swiss Guards burst into the room and took Romer privately aside. A moment later, an embarrassed-looking Romer turned to Legnano: 'We've found the pilot and co-pilot of the helicopter. They were gagged and bound late last night, in the garden, near the Lourdes grotto.'

'Incredible,' said Legnano, feeling the anger rise within him. 'Tell me, colonel. How did these kidnappers get past your Swiss Guards?'

'We're looking into that, your Eminence,' said Romer.

'Did they get a description of the men?' asked Guadagni to the Swiss Guard. 'No, they were hooded.'

'Did they see or hear anything that could help us identify them?'

'Apparently, they knew exactly where to go,' said the Swiss Guard. 'As if they were familiar with the layout of the gardens. Oh, and they spoke French.'

'Great,' replied Guadagni.

Legnano threw an inquisitive glance at the policeman. 'Any news from the Italian armed forces?'

'We're waiting to hear from the Air Force and Coast Guard. Your Eminences, there is no use for you to stay here and worry,' said Guadagni. 'The constabulary forces are doing all they can to locate the helicopter. Meanwhile our forensics people are combing the papal apartments and grounds for any traces left by the kidnappers. Colonel Romer and I will contact you immediately once we have any developments.'

'I suppose you're right,' replied Legnano. 'Your Eminences, we should let the police do their work. Let's reconvene here once they give us news.'

'But surely, there is something we can do,' said Brentano.

'Yes,' replied Legnano. 'We can pray.'

The other cardinals, Romer and Guadagni, left Legnano's office and, exhausted, Legnano retired to his bedroom. Later, unable to sleep, Legnano returned to his office and tried to busy himself in his work. The specter of the Pope's death kept creeping into his thoughts. At 9:30 a.m., his phone rang.

'Yes?'

'Inspector Guadagni, your Eminence.'

'You have news?'

'Your Eminence, we have an initial report from forensics. They've found traces of dobutamine mixed with arbutamine in the Pope's water glass.'

Legnano waited in silence.

'They're used in cardiac research. They induce heart attack symptoms.'

Legnano slowly put the receiver down, and sat transfixed, staring blankly at the wall across the room. After a moment, he crossed himself slowly. Regaining his composure, he walked over towards the full-length window and looked outside to the gardens below. It was raining slightly. The morning light was beginning to fade, invaded by an ominous, low-flying thunderstorm cloud.

That evening, as Cardinal Legnano's limousine twisted through Rome on its way to the Vatican, Dulac turned to Harris. 'I'm curious. Why me?'

Before he could reply, Cardinal Legnano interrupted. 'I'm the one responsible for your presence here, Mr Dulac. Your false modesty is out of place. I need hardly remind you of your solving of the Archbishops Salvador and Conti murder cases. Rather brilliantly, I might add. Cardinal Signorelli planned your—'

Abduction, Dulac thought.

'—trip. I must say that Secretary Signorelli's resourcefulness never ceases to amaze me. When Mr Harris told us you were vacationing in Canada, Signorelli phoned Vasari, the Italian Minister of Defense. He in turn contacted the Canadians, who gave him instant clearance for the jet. They organized the helicopter pickup. Very simpatico, these Canadians.'

'You'll find some fresh clothes in there,' said Harris, pointing to a suitcase at Dulac's feet.

'Thanks. Wouldn't want to breach Vatican protocol.'

'You can change in the antechamber of my office,' said Legnano, his tone gruff.

Just then, the papal limo reached the San Pietro entrance, was waved past by the on-duty Swiss Guards and came to a stop in front of the Basilica's steps. The chauffeur opened the door and a balding priest with a gaunt face greeted them. They followed him down a long corridor, at the end of which the priest pulled Dulac aside and showed him to an antechamber, waiting outside while Dulac changed. Moments later, Dulac was shown into Legnano's office, where the cardinal wasted no time in introducing Harris and Dulac to the other members of the Curia.

' . . . and you remember Inspector Guadagni,' said Legnano.

'How could I forget? Seems you can't do without me,' said Dulac, looking at his colleague.

'Always so humble,' replied a somber-looking Guadagni.

Dulac sat down next to Harris and absorbed the atmosphere, a mixture of collective guilt, embarrassment and anxiety.

'Mr Harris, your preliminary thoughts on who could have done this?' asked Cardinal Signorelli.

Harris turned towards Dulac. 'I will defer the answer to your question to Mr Dulac. After eight years as General Secretary, my investigative skills are a little rusty.'

'Your Eminence,' said Dulac, 'the planning alone of this abduction tells us of their degree of sophistication. That narrows the field to, let's say,' — he looked up at the ceiling — 'a couple of hundred crime organizations perhaps?'

Signorelli's face went as red as the fascia around his generous waist. 'Mr Dulac, this is no time for facetiousness. I—'

'I wasn't being facetious, your Eminence. Simply pointing out the odds. Gentlemen, Cardinal Legnano has briefed me on today's events. Inspector Guadagni, has your forensic team investigated any purchase of dobutamine or arbutamine in the last two months.'

'Why only two months?'

'I believe that's their shelf life. Colonel Romer, what's the Huey's range?'

'About 400 km. We've contacted all military air bases and airstrips within that radius. They're combing the area now,' answered the tall, rosy-complexioned Swiss.

'Fine. What direction did the Rome control tower see the helicopter travel in?'

'South-east,' said Guadagni.

'They may have headed for the coast,' said Dulac.

'Or Sicily,' replied Guadagni, scratching his scalp.

'In any case, they've abandoned the chopper, and perhaps destroyed it,' replied Dulac. 'Now, gentlemen, you must decide.'

'Decide?' said Legnano.

'When do you go public with the Pope's abduction?'

The cardinals looked at each other warily, no one daring to speak first.

Cardinal Legnano finally spoke. 'Gentlemen, we've had a long, stressful day. We are all very tired. Let's reconvene at 8:30 a.m. tomorrow morning in the Segnatura room.'

Dulac gave Legnano an inquiring look.

'We use it for video conferencing, Mr Dulac.'

As the policemen and the five cardinals left Legnano's office, Dulac imagined the collective outrage of a billion Catholics when hearing that their leader, pastor and beloved pontiff had been kidnapped.

In the taxi back to the hotel, neither Dulac nor Harris spoke. Dulac felt himself occasionally nodding off, his head heavy with stress and sleep deprivation. Harris finally broke the silence.

'I'm off to Lyon tomorrow morning. For the moment, there's nothing more I can do here. Besides, all hell is going to break loose at head office when the news gets out. We'll be more efficient if I coordinate from there.'

CHAPTER 5

Vatican, Segnatura room, 8.20 a.m., Tuesday 23 May

Dulac entered the room and his attention was immediately caught by the huge video monitor at the far side of the room. Next to it, a technician looked up for a moment, glanced inquisitively at Dulac, who gave him a knowing nod of authority, and the technician resumed switching the video from one channel to the other, seemingly testing the audio and video functions of the monitor.

'Sì, sì, no, a little sharper. Yes, OK, there,' said the technician to his counterpart on the video screen. 'I'll get back to you.'

While the technician continued his tests, Dulac wandered about the room, admiring and absorbing Raphael's precocious genius on the walls of the Segnatura, the most intimate of the Stanze rooms. Remembering his art classes at Montpelier University, Dulac recalled his professor's passionate words: the Segnatura is ineffable. It contains Raphael's most beautiful early frescoes. They mark the beginning of the High Renaissance in Italy.

Dulac paused and looked up at the ceiling. Eternal Good, Truth and Beauty, represented by the frescoes of three young men, looked back down at him with expressions of naiveté mixed with unalienable faith. Dulac wondered how the worldly Raphael had achieved such exquisite balance between his religious and artistic ideals.

The sound of conversation behind him close to the room's entrance jolted Dulac from his divine reverie. Guadagni and Romer entered, bringing Dulac down to earthly realities. Moments later, Legnano walked in, followed by the other cardinals. Legnano motioned them to the seats around the large oak table.

Guadagni eyed the technician, sitting next to the video monitor, and said. 'Everything ready?'

'Sì, Inspector.'

'Your Eminences, gentlemen,' said Guadagni, 'we are in contact with the Ministry of Defense, the Coast Guard, Interpol Central, the Italian President's office and all airports within a 400 km radius. We will be immediately advised of any developments.'

'I must put one caveat on this,' said Legnano, his tone imperious. 'We in the Vatican will consult everyone. But we alone will make any decisions concerning the Pope. Is that clear?'

'Of course, your Eminence,' said Guadagni.

Dulac held back, but the opportunity presenting itself in the form of silence couldn't be passed up. He said: 'While we await news, I suggest we discuss what is on everybody's mind: disclosure.'

'Yes, yes,' said Legnano, hands on the table while he nervously fidgeted with his rosary. 'Mr Guadagni, what do you say?'

'Your Eminences, so far, you've already decided not to disclose. I think that's a mistake. The longer we wait, the less chance we have of the people helping us find the best known man on the planet.'

'I disagree,' said Dulac, looking at Legnano, then the other prelates, while trying to avoid Guadagni's hostile stare. 'If we reveal now to the world at large, we'll be swamped with calls. Well-wishers, people who want to see him, think they saw him, pranksters, even the kidnappers. We'll be chasing our tails. They'll paralyze our forces. Not to mention the worldwide impact on a billion Catholics. Besides, if the kidnappers want to start a holy war, this is playing right into their hand. You'll have riots in the streets. Think of Belfast. Think of Beirut. My advice is to keep this information contained to the police forces directly involved for as long as we can.'

'But Mr Dulac,' said Legnano, 'the Pope is due to appear tomorrow evening from the balcony for his weekly Angelus blessing.'

'I see,' said Dulac. 'Surely he's missed some of his appearances before. Surely you can prepare a communiqué to the effect that — I don't know — the Pope is overworked and resting in Castel Gandolfo?'

'I suppose,' said Legnano, sounding unconvinced.

'Cancel his appointments,' continued Dulac. 'Advise the minimum number of people and swear them to secrecy. By the way, did someone contact the staff at the hospital? They must also be sworn.'

'Everybody on the tenth floor signs a confidentiality agreement upon hiring,' said Legnano.

'Let's hope it buys us time,' said Dulac. 'Every hour without disclosure is worth gold.'

Legnano, still fidgeting with his rosary, turned to the cardinals, 'Any comments, Monsignori?'

The cardinals looked at each other in utter silence. 'I will take that as agreement,' said Legnano.

Sicily, 8.15 a.m.

The middle-aged spinster Paola Bragante had been instructed by her brother-in-law Piero Vespoli, to attend to the pontiff. She was to serve him meals, which he was to take in his room. She rapped twice on the door and entered the pontiff's room.

'I've come with your breakfast,' she said. Bragante entered the windowless, sparsely lit room carrying a tray of fruits, yogurt and coffee. The Pope, dressed in an oversized burgundy nightgown, sat on the edge of the bed, his shoulders slumped. She deposited the tray on the small night table beside the bed.

'Thank you,' said the Pope. 'And your name is?'

'Paola. Paola Bragante.'

'Thank you, Paola.'

An atheist, Paola felt strange at meeting this man whose faith she had long ago rejected. Yet she sensed the immense attraction and power of the persona, radiating through his air of sadness and resignation. On the other side of the bed, the white cassock she'd laid out the previous day had remained untouched.

The Pope cleared his throat. 'Tell me Paola, is it a nice day outside?'

'Cloudy.'

'And where are we exactly, Paola?' he said. She remained silent and started to turn away.

'And where are you from, Paola?'

'Prizzi,' she said proudly.

'Near Palermo?'

'Sì.'

'So we are in Sicily.'

His smile looked so kind, so inviting. She thought of Vespoli and suddenly got a grip on herself. 'I, I have to go.' She knew she'd talked too much already. Vespoli's instructions were clear: Do not engage in any conversation with him, he'd said, his cold eyes menacing under the small brow and short cropped hair. She wiped her hands on her apron and started backwards towards the door.

'Yes, of course,' said the pontiff.

She turned to leave, and heard the voice behind her say, 'God bless you, signora.'

The pontiff took a few spoonfuls of yogurt and, as he finished his coffee, he heard a short, aggressive knock on the door. Before he could rise to answer, a stocky man dressed in brown fatigues, his brownish hair cropped close, entered the room.

'Come with me.' The man grabbed the prelate by the arm and ushered him into the corridor. 'You'll meet your host,' he announced gruffly, as he led the Pope to the small elevator.

They went down one floor along a corridor and Vespoli opened the door to a small, crescent shaped room with a stage. A television monitor had been set on a table at the center of the stage.

'Sit here,' the man ordered, showing the Pope to the first row seat.

The Pope sat down and waited, as the man turned and left the room. Clement XXI stared at the garish drapes, thinking they gave the room the look of a cheap funeral parlor, when suddenly the monitor flickered to life. Only the shadowed outline of a man's head and shoulders appeared. The Pope waited anxiously for the man to speak. Nothing.

Finally deciding to break the oppressive silence, the pontiff asked, 'Why am I here?' The shadow didn't answer, but a woman came into view and placed a small, shiny microphone in front of him. He tapped the microphone to test the audio and the woman nodded. 'For many reasons,' said the electronically-altered voice.

'What do you want from me?' said the pontiff, trying to stay calm, yet resolute.

'What we want, I doubt you can give us.'

'I presume this is about money?'

'You should presume nothing.'

The pontiff shifted in his seat, grasping the armrest. 'What do you intend doing with me?' he asked, and tried to detect movement from the shape.

'That depends on you and your cardinals.' The voice sounded automatic, almost preregistered.

'What do you mean?'

'Life, to continue, must change. All of us must choose.'

The Pope felt his pulse quicken, 'Between?'

'Simply put, between stagnation and progress.'

'I don't follow,' said the pontiff.

The voice hesitated, as if the man wanted to say more, but said simply, 'I know.'

'How, how long do you intend keeping me here?'

Silence. The Pope felt sweat form under his armpits and he leaned forward, clasping his hands nervously. He summoned his courage and asked, 'Do you intend to . . . to?' his voice trailing off to a whisper. Before he could finish, the screen went blank.

The Vatican, 9.15 a.m.

It had been agreed between the cardinals and the policemen that until further news as to the Pope's whereabouts or contact from the kidnappers, Guadagni and two of his men would stay in the Segnatura room to coordinate incoming developments and keep everyone advised, and the cardinals would resume their functions as if nothing happened. If it bought them an hour or even half a day more of non-interference by the media, so much the better.

Meanwhile Dulac had his own agenda: the delicate business of investigating and questioning some of the most powerful and secretive men in the world, members of the Vatican Curia. It was said they practiced omertà more effectively than the Mafia.

As the cardinals, Dulac and Romer left the Segnatura room, Romer in the lead, Dulac shot a side-glance at Legnano, whose quick pace he was barely keeping up with.

'Monsignor Legnano,' Dulac said. 'I'll need a small, quiet room to carry on my investigation.'

'Let's see. You can use the papal library,' said Legnano.

'Fine. In the meantime, can we go to your office, your Eminence? I have some matters to discuss with you.'

'Yes, of course, but—'

'I'd like Colonel Romer to join us,' Dulac said, loud enough so Romer, walking a few steps ahead of them, could hear.

Romer looked back, glaring at Dulac. 'Colonel, if you please,' said Legnano.

Romer gave a quick hunch of his shoulders in a mix of disdain and reluctant acceptance. They entered Legnano's vast, Venetian-style office.

'Gentlemen,' said Legnano, offering the police officers the large sofa in the center of the room.

Dulac waited for Romer to sit. 'Colonel,' said Dulac, towering above Romer, 'can you explain how those two potent drugs, any drug for that matter, got past your security and into the Pope's water?'

Romer fidgeted with one of the buttons of his suit. 'We check all food and drink before they enter the main kitchen. Sister Vincenza is responsible for the Pope's medication.'

'Presumably you check the water?'

'It's filtered twice before reaching the main intake.'

'I'm talking after it enters the Apostolic Palace,' Dulac said, walking across the room to the full-length window.

'No.'

He turned to face Romer. 'So the drugs could have been put in the water after it reached the kitchen and before Sister Vincenza gave him the glass?'

'Possibly. In any case, the Pope always drinks bottled water.'

'Always? You know that for a fact, Colonel?'

'Well, I mean he usually does.' Romer leaned back and crossed his arms.

'I also drink bottled water, Colonel, but I have been known to supplement it with tap water when I run out of the bottled stuff.'

'I guess that's possible.'

'In any case, as you seem to suggest, a drugged bottle could have been planted, yes?' Dulac said, irritated at the smugness of Romer's replies.

'We can't take a sample of every bottle entering the Vatican.'

Dulac walked towards the sofa, eyeing Legnano briefly as he approached Romer. 'Tell me, Colonel, have you started a sequence-of-events investigation from, say, twenty-four hours before the Pope's kidnapping until the time of the abduction?'

'We have.'

'People stream, food analysis, the water bottles' seal check, their date of bottling and—'

'Mr Dulac, we don't have the resources of Interpol. I already have three men preparing a security critical path analysis. We can't be everywhere at once. These issues will be dealt with in due course.' Romer rose and turned away from Dulac's stare.

'What's the hurry, Colonel?' Dulac said.

'Inspector, I'm not under investigation here. Your Eminence.' Romer gave a quick bow to Legnano, turned and started towards the door.

After Romer left the room, Legnano said, 'You were a bit harsh.'

'Really? I thought I was restraining myself. By the way, I'm ordering a full security crosscheck on everyone who saw or came near the Pope within the last forty-eight hours.'

'But Colonel Romer—'

'Crosschecked by Guadagni.'

'Surely you don't include Sister Vincenza or . . . or Cardinal Signorelli?'

'Everyone.'

'That would include me.'

Dulac smiled at the cardinal.

Dulac entered the simply decorated papal library, its white and gold wall-papered walls adorned with the papal crest. He walked to the oak desk below Perugino's painting of the Resurrection and sat in the uncomfortable, high-backed chair, usually reserved for the Pope.

Moments later a diminutive nun dressed in a gray frock appeared in the doorway. 'I am Sister Vincenza. You wish to see me?'

'Yes, yes, good morning, Sister. Please be seated,' he said, offering the gray-haired nun a chair across the desk.

She issued a faint smile of acknowledgment and sat down hesitantly.

She's insecure. Make her feel comfortable. Establish a bond quickly.

'Sister Vincenza, thank you so much for coming. I know this tragedy must be hard on you. I assure you that—'

'Mr Dulac. I am here to help. What is it you wish to know?' she said in a gentle yet no-nonsense voice.

'Very well, Sister. I'm glad of it. Let's get to the heart of the matter,' said Dulac, slightly off guard. 'What is the Pope's routine before he retires for the evening?'

'I speak with the Secretary and prepare the small tray—'

'Cardinal Signorelli?'

'Yes. Sometimes, in his absence, his assistant, Archbishop Ferris. I ask him when the Pope will be retiring, and if His Holiness has any requests.'

'What kind of request?' Dulac thought he sensed her distrust slowly melting.

She cleared her throat. 'He sometimes suffers from insomnia, so I give him aspirin.'

'Aspirin? I'm a little surprised, sister. To my knowledge, aspirin isn't a sleeping aid,' said Dulac, trying to disguise his disbelief behind a hint of curiosity.

'For him it is. He says it relaxes him. Particularly when he's had a stressful day.'

'So you put the aspirin on the tray only when requested by the secretary?'

'Yes.'

'And who keeps the bottle?'

'I do.'

'And after you have finished, where do you store it?'

'In the medicine cabinet, in my room . . .' she said, her voice trailing off.

'I'm sorry. Where?'

'In my room.'

'I see. Is the access to your room guarded?'

'Well, yes but . . . no, not really.'

'What do you mean?'

'There's the Swiss Guards, but they're down the corridor.'

'So someone could — excuse me, let me rephrase that. As far as you're concerned, they don't always see you enter or leave your room.'

'Sometimes yes, sometimes not.'

Dulac wasn't getting the answers he wanted to hear. He couldn't believe the lack of security around the leader of the Catholic world.

'Sister Vincenza, did His Holiness take aspirin last night?'

'Yes, he did.'

'And who requested it?'

'The Secretary, Cardinal Signorelli.'

'I see.' Dulac paused for a moment. He knew he couldn't continue in that line of questioning. She might perceive the next question he had in mind as discrediting Signorelli, and he didn't know, couldn't gauge the amount of trust between them. He needed the nun's cooperation. If anyone in the Pope's entourage was beyond suspicion, it was her. It was common knowledge that she'd been Pope John Paul I's assistant as well, and had been first to see his body after his fatal heart attack.

'Sister Vincenza, at approximately what time did you leave the tray at the Pope's door?'

'At about 10.30 p.m., as I always do.'

'Did you happen to see His Holiness?'

'Yes, he looked tired,' she said, looking tired herself.

'Did you happen to notice the Swiss Guards on duty when you left the tray beside the papal apartments?'

'They were both there.'

'Who would that be, sister?'

'It was Haeker and Dumont, I think, no, I'm sure.'

'Was it the same two when the Pope buzzed for help?'

'I didn't notice. But you can check their time of rotation. Colonel Romer has the schedule.'

'Yes, of course.' He saw the beginning of a smile on her worn face.

I've got her trust. Don't rush her. Don't break the trust.

'Sister Vincenza, how long have you known Cardinal Signorelli?'

She paused. 'About two years. His nomination is quite recent.'

'You didn't know him before that?'

'No, only when he took office.'

Dulac paused. 'Sister, that will be all for now. You've been very helpful.'

As she rose to leave, Dulac knew he had to ask his last question. 'Sister Vincenza, one more question. Could Cardinal Signorelli have had access to your room?' He didn't like the way it sounded, but there was no other way of putting it.

'Mr Dulac!'

'I only want to know who could possibly have had access to that bottle. The drugs found in the Pope's glass could have been put in that bottle.'

'I see. So you also suspect me and the Cardinal?'

'Unfortunately, I suspect everyone. It's my job.'

'I rarely lock the door, if that's what you wish to know.'

'So others might have access also.'

'Yes.'

'That's all I wanted to know.'

'Good day, Mr Dulac,' she said and turned to leave.

Great, now I've offended the hell out of her.

'Sister, before we finish, could you please get me the bottle of aspirin?'

'Of course,' she snapped.

As he waited for the nun to return, Dulac thought: maybe I should have held back and continued later. He knew that the trust he needed so badly was now, if not broken, at least seriously damaged. Suddenly, the nun rushed in.

'I . . . I was sure I . . . I cannot find it anywhere. It's gone.'

CHAPTER 6

While Dulac waited in the library for Dumont, the Swiss Guard, he went through the logic of the kidnappers' plan. If drugs had been exchanged for the aspirins, how could they be sure the Pope would take them? The timing included the kidnappers' infiltration onto the grounds and neutralizing the helicopter pilot and co-pilot. It also depended on the absolute certainty of the appearance of the Pope's falling ill that night, between 10.30 p.m. and early morning, before the pilot and co-pilot would be missed. Only one thing was certain: the Pope drank water every night. Dulac couldn't even be sure the pontiff had taken only the bottled water. Then there was the missing aspirin bottle. Had it been used to smuggle the drugs by someone having access to sister Vincenza's room? Cardinal Signorelli . . . Yet others could have had access to her unlocked room. But the kidnappers couldn't know for sure that the Pope would take aspirin that night. Predictability was essential to their plan. Yet Cardinal Signorelli had ordered . . .

Someone coughed. Dulac looked up to see the Swiss Guard, dressed in a blue uniform, standing in the doorway.

'You must be Dumont,' Dulac said.

'Yes,' said the blond, pale-complexioned young man.

'Come in, come in. Please.' Dulac offered him the chair in front of the desk. 'Mr Dumont, I am Inspector Dulac of Interpol. Do you know why you're here?'

'Yes, Colonel Romer has briefed me. He mentioned that the Pope is resting in Gandolfo, but that an attempt may have been made on his life.'

'Correct. Did you see anything unusual last night? Anything out of the ordinary?'

'No,' the guard said, as he squirmed uncomfortably in his chair.

'Mr Dumont, how long have you been a Swiss Guard?'

'Two years,' said the young man, looking like an about-to-be-chastised schoolboy.

'About the same time Cardinal Signorelli became secretary?'

'He was already here when I joined.'

'And what did you do before becoming a Swiss Guard?'

'I worked on the family farm.'

'Where?'

'In the Valais, near Sion.'

'I see. Apart from last night, has anything unusual, out of pattern, happened in the past, say, two months?'

'Not really, except we've been asked to extend our shifts by an hour.' Dulac smiled at the guard's perception of the unusual.

'By whom?'

'Colonel Romer.'

'And why is that?' Dulac said, elbows on the desk, hands clasped.

'He says he has fewer men. We must make do. How is the Holy Father?'

'He's fine. That will be all, for now. Thank you for coming. If anything comes to mind, call me.' Dulac handed him his card.

The interview with Haeker, the other Swiss Guard on duty that fateful night, had proven just as inconclusive. Dulac now squarely faced the delicate prospect of questioning Cardinal Signorelli. He knew the reputation of the Vatican's diplomats. Secrecy, evasiveness and ambiguity were their stock in trade. Inside the muted corridors of the Vatican, the saying went:

If you can avoid it, don't even think it.

If you think it, don't say it.

If you say it, don't write it.

If you write it, well, don't be sorry.

'Good morning, your Eminence,' said Dulac as he rose from behind the desk. He pointed to the chair. 'Please.'

The cardinal sat down slowly, his corpulence overflowing on either side of the small seat. The prelate was a tall man for an Italian. His chin, barely distinguishable under layers of fat, had a shallow dimple to remind one of its past location. The quiet brown eyes surmounted by overlapping, tightly drawn eyelids, his sensuous-lipped, enigmatic smile only heightened Signorelli's resemblance to an overdressed Buddha. Dulac was about to discover, however, that behind the benign-looking facade resided a razor-sharp mind and a stratospheric IQ.

'Have the staff been advised and sworn to secrecy?' said Dulac.

'Yes. The official line is that the Pope is resting in Castel Gandolfo. It's being told on a need-to-know basis.' Signorelli crossed his hands over his prominent belly and gave Dulac a condescending sneer.

'Any reaction?'

'Mr Dulac, it's not the first time the Pope has interrupted his schedule to rest at Castel Gandolfo.'

'But the swearing to secrecy. Didn't that arouse suspicion?'

'Not really,' Signorelli said, looking bored.

'What do you mean?'

'We often require members of the staff to assure us, let us say, of a certain amount of discretion.'

'Meaning?'

Signorelli leaned forward slightly and took the loose end of his fascia, as if to check its state of wear. Without looking up he said, 'You might be surprised to learn, Mr Dulac, that not everyone wishes it to be known that they visited the Pope.'

'I see.'

Signorelli dropped the end of the fascia and looked up at Dulac. 'And vice versa.'

'I was about to ask.'

Signorelli's air of condescension had been replaced by a cold, hard stare. 'Mr Dulac, you didn't request this discussion purely to find this out, surely?'

'Not exactly. Would you go through again, the sequence of events—'

'Mr Dulac,' interrupted the cardinal, 'am I a suspect in this matter?'

Dulac waited an instant before answering, trying to regain the tempo of the questioning. It wasn't the first time a VIP had tried to embarrass him by cutting to the chase. 'Does it make any difference if I say no?'

'I suppose not,' said Signorelli, his air haughty again as he inserted both thumbs between the part of the fascia around his waist and his bulging black cassock.

'Glad we understand each other, your Eminence. So when did you enter the Pope's apartment?'

'I think around quarter to three. Cardinal Legnano phoned me.'

'Did you see anything unusual in or outside the apartments last night?'

'Not really, no.'

'And before?'

'Mr Dulac, you don't have to pry from me the slightest anomaly or unusual behavior of anything or anyone. I'm as deeply concerned about this as you are, and have been racking my brain to see what and how this happened. Unfortunately, I've come up as empty-handed as you seem to be.'

Swallowing the insult, Dulac smiled, his eyes still locked onto the cardinal. Dulac leaned forward, shoulders hunched, hands clasped on the desk. 'Your Eminence, we both realize how delicate this is, but I've learned in my job that the mind plays tricks on the best of us. Something I might ask or say might trigger some seemingly insignificant thought or comment, which I might find vital. I know this is embarrassing, but it is necessary.'

The cardinal sat silent, arms crossed, giving Dulac that supercilious smile of his again. Dulac changed gears and went for the jugular. 'Did you have access to the Pope's drinking water last night?'

The prelate looked away, paused then said, 'I suppose I did.'

'When?'

'Mr Dulac, if you are insinuating that I put the drugs in the glass, I would first have to know when the water would be poured in order to avoid detection, wouldn't I?'

'Which you didn't?'

'No. My access would be limited to the time when Sister Vincenza poured it, and the Pope drank it. I would have either had to go to Sister Vincenza's room before she poured it, in which case she would've seen the drugs in the glass, or between the time she delivered it and the Pope opened the doors to his apartment and took the trolley.'

Dulac saw instantly where the Cardinal was leading him. 'And the Swiss Guards would've seen you.'

'Go to the head of the class, Mr Dulac.'

'Unless they weren't there. Did you order aspirin for His Holiness last night?'

'As a matter of fact, I did. He said he felt stressed, so I spoke to Sister Vincenza. But you already know that since you interviewed her.'

'I'm told she rarely locks her room. So anyone on that floor could have had access and substituted the dobutamine and arbutamine for the aspirin.'

'I suppose.'

'Including you?'

'I find your question insulting, inspector. I won't even consider answering it.'

'You already have, your Eminence. Thank you.'

Inside the lower echelons of the Vatican's administration, a vague, strained unease could be felt, but not identified. Following the Curia members' meeting with the policemen, Sforza had returned dejectedly to his office. Unable to resolve the battle within his conscience between the divulgation and the keeping secret of the kidnapping, he'd requested another meeting with the cardinals in Legnano's office.

An hour later, Sforza entered the ornately decorated room, only to find the cardinals already waiting, an air of impatience sketched on their faces.

'Where is Cardinal Signorelli?' asked Sforza.

'With Inspector Dulac,' answered Legnano from behind his desk. 'He'll join us shortly.'

'I'll get right to the point, your Eminences. I think we are making a mistake. I think we should announce the kidnapping,' said Sforza.

Legnano bolted up from his chair. 'We agreed not to, cardinal.'

'People are already questioning the Castel Gandolfo story,' said Sforza. 'There's bound to be a leak, and we will be seen, once again, as hiding the truth.'

'Cardinal, may I remind you of St. Thomas Aquinas' wise words,' said Legnano. 'When two moral principles oppose each other, find in your heart the greater one and apply it. Our greater responsibility here is to protect the Pope by helping the police.'

An uneasy silence permeated the room.

Undeterred, Sforza continued, 'What if the Holy Father dies and we haven't told the world about his abduction?'

'Please, Monsignor, let's not panic,' said Legnano. 'If we can buy another day for the police, we increase our chances of finding him, hopefully alive.'

At that moment, Cardinal Signorelli entered the room.

'Ah, cardinal,' said Legnano. 'We are debating whether or not we should reconsider disclosure. What do you think?'

'Absolutely not. We must give the police every opportunity to find His Holiness,' said Signorelli.

'Any other votes for disclosure? None? The matter is settled,' said Legnano. 'We will announce only the theft of the helicopter. Cardinal Signorelli, please prepare the press release accordingly. It's 11.55 a.m. Let's reconvene at 1 p.m. and review the draft.'

The Cardinals were preparing to leave when Archbishop Ferris, Cardinal Signorelli's assistant, suddenly burst into the room. 'Monsignori, I have a reporter from Corriere Della Sera on the line. He says he's received information from a credible source that the Pope has been kidnapped. He's asking us to confirm or deny.'

CHAPTER 7

Sicily, 10.30 a.m.

The morning's rays were shining through the villa's angled porch windows and reflecting off the wall mirror, illuminating the dining room with their harsh light and casting a reflection on the video monitor encased into one of the walls. Sitting at the head of the table, Vespoli ordered Paola to close the shutters. While they waited for the videoconference to begin, the men sitting around the table conversed in hushed tones, acutely aware of the importance of the impending moment. Suddenly the video screen came to life. A dark human outline appeared on the screen and an electronically-altered voice spoke. 'Messieurs, bonjour. I'm pleased to announce that Alpha phase was successfully completed yesterday, without incident. Beta phase has begun, and our guest is well. I spoke with him after breakfast yesterday and he asked the anticipated questions.'

'Does he suspect—' asked Vespoli.

'Do not interrupt,' said the voice. 'As I foresaw, the Vatican chose not to divulge, trying to buy time. This morning, we forced their hand. Gamma phase has started. It will run concurrently with Beta. Meanwhile I have news from Gstaad. All is on schedule and I will be leaving for Switzerland to see for myself. Any questions?'

'What about the doctor? Shouldn't we get rid of him?' said Vespoli.

'He stays healthy,' said the voice.

'But he can identify any one of us.'

'We will deal with that later. In the meantime, Vespoli, take good care of our guests, à bientôt.' The video screen went blank.

Dulac was downing a quick lunch at the Hotel Dante when the news of the Pope's kidnapping hit the streets. Legnano called and summoned him back to the Vatican immediately. As Dulac's taxi driver punched incessantly at his horn, trying to weave through the traffic on Via Della Conziliatione leading to St. Peter's Square, Dulac's cell rang.

'It's me,' said Karen. 'I just heard the news on France 2 TV.'

'I couldn't phone you. All hell is about to break loose. Up till now, we were all on a mum's-the-word, need-to-know only basis.'

'I understand.'

'They're preparing a press conference and a public address by Cardinal Fouquet, the Camerlengo. I'll call you later.' He flipped his phone shut.

Dulac's taxi approached the Vatican's Sant'Anna entrance, and Dulac saw the thousands of faithful already milling about the square in anxious expectation. At the far end, atop the steps leading to the Basilica, Swiss Guards had formed a line to prevent access.

Dulac showed his pass to the guard at the entrance, and made his way to Legnano's office.

'Buongiorno, Mr Dulac,' said Legnano as Dulac entered and nodded to the assembled prelates, Colonel Romer and Inspector Guadagni.

'Any news from the armed forces?' Dulac asked Guadagni.

'Nothing, except a suspicious radio transcript overheard by a Rome weather station. We're trying to trace it,' said Guadagni.

'What did it say?' asked Dulac.

'The voice said: "Tout va bien, Alpha phase now complete."'

'Monsignori, gentlemen, may I have your attention,' said Legnano, a deep furrow on his brow and lines of stress along his cheeks and mouth. 'Since we've been forced to go public, we have convened the press conference for 2 p.m. at the Old Study Room. Cardinal Sforza and his people are working on the press release now.' He turned to the two inspectors. 'Gentlemen, I ask that you join us for the conference.'

'Of course, your Eminence,' said Dulac. Guadagni nodded.

'Fine,' continued Legnano. 'I will chair the meeting and direct questions, as appropriate. I need not remind you that we must be truthful, but reserved. If you don't know the answer, don't speculate. I will read the opening statement. Are there any questions? None. We'll convene at the Old Study Room, at 1.50 p.m.'

As the prelates started to disperse, Romer took Dulac aside and handed him an envelope. 'It's the people stream report on the Vatican's personnel in the Pope's immediate entourage, during the twenty-four hours preceding the abduction.'

'Has Guadagni seen it?' said Dulac, opening the envelope and taking out the thick report.

'Yes,' Romer said dryly.

'Colonel, why don't you save me wading through all this and give me a quick summary,' said Dulac, pushing the report back into the envelope.

'Very well. As far as we can find out, only four persons had access to the water supply between the time the bottle was opened and poured into the glass: the two Swiss Guards, Cardinal Signorelli, and sister Vincenza.'

'That doesn't get us very far.'

'Except for one thing.'

'Yes?'

'There is a permanent video camera taping the Swiss Guards during their rotation on guard. There is no sign of them, or anyone else for that matter, coming close to the tray at any time.'

'Which suggests, if it's the bottled water that was tampered with, it was done before that?'

'Yes.'

'And of course you don't have a report on the tap water.'

'Not yet.'

'By the way, Colonel, where were you during that period?'

'I knew you would ask. It's in the report, page thirteen.' Romer turned briskly and walked away.

Not since Pope Pius VII in 1809, had a Pope been abducted. The world's police forces were now reacting, inundating the Vatican's security services with offers to access their data banks, alert functions, search and rescue teams, crisis management teams, forensics labs, and research centers. The overwhelmed Secretariat of the Vatican had urgently requested the help of Rome's main police station, the Questura Centrale di Roma, to help sort out, prioritize, and redirect the huge volume of incoming calls. An otherwise divided world seemed to be galvanizing its efforts in a desperate search to find Pope Clement XXI, preferably alive.

From his previous visit to the Vatican, Dulac remembered that the Old Study Room stood out as somewhat of an anomaly amidst the customary opulence of the Vatican's richly decorated halls and rooms. Its bare columns supporting undecorated vaulted ceilings gave the place an impression of almost monkish, cloister-like austerity. Underneath, rows of wooden desks normally hosted scholars of the Vatican's so-called Secret Archives, no longer very secret.

Dulac followed Legnano, Sforza and the others as they entered and walked towards the table and chairs that had been set up temporarily at one extremity of the room. They were soon engulfed in chaos. Some reporters, seated at the rows of desks, were shouting like schoolboys while others, not content with the view, were standing on the desks, to the outraged but largely ineffective yelling of 'sit down' by their colleagues. To the sides, TV crews were busy setting up their cameras and microphone booms. The mob's cacophony resonated loudly within the room's arched colonnades and reverberated off its high-domed ceiling.

The prelates and policemen sat down and waited for the din to subside. To no avail. After five minutes, exasperated, Legnano rose, signaling the others to leave. Sitting two seats away from Legnano, Dulac was getting up when the tumult began to subside.

Legnano resumed his seat, pushed back his bifocals to the top of his aquiline nose and adjusted the microphone. 'Thank you. Ladies and gentlemen, I am Cardinal Legnano, Secretary of State of the Vatican.' Legnano proceeded to introduce the others, and handed the microphone to Sforza, sitting next to him.

'Thank you, Cardinal Legnano. I will give my address, and I ask that you keep your questions till the end.' The diminutive, balding Sforza lowered the microphone slightly, cleared his throat and began reading his notes. 'The Pope was abducted yesterday morning early, along with Dr Bruscetti, the Pope's personal physician. As of now, we do not know the kidnappers' identity, or their motive.' Sforza looked up briefly then continued. 'We have alerted all police and military forces in Italy and have requested the help of Interpol, as we cannot rule out the possibility that this crime transcends Italy's borders. We have not received any communication from the kidnappers. At this point in time, this is all the information we have.'

A forest of hands shot up.

'Yes?' said Sforza, singling out a small woman in front of him with plastered down brown hair and large horn-rimmed glasses.

'Your Eminence, how did the kidnappers get through the Swiss Guards?' Sforza turned sideways and looked at Romer.

Romer grabbed the microphone. 'Ah, they, they broke in at the northern end of the Vatican—'

'I'm sorry,' interrupted the woman. 'Perhaps my question wasn't clear. What I meant to say is how did they get into the papal apartments? Aren't they guarded 24/7?'

Romer looked at Sforza, then at Dulac, as if to seek their approval. 'Well, yes that's correct, there are two—'

Dulac grabbed the microphone from Romer. 'No comment.'

'Don't you think the public has the right to know?' said the woman. After all—'

'Madame, in this case the public's right to know is trumped by the sensitive nature of this investigation,' said Dulac. 'We won't endanger its progress by revealing classified information.'

'Classified by whom?' she said.

'By me.'

Sforza pointed to a blond-haired man wearing a dark-blue blazer and a bow tie, his hand insistently waving.

'Your Eminence, John Irvine from Associated Press. Who is in charge of the investigation?'

Sforza took the microphone from Dulac. 'Inspector Guadagni.' Sforza eyed Guadagni to his left.

'Does that mean you don't trust your own security forces, your Eminence?' said Irvine. Sforza hesitated. Legnano leaned over and grabbed the microphone. 'Not at all. Quite to the contrary. You must understand that we at the Vatican are not equipped to handle an investigation of this magnitude. Colonel Romer will give inspectors Guadagni and Dulac his full support.'

'I see,' said Irvine, continuing his thrust. 'Colonel Romer, has there been a breach in Vatican security? If so, please explain why.'

Romer took the microphone. 'No comment.'

Sforza recognized a middle-aged red-headed woman standing in the second row of desks. 'Yes?'

'My question is for Inspector Guadagni. Inspector, is Doctor Bruscetti a suspect at this time?'

Romer handed the microphone to Guadagni. 'No comment.'

Legnano stood up and in a loud voice said, 'Ladies and gentlemen, this is all the information we can share with you at this time. I ask for your patience and forbearance during this traumatic time. We will address the public at 4 p.m. at the Great Hall, followed by a mass at the Basilica. Thank you.'

CHAPTER 8

Rome Termini Railway Station, 10.30 a.m.

That goddamn Ascari, I should have never trusted him.

Standing in front of track eleven, Mecem Aguar looked furtively and expectantly about the passengers rushing to and from the trains, cellphone glued to his ear, desperation seeping in as he waited for Ascari to answer.

'Hello?' said Ascari finally.

'What the hell is coming off? You were supposed to be here at 10 a.m. My train leaves in less than half an hour. I'm—'

'I tried to phone you. I—'

'Bullshit. I've been waiting here for over an hour.' Aguar grabbed a kerchief from his pocket and wiped his brow with his free hand.

'Listen. It's not that easy to gather $200,000 US cash without the risk of a trace. It takes time. I've had to go to different banks and—'

'Not my problem. You should have thought of that earlier. If I miss that train, I'm screwed. Today was my day off. When I don't show up at the Vatican tomorrow morning, they'll send their dogs after me.'

'Relax, Mecem. You'll get your money. I just need another day.'

'Another day? Are you crazy? My ass will be sticking out there like a red flag to a bull.'

'Cool it, Mecem. How will they know to look for a simple busboy? You're not exactly tops on their list of suspects.'

'Don't fuck with me, Umberto. You'd better show up tomorrow morning here with my cash. Don't you fuck with me, or I swear I'll whack you if it's the last thing I do. I'll—'

The line went dead.

Bruscetti had obtained permission from Vespoli to visit his patient. Medical bag in hand, he knocked on the door.

'Yes?'

'Doctor Bruscetti, your Holiness.'

'Come in.'

Bruscetti entered the small, windowless room and said, 'How do you feel, your Holiness?'

'Better I suppose. Perhaps it was indigestion after all.'

'First, let's take your pulse and blood pressure,' said Bruscetti, taking his stethoscope out of his bag.

The Pope rolled up the right sleeve of his cassock. Bruscetti wrapped his patient's arm with a Velcro strap and inserted the tube of the small air pump.

'I would have never thought . . . What do you make of all of this?' the pontiff said, eyes probing into the doctor's frown.

'It's extortion, surely. They know that those Iraqi kidnappers obtained millions for the return of Archbishop Casmoussa. These ones will be demanding much more for the most loved man on the planet.'

The pontiff stiffened. 'Please, Doctor, no flattery.'

'I'm sorry. I was just trying to imagine what they think you're worth.'

'That's not important. I'm not for sale.'

'The cardinals may differ.' Bruscetti pumped the air into the strap, then opened the bleeder valve slowly, looking at his watch.

'Then I haven't been a very good leader.'

'Your Holiness, I don't want to think of the consequences if these criminals were to carry out any, any . . . threats.'

'Say it, doctor. You mean kill me.'

Bruscetti didn't answer, trying to avoid the pontiff's stare. He took off his stethoscope and started to remove the strap from the Pope's arm. 'Your vital signs are completely normal. Of course they could be religious extremists.'

'Possibly,' said the pontiff.

'Possibly?'

The pontiff rose from the bed, walked to the door and turned to face Bruscetti. 'Following the kidnapping of our bishops in Africa and Iraq a few years ago, the Vatican had experts prepare a report, to see if we could protect our prelates against future kidnapping attempts. The report concluded that each situation was different. Different kidnappers' profiles, different motives, different outcome. There is no set pattern.'

'I see.'

'The one common thread was that if you could begin a dialogue, you had a better chance of surviving. We must talk to these men, doctor. We must find out more about them, what their beliefs are. Do they have wives? Children? Is it me they hate? The Church? I must try and reason with them.'

Rome, 5.45 p.m.

After mass at the Basilica, Guadagni had offered Dulac a lift back to the Hotel Dante. As the dark-blue Alfa Romeo headed into the traffic jam ahead, Dulac turned to Guadagni, 'Can we drop by the Questura Centrale first?'

'Of course, but why?' asked a perplexed-looking Guadagni.

'I'd like to talk to your forensics people.'

'Something new?'

'Something I've been thinking about that troubles me.' Dulac looked outside, his right hand gripping the plastic indentation in the door as the Alfa took a right turn. 'You see, the kidnappers seemed sure the Pope would take water, but weren't sure if he'd take bottled water, or tap water for that matter. Also, they couldn't insert drugs in every bottle. And preferably the seal had to be left intact. A broken seal might arouse suspicion, and the bottle would be put aside. Every element of their plan had to be predictable, otherwise it wouldn't work.'

Guadagni shot a side-glance at Dulac. 'What about the aspirin? They could have substituted the drugs.'

'Correct. But unless they had divine insight, they couldn't be sure the Pope would take aspirin that night.'

'I see. So where does that lead you?'

'To the Pope's water glass.'

'What do you mean?'

'What if it had already been coated with some invisible, transparent substance containing the drugs, prior to the water being poured?'

'Mannaggia la miseria.' Guadagni grabbed his cell and dialed the Questura's number. 'Guadagni. Get me Cortese.'

Guadagni led Dulac into the main floor's open-room, and Dulac saw a short man with crew-cut black hair wearing a lab coat approach quickly from one of the side corridors.

'Dr Cortese,' said Guadagni, 'meet Inspector Dulac. He's with Interpol. He has a few questions.' Guadagni's tone was anything but sympathetic.

'Buongiorno, 'spector," Cortese said.

'Are you the one that found traces of the drugs on the Pope's water glass?' said Dulac.

'Sì. That is correct,' said Cortese, beaming with pride.

'Tell me doctor, can dobutamine or arbutamine be finely ground into some kind of paste and mixed with a gel?'

'Yes, but we would have seen that.'

'What if they added a masking agent?'

'Very difficult to mask a gel, 'spector.' Cortese's air of infallibility started to show a small crack.

'But it is possible.'

'With today's chemicals, anything is possible, 'spector. That does not mean it is likely,' he said impatiently.

'So if you weren't looking for the gel, or if it were masked with another substance, you might have missed it?'

'I suppose,' Cortese said reluctantly.

'I don't suppose you checked for any traces of gel or masking agent in the Pope's glass?'

'We were asked to do a preliminary report. I—'

'*Mannaggia la miseria*,' exclaimed Guadagni, glowering at Cortese. 'You'd better still have that goddamn glass.'

'Of course. I'll . . . I'll run another test right away.'

Dulac turned to Guadagni. 'Have Romer send the Pope's other glasses over here immediately. Get Romer to identify anyone dealing with or near those glasses for the past week.'

Dulac caught a cab back to the Hotel Dante. As he sat in the worn, uncomfortable rear seat, Dulac ran his fingers through his hair, replacing a recalcitrant lock back where it belonged. With the background noise of the traffic, Dulac could make out only bits of information over the cabbie's radio, as the spokeswoman gave the latest news on the Pope's kidnapping.

''orrible. 'orrible. Who would do such a thing?' the driver said, throwing a quick glance at Dulac through his rearview mirror.

'Many.' Dulac looked distractedly out the window at the onrushing traffic.

Suddenly, the cabbie's dispatcher overrode the radio program with staccato burst of his loud voice interspersed with ear-shattering static.

'Sì, sì,' replied the cabbie. He eyed Dulac in the mirror. 'Airport again. My eighth time today. Reporters and TV people. It's worse than when John Paul II died.'

'Good for business though,' said Dulac.

'I don't need it. I have enough without it. You know what I think? It's the Muslims.'

'Why is that?' Looking in the taxi's rear view mirror, Dulac caught that air of undoubting authority that cabbies acquire due to their position of temporary control over their passengers.

'The newspapers. They say it's the start of the Holy War. The one before Armageddon. It's predicted by Nostradamus. The Muslims, I'm telling you, it's the Muslims. Nostradamus says it will start with the kidnapping of Jesus's successor. Then the Antichrist will rise and reign for twelve years. It's all right there. Nostradamus. He's always right.'

Before Dulac could reply, the cabbie turned down Via Canaletto. Dulac saw the Hotel Dante's welcoming shape and breathed a sigh of relief. Dulac paid, entered the hotel lobby and walked briskly to the elevators.

Just as he entered his room, his cellphone rang. He closed the door and flipped it open. 'It's me. Karen. How did it go?'

'I'm wiped out.'

'You sound it. Listen, I've got some good news. I've just received a mandate to oversee a master's thesis on Roman animal mythology. I'm meeting my student Laura for lunch in Rome tomorrow. How about dinner, or . . . whatever?'

'I'll have the whatever.'

That musical laughter of hers burst into full song. 'And I thought you French had invented foreplay. I'll meet you at six tomorrow in the lobby.'

Dulac thought of those long, fit slender legs and suddenly felt reinvigorated. He went to the small desk, opened his laptop and scrolled down to the headlines of the world's major newspapers. The Pope's picture jumped out from every front page.

'Kidnappers abduct Pope Clement the 21st. Their identities and motive remain unknown,' said the *New York Times*. 'Pope Clement 21st target of abduction,' read the *Daily Mirror*. 'Is he still alive?'

'Curia members appeal to kidnappers: give us back our beloved pontiff,' read *The Sun*. 'Interpol brought in to find Pope,' said the *Herald Tribune*. 'No leads on the kidnappers.'

Dulac searched quickly for any encrypted e-mails from Interpol. Nothing. He went over to the minibar and poured himself a scotch. Too tired to change, he sat on the bed and leaned back against the pillows propped on the oak headboard and sipped his drink slowly. Soon, his head fell forward, the empty glass rolled from his hand onto the bed and he dozed off into a dreamless sleep.

The following morning, the shrill pinging of the hotel's phone snapped Dulac, still dressed, upright in the bed.

'Guadagni. My forensics people were up all night. The Pope's glasses, they're all coated with dobutamine and arbutamine mixed with a gel and a masking agent, some hydra-di-tetra something or other. Don't ask me to repeat the name. Very sophisticated chemistry, according to Cortese.'

'Ha!' For a brief moment, Dulac couldn't resist enjoying that warm smug feeling of being right.

Guadagni continued. 'We have another problem. The busboy, the one who cleans and places all the utensils and dinnerware in the papal kitchen . . .'

'Yes?'

'We can't find him. He hasn't been back at the Vatican since the day of the kidnapping.'

'Christ. Why didn't Romer mention it in his people-stream report?'

'Apparently, he had a day off yesterday so he wasn't missed. I put out an all-points search for him.'

'What's his name?' Dulac leaned over the desk and pulled out a cigarette.

'Paolo Valetta. At least that's the name on his job application. We're doing a profile search.'

'While you're at it, forward the profile to our guys at Lyon. Any news from the Air Force or the Coast Guard?'

'No sightings whatsoever. They've been busy combing a 500 mile radius with everything from Coast Guard vessels and helicopters to fighters and surface ships. Nothing. That helicopter has vanished into thin air.'

CHAPTER 9

The Vatican, 4.50 p.m., Wednesday 24 May

The Swiss Guard hurried from the Vatican's Sant'Anna entrance directly across to the barracks' office and handed the small package to Colonel Romer, sitting at his desk. 'It's for Cardinal Legnano. It was delivered by courier ten minutes ago. We checked it through security. It's safe. It's a DVD.'

Romer read the inscription in bold red letters on the lower left side of the small package. 'Urgent. Hand deliver only.' He rushed to Legnano's office.

Under Romer's expectant gaze, the cardinal opened the package, took out the DVD and inserted it into his computer. 'Mio Dio,' he exclaimed. Legnano pushed the stop button, picked up the phone and called Sforza. 'Come to my office quickly. I'll phone the others.'

Moments later, the prelates and Romer looking over his shoulder, Legnano hit the play button of his computer again. The picture of a seated man, dressed in a plain white cassock, appeared on the screen.

'It's His Holiness,' exclaimed Sforza.

'He's alive!' chimed in Brentano and Fouquet. Legnano called for silence as the video continued.

'Monsignori,' said an electronically-altered voice. 'We are taking every precaution to keep your pontiff in good health. His remaining so depends on you. We must receive the sum of $310 USD million, hot wire transfer, by 5 p.m. Rome time Friday May 26. You will receive our deposit instructions shortly. If you do not pay, we will destroy the pontiff. We have access to worldwide TV coverage.'

Legnano shouted to his secretary, 'Call Dulac. Call Guadagni. Tell them to come immediately.'

Seated at his hotel-room desk, Dulac had been busy coordinating between the Vatican and Interpol a system of classification of outside calls. He'd ensured that they be filtered through Interpol's Lyon headquarters, to check their credibility and authenticity: Code three was for pranksters, nut cases and known fame-seekers. Code two for the vast majority of well-meaning, well wishing, but not necessarily helpful calls from the world at large. Code one was reserved for the verified, authenticated calls from law enforcement agencies, local, national and international, including Italy's security agency SISMI, the FBI, the French Bureau and the Russian FSB.

Dulac had just received two code one calls when he recognized the Vatican's number on his encrypted cell. It was Legnano.

Twenty minutes later, Dulac hurried through the Sant'Anna entrance, flashing his credentials to the Swiss Guards. Cardinal Legnano's secretary was waiting inside and they rushed to Legnano's office. Guadagni, his hair disheveled, entered moments later, and stood next to Dulac in the center while the other cardinals milled about expectantly.

'$310 million USD! That's what these criminals want for the pontiff,' said Legnano as he paced back and forth in front of the large window, throwing his hands in the air and casting a glance at Dulac. 'Do they think we're the US Federal Reserve?'

Dulac eyed the Cardinal and feigned a look of sympathy. He knew this was pocket change for the Vatican Bank, one of the world's biggest. 'Your Eminence, I'd like to see the video,' he said calmly. 'By the way, you should have called us before opening the package.'

'Oh? Why?' said Legnano.

'Because you've probably compromised the evidence. The kidnappers might have left fingerprints.'

Legnano looked at Romer accusingly.

'The damage is done. Let's have a look,' said Dulac.

'Sì, sì. Come over here, gentlemen,' said Legnano to Dulac and Guadagni, as he walked back to his desk before pressing the start button.

He's worn out, thought Dulac as he saw the Pope sitting expressionless, shoulders hunched. 'We'll see if our technicians can get something out of this. That voice can be unscrambled. We may be able to trace the disk if it's not too old. Also, this might be a clever montage. We've been duped before. In the meantime, have your secretary copy me a DVD,' said Dulac.

'What do you think of these, these supposed accounts?' Cardinal Sforza asked Dulac.

'They're smart. That's why they are creating a time lag between now and payment time. They won't create those accounts until the last possible minute, so we can't trace them,' said Dulac. 'They'll have trustees with false identities set them up, and when their dirty work is done, they'll disappear into space. Once the money is distributed, the accounts will self-destruct. For the outside world, it's as if they never existed.'

'Can't you do anything to stop them?' said Legnano, his voice strident.

'It depends on how sophisticated they are. From what we've seen so far, I wouldn't bet on it.'

'You're saying that once the money is transferred, we have no hope of retrieving it, or tracing it back to the kidnappers?'

'Unfortunately that's correct, your Eminence,' replied Dulac. 'They'll probably create an instant bank or offshore foundation and do some corporate layering to mask the ownership structure. Then they'll distribute small amounts to accounts in other countries. They'll make sure those amounts are under the reportable thresholds of the receiving banks, then they will collapse the sending bank the same day. That's the standard pattern. It'll take us anywhere between two to six months just to clear the jurisdiction hurdles, before we can even begin to investigate.'

For a moment, Dulac felt he would give way to the urge of telling the cardinals that $310 million was a mere pittance in the secretive world of offshore money transfers, but resisted the temptation.

'Mr Dulac, what do they mean by hot wire transfer?' said Sforza.

'It's like hot-wiring a car to start it. Short-circuiting all the checks and balances of the SWIFT wire transfer system, and local banking security regulations, such as they are in these offshore countries.'

The expressions on the cardinals' faces grew somber, as they seemed to absorb the fundamentals of international money laundering for the first time. Legnano leaned back in his chair, and then looked at the other cardinals. 'Monsignori, we have a basic decision to make. Any preliminary thoughts?'

Fouquet spoke first. 'How do we contact them? We cannot—'

Dulac interrupted him. 'Don't worry, your Eminence. They'll contact you. Probably shortly before 1 p.m. Friday. They know it takes some time for even a hot wire transfer to go through.'

'That's only two days away,' said Sforza. 'If we start—'

'This is completely immoral,' interrupted Cardinal Brentano. 'We don't deal with criminals.'

To be expected from the keeper of the Church's doctrine, Dulac thought, as he waited for a reaction from the other cardinals.

'Are you suggesting we sit here and do nothing? Call their bluff?' said Legnano, glaring at Brentano.

'I'm not suggesting anything of the sort. But we can't just simply hand them the money. The Church would be seen as condoning extortion,' replied Brentano.

Fouquet spoke up. 'I'm sorry but I won't stand here on high moral ground and risk signing the Pope's death warrant. These criminals know they have all the cards.'

'Not necessarily, your Eminence,' said Dulac.

'What do you mean?'

'Do you remember the Bulgarian hostage taking of the Korean nurses?'

'Of course.'

'After the French intervened and got the hostages out, the French government officially denied any payment of ransom, saying they used a mole to get the nurses out.'

'But surely, the government must have paid,' said Legnano.

'Did it? No proof of where that payment came from, or even if there was any payment,' said Dulac.

'I suppose, but we all know that someone must have,' said Legnano.

'Your Eminence, surely you're aware that ransom demands can be met in other, shall I say, creative ways.'

'What do you mean?' said Legnano.

'The Canadians rescued one of their kidnapped diplomats from Bolivian terrorists by giving a large chunk of money to a so-called humanitarian organization in Bolivia. That way, they were able to categorically state that they never paid the ransom. A few years later, Interpol traced an arms deal between the Bolivian rebels and a Canadian arms dealer for exactly that amount.'

'I see,' said Legnano.

'Don't get me wrong. I'm certainly not suggesting that you contact an arms dealer. My question to you is simply the following: can the Vatican live with the perception, but not the proof of the reality by the world at large?'

'Certainly,' said Sforza.

Dulac knew that in today's faltering faith, the Vatican's very existence and survival depended more than ever upon perception. Perception of its God-given authority, perception of the Pope's infallibility, perception of ultimate good and justice crushing the forces of evil, and most important, perception and promise of eternal bliss.

'What are you suggesting Mr Dulac?' said Sforza.

'I'm asking you not to exclude negotiating, when the opportunity arises.'

'You said, "when", inspector?' interjected Legnano.

'Yes. When. When you send them the down payment on Friday.'

CHAPTER 10

As Dulac and Guadagni waited beside the stand at the entrance of *Il Cortile*, Dulac could see the customers fighting for the attention of the two blasé waiters, taking their sweet time only as Italian waiters can, flagrantly oblivious to the hand-signaling and clamors of their expectant clients.

'Reservations?' asked the maitre d'. Guadagni flashed his credentials. 'Yes, inspector. Right this way.'

Guadagni and Dulac followed the maitre d', past the now angry couple who had been waiting for the sole remaining table.

Guadagni sat down and said, 'You seem confident that—'

Dulac suddenly hit his forehead with his right hand. 'Shit. Shit. I'm in deep shit.' Dulac grabbed his cell and dialed the hotel's number. 'Ms. Dawson please, room 348.'

After a moment the receptionist said, 'There is no answer.'

'Please leave her the following message: Sorry about dinner. I'll explain later.'

'You were saying?' Dulac said, turning back to Guadagni.

'You seem confident these people will negotiate.'

'The cardinals are in a tough spot,' said Dulac, unbuttoning his jacket and relocating his unruly lock off his forehead. 'They can't condone extortion, yet if they don't pay, these kidnappers might do something stupid.'

'Like those who murdered Archbishop Kaharo in Iraq.'

'I'm sure the thought crossed everyone's mind at the Vatican.'

'I hope you're right,' said Guadagni, putting on his bifocals and reading the menu. 'Their calf's sweetbreads in butter are simply delicioso.'

'I'll pass. I'm up for some spaghetti.'

'Spaghetti? In Italy? Suit yourself,' said Guadagni, obviously unimpressed by Dulac's mundane selection.

Fifteen minutes later, the waiter arrived with their orders, and Dulac inserted his napkin between collar and neck, to Guadagni's unconcealed amusement.

'I know. But it saves me a dry cleaning later,' said Dulac.

After dinner, as they waited for their coffees, Dulac opened his laptop and typed Paolo Valetta's name into the encrypted Interpol search engine. After a moment, he said, 'Just as I thought. Your busboy isn't Italian at all. He's gone under a half dozen names, the last of which is Mecem Aguar.'

'Sounds Bulgarian.'

'Turkish. I've got about a dozen crime organizations, anyone of which could have hired Aguar. Let's see, he's worked for the Basque's ETA, the Medellin boys, even the Russian FSB. That's only the ones we know.'

'What's his background?'

'Just a second.' Dulac scrolled down. 'Here. Chemistry. Our man got his PhD in pharmacology at the University of Ankara. Hmm, interesting, he's probably in shape. He tried out for the Turkish wrestling team for the 1988 Olympics. A bit overqualified for a simple busboy, wouldn't you say?'

'Why the hell didn't Romer pick all this up before hiring him?' said Guadagni.

'My very thoughts,' said Dulac, removing his napkin from his collar.

'I guess a busboy doesn't get a high-level screening in the Vatican.'

'Even if he can poison the Pope?' said Dulac.

'I'll get the details of Aguar's hiring from Romer.'

'While you're at it, you might check Romer's also,' said Dulac, his eyes searching for the brunette.

'You can't be serious.'

Dulac looked at Guadagni. 'Dead serious.'

Dulac had left two more messages for Karen and was heading back to the hotel.

'Code One call for Inspector Dulac,' said the voice on Dulac's encrypted cellphone, as he got out of the taxi.

'Speaking,' said Dulac, taking quick strides towards the hotel's entrance.

'David Béland, Interpol Intercept Division. We received a Code One from an Inspector Maurice Shabbat, in Casablanca. They apparently have a voice transcript of a video-voice signal between an unknown source and a receptor in Sicily. They intercepted a short exchange between the two. Initial unscrambling shows the Sicilian source could be a match with the Pope's voice.'

'Fantastic. Send it to Gina at forensics for corroboration.'

'She's already on it.'

'Good man. Did Shabbat get the longitude-latitude coordinates?'

'No, the call was too short.'

'When can you get confirmation?'

'Hard to tell. Gina says the unscrambling may take hours, maybe days. It depends on the degree and complexity of the scrambling.'

'What about the sender's identity?' said Dulac, stopping in front of the revolving door.

'Impossible. It's a frequency-modulated, computer-created voice. Very latest equipment.'

'Let me know.' Dulac took a few steps away from the hotel entrance, stopped and punched Guadagni's number at the Questura Centrale. 'Dulac. We have a Code One that the Holy Father may be in Sicily.'

'That's a big piece of territory.'

'What is your situation there?'

'We're pretty thin. Plus, we're fighting a resurgence of the Cosa Nostra.'

'Could they be involved?' said Dulac.

'I doubt it. They're staunch Catholics, Sicilian style: go to confession on Sunday, commit a murder or two on Monday. Kidnapping prelates is not their style. But we have, shall we say, contacts, yes contacts within the Familia in Sicily.'

Dulac smiled at the thought of the unholy, perhaps incestuous alliance.

'I'll order air and sea coverage on Sardinia and Sicily. We'll cover all the ferries, ports, public and private landing strips, even yacht clubs. I don't want a mosquito to leave without us knowing.'

'Call me when you have news,' said Dulac as he headed through the revolving door into the Hotel Dante's lobby.

As she sat sipping her glass of Cabernet-Sauvignon at Hotel Dante's bar, trying to control her anger after Dulac's latest slight, Karen immersed herself into her student's thesis.

'Is this seat taken?'

Jolted, she turned to face Dulac, who hadn't waited for an answer before placing his computer satchel on the bar and sitting down beside her.

'You could have at least called,' said Karen, trying to fix her most reproachful gaze on Dulac.

'I did. I left messages at the reception. Didn't they reach you?'

'That's the lamest, most overused attempt to shift the blame I've heard in a long time.'

'I really had a terrible supper with Guadagni, if that's any consolation. Have you eaten?'

'The Black Sea caviar was fantastique. So was the lobster risotto. The Neapolitan mousse was out of this galaxy. By the way, you paid for all of it.'

'Of course. Anything else?'

'A grappa might be a good start. A Nardini Riserva Speciale to be exact.'

Dulac signaled the bartender. 'You heard the woman.'

Moments later, the bartender returned with a bottle of one of Italy's priciest liqueurs and showed it to Karen, then Dulac, who nodded reluctantly.

The bartender filled her glass, then Dulac's.

'With my apologies,' said Dulac, toasting her.

'I'll consider the matter.'

Time for the sympathy tack, Dulac thought as he put down his glass. 'You know, I'm getting too old for this harried, suitcase living. Hotels and more hotels. The airport lineups. Late planes that sit for hours on the tarmac. Fat, sweaty passengers. Why do I always get the fattest, sweatiest, smelliest slob sitting right next to me? It's as if the girls at the flight desk think, "Well, he looks thin enough. We'll put him next to fatso. That way, things will even out on that side of the plane."'

'Yeah, sure,' said Karen.

Dulac thought he saw the beginning of a smile forming from Karen's generous lips. 'Soft hotel beds, hard beds, showers that run cold, suits pressed inside out, trousers with double creases, lost shirts and underwear, shrunk socks. I can't count the number of times I've gone to meetings in dirty underwear.' He took a sip of grappa. 'I can't take much more of this.'

Karen emitted a small guffaw. 'Pure Hell, Thierry. How can you stand it? Give me a break. You have the biggest challenge a man could have. The Pope's life is at stake and the world's police forces are at your fingertips, and—'

'I know, I know. I complain. I can't help it. It's in my genes. You must understand. The French have got to complain, or die. We've developed the reflex over centuries. We've been given realms, just to shut us up. When the French and the British signed the Treaty of Versailles, when was it?' Dulac paused and scoured his memory. '1763 I think.

Yes, 1763. The Brits gave us half the world. Christ, we'd lost the war! But we won the argument. Same thing after World War II: France lies in ruins and de Gaulle talks the country back into glory. We French bluster our way through, and the world loves us for it.'

Karen flicked back a wisp of hair from her forehead. 'Glad you think so. Getting back to business. What's happening with your case?'

'We're trying to trace a guy named Aguar who might be the person who drugged the Pope.'

'Trying to, might be. Sounds about as firm as hot Jell-O, inspector.'

Dulac leaned conspiratorially towards Karen and whispered in her ear, 'Since we're on that subject, care for something harder?'

Aboard the Rome to Zurich train, later that day

As the train to Zurich twisted and turned through the foothills of the Apennines, Aguar, tense and tired, would doze off then wake fitfully, to catch a fleeting glimpse of one of the many pastel-colored renaissance palaces and Romanesque churches that dot the Upper Ticino valley. Suddenly the squawk of the train's intercom jolted Aguar from his light sleep.

'Attention all passengers,' said the harsh voice. 'We will be stopping in Chiasso to change locomotives. Please have your passports ready.'

Damn. Aguar slammed his fist against the side of the compartment, underneath the window. This was supposed to be a non-stop trip. They don't check passports on non-stops. He felt beads of sweat forming on his forehead as the train snaked its way slowly into Chiasso's triage yard, its multiple rail sidings stretching out like the giant fingers of a steel hand, ready to clutch him in its vice-like grip. Gradually, the train came to a full stop.

Aguar took out his handkerchief and wiped his brow.

Moments later, a border guard entered Aguar's railcar and started to check passports. The short, middle-aged man, his beer paunch straddled by his suspenders, made his way through the rows of seats, chatting with the passengers sometimes in Swiss-German, sometimes in Italian. Aguar tensed, his heart pounding like an out-of-control jackhammer.

The guard smiled down at him as Aguar handed him the passport. 'Ah, you are from Montreal?'

'Yes.'

'I know it well. My brother works there.' Aguar nodded knowingly.

'What brings you to Zurich?'

'Business.' Aguar could feel the perspiration forming on his upper lip and brow.

'What kind of business?' said the guard, his tone still cordial but firm.

'Investment banking.'

'Anything to declare?'

'No.' As the word left his lips, Aguar knew the 'No' had been one decibel too many.

'I see,' said the guard, looking suspiciously at Aguar, then at the leather carry-all above him on the rack. 'Is this yours?'

'No,' said Aguar, hunching his shoulders in ignorance.

'Really? You're the only passenger—'

Aguar had a millisecond to react. He sprang up, shoved the guard across the aisle onto a seated, bewildered woman, grabbed the carry-all and made a run for the door.

'Stop!' yelled the guard.

Aguar heard the loud, strident whistle as he jumped off the train onto the cement platform. He stopped for an instant, looking for an escape route. Directly across the sets of tracks, about a hundred yards away, a small concrete wall separated the triage yard from Chiasso's busy streets. If he could get there, he could easily bolt it. Carrying the bag in his left hand, he ran towards the wall, careful not to trip on the tracks.

Only three more sets of tracks and . . .

Suddenly, he heard a dog's furious barking, getting louder.

One more set. The dog was right behind him. Aguar turned, only to glimpse a mass of German shepherd fury hurtling through the air, its open jaws aiming at his left arm. He brought up the bag, trying to fend off the dog with the bag. He missed and the dog's jaw clamped onto his left forearm. Aguar dropped the bag and fell backwards, hitting the top of the cement wall with his lower back. He felt the pain jab through his kidney like a sword. The dog went down on top of him, tearing back and forth at Aguar's forearm while Aguar tried desperately to grab the dog's throat. The dog snapped viciously at Aguar's hands, then bit into his right forearm. Two guards rushed up to Aguar and drew their pistols as one of them called off the dog.

Aguar, his forearms and hands bloodied, lay panting and very, very still.

CHAPTER 11

Lying naked in bed under the comfort of the duvet, Karen and Dulac watched the news on the hotel room's TV. The raven-haired woman with the rectangular-rimmed glasses from France 2 went on impassively, as the camera focused on an ambulance near the entrance of a mosque . . . 'there is fear of more reprisals for the Pope's abduction, as in Bercy this evening eleven Islamic students were gunned down in the Al Fatih mosque. As of now, there are six confirmed dead, and two more are in critical condition. According to witnesses, four masked gunmen opened fire at the faithful while they prayed . . .'

The camera zoomed onto a white placard on the ground while she continued, 'They left this warning at the entrance of the Mosque.' The placard read: 'For the Pope — we will return.'

'Now it starts,' said Dulac. Suddenly his cell rang. He leaned over the night table and grabbed it, recognizing the Questura's number.

'Dulac.'

'Guadagni. The Italian border guards caught Aguar. He was trying to escape to Switzerland by train.'

Dulac sat up in the bed. 'Guadagni, you've made my day. Where is he?'

'He's being shipped to the Questura Centrale as we speak. He should be here within the half-hour.'

'Be there in a bit.' Dulac hung up and turned to Karen. 'They've caught Aguar.'

Dulac dressed quickly and put his laptop in the black, worn satchel. He turned to see the svelte honey-blonde stretch catlike in the bed, open her arms toward him, her eyes inviting, her lusting body bordering on the irresistible.

'Wish I had time. Keep the engine running, Dr Dawson.'

'Aren't we a bit formal?' said Karen, pouting slightly.

'Surely you still enjoy the title.'

'Not coming from you.' She turned away and coiled up on her side in a prenatal curl. 'Note taken.'

Dulac leaned over the bed, parted her hair slightly and kissed her on the back of the neck. He grabbed his laptop, headed for the lobby and ordered a taxi from the concierge. As he stood outside waiting, the crisp dusk air invaded his lungs briefly, reminding him of his craving for that delicious evening cigarette. 'The Questura Centrale. On Piazza del Collegio Romano,' he instructed the cabbie.

'I know where it is,' answered the driver, with an Italian hand gesture Dulac didn't fully understand. Moments later, Dulac, laptop satchel slung over his shoulder, hustled up the worn limestone steps of Rome's main police station, to see a smiling Guadagni standing proudly at the entrance. 'One of the border guard dogs caught him just before he got to the triage yard fence. He's in bad shape.'

Guadagni led Dulac past rows of cells, the recurring habitat of Rome's finest, to the elevators at the end of the corridor. They took the elevator to the second floor and walked towards two guards standing in front of the door of a small cell. Upon seeing Guadagni, they snapped to attention. Guadagni acknowledged their salute with a curt nod.

Lying on his cot, the dark-complexioned man inside the cell sat up, his stare expressionless. Mecem Aguar was a short, heavyset man in his early forties. With his narrow brow, stubby nose, crew-cut graying hair and wide shoulders bursting out of his undersized brown sports jacket, he looked like an ageing football player turned sports commentator. His bloodied, bandaged hands and forearms bore testimony to the guard dog's efficiency.

'I've asked for the Vatican's employee file on him,' said Guadagni, as they stood in front of the cell.

'Probably pretty thin, from what I've seen. I'll work with Interpol's.'

'Well, there's no need, since I'll interrogate,' said Guadagni peremptorily.

'Don't think so,' said Dulac.

'What do you mean? We have jurisdiction,' said Guadagni, his tone rising to Dulac's challenge.

Dulac smiled. 'Not really. Read the Interpol-Italy Cooperation Agreement, section 23. Since the presumed crime is cross-border, Interpol has jurisdiction. You can witness my interrogation if you like.'

'Listen, this is my jail, my turf. I do the questioning here.' Guadagni stood four centimeters from Dulac's face. The prison guards looked on, slightly embarrassed but ready to support Guadagni.

Dulac retreated slightly. 'Fine. I'll call my friend Paolo Nulti. You know, the Italian Minister of Justice. Haven't talked to him in a while. Let's see what he thinks.' Dulac opened his cellphone.

Guadagni backed down. 'Well, there's no need to get all formal. We can work him together. Why don't you loosen him up a little first, then I'll go in for the kill.'

'Good.' Dulac smiled and closed his cell. Although he remembered hearing Nulti's name in a recent Radio Roma interview criticizing the slowness and inefficiency of the Italian courts, he didn't have the faintest idea what Paolo Nulti looked like.

Guadagni had one of the guards open the cell door and Dulac went in, followed by the guard.

The cell door closed behind them. Dulac pulled up the wooden chair next to the table, set his computer on it in front of Aguar and opened it. He scrolled down. 'Ah. Here it is . . .' After a moment, he raised his eyes to Aguar's level. 'Hello Mecem, or is it Hamir, or Dmitri, or Victor? You're hard to keep up with, these days.'

Aguar sat expressionless on his cot, arms crossed, staring at Dulac from across the table. 'How do you ass-fucking Turkish sons of whores get your jollies going after Popes? First it was John Paul II, and now this one?'

Aguar remained impassive, but from the corner of his eye Dulac saw Aguar's right bandaged hand contract almost imperceptibly.

'Just as I thought. You do understand English.'

Aguar brought his hands up and stretched. He reclined slightly and reclosed his arms carefully over his barrel chest.

'We know about the dobutamine, arbutamine and the gel. Quite imaginative, I must admit. And there's the small matter of $200,000 USD you were carrying illegally across the border. What did you say that was for?'

Aguar remained expressionless and silent.

'Of course, you didn't say, did you?' Dulac hardened his gaze and locked onto Aguar's. 'Next you'll probably tell me you want to see your lawyer. Well, let me give you my take on this. It's the only free legal opinion you're ever going to get. The way I see it, assuming the Pope is still alive, you're a conspirator to kidnapping. Not great, but it could get worse. If the Pope dies, you're facing a murder charge in an Italian court.'

Dulac paused, his eyes still locked onto Aguar's. 'Not good, Mecem, definitely not good. You know the Italians. They can get pretty nasty when you attack their faith. Do you really want to play out that script?'

Aguar remained silent, impassive.

'You cooperate with us now, give us your contacts, and you'll save yourself a lot of prison pain, front and back, if you know what I mean. We get the judge onboard and the worst you'll do is a couple of years in a cushy minimum security prison in Padua. Best deal you'll ever get.'

Aguar stared, expressionless.

'I see, still playing dumb. Up to you Mecem, but you know these people. You poisoned their pope? Another Turk? Not a pretty picture. Yes, I know you'll tell me you're a dead man if you speak. I'll admit it's not an easy choice: rot away slowly in custody, or die quickly by the hand that hired you.'

Aguar's head reclined in defiance. 'You have no proof. I did nothing.'

'Well, well. The dumb miraculously speaketh! But we do, you see, we do. Funny thing about latex gloves. Who would ever think we could pick up imprints on the inside? You did use latex gloves didn't you, when handling the Pope's glasses? Of course you did. You threw them away in the garbage can. You've got to give the Italian police credit for being meticulous. Dumb move, Mecem, dumb move. We have a 98% match on two of your fingers. But we have even better: there's enough of your dried sweat on those latex gloves to do about 50 DNA tests. Any bets on the results?'

Aguar's face reddened. 'I admit nothing. I want to see a lawyer.'

'Later. Later. You'll be speaking to as many lawyers as you want. For the rest of your short life.'

'I'll take my chances.'

'Suit yourself.' Dulac smiled and put his computer back into the satchel. He rose and signaled the guard to open the door. Looking at Guadagni he said, 'Your turn.'

After a half hour of questioning before a bemused Dulac, Guadagni threw in the towel. Guadagni slammed the cell door behind him. 'Thinks he's tough. He hasn't gone through a couple of all-night redeyes yet.'

'Do I want to know what an all-night redeye is?' said Dulac.

'Probably not.'

They made their way down the corridor back toward the front desk. As they approached, loud voices could be heard coming from the front desk area. 'That'll be the bloody press,' said Guadagni.'

'Already?'

'They saw the special escort vehicle outside. Like a pot of honey to a bear.'

'Do they know he has anything to do with the Pope's kidnapping?'

Guadagni glanced at Dulac. 'Ha! Believe me, they know. Any bets?'

'No bets. Your turf, remember?' said Dulac, smiling. In an instant, the hungry horde had surrounded them.

'What's his name?' asked a blonde woman reporter from Corriere Della Sera to Guadagni.

'Dimitri. Or Victor. I forget,' he answered.

'Has he been charged?'

'Not as of now.'

'What is his role in the Pope's kidnapping?'

'Who says he has anything to do with that?' said Guadagni, smiling.

'Come on, inspector, we're only doing our job. Where is he from?'

'The middle-east,' said Guadagni.

'Do you believe the Pope is still alive?' said the reporter from Giorno Napoli.

'We have no reason to think otherwise.'

'Will the Vatican give in to the ransom demand?' said the Corriere woman.

'You'll have to ask them.'

'So you're no further ahead than yesterday?' she replied.

'I wouldn't say that.'

'You don't have to.'

Guadagni put up his right hand, indicating closure. 'Ladies, gentlemen, that will be all for today.'

CHAPTER 12

Central American Jungle, 11.05 a.m.

Still unshaven, the man put aside his cup of tepid coffee, rose from the wicker chair and walked to the veranda. He stretched and, arms akimbo, began his twenty torso rotations. His daily ritual finished, he reached into the water basin beside the bamboo separator and aspersed his face.

He looked up just as the sun broke over the mountains' horizon. He walked over to the edge of the veranda, put his hands on the wooden railing and gazed into the distance. Engulfed in the folds of the valley below, the river snaked lazily along, its meanders of dull silver weaving through the green of the lush, sub-tropical forest. Below and to the left of the veranda, two guards were patrolling inside the barbed-wire perimeter of the compound. Except for their short, muted exchanges and the occasional crowing of a macaw, the jungle was quiet.

He took in deep breaths, absorbing the fresh morning air. The man looked at his watch. He left the veranda, walked through the salon and went downstairs to the closed-circuit video conference room.

It was time. Time to speak to his 'guest' again, then to Vespoli.

Sicily, 7.10 p.m.

The Pope sat uneasily, hands crossed in his lap, waiting for signs of life from the TV monitor. Finally the shadow appeared.

'You wish to speak to me?' inquired the video voice in an electronically-altered monotone.

'Yes,' said the pontiff, his voice firm. 'I have a right to know why I've been brought here.'

'You'll find out in due course.'

'Is it about money?'

The shadow didn't answer.

'Is it about the Church? About me?'

'Partially.'

'What, specifically?' said the pontiff, trying to hide his growing discomfort caused by the impersonality of the voice.

'Your arrogance, your lack of openness, your rigidity, your lack of vision, but most of all your hypocrisy. You should never have been elected Pope.'

The pontiff felt a surge of anxiety, and fidgeted with his tunic. 'Why?'

'You preach against genocide. You constantly denounce the regimes practicing it. Do you remember your last condemnation?'

'You mean the Mugabe regime?'

'What right do you have to condemn others? After what you did? I quote to you John 8:7: "And Jesus said unto them: he that is without sin . . . let him cast a stone . . ."'

The Pope felt the blood rush to his face. A throbbing constriction began to tighten the muscles and skin over his temples. His mind went numb. He feared he knew the answer to the question he was about to ask, but had to utter it.

'What do you mean?'

'We have the diary.'

'*Mio Dio!*' The Pope put a hand to his mouth and felt his hand begin to shake. After a moment, he said meekly, 'And . . . and what do you intend to do with it?'

'That depends on the Curia.'

The shadow's image dissolved and the monitor went blank.

Vespoli had just finished escorting the Pope back to his room and had hurried back to the video conference room, this time alone. It was time for their prescheduled video conference, and as he sat down in one of the plush velvet seats, Vespoli fought back the increasing panic with every fiber of his body. Little droplets of sweat were forming on his upper lip and he wiped them away with the back of his hand. He tried to calm his frayed nerves by closing his eyes, drawing a blank in his mind, and holding it. He hated the impersonality of the electronically-altered voice and shadowed outline format of the transmission, but recognized the need for utmost safety precautions to hide the identity of the parties.

The monitor flickered to life. At the sound of the static, Vespoli jumped.

Gathering his wits, he said to the shadowed outline on the screen, 'We have a problem, sir.'

'Problem?' answered the electronically-altered voice.

'They've arrested Aguar.'

A long silence. Vespoli felt the muscles of his throat tighten.

'Where is he?'

'According to our contact, they've taken him to Rome, to the Questura Centrale.'

'I trust you have an immediate solution to this problem,' said the voice, dispassionate.

'He was crossing the Swiss border and—'

'Where is Umberto?'

'Ah. We . . . we don't know. He was to meet Aguar at the train station. He hasn't reported in.'

'Then you have two problems.' The voice's tone changed, more forceful.

Vespoli could feel the sweat running down from his armpits. Another long, oppressive silence. Vespoli heard the shadow inhaling and exhaling breaths through the electronic voice modifier. It sounded like the last rasps of a dying man.

'What does Aguar know? How far up?' said the voice.

'Only to Umberto.'

'You're sure?'

'I swear.'

'You'd better be right. I want this resolved quickly, Vespoli. Before I arrive in Switzerland tomorrow. Get Tomaso on it.'

'Yes, sir.'

'I don't need to remind you that we're on a very tight schedule.'

'No, sir.'

'No more screw-ups Vespoli, is that clear?'

'Perfectly, sir. I'll get Tomaso on it right now.'

The screen went blank. Vespoli rose from his seat and felt the numbness in his legs slowly dissipate. Raw, deep fear overtook him. He knew the man didn't have a high tolerance for error, sometimes exacting a heavy price from those who had ventured beyond those limits. Vespoli knew he was at that threshold. He was responsible for all men under his command. Their errors were his. Damn that Aguar. Vespoli thought for a moment, searching for options. No, Tomaso had to be called. There was no other way.

Yet Vespoli still hesitated, fearing the call to Tomaso would also trigger his own death.

CHAPTER 13

Hotel Dante, 8.05 a.m., Thursday 25 May

Dulac had returned to the hotel, exhausted and frustrated. The clock was ticking and the investigation was stalled. Even if Guadagni made Aguar crack, apart from his role, Aguar probably didn't know much. Dulac knew the kidnappers would have compartmentalized each and every of their accomplices' tasks, to avoid any linkage. At best Aguar would know the name of his immediate superior, and it would undoubtedly be false. To go up the chain would take time, a commodity Dulac didn't have.

After a quick breakfast with Karen and seeing her off to her meeting with her graduate student, Dulac returned upstairs to his room. He poured himself a coffee from the cheap mixer and lay back on the unmade bed. He lit a Gitane. For a long moment, he stared across the room, blowing bluish puffs towards the cheap copy of the painting of Notre Dame by Monet. Something bothered him about the kidnappers' message. He took the copy of the DVD Legnano's secretary had made for him, went to his computer and played the disc again.

The Pope's familiar outline came alive, as did the disquieting voice. 'We are taking every precaution to keep your pontiff in good health. His remaining so depends on you. We must receive the sum of $310 USD million, hot wire transfer, by 5 p.m. Rome time Friday May 26 . . . If you do not pay, we will destroy the pontiff. We have access to worldwide TV coverage.' Jesus, Today is Thursday. The Curia has a day to decide, thought Dulac. The idea of the Pope being murdered in cold blood chilled him to the marrow of his bones. The consequences were unthinkable. He replayed the video again.

'We will destroy the pontiff . . .'

'Merde!' He jumped up from his desk and, grabbing his cellphone, walked quickly towards the window. He dialed Cardinal Legnano's number. 'Your Eminence, I want to meet the members of the Curia. Today.'

'Mr Dulac, this is quite sudden. The members of the Curia and I will be attending meetings of the highest order.'

That could only mean with the President of Italy, Dulac thought. 'We have to decide before tomorrow,' said Legnano.

'I know, but this is urgent, your Eminence. It might even have a bearing on your decision.'

'I'll see what I can do. What's this all about?' asked Legnano.

'I'll tell you when we meet.'

Dulac left his room and went to the lobby, waiting for Legnano's call. What's taking him so long? It's about the Pope, damnit, Dulac thought as he lit a cigarette and reclined in the wraparound imitation leather seat. Suddenly, his encrypted cellphone rang. Dulac looked at the number appearing on its small screen: Harris.

'We've got a lead,' said Harris, excitement in his voice. 'Bergson in Panama City says he's been tipped off.' Harris coughed. 'Four banks are going to receive large deposits through a single hotwire transfer. It's going down this week.'

'What's so unusual about that?'

'They generally stagger hotwire deposits to avoid detection. They don't bunch them up in one operation.' said Harris.

'Could be a coincidence.'

'Four banks? That's a hell of a coincidence.'

Dulac thought quickly. 'If you're right, it would mean that the Vatican already knows where to deposit the money, that the kidnappers have contacted them and that Legnano and company are suddenly acting behind our backs. Plus, would they have prepared a single hotwire transfer and been stupid enough to let us in on it? It's not impossible, but it's a bit unlikely, don't you think?'

'I'm not taking any chances. I'm putting two agents in every one of those banks. Once the money is in, we'll freeze the bloody accounts. We'll freeze the balls off those bankers.'

Dulac slumped into the seat, all the while exhaling circular, bluish puffs of Gitane smoke. He tried another tack. 'If the kidnappers are behind this and get wind of our agents going in, they'll call it off. Those bankers talk to each other,' Dulac said. 'There's a good chance of a leak.' Dulac paused and for an instant, thought he heard the sucking sound of Harris taking the bottle from his lips.

'I'll take that chance,' said Harris.

'You'll have to pull units. That'll weaken our already thin network. If the kidnappers have other plans—'

'We can't just sit and wait. We have to be seen as reacting,' said Harris.

He's been hitting it hard.

'Frankly, if this is related to the ransom, they're obviously baiting us. Panama is bait. Bait and switch at the last minute.'

'I can't take the bloody risk. Risk they won't use Panama. They want us to think exactly what you're thinking. In that case, it's Panama.'

'I doubt it.'

'Why?'

'Too obvious.'

'So where do you think this will happen?'

'No idea.'

'No idea? That's the best you can come up with? I'm being hammered left and right: politicians, the press, the Vatican, you name it. They're all taking shots at me, and all you can say is no fucking idea? They say we're not doing much. You know, I think they're right. Well, I'm gonna show them, Dulac. I'm definitely gonna show them.'

'Yes sir. That you will.' The line went dead.

Drunken bastard!

Dulac extinguished his cigarette. Harris's 'we' was meant to be a 'you'. You, Dulac, aren't doing much. He phoned his assistant in Paris, Daniel Lescop.

'Eight units to Panama? Is he nuts?'

'Would you mind telling him that? I'd appreciate it,' said Dulac. 'Yeah, sure. What if Panama is bait?'

'My thoughts exactly. I'm giving you a heads up. There's a good chance you'll be among the chosen few. You know Panama well.'

'Thanks for nothing.'

Having realized he'd forgotten his computer in the room, Dulac got up and started towards the elevators, only to reopen his buzzing cellphone.

'Dulac.'

'Guadagni. I have news. An hour ago, my men found a man with a bullet in the back of his head, lying along the Rome-Naples Autostrada. His name is Umberto Ascari.

'Sounds like a Mafia hit.'

'We thought so too, until my men went through his boots.'

'Boots?'

'We're more thorough than his killers were. Ascari had bought two one-way plane tickets from Zurich to Mexico City: one in his name, the other in the name of—'

'Mecem Aguar!'

'Exactly.'

'He's not going to Mexico anytime soon. I— Sorry, I have another incoming call,' said Dulac. 'I'll get back to you.' He pressed the button. 'Dulac.'

'Cardinal Legnano. I've arranged for you to meet us at 10 a.m. in the Segnatura room. We'll give you have half an hour, no more.'

'Yes, your Eminence. I'll be right over.'

The taxi drive from the hotel to St. Peter's Square usually took the better part of ten minutes, but soon Dulac's taxi was sitting immobile in Rome's mid-morning gridlock, enveloped by vapors of gasoline and diesel fumes. His cabbie was swearing as only Italians can, imploring the Saints without really offending them. 'Santa Margherita Ligure, can you believe these idiots? Why don't they stay on the right? They're blocking everything. Santa Lucia, look at this imbecile trying to turn left.' He pounded the horn twice with his right fist and kept it there, to ensure his participation in the rising cacophony.

Dulac grabbed his laptop, reached into his pocket and handed ten Euros to the cabbie. 'Here. I'll walk.'

The driver took the money and put it on the console, then threw up his hands in a dramatic gesture of abandon.

Twenty minutes later, Dulac showed his pass to the Swiss Guards at the bronze doors entrance to the Vatican, trading the noise of Roman traffic for the muted, discreet shuffling of prelates within the Vatican's narrow streets and corridors. Moments later, he entered the Segnatura Room.

'Ah, Mr Dulac, finally. We don't have much time,' said Legnano as he glanced at the clock on the mantelpiece and showed Dulac to the empty chair. The members of the Curia, already seated around the table in animated discussion, stopped talking and stared inquisitorially at Dulac.

'Your Eminences, sorry for the delay. Your traffic was deadlier than usual.' Dulac tried to act as casual as possible. His next question would light the fuse, either way. 'Oh by the way, before we begin, have any or all of you been in touch with, or received instructions from the kidnappers?' He eyed the prelates one by one, trying to seem offhand about his query.

The cardinals stared back at Dulac in bewilderment.

'Mr Dulac. Is this your idea of a joke?' said Legnano, eyes suddenly ablaze. 'If you've convened us to—'

'Sorry, your Eminence. Just wanted to clear up an in-house misunderstanding. Please don't take offence.'

Dulac sat down, reached for his laptop and opened it. 'Your Eminences, I want to show you the DVD again.' He inserted the disc, pushed the play button and turned the computer around so the cardinals could see.

They watched in silence while the DVD played till the end. 'Does anything seem odd to you?' asked Dulac.

'Get to the point Mr Dulac,' said Legnano, his tone edgy.

'They say they will destroy the pontiff. Why not say kill the pontiff?'

'Are you suggesting they will not kill him?' said Brentano, shuffling in his seat.

'I'm saying perhaps I jumped to that conclusion early.' Dulac eyed the prelates again one by one. 'The term "destroy" seems odd in this context. I'm thinking one destroys a person's reputation, his career perhaps, by revealing something about that person, something secret.' Dulac paused, then continued. 'Your Eminences, tell me, is there something I should know about Pope Clement XXI?'

The prelates sat expressionless, occasionally looking at each other discreetly. Dulac knew he'd hit a nerve. Finally Legnano looked at his watch, got up and said, 'Mr Dulac, we must leave. We have another meeting starting in two minutes. Would you please excuse us?'

By Legnano's tone, Dulac knew the cardinal wasn't really asking.

Gstaad, Switzerland. 10.15 a.m.

Gstaad. Its very name slips so sweetly off the silvered tongues of the wealthy. Longtime Swiss playground of European royalty touring down its narrow streets in horse-drawn calèches, the sparkling, quaint village now resonates with the rumble of black limousines carrying statesmen, oil sheiks and vodka barons to its pastel-hued, turn-of-the-century hotels. A kilometer south of the village, down a narrow country road, the Lorenz Institute, an austere mid-50s building of indeterminate architecture, stands perched on a small hill overlooking the Saâne valley. The Lorenz is world-renowned for the facial reconstruction of the severely burned.

From the rear seat of his chauffeured Opel limo, the passenger could see the Wasserngrat peak towering majestically and the greenness of spring encroaching on the receding snowline of its upper slopes. The limo arrived at the institute's entrance and stopped. A gray-uniformed woman stepped out from the portico and hastened to open the limo's back door. The passenger rose quickly, uncoiling his frame in one smooth, effortless movement.

'Welcome to the Lorenz,' said the woman with a guttural, Prussian accent, smiling at the visitor. 'Dr Malenski is waiting for you.'

He followed her as she led him past the entrance and the glassed-in registration desk, down a long corridor lined with private rooms. Through a door left ajar he caught a glimpse of a heavily bandaged patient lying mummy-like in one of the baldaquined beds.

Moments later, a short man with a thin slice for a mouth and a recessed chin, dressed in a white lab coat, emerged from one of the side corridors and proffered his hand to the visitor.

'Good afternoon, sir, how was your trip?' he said in a guttural voice that reverberated off the granite floor.

'Exhausting. I haven't much time, doctor. Show me to his room.'

Malenski dismissed the woman with a nod and turned to the man. 'He's resting now. After the last operation, we almost lost him.'

'After all the time and money we've spent on him, that would be disastrous, doctor.'

'Ya, now please, come with me.' Malenski led the visitor past some cubicles and laboratories towards the rear of the building.

'Was it the pain?'

'Nein. You see, our work here makes us excellent pain managers, yes? Otherwise we lose our clientele, yes?' Malenski said, emitting a small guffaw. 'We are experts at it,' he said proudly.

'Is he ready to leave?'

'Nein, nein. We keep him here a few more days, to make sure.'

'Impossible. We don't have that luxury, doctor. He must be there Friday.'

'But that's tomorrow.'

'No discussion, doctor.' The visitor wagged a remonstrative finger at Malenski and quickened his step.

When they reached the end of the corridor, Malenski turned right and they faced a door marked 'Authorized personnel only'. Malenski took out his key, opened it and they descended a narrow, steel staircase leading to another door, before which stood a woman in a blue frock reading a thick document. She stepped aside and Malenski led the visitor into the small room, dimly lit by a single fluorescent light in the middle of the ceiling. They could make out a man's shape, lying on a bed at the far side. He seemed to be asleep. As they drew nearer, the man's face became visible. The visitor stared for a moment, then smiled.

'My congratulations,' he whispered to Malenski.

'Good, yes?' said the doctor, his eyes twinkling behind the rimless glasses.

'Yes. Very good.' The visitor looked at his watch. 'I must go,' he said as he turned and started back towards the staircase. 'Is the package ready?'

'Of course,' said Malenski. 'It is in the lab. I will call for it.'

Malenski stopped at one of the wall-mounted intercoms and moments later, a young red-headed woman met them in the corridor, carrying a small, brown rectangular parcel. Malenski gestured her to hand it to the visitor.

'It's vacuum packed. Keep it frozen and it will not deteriorate for a week,' said Malenski.

'Fine.' The visitor and Malenski walked through the reception area, towards the revolving door of the entrance.

'Ya. We will accelerate the healing with doses of—'

'I don't have time for details, doctor. Remember. Tomorrow is Friday.'

Rome, Questura Centrale police station, 4.30 p.m.

'Your name?' said the woman desk sergeant, obviously bothered by the untimely interruption of her reading a thick report.

'Good afternoon, signora. It's Nervi, Dottore Alberto Nervi,' said the man, pushing up his nose a pair of oval, wire-framed spectacles.

'What do you want?'

'I'm here to see my client, Mecem Aguar. I'm his lawyer.'

'Identity card.'

He opened his wallet, took out a card bearing his photograph, and handed it to her. It read: 'Dr Alberto Nervi, lawyer, member #17786, Roma Bar Association, years 2005-2006.'

She looked at the card, then at him. 'What's that?' she said, pointing to the elegantly wrapped box.

'Oh, I forgot. It's chocolates for my wife. I just bought them at the—'

'They stay here.'

'Of course.'

She was busy copying the details of the card, when two policemen approached the desk, shouldering between them with great difficulty an obese woman wrapped in a dripping wet blanket.

'She's American. She's drunk,' said the younger policeman. 'She apparently fell, or jumped off the Ponte Sant'Angelo bridge.'

'Momento,' said the sergeant, holding up her right hand. 'I don't want her dripping all over my desk.' She turned to the lawyer. 'I'll give you twenty minutes.'

'That should be enough.'

'Nina,' she said, calling over a small frail woman in uniform. 'Show him to 12B. He's here to see Aguar. Don't let them out of your sight.'

'But I must be assured confidentiality. I have to discuss—'

'Nineteen minutes.'

'All right, all right,' he said.

The woman sergeant turned towards the two policemen still propping up the large, wet woman. 'Get her into cell 3A. I'll talk to her tomorrow when she's sober.'

Pushing the ill-fitting, rimmed glasses upwards again on his nose, Tomaso followed the small woman through the metal detector and down a corridor lined with cells filled with Rome's rejects, while they vied for Tomaso's attention. 'Hey, you a lawyer? You any good? I pay well,' laughed an old prostitute, pumping lewdly with her pelvis and plumping up her sagging breasts.

They took the elevator up to the third floor. Its doors opened, and two guards stood before them, blocking the corridor. She showed them her identity card, and the guards let them through. He followed her to a large cell, before which stood two more guards, their Uzis at the ready. Rome's 'policia' weren't taking any chances. One of them frisked him.

'What's this?' said the guard, pulling out a wrapped chocolate from Tomaso's pocket.

'Oh, I forgot. I left the box at the counter. I—'

'OK, OK,' he said, handing Tomaso the chocolate. 'Be quick.'

'Yes, of course. Thank you.'

The guard unlocked and opened the heavy metal door.

'You have a visitor,' said the woman to Aguar as she stood beside the entrance. Aguar looked puzzled.

'Me? Why?'

'Your lawyer.'

'But—'

'Nervi, Mr Aguar, Dottore Alberto Nervi,' he said and entered the cell. 'I'm here to help you.'

'You were sent by—'

'Quiet,' said Tomaso, putting a forefinger to his lips, then taking Aguar by the arm to the back of the cell. 'It's probably bugged.'

'Sorry. I didn't think.'

'What did you tell them?' whispered Tomaso, his head bowed, his lips barely moving.

'Nothing. They want to deal. They're offering a reduced sentence if—'

'That would be most unwise,' interrupted Tomaso.

'They know about the gel on the glasses,' whispered Aguar.

'I see. Anything else?'

'They found my fingerprints inside the latex gloves,' said Aguar, looking scared. Tomaso thought quickly.

'And you believed them? That's an old trick. Trust me. If they tried that, they don't have a case.'

'Can you get me the hell out of this shithole? I suppose you . . . I mean, you must know people?'

'Of course we know people.' Tomaso said.

Tomaso reached into his jacket's left pocket, took out a chocolate, unwrapped the blue tinfoil and popped it into his mouth. He chewed briefly, swallowed and said, 'the right people.' A look of relief started to form on Aguar's face.

'Good. That's good. When can you—'

'Soon. Very soon. Don't worry,' Tomaso said, putting his left hand on Aguar's shoulder reassuringly. Tomaso then reached into his jacket right pocket and took out a chocolate, wrapped in white tinfoil. 'In the meantime here, have one of these. Good for the morale.'

CHAPTER 14

Béziers, France, 20 May 1966

'Come, son, let's go to the library.'

The boy followed his father who, at sixty-eight, his hair white, his gait hesitant, looked ten years older. As they entered, the boy could smell the familiar scent of nutmeg and must emanating from the worn books. A soft summer light intruded between the heavy, velvet drapes, its rays warming the library's threadbare Persian carpets. The boy anticipated these weekly sessions with a certain apprehension: the fascination of new knowledge brought with it a sense of growing responsibility. It was becoming increasingly clear this was preparation. Preparation for the role he would play in the Cathar faith's survival. Every week brought an extra brick of information that fitted into the walls of his ultimate destiny. There was no escape.

His father reached up and took down a tome with a faded red velvet cover, amid a row of brown leather books. He dusted it slightly and opened it.

'This is the life of Pierre de Combel,' his father said, 'your ancestor. He wasn't much older than you are now when he miraculously survived the massacre at Montségur. It's time you read about him. I think you'll find he was quite a remarkable man. Courageous, very courageous, yet cunning.'

'Cunning?'

'Yes cunning. Because under the masquerade of his Catholic knighthood, he quietly went about organizing what was to become the Cathar resistance movement. De Combel and, and a few others . . .' The old man bent over and coughed heavily, his face turning to an alarming red as he gasped for air between spasms.

'Father, are you all right?'

'Yes, yes I'm fine. Just a bad cold.' His father regained his composure and continued. 'Most important, de Combel set new rules for the survival of our faith,' he said, closing the book and waving it slightly.

'How is that?' said the boy.

'I'll get to it in a moment. You see, Pierre de Combel was entrusted with one sacred treasure. No, not that ridiculous piece of tin and silver that frauds and pseudo-historians like that Otto Rahn have written about. This Holy Grail and its supposed gift of eternal life. What nonsense! No, de Combel's treasure was far more valuable, and even harder to secure: the preservation of our faith, so that our promise could eventually be fulfilled.'

'Le pré reverdira. Our time will come again,' said the boy.

'Correct. You've learned your lesson well, my son. But what I'm about to tell you now will surprise you, might even shock you. To protect his sacred trust, Pierre de Combel wasn't afraid of using violence if necessary.'

'Violence?' said the boy, looking at his father with an air of curiosity mixed with disbelief.

'I know. So far, you've learned that one of the basic tenets of our faith is non-violence.'

'Of course.'

'Not of course. Following the massacre at Montségur, de Combel realized that passive non-violence had only led to the useless slaughter of three hundred men, women and children, who believed their immolation was inevitable, the will of God. De Combel realized that for the Cathar faith to survive, he had to take the initiative. The Cathars had to fight fire with fire. So he organized a sort of Le Maquis against the Catholic oppressor, much like the French resistance movement did against the Germans during WWII. De Combel's actions against the Catholics are well documented in this book.'

The boy stared at his father, unsure as to what degree he was to believe what seemed to go against everything his Cathar teachers had taught him.

'You look skeptical.'

'No, it's that it's quite difficult to—'

'To believe? I'll give you an example. In 1267 AD, the Archbishop of Albi, Villebet was his name, proclaimed that any Catholic who knew a Cathar within the city's walls and didn't denounce the heretic, such Catholic, when found out, would be ipso facto excommunicated. I don't have to remind you that excommunication, in those days was feared worse than death. To a Catholic, it meant eternal damnation. For the Albigese, in a city where the two faiths co-existed side by side, it was a difficult, untenable choice. The Archbishop was forcing brother to turn on brother, friend against friend. After Villebet's proclamation, de Combel decided to eliminate the Albigeses' dilemma. He—' His father started coughing again, a dry sickening rasp coming from the bottom of his lungs. The old man leaned backward, gasping for air.

'Father, I . . . We can maybe continue some other—'

'I'm fine. Just get me a glass of water.' Grasping the book with both hands, the old man slumped wearily into the sofa, his small, fragile frame almost lost amid the sofa's vertical ribs of padded leather.

The boy went to the kitchen and returned with a glass of cold water. Taking the glass with a trembling hand, his father took two sips and placed it on the table next to the sofa.

'Here, son, sit down next to me,' said the man as he patted the cushion with his skeletal, arthritis-ridden hand.

'Where were we? Ah yes, the Archbishop. Two days after his proclamation, Villebet was found crucified on the altar, in his cathedral. They never found out who did it until much later, 250 years to be more precise, when de Combel's biographer pieced the evidence together. It was definitely de Combel. But getting back to my story, Villebet's successor was wiser. He immediately annulled the proclamation.' His father took another drink of water. 'Later on during those troubled times, because of his high position within the knighthood, de Combel saved many Cathars from execution, often at the peril of his life. We owe him a lot. Some go as far to say the very survival of our faith.'

'I see. But apart from a lesson in history, what has this got to do—'

'With you? You're going to learn, son, that all great endeavors are built on a strong historical foundation. Lenin and Mao read Marx and Rousseau. Jefferson read Aristotle and Sophocles, Patton was taught by Alexander the Great and Napoleon, and—'

'I understand, Father.'

'If you are called eventually to become our leader — and I believe you have the qualities necessary for the post — you must first acquire the tools, the skills and the judgment essential to the faith's survival and growth. You'll have many enemies, starting with those from within. Our current leadership is passive and weak. I wish I had the strength to fight them, but I'm afraid my time has passed. I suppose I was too busy acquiring this.' The old man waved his hand at the rest of the room, and, the boy imagined, at the rest of his possessions and fortune. 'All of this will be yours someday.'

A sudden dread filled the boy's heart. 'Father, your cough. Is it . . . ?'

'The doctors say a good rest will cure it. If you believe them. These quacks, what do they know?' His father's weak smile did nothing to dispel the boy's fears. 'You see, de Combel was in much the same situation then as we Cathars are in today. The threat is all the more sinister now that it is hidden, pervasive, veiled in the cloak of so-called tolerance. Of course the weapons and skills of combat have changed, but make no mistake, it is, and will always remain, war. War that every oppressed minority must wage if it is to survive.'

'But, sir, how, how will I know when?'

His father took on that reassuring look that the boy knew so well, always a safe harbor from his anxieties and dilemmas.

'In time, son, in time. All in due course. You and you alone will feel when you're ready, when the circumstances are right. Let God and Spirit inspire you, guide you. You will feel it, know when it's time. My task is the easier one. It's to prepare you for that moment. When you become their chosen leader, I ask only one favor of you.'

The boy looked quizzically at his father.

'That you take the name of Pierre de Combel, in memory of our illustrious ancestor. That name belongs to our family, and it is time to restore it to its full glory again.'

'Yes, Father.'

'In the meantime, read the book and let me know what you think. I warn you. The end is quite disturbing.'

The boy never got to talk about the book with his father. One month later, the old man was dead.

CHAPTER 15

Legnano's office, 8.30 p.m., Thursday 25 May

The resumption of Dulac's morning meeting with the members of the inner Curia had been postponed to later that evening. Before him, the members of the Curia continued to look at each other in silence, no one willing to break it.

'Well I'm waiting, Monsignori. What could destroy the pontiff?' Dulac said.

Finally, Brentano spoke: 'Mr Dulac, I'm not aware of any particular circumstance that could destroy the Pope's reputation, if that is what is meant by the message. But of course, before our call to the priesthood, we were . . . men. Some of us may have had a few rattles in the closet,' he said, looking at the other cardinals with a knowing smile.

'Skeletons. You mean skeletons, your Eminence. There's a difference between a few skeletons and a cemetery,' said Dulac. 'The message says the Pope will be destroyed. I'm telling you what to expect if you don't deliver. It's your decision.'

'And your job is to prevent this from—'

At that moment, Dulac's cellphone rang. He looked at the number: Questura Centrale. 'Sorry your Eminences, it's Guadagni.'

He took the call. 'Inspector, I'm in a—'

'We went to interrogate Aguar again tonight,' said Guadagni.

'Get anything out of him?'

'He's dead.'

'What?'

'Poisoned. Someone posing as his lawyer gave him chocolates laced with enough trichloromethyl cyanide to kill an elephant.'

Dulac's eyes rolled up towards the ceiling in disbelief. 'Christ, Guadagni, our one suspect, our only source, and he gets murdered in your jail? By a lawyer?'

'They frisked him—'

'Great. Just pissing great.' Dulac hung up.

The members of the Curia looked at him expectantly. 'They murdered Aguar.'

'God have mercy,' said Sforza.

Dulac eyed the prelates and pounded his fist onto the table. 'Why don't you tell me the truth? This is no time for omertà. Clement XXI may die. For God's sake, tell me what you know.' The silence that followed could have lasted for minutes, hours, while the cardinals looked at each other, no one daring to speak. Dulac didn't care anymore. He rose to leave.

Legnano finally spoke: 'All right, Mr Dulac, all right. Please calm down. I will explain.' He looked nervously at the other cardinals. 'We'll go to the Pope's library. What I have to tell you . . .'

Will embarrass the hell out of all of you, Dulac thought.

' . . . is more appropriately told in private.'

'Now we're getting somewhere,' mumbled Dulac, rising from his chair and following Legnano out of the room.

The cardinal hastened his step and they arrived before the Pope's library adjacent to the papal apartments.

'Please,' said Legnano, ushering Dulac into the sparsely decorated room.

They faced each other on either side of the large oak table, Dulac in one of the spindly-legged Louis XV chairs,

Legnano in the Pope's high-backed chair, directly under the large painting of The Resurrection by Perugino.

He looks quite at ease, sitting in the Pope's place, thought Dulac.

Legnano crossed his arms and said, 'Mr Dulac, I will be frank. It is possible that these men, these kidnappers might have found out something we discovered several years ago. To be exact, three years after the election of Pope Clement XXI. Until now, we, the members of the Curia, thought we were the only ones to know about this, this diary.'

'A diary? Whose diary?' Dulac said, offended at the cardinal's lack of transparency.

'A German officer's diary.'

'I don't follow.'

'Before I speak, swear to me that this information will never pass your lips.'

'Of course.'

Legnano cleared his throat, leaned forward, hands clasped and forearms resting on the desk. 'In 1943, in Naples, a young 13-year-old orphan boy named Paolo was trying to survive the bombing raids of the allies. He was one of the many facing starvation. He had a younger sister Maria, and they were living in a corrugated tin roof shack. She was sick, very sick. Prior to the war, Paolo lived near the synagogue on Via Cappella Vecchia and had befriended a young Jewish boy named Eli Tannenbaum. They often played soccer together in the courtyard near the synagogue. When the war erupted, the Jews of Naples abandoned the synagogue and went underground, but Paolo got news of Eli's whereabouts through a friend.'

Dulac sat immobile, feeling the muscles of his jaw tighten slightly.

Legnano continued. 'When Maria couldn't walk anymore, feverish with dysentery, Paolo went looking for Eli. He knew where the Jews had retreated to, but going there meant crossing the whole city, and risking running into one of the German patrols and probably being followed. Besides, he'd heard that the Jews were also desperate for food. He waited. But at the end of the third day, his sister burning with fever, he decided he had only one hope left: the Germans themselves. He went to the nearest command station twice, begging for food. They turned him back. The third time, he offered them something he knew would interest them: his friend Eli's address.'

Dulac leaned forward, his anxiety growing.

Legnano continued, a frown furrowing his generous forehead, 'After the war, Paolo found out that the Germans tortured Eli, and as a result of his confession, arrested 450 Neapolitan Jews and sent them to Auschwitz. Eli's entire family perished. Eli was spared, but committed suicide shortly after the end of the war when he found out what the Nazis had done. Paolo and his sister Maria were nourished by the Germans and survived the war. After the war, Paolo eventually became a priest, and rose quickly within the ranks of the Church.' Legnano paused and took a deep breath, his gaze locked onto Dulac: 'Paolo Volpini, Mr Dulac, is Pope Clement XXI.'

Dulac sat, mouth slack, staring at Legnano.

The cardinal continued. 'We were sent extracts of the diary by the Catholic son of a German officer serving under the commandant in Naples, who had gotten hold of his father's diary. The officer had meticulously noted the names and addresses of the deported Jews. Twelve of them survived. Their account corroborates the dates in the diary. They think Eli was the traitor. They don't know about Paolo Volpini.'

Legnano clasped his hands and leaned forward on the desk: 'I don't have to remind you of your oath of confiden—'

'What happened to the diary?'

'I don't know. We have only extracts. We tried to get in contact with the officer's son, but he has disappeared.'

'Hence the kidnappers' reference to "destroy" instead of "kill"?'

'You don't have to remind me of that, Mr Dulac,' said Legnano, the frown on his forehead deepening. 'We had already come up with that premise before you "hammered the point home", so to speak.'

'I presume you've had this story corroborated by the Pope?'

'Mr Dulac, how do the Americans say, we are between a mountain and a rocky place. If the Jewish community, or for that matter the rest of the world . . .' Legnano's voice trailed off slightly.

'Explosive diary.'

'We must get that diary, Mr Dulac.'

CHAPTER 16

The following morning, Dulac awoke to the insistent ache of his arthritis, which had invaded the rest of his once supple pianist's hands. Dulac rose, went to the bathroom and took two aspirins. Moments later, he dressed and walked downstairs to the breakfast room, where hotel guests, from business-suited executives to T-shirted tourists, were already standing impatiently in the buffet queue. After a perfunctory breakfast washed down with remnants of the hotel's battery-acid coffee, he went outside and hailed a cab.

Fifteen minutes later, Dulac entered the Segnatura room where the members of the Curia awaited, some seated, others standing. Sforza, fidgeting with his rosary, stood underneath Raphael's fresco depicting Ultimate Truth. How ironic, thought Dulac.

Brentano, seated, kept clasping and unclasping his hands, like Pilate washing himself of the whole mess. Legnano paced back and forth, hands behind his back, his traditional scowl creasing his forehead and lines tugging at the sides of his mouth, transforming it into an inverted crescent.

Sforza spoke. 'We will receive their bank transfer instructions at any moment. We must decide now.'

'You're saying we should comply with their demands?' said Brentano, his face flushed with animosity. 'Condone extortion?'

Dulac sat dumbfounded. The kidnappers want $310 million before five and the cardinals haven't decided whether or not to pay?

'Monsignor,' said Sforza, his glare locked onto Brentano, 'Cardinal Legnano and I have consulted with the Italian security force SISMI and the French Bureau's ransom experts. They agree with Mr Dulac's recommendation. We must get these kidnappers to the table. It is essential that we find out who we are dealing with.'

Sforza looked at the other prelates for approval. 'Monsignori, we just can't take the risk that they—'

Legnano stopped pacing and raised his right hand in protest: 'Enough, Monsignor, enough.' His tone was peremptory. 'Thirty million USD, that's what the Italian government has agreed to send them once we receive the deposit instructions. That will bring these criminals to the table. Besides, Mr Harris informs us Interpol will cover every bank in Panama City. They'll trace the movement of the funds tomorrow.'

'I don't think it will be Panama City,' said Dulac.

'Oh, and why not?' said Legnano, eyeing Dulac quizzically.

Dulac leaned forward, his hands palm down on the table. 'Simply because the kidnappers know we can't afford to think it isn't.'

'So you think they, how do you say, set us up?' said Legnano.

Dulac ran his fingers through the misplaced curls falling on his forehead and gave the cardinal a quick smile. 'Yes.'

The bubble-wrap padded beige envelope had been delivered to the Swiss Guard at the Sant'Anna entrance, addressed to Cardinal Fouquet. 'Hand deliver personally urgent' said the red inscription on its front. After checking the envelope through security, the guard brought it to Fouquet's personal secretary, Monsignor Dudec. 'It's a DVD disk,' said the guard. The elderly prelate rose and made his way slowly to the Segnatura room. He entered and handed the cardinal the package.

The assembly looked on expectantly as Fouquet opened the envelope and slipped the disc into the computer. The projector flickered to life and the unfocused images of two men appeared, until the camera zoomed in on a hooded man, then switched to the Pope. Dressed in a simple white cassock, he stared at the camera, his expression one of calm and resignation.

'Monsignori,' the hooded man said, 'as you can see, we are treating your pope well. His continued good health depends on you. You will remit the $310 million in five deposits by hot wire transfer to the bank indicated here, receipt of which we will confirm today on closed-circuit TV, 5.10 p.m. Rome time. Our technicians will contact the Vatican's shortly. Any attempt to trace the origin of our transmission will cause extreme prejudice to the hostages.'

The camera focused onto the inscriptions on a tripod-mounted clipboard, which read:

Account number:
380-4625 — $90 million
273-4723 — $55 million
337-0462 — $55 million
214-0676 — $60 million
395-7837 — $50 million

Hot wire transfer number: 175-362-426-4066
Recipient: Blue Sky International Bank.

The camera refocused on the hooded man once again: 'Upon receipt of the above, Clement XXI and Dr Bruscetti will be delivered to you unharmed, at a place we will disclose.'

The video screen went blank.

The prelates shot furtive glances at one another in nervous silence. Legnano turned to Dulac. 'Where is this Blue Sky Bank?'

'I'm sending the information request now,' Dulac said as he typed the name into his laptop, linking him to Interpol's encrypted databanks.

Legnano continued. 'So Monsignori, we agree to proceed?'

'We are condoning blackmail,' said Brentano. 'They wouldn't dare harm the Pope.'

'And you want to play Russian roulette with the Pope's life?' said Sforza.

'I have the location of the bank,' said Dulac. 'It's a class B restricted offshore bank in San José, Costa Rica. The owner is a numbered company, whose shareholders have bearer shares. It was incorporated three days ago.'

'If I understand correctly, they will have complete anonymity,' said Legnano.

'Correct,' said Dulac.

'What can we do?' said Brentano.

'In a few hours, not much,' said Dulac.

'Don't you have an Interpol agent there? Won't the local authorities cooperate?' said Sforza, his voice a mix of frustration and anger.

'To answer your first question, Monsignor, no. He was killed three weeks ago in a car accident. We haven't replaced him yet. As to your second question, we'll contact the local authorities immediately, but I wouldn't get too optimistic.'

'Why is that?'

'They receive large bank transfers every day. This one is small in comparison. They can't risk paralyzing their transfer system unless and until they have proof of a crime. That will take days, and a court order. By that time it'll be too late. The money will have come and gone.'

Sicily, 4.30 p.m., Friday 26 May

The chopper was due to land in a farmer's field near Loresia at any minute. Moments later Vespoli, seated in the van, watched as the Alouette came into view and he recognized the fake, recently painted call sign on the chopper's tail. The helicopter landed and within minutes, the door opened. Dressed in a beige desert shirt and khaki pants, a man appeared, his lithe frame uncoiling with the ease of a cheetah as he jumped to the ground.

Hastening to meet him, Vespoli felt his heartbeat quicken. 'How was your trip, Mr de Combel?' inquired Vespoli to the man with dark lustrous hair and fine, chiseled features.

'Tiring.'

They walked briskly towards the van.

'And the problems?' the man shot a side-glance at Vespoli with eyes colder than black ice.

'Resolved,' said Vespoli, his semblance of assurance belying his profound dread.

'Good. I trust all the others are here?'

'They're waiting at the villa,' said Vespoli.

'The Bellerophon. Has it arrived?'

'It's waiting at anchor in the Bay of Augusta.'

When they reached the van, de Combel looked at his watch: in less than an hour, the Vatican would be transferring the money.

'Keep it frozen,' he said, handing Vespoli Malenski's package, then entering and sitting in the back seat.

'Go,' Vespoli ordered as he sat next to the driver and closed the van's door.

The van started up the narrow, bumpy dirt road to the villa. Ten minutes later, the cream stucco villa and its cantilevered steel veranda, jutting aggressively over the cliff, came into view. The van stopped in front of the garage and the passengers exited.

'Take the package upstairs, and put it in the freezer,' said Vespoli to the driver.

'Damn, Vespoli, you take it,' said de Combel, pointing a forefinger at Vespoli.

'But I thought—'

'Don't think. Don't take your eyes off that package. Is that clear?'

'Yes, sir.'

From the underground garage, the threesome made their way up the narrow wooden staircase, through the hall and into a large room.

De Combel looked about and smiled. Before him, fifteen descendants of the Cathars who had escaped the massacre at Montségur sat around an oval table. They rose in unison.

'Good evening, ladies and gentlemen. Please sit down,' said de Combel. 'For those of you I haven't met, my name is Pierre de Combel.' He walked to the far side of the table and sat down. 'After these years of planning, this is a moment of great joy for me.' He paused for a moment. ' . . . And of course, for you. My dream, I'm sorry, our dream is finally becoming reality. Our prophet once announced "*Le pré reverdira*". "Our time will come again." It is now that time. The Cathar martyrs, your ancestors, my ancestors, will not have died in vain. Today, a new era has begun for us. From my — our project, Alpha, Beta and Gamma phases are complete. Delta will begin this evening. So far, we've been fortunate. We've only suffered minor, inevitable collateral damage.' He eyed Vespoli. 'With a plan as bold as ours, that may not always be so.' He eyed the table. 'I see that Mr Vespoli has prepared the next phase. You've noticed that some of you have hoods before you on the table. Before Delta begins, you'll be required to put them on. Vespoli, is the hookup with the Vatican ready?'

'Yes, sir.'

'Secure?'

'Yes. Our technicians assure me they've finished testing the camera and linking of the transmission path through six secure stations. The seventh will be the Vatican.'

De Combel looked at the other Cathars. 'As you can see, we're taking every precaution.' He turned to Vespoli. 'And how is our guest?'

'He's in his room. He says he refuses to cooperate with kidnappers. We've had to drug him.'

'I see. Not enough to render him unconscious, surely?'

'No, no, just enough to handle him. But he can't talk.'

'Good,' de Combel said, rubbing his hands together. 'As long as he can sit. Is Godefroi here?'

'That's me,' said the bald man with the bull neck, raising his hand.

'You know what you have to do?'

'Yes sir, I do.'

'Fine. Vespoli, distribute the documents.' De Combel paused for a moment then continued. 'You have before you the detailed description of two new scenarios, one of which will be played out today, depending on whether the Vatican complies with our demands. There have been some modifications to prior plans. Take a moment to look at them. I don't want any panic.' After a brief moment, he continued. 'Are there any questions?'

The Cathars looked at each other in silence, a look of dread on many of their faces. Finally, a man wearing a dark-blue shirt stood up, trembling. 'I, I can't be a party to this.'

'Really? And why not?' said de Combel.

'I have a young family . . .' His hand holding the paper started to tremble. 'This is going too far . . . Surely you aren't going to, to—'

De Combel's right hand pointed towards the door. 'Out!' he said. 'Vespoli, keep him under guard. He must not leave the villa.'

'Yes, sir,' said Vespoli as he escorted the visibly upset man out of the room.

De Combel turned and challenged the others. 'We must be united,' he said, banging his fist on the table. 'Anyone else?' De Combel looked at the Cathars one by one. Nobody spoke.

Suddenly, the chime of a cellphone broke the silence. It was Vespoli's.

'That must be the agent from Blue Sky Bank.' He looked hesitatingly at de Combel.

'Then take it, damnit.' shouted de Combel.

'Vespoli. Yes, he's here. Just a minute . . .'

De Combel grabbed Vespoli's phone. 'De Combel'.

Vespoli and the others watched, as de Combel's expression became somber. After a moment, his face turned to crimson, his eyes went black. Vespoli could see, feel the anger as the muscles around de Combel's mouth contracted and his lips narrowed into a thin slit: 'Thirty . . . ? You said thirty total? You're absolutely sure? I see. No other transfers coming in? None.' De Combel flipped the encrypted phone shut. He paused for a moment, his head bowed. Then slowly he looked up, his jaw jutting forward in defiance. 'Damn them. $30 million. They're insulting us.' He turned to Vespoli, then the others. 'They leave us no other choice.'

A Cathar spoke, looking around at the others seated around the table. 'Surely we, we must wait a little longer. They may send another transfer . . .'

'Nonsense. The Vatican thinks we're bluffing.' said de Combel.' We'll show them.' His eyes sparkled with rage as he shook his fist in the air. 'We will show them.'

'But, Mr de Combel, we can't—' said another Cathar.

'Those of you with hoods, put them on now,' interrupted de Combel. 'The rest of you, leave us. Vespoli, make the preparations.'

'Yes sir.'

De Combel walked over to a small drawer beside the dining room entrance, where clothing had been placed. He took one of the dark fatigues and slipped it on easily, as if he'd practiced the move before. He picked up the black hood and put it over his head. After a moment, the door of the dining room opened again and a technician accompanied by a cameraman walked to the side of a small platform, which had been placed along one of the walls away from the dining room table.

In the Segnatura room, Dulac, along with the members of the Curia, the Minister of State of Italy, Guadagni and Romer, sat nervously around the conference table. Outside, two Swiss Guards guarded each of the room's two entrances.

No one was to be allowed in, under any circumstance. Dulac watched the prelates, sometimes glancing at each other, sometimes at the two video monitors resting on wheeled dollies along one of the walls. Legnano, sitting next to Dulac, looked particularly anxious.

Dulac turned and said, 'Anything wrong, your Eminence?'

'The Italian government should have confirmed the bank transfer by now. What's taking them so long?'

Suddenly, the monitors came alive. The screens vacillated for a moment, then the picture came into focus: seven hooded figures dressed in dark brown fatigues were seated behind a small platform onto which had been set a microphone and a single chair, empty. Dulac felt a cold chill run up his spine. A mock trial, he thought. A hooded man wearing black fatigues appeared, stood before the microphone for a moment, before reaching down and adjusting its height. He seemed to signal to someone to the side of the platform, invisible to the camera.

Then a large, hooded man wearing black fatigues walked onto the platform followed by two shorter men supporting a white-robed figure between them. They sat the man down brusquely in the solitary chair, and the camera focused on the lonely figure, stooping slightly, his jaw slack, his head leaning to one side. 'It's His Holiness!' said Sforza.

They've drugged him, thought Dulac, fear seizing his brain like a vise. Not good. The man in the brown fatigue grabbed the microphone: 'Men of little faith, you dare challenge us? Did you think we weren't serious?' The electronically scrambled voice was a chilling, otherworldly monotone. 'Your token gesture is an insult. Do you hear? An insult.' The voice's pitch rose slightly. 'To us, to your Pope, to the world. Our demands were clear, and you chose to ignore them.' The voice paused for a moment and the hooded man pointed to the pontiff sitting below him. 'Now, your Pope will pay the price.'

Dulac's stomach knotted. He could hear the hushed rumblings of the incredulous prelates spread like a trail of lit gunpowder.

Legnano, his eyes glued to the monitor, leaned over towards Sforza sitting next to him and whispered, 'They're going to disclose the diary.'

'They're not going to, to harm him?' said Sforza.

The hooded man in brown gestured to the burly man in black, who walked over and stood behind the seated pontiff. At the man's command, the burly man grabbed the side of his belt and unsheathed a large scimitar in a quick, smooth motion. For an instant, a flash of light reflected off the wide, curving blade.

The Segnatura room's occupants sat transfixed, mute, holding their collective breath. 'Jesus Christ, they're not going to decapitate him?' said Guadagni, as he crossed himself quickly.

The burly man raised the scimitar above his head with both hands. '*Mio Dio!*' exclaimed the Minister of State.

The burly man waited. After what seemed an eternity, he looked sideways to the other man. The man nodded.

'NO! NO!' the voices of Brentano, Fouquet and Sforza shouted in unison, as they jumped up from their seats.

The monitors' image blurred for an instant and caught the scimitar's arc as it sliced downwards. A collective gasp rose from the room.

The Pope fell forward, blood spattering onto the camera's lens.

The Segnatura room's occupants sat motionless, transfixed. No one uttered a word. All stared, hypnotized by the screens of the TV monitors, now blank. After an endless moment, Fouquet crossed himself slowly and broke into tears. 'In God's name, why? Why?'

Dulac sat, staring into space. He didn't dare make eye contact with the Cardinals. After what seemed an eternity, Legnano said in a barely audible voice: 'I never thought . . . They are mad . . .' Legnano turned to Dulac: 'Who are these barbarians? Who in God's name would take the pontiff's life? Why, Mr Dulac? Why?' Legnano took his head in his hands.

The other members of the Curia simply sat, looking at each other, unsure as to what to do next. Finally, Brentano broke the mournful gloom. 'We . . . we must prepare a statement for the press.'

'The press? Is that all of you can think of?' said Sforza, indignant.

'We aren't sure that the Holy Father . . . I mean, we can hope that . . .' said Brentano.

'Do you need to see the body?' said Fouquet, his voice cracking with emotion.

'Barbarians. They're insane. They butchered an innocent man,' said Guadagni.

The Italian Minister of State rose solemnly from his chair and said, 'Gentlemen, your Eminences, you have my condolences. I will advise the President immediately. Cardinal Legnano, rest assured we will wait for your permission before advising anyone else.' From the corner of his eye, Dulac caught a glimpse of Guadagni trying to get his attention: 'Partial payment, eh, Dulac. That was your recommendation.'

Dulac felt his face reddening and steeled himself not to meet Guadagni's stare.

'What do we do now, Mr Dulac?' asked Sforza, his voice breaking.

'I wish I knew, your Eminence. I wish I knew,' Dulac said, feeling the weight of a horrible guilt pressing upon his chest.

As the Cardinals sat in oppressive silence, suddenly, loud voices and a commotion could be heard coming from outside the room.

Sforza got up, walked to the door, and opened it slightly. A handful of reporters were in a heated discussion with the Swiss Guards.

'What is it?' asked Sforza.

'They say the Pope has been assassinated. It was on Al Jazeera TV ten minutes ago.'

Amid the ensuing chaos, Dulac had made his way out of the Vatican and regained the relative quietness of his hotel room. Sitting at the desk eating a sandwich, Dulac was on the phone with Henri Bléguet, Head of Interpol's data center in Lyon, while the Cray computers analyzed, crunched, filtered, and digested the raw data regarding the Al Jazeera transmission, and preliminary results trickled in. The news was not good. The transmission's security codes and firewalls were resisting Interpol's computers' attempts at descrambling, and the bouncing off restricted satellites before reaching Al Jazeera's newsroom was making the transmission impossible to trace.

Dulac rose and turned on the TV. The blonde anchor-woman, a look of professional concern on her face, announced that a special news broadcast from the Vatican's Old Study Room was about to begin. The scene switched to the Vatican, the camera zoomed in onto Sforza, then Legnano, sitting behind a white cloth-covered table. Slightly beneath and in front, reporters and journalists waited for the press conference to begin, to the incessant flashing of camera lights.

Legnano reached for the microphone and started to read his notes, his hand shaking slightly, his voice broken. 'Ladies and gentlemen, we have all witnessed today an abominable, barbaric act. We believed we could initiate a meeting with the kidnappers, in order to negotiate the release of His Holiness Pope Clement XXI and of Dr Bruscetti. We had no reason to think they would carry out this wanton, savage killing. We do not understand what they have gained by this . . . this . . .' Legnano stopped, upset. He wiped a tear with his hand, then reached for a glass of water. 'Words cannot describe the pain and sorrow that I feel, that I'm sure you all feel. The loss we must bear is all the greater in that his death was gratuitous.' Legnano paused and took another sip of water. 'In a moment such as this, it is inevitable and natural that we feel anger and frustration and want to exact revenge on the perpetrators. But this is not what our Holy Father would have wished. That is why we ask that you find it in your hearts to forgive those who have done this, as Jesus, our Savior did some two thousand years ago. In the words of Christ: 'Father, forgive them, for they know not what they do.' We in the Curia share your grief, pain and sorrow on this somber day for all of humanity. Please join us in prayer, prayer that His Holiness finds everlasting peace in the arms of our Lord. Amen.'

Legnano and Sforza started to leave when some of the reporters cut them off at the exit of the Old Study Room, pushing aside the Swiss Guards and poking microphones in the prelates' faces.

'Why didn't you pay the whole ransom? Did you not think the Pope's life was worth it? Don't you feel partially responsible for His death?'

'What kind of principle are you applying when you pay a down payment only?'

'No comment. No comment,' was the recurring answer from the unprepared cardinals.

Dulac turned off the TV, went to the bed and lay down. A while later, unable to sleep and fed up of staring blankly at the ceiling of his room, Dulac went downstairs and sat at the hotel's bar. 'Double scotch.'

'Yes sir,' said the thin, bald bartender. 'Say, aren't you the Interpol inspect—'

'And no goddamn ice,' growled Dulac.

'Yes, sir,' the bartender said, recoiling.

Dulac took a deep drag from his Gitane. His cell rang, and he pivoted away from the bar before answering.

'Hi. It's me.'

'Hello Karen.'

'I still can't believe it. Why? What do they have to gain?' she said.

'I really don't feel . . . I'm not up to talking about it just now.' Dulac caught a glimpse of the bartender, trying to listen in. He stood up and walked away from the bar.

'You're not taking this personally, are you?' said Karen.

'I proposed the partial payment. I was sure they would negotiate.'

'Surely the Curia checked with ransom experts before making their decision?'

'Still, I suggested it.'

'Thierry, it was their decision.'

'I thought we were dealing with rational, intelligent human beings, not twisted psychopaths. I trusted my instinct. I was wrong, dead wrong.'

'By the way, did you look at that video closely?'

'What do you mean?'

'I'm not sure, but I think I saw a flash, a ring or something on the finger of the man with the electronic voice, when he adjusted the microphone.'

'A ring? Yes, I suppose . . .' In a nanosecond, thousands of neurons made two million connections in the world's fastest and most efficient computer, the human brain, and reached into the faraway depths of Dulac's data bank, his memory. The idea formed and struck him like a lightning bolt. 'Jesus. I'll call you back.'

He hung up, downed the scotch and punched Interpol's single digit, quick-dial Lyon number. 'Get me Gina at forensics.'

'Hello?'

'It's me, Dulac. Do you have a copy of the Al Jazeera video on your computer?'

'Just a minute. Yes, I have it.'

'The left hand of the tall man, when he adjusts the microphone. Get a close-up of it.'

'Got it.'

'Can you see a ring?'

'Yes, sort of. It looks like a small seal.'

'Any inscription on it?'

'It's too fuzzy. I have to do a micro-reconstruct by computer. It'll take a couple of minutes.'

'I'll wait.' Dulac put the phone to his shoulder and lit another Gitane.

'There, I've got it now,' said Gina.

'What do you see?'

'A small animal. Some kind of strange animal, I think. Yes. Head of a lion, body of a goat, and—'

'The tail of a snake? A Chimera?'

'That's it.'

'Goddamn de Ségur. It's de Ségur. He's behind this. He and his ultra-right-wing Cathars. Why didn't I think of it before? Do a kinetics-anthropomorphic comparison with the man in the black fatigues. I'm sure that's him.'

'We've already started a voice deconstruct and rebuild from the video. With this input, it shouldn't take long,' said Gina.

'Call me.'

Dulac took the elevator back up to his room, his third scotch slowing his usually determined gait. Walking down the corridor, the memories of his arch-nemesis, the man Dulac had uncloaked and laid bare as a murderer, the man responsible for Gladio's resurgence and deadly agenda throughout Europe in the eighties, Dulac's struggle and ultimate failure to bring de Ségur, the French billionaire, to justice, all the memories of Dulac's ill-fated case resurfaced and flooded his brain. De Ségur, the ex-CEO Of Miranda Group, the murderer of Archbishops Salvador and Conti. Dulac felt the anger mount and tried to remain calm.

After a tepid shower to cool his temper, he phoned his assistant Daniel Lescop in Paris. 'It looks like de Ségur,' said Dulac. 'I'm having a voice video and anthro-analysis done.'

'De Ségur? Why on earth him?'

'Try revenge. Besides, murder has never stopped him before.'

'I suppose. Who is doing the anthro?'

'Gina.'

'She's the best. So you believe de Ségur and his Cathars kidnapped the Pope and murdered him when their ransom demands weren't met?' asked Lescop. 'Doesn't sound rational.'

'Since when are these fanatics rational?'

By evening, the horrific, sequential pictures of the scimitar on its downward trajectory toward the Pope's head were on all of the TV news channels of the world and the special edition front pages of the world's major newspapers. 'Kidnappers kill Pope Clement XXI. Ransom not paid in full. World shocked by live coverage of assassination,' the blood-red Corriere Della Sera's headlines blurted.

As usual, the Evening Standard hit the streets of London first: 'Pope Clement XXI executed live on Al Jazeera.'

CNN reporter Dave Anderson was broadcasting live from St Peter's Square.

'Hello Larry, I'm here in front of the Basilica. People are streaming in by the hundreds, most of them still in shock. It reminds me of when Pope John Paul II died.'

'Any more news from the Vatican yet?'

'Larry, the Vatican press secretary has told me that they won't be making any further announcements today.'

'What about the police? Do they have any idea who did this?'

'We haven't been able to contact them yet. At headquarters in Rome here, they say they're too busy coordinating with other police forces to talk to us.'

'How are the people in the square reacting?'

'Larry, people are still in shock. A lot of them can't believe this has happened. I spoke to a woman who witnessed the attempt on Pope John Paul II's life, and she says she never thought she would see this again. She's confused and angry.'

'Understandably. Aren't we all? Keep in touch Dave. Now, a word from our correspondent Nancy Price in Washington for a reaction from the White House. Nancy . . .'

The Vatican's Secretariat was once again flooded with calls. World leaders reacted swiftly, phoning, faxing, e-mailing their anger and shock, and expressing condolences to the members of the Curia.

'The Vatican has received more than 1000 calls within the last five minutes', said Sforza to Brentano. 'Even the new circuits are overloaded. The lines are completely jammed.'

Back in his hotel room, Dulac put down the glass he was about to bring to his lips, and answered his cellphone. He recognized the number: it was Interpol's forensics section.

'Mr Dulac?' said the woman's voice.

'Yes, Gina.'

'The audio lab people have made a spectrogram deconstruction and analysis of the voice heard on Al Jazeera. They compared it with the—'

'So whose voice is it, Gina?'

'It's not that simple. Due to the heavy masking of the voice, they had difficulty in establishing definite patterns and comparing them with known exemplars of de Ségur.'

'Exemplars?'

'Samples, if you prefer. Parts of speeches recorded when he was CEO of Miranda Group a few years ago. The diphthongs and inflections—'

'Gina!'

'Let me finish. The diphthongs and inflections show up on the spectrogram along with the occlusives, such as Vs and Ps, along with their wavelength, wave amplitude and intensity. All those compare favorably with the ones on the exemplars.'

'The point being, Gina?'

'We have an 80% match with de Ségur's voice. But—'

'Good enough for me.'

CHAPTER 17

Sicily, 6.40 p.m.

Hugues de Ségur, alias Pierre de Combel, had planned to evacuate shortly after the live TV transmission. He knew that the worlds' intelligence agencies and security forces' super computers were already busy trying to break the firewalls, decipher the codes and hunt down the latitude-longitude coordinates of the transmission.

Amidst the flurry of preparations for departure, de Ségur was talking to the bull-necked Godefroi when suddenly Vespoli, phone in hand and looking embarrassed, entered the dining room: 'Sir, it's the helicopter pilot.'

'What is it?' said de Ségur.

'We have a problem. The pilot had a mechanical at Saanen. He had to lease another helicopter and it has a different interior configuration.'

'So?'

'The stretcher doesn't fit.'

'What?'

'I'm sorry, sir. I—'

De Ségur grabbed Vespoli by the lapels of his jacket and shook him violently. 'It was your job to check and counter-check all of the transportation requirements, you numbskull.'

'I know, sir, but—'

De Ségur released Vespoli's jacket and calmed down. 'Now what do we do with him?'

He turned away, thought for a moment, then faced Vespoli again. 'Take him on the Bellerophon.'

'Yes, sir.'

Twenty minutes later, de Ségur boarded the helicopter, destination Benghazi. Before leaving, he'd confirmed his instructions to Vespoli that he and the others would leave on the Bellerophon, a charter yacht standing by in the Bay of Augusta. They were to meet him the next morning in de Ségur's desert compound near Suluq, 10 km south of Benghazi.

Vespoli, still unnerved by the confrontation with de Ségur, walked downstairs and entered Bruscetti's room. 'Quick, get your things. We're leaving.' he ordered.

'But I have just finished—'

'Now.' Vespoli handed him a one-piece dark brown fatigue. 'Here, wear this.'

Bruscetti walked to the bathroom. Moments later, he reappeared, his round belly molded tightly by the ill-fitting one-piece suit.

'Where are you taking me?' he said. 'Where is His Holiness?'

Vespoli didn't answer. He took Bruscetti firmly by the arm, and led him up the stairs and outside to the white van, its motor running. They climbed into the van and seated themselves among the other passengers. The other van was already in motion when Vespoli signaled the driver to follow it.

Thirty minutes later, Bruscetti looked out of the van's window and saw the outline of a yacht, anchored in the bay, surrounded by a sea of setting sunlight. The van stopped alongside the pier and disgorged its clandestine cargo, while three men, their Uzis at the ready, looked nervously about.

Vespoli led Bruscetti and the other passengers down the pier towards a small launch. Reaching it, Vespoli started to usher them aboard when Bruscetti, about to board, stopped and said: 'I demand to know. Where are you taking me?'

'Get in,' ordered Vespoli, shoving Bruscetti down the launch's narrow steps.

Falling into the launch's wooden cockpit, Bruscetti lunged for the handrail, catching it at the last moment. He sat down on the uncomfortable bench, nervously looking at the two armed men sitting across from him. The launch's motor rumbled to life and the crew cast off the lines from the pier. Five minutes later, the launch was pulling alongside the stern platform of the yacht. Bruscetti could see, inscribed on its stern, Bellerophon, and beneath it the name of its home port, Toulon. He and the others took the boarding ladder up to the yacht's main deck. Halfway up the stairs, Bruscetti heard the launch leave, turning to see it head back towards shore.

As he stood on the deck and waited, Bruscetti's attention was drawn to the man standing alone on the bridge above, giving instructions on the intercom. Must be the captain, he thought. Moments later came the distinct clanking sound of the anchor chain passing through the hawse pipe. Bruscetti looked at his watch: 7.45 p.m. He felt the yacht begin to move, slowly at first, then more rapidly. He looked astern and saw the coastline slowly disappear into the distance. Surrounded by a halo of cloud, the premature moon looked foreboding.

Bruscetti felt someone grab his arm from behind.

'Come,' said Vespoli, as he proceeded to lead him down the companionway. Upon reaching the level below, Vespoli turned left down the sparsely lit corridor and stopped before an open doorway.

Vespoli gestured to the empty room. 'Your cabin. Get some rest. You'll need it.'

Bruscetti entered and turned towards Vespoli. 'Where are we headed? Where is His Holiness?'

Vespoli didn't answer and closed the door in Bruscetti's face. The doctor heard the lock click.

An hour later, Vespoli made his way up the companionway and the narrow stairs to the bridge. 'When do we reach Benghazi?' he asked the captain.

'In about fourteen hours. That's if the weather holds,' said the short, swarthy Egyptian with the large, cocker spaniel eyes.

'What do you mean?'

'There's a Force 10 Beaufort sirocco working its way up the east coast of Tunisia. It could veer west and hit us.'

'That's all we need,' said Vespoli. As navigator of a Hercules C130, he'd been tossed around like a rag doll inside its cockpit, as the plane plowed through a Force 10 Beaufort storm. He'd felt first-hand the unimaginable power of gusts of over 130 km an hour. 'Can the Bellerophon take it?' he said.

The captain nodded, as he continued staring ahead into the unknown.

Rome, 5.35 a.m., Saturday 27 May, the day following the TV broadcast

The hotel phone rang loudly, jolting Dulac out of a heavy sleep. He groped for the receiver, and the phone fell off the night table. 'Christ!'

'No, Guadagni.'

Dulac replaced the phone on the table. 'Don't you ever sleep?'

'Romer's dead. They found him this morning in his room.'

'Jesus.'

'No signs of violence. We've ordered an autopsy.'

'Who had access to his room?'

'About 50 Swiss Guards. He slept near the barracks.'

'Great. Just pissing great.'

'Ah, and another thing. I've got that preliminary report on him. The one you ordered a week ago.'

'On the pre-hiring investigation?'

'Yes. You won't believe this, but apparently he was a Cathar.'

'What?'

'Our source says he was registered in Sion, Switzerland, as a practicing Cathar.'

'Unbelievable.' Now sitting on the edge of the bed, Dulac absorbed the impact of the news. For the Vatican to allow the Swiss Guards, staunch Roman Catholics to a man, to be headed by a Cathar, was embarrassing, inexcusable. Someone would have to answer for the laxity. Perhaps a cardinal or two.

'I know. As incredible as it may seem, he was in regular contact with the Cathar bishop of Switzerland, a monsignor Pierre Comtesse. Romer being head of the Swiss Guards, nobody bothered to check.'

'Nor had anyone reason to. Up till now. Who checked his credentials when he applied for the post?'

'That's going to take a lot more digging.'

'That explains why Aguar had no difficulty in getting hired, why the kidnappers knew about the ambulance being out of service, had access to the helicopter landing pad. Christ, the kidnappers had inside info on everything. Just pissing great.'

'It all falls into place.'

'So Aguar, dead, Romer, a Cathar, dead. De Ségur, a Cathar, very much alive. He and his bunch of hoods have killed the Pope, and we have their lat-long fix in Sicily. What the Christ are you waiting for? De Ségur's personal invitation?'

'Your sarcasm I don't need, Dulac. You didn't let me finish. Yesterday, the Palermo police raided the villa corresponding to the latitude-longitude fix.'

'And?'

'It's empty.'

CHAPTER 18

Somewhere in the Mediterranean, 4.42 a.m.

The wind was now shearing plumes of phosphorescent foam off the mountainous wave tops. The captain glanced at the fine-featured Tunisian helmsman standing slightly ahead of him, not getting any reassurance from the worried look on the helmsman's usually jovial face.

'Everything OK?' said the captain coolly, as the Tunisian swung the wheel to starboard, to counter the force of an oncoming wave.

'OK. I'm OK,' said the Tunisian nervously, overcorrecting to port.

Spews of spray were exploding off the Bellerophon's bow, hitting the bridge's windows with increasing regularity and force. The wipers weren't keeping up. Instead, a greasy film of sand and saltwater was forming on the glass, reducing the Tunisian's visibility. Now and again, he would emit a muffled curse in Arabic, leaning over to the side window to get a better view of the oncoming waves.

The captain looked at the anemometer's dimly-lit dial directly above him. Its needle was oscillating between forty-five and fifty knots. The occasional gust would bring the needle perilously close to sixty knots.

'It's veering south-east,' said the Tunisian. 'It's already 20 degrees off the port bow.'

'Take her down to ten knots,' ordered the captain.

The pounding of the waves on the vessel's hull had awakened Vespoli in his cabin. Hearing the motors slowing, he'd dressed and rushed up the companionway. At the top, he opened the door leading to the deck only to meet a wave hitting the side of the Bellerophon and drenching him from head to foot. He clambered up the open staircase and made his way to the bridge.

'What's the situation?' he asked the captain.

'We have a gale. And the wind is increasing.'

Vespoli looked at the current position of the Bellerophon on the illuminated GPS chart plotter next to the helmsman, then looked at his watch. 'We're over an hour behind schedule. Can't you get more speed out of her?' The sight of an irate de Ségur waiting for him near Suluq darkened Vespoli's mind briefly.

'Forget it,' said the captain. 'Does the yacht "Estée Lauder" mean anything to you?'

'No. Should it?'

'She was caught by a Force Ten storm in the Straights of Messina. She tried to go head-on through it, got hit by a wave that sheared off half the bridge.'

'And?'

'She went down like a rock.'

Vespoli didn't react, looking straight ahead. With the slowing of the engines, the Bellerophon was now hobby-horsing, its bow lifting high above the water before plunging down the face of the next wave. Just then, a wave slammed into the half-inch thick window with the force of a wrecking ball. The whole bridge shook violently.

The captain grabbed the wheel from the helmsman and pulled back the throttle.

'Get the crew up here. Check the panes for cracks,' said the captain to the helmsman. Suddenly, a voice crackled on the intercom.

'Captain, the lower deck has three broken ports and we're shipping a ton of water.'

The captain glanced at the ship's anemometer. It was locked at the maximum, 70 knots. 'Get me Tripoli Coast Guard,' said the captain to the radio operator behind him.

Vespoli pulled out his Glock 7 mm pistol from his jacket and put it to the radio operator's temple. 'Do that and those will be your last words.'

The radio operator looked wild-eyed at Vespoli and froze.

'Are you crazy? You're risking all our lives,' shouted the captain. 'The next wave can take us out.'

Vespoli had survived de Ségur's wrath twice. De Ségur had made it very clear there would be no third time. To dock into Tripoli Harbor under Coast Guard escort would blow their cover, kill the mission and sign Vespoli's death warrant. The risk of the Bellerophon being damaged by an out-of-phase wave paled in comparison.

'Get your speed to 10 knots, or I will,' said Vespoli, now aiming his Glock at the captain's head.

'This is madness, complete madness.' The captain obeyed, slowly moving the throttle forward. The yacht lurched and plunged directly into the sea's increasing fury.

At that moment, the door of the bridge opened and two Cathars entered, disheveled, and soaked.

'Captain, everyone below is sick. Can't we go slower?' said the man in the wet brown shirt.

The captain looked at Vespoli and before he could answer, the crackling of the intercom interrupted again.

'Captain, we're flooding. The bilge pumps can't handle the volume,' said the now-desperate voice.

'How far are we from Libya?' said Vespoli to the captain.

'About 30 nautical miles from Benghazi.'

'So the waves should get smaller as we get nearer the coast.'

‘Shorter but steeper and more powerful. Like a herd of bull elephants.’

The intercom crackled to life again: ‘Captain, the engine room is half flooded. We must slow down.’

The bow was now rising clear of the water, and then submerging completely under tons of deadly water. The whole ship shuddered violently on every impact.

‘Slow her to 8 knots,’ Vespoli ordered.

‘That’s not enough! We must reduce to minimum steerage,’ said the captain. Between torrents of water lashing at the bridge’s windows, Vespoli would catch a glimpse of the Bellerophon’s bow rising up the steep cliffs of water, coming to a halt on the crests, then accelerating down the waves’ backsides. The intercom crackled again: ‘Captain, both generators have shorted out. We’re on battery power only.’

Suddenly, a large cross-wave hit the Bellerophon on her port quarter and she started heeling in a continuous, sickening roll. Vespoli grabbed the handrail over his head with his free hand, still pointing his Glock at the captain. The yacht veered to starboard, exposing its port flank broadside to the waves’ fury. The captain flung the wheel hard to port and shoved the throttle full forward, in a desperate attempt to bring the bow back, perpendicular to the waves.

‘Come on. Come on, you can do it,’ coaxed the captain. The Bellerophon shuddered as she slowly righted herself and struggled back onto her course.

There was a moment of relief, and the captain reduced speed again. Vespoli relaxed his grip on the overhead metal handhold.

The Bellerophon‘s hobby-horsing had assumed a steady rhythm, when suddenly Vespoli sensed an eerie darkness invading the bridge. ‘What the . . . ?’ said the captain.

Vespoli looked up and saw it: ‘Mother of God!’

The enormous rogue wave, three times the size of any previous wave, started to engulf the ship’s bow, the mountain of falling water obliterating the morning light.

The men on the bridge stood paralyzed, hypnotized by the onslaught of the incoming monster.

'Hold on,' yelled the captain.

Those were the last words Vespoli ever heard.

The wave hit the bridge with the force of a freight train, shattering windows and sending missiles of broken glass through wood and flesh. Men were sent flying onto the steel-paneled rear wall of the bridge, hitting its protruding beams with their arms, torsos and heads, their broken bodies collapsing onto the floor. Water gushed through the windowless ports, flooding the bridge. The few men who had survived the impact were trying to escape the torrent, their screams muffled by the inrush of water. Minutes later, the bridge lay half-submerged, filled with bloodied bodies and drowning men.

Then, the Bellerophon began a slow, inexorable roll to starboard. Her fate seemed sealed when suddenly, as if by held by a giant hand, her rolling stopped. The yacht lay on its side, wallowing in the waves like a mortally wounded whale. Below, suffocating men were fighting to get out from the rapidly flooding entrails of the ship. Then, an out-of-sync wave hit without mercy, submerging the bow under tons of water. The doomed ship began its inescapable descent, sinking slowly at first, then quickly, as the bow dove steeper, deeper into the abyss.

Below in his cabin, Bruscetti was thrown across the room onto the small commode of the stateroom. He tried to regain his balance, only to fall down on the lopsided floor. The water was gushing in under the doorsill. He clambered towards the door, fighting the inrush of water. He grabbed the door handle and pulled himself up, working the door handle frantically until finally it broke off. He grabbed the bottom of the door and tried pulling. It was no use. 'Help! Help me,' he yelled. He pounded desperately on the door, to no avail. Finally, the water pressure burst the wooden door off its hinges and Bruscetti was thrown clear across the cabin, the door crushing his chest and pinning him against the wall.

As he tried in vain to free himself, the water level quickly reached neck-level. He tried to breathe but choked, again and again, his body's autonomous reflex attempting in vain to expulse the deadly liquid. As his lungs filled with water, he began to feel dizzy. Now he could barely see the cabin lights, flickering in the increasing obscurity. The cabin was almost fully submerged, when the door finally released its deadly grip and fell slowly to the floor. By now, Bruscetti's world had swung ninety degrees: he was standing nearly fully submerged on one of the cabin's walls, the doorway was now horizontal and completely submerged, and the edge of the water was lapping at his chin. I must try now! For Maria. He took a last gulp of air, ducked underwater and began swimming towards the cabin's doorway. He was halfway out the doorway and trying to resurface when he felt his clothing catch on something. He looked down: he'd caught a loop of his fatigue around the leg of an overturned chair. He pulled hard to free himself, only to tighten the loop around the chair's leg. He panicked, letting out the precious air from his searing lungs. He choked and swallowed more water. There was no more air. He pulled desperately one more time, as his lungs burst with pain. Nothing. It was useless. He was caught. He swallowed again.

Slowly, inexorably Bruscetti felt a feeling of abandon overtake his will to survive, giving way to a sense of resignation and peace. As the lights flickered erratically underwater in the corridor, the last thing Bruscetti saw was a white blur, being carried away by the water. The blur was struggling in slow-motion, trying to surface. It looked like an angel.

Then, darkness fell.

Suluq, 20 km south of Benghazi, 6.05 a.m.

In the Libyan Desert, the earliest warning of a sirocco comes invariably too late. Awakened in the middle of the night by the eerie whistling sound of the wind, de Ségur had ordered the Berbers to barricade the doors of the house, and secure the Alouette helicopter by tying it down with sisal ropes anchored to small stones. When the 150 km-an-hour wind hit the helicopter, it ripped the ropes free in minutes. Flogging wildly about like sails in a storm, the loose ropes eventually flipped the helicopter onto its side like a toy in a sandbox.

Two hours later the wind finally abated, and one of the Berbers had to crawl through a window to remove the pile of sand blocking the front door. De Ségur stepped outside, looking forlornly at the remnants of the Alouette: the helicopter lay half-buried in sand, two of its blades badly bent. The force of the wind had blown off the jet motor's intake cover, letting in large amounts of sand. De Ségur was looking at the useless piece of wreckage when his satellite phone rang.

'Yes?'

'Sir, there's still no sign of the Bellerophon.' De Ségur recognized Antoine's voice. 'She should have been here an hour and a half ago.'

'Any radio contact?' said de Ségur.

'Nothing. We tried hailing them on channel 76 and emergency channel 16. They must have been hit by the sirocco. It went through here about two hours ago. There's big damage to the docks. Three fishing trawlers were sunk here in Quaminis Bay.'

'Give them another hour, and then get back here,' said de Ségur to Antoine, the van's driver. 'We've got to make other plans.'

De Ségur returned inside to face the eight Cathars seated in the small, stuffy room: 'They're almost two hours late. The sirocco must have hit them.'

'Mr de Ségur, we looked outside,' said a young Cathar. 'Is the helicopter . . . ?'

'Finished.'

The young man was silent, waiting for de Ségur to continue.

'We still have the vans,' said de Ségur as he sat down, absorbing the air of disquiet on the Cathars' faces. For the first time, he felt their confidence in him wavering.

'Sir, the Bellerophon. Could it have altered course to another port?' asked the burly Frenchman in the brown desert shirt.

'Vespoli would've contacted us,' said de Ségur.

'Their radios could be temporarily out of order,' said a bespectacled, bald man.

'Not all of them,' said de Ségur.

Jean Gaspard, treading water, half dazed and coughing out a lungful of salt water, looked desperately for floating debris from the Bellerophon. Waiting for a wave to pass, he pivoted on himself and searched the horizon. Nothing. Another wave caught him off guard and he swallowed more water. He knew that every time he did, he was getting a little closer to drowning. He turned again slowly, careful to keep his timing and to inhale only when on top of a wave. Again, nothing. Desperation was setting in. He had to find something, anything that could help him float. He pivoted one more half turn, and saw it: a couple of hundred yards away. First an orange blur between each passing wave. He focused and waited for the next wave. He rose with it. Yes. A life raft! He suddenly felt a surge of elation. He started swimming vigorously towards the raft. After a dozen strokes, he realized he wasn't closing the distance. It seemed the wind and waves were pushing it at a slight angle away from him. He realized he had to aim not at the raft but in front of it. If he swam quickly, he could still intercept it. He knew he had but one try before the raft would sail away. He swam forcefully towards the raft, marshaling every bit of energy, when suddenly a wave flipped the raft onto its side. The raft began to sail away more quickly. Gaspard swam furiously, fear and adrenaline his only fuel. He was catching it. His arms and lungs seared with pain but he kept hitting the water with rapid, purposeful strokes. A few more yards. He was there. With a last, desperate lunge, he grabbed the rubber tubing of the raft's side. As he tried to right the raft, his hand slipped, and a wave pushed the raft out of reach. Exhausted, his arms heavy with lactic acid, he swam after it, but another wave pushed the raft further away. In a matter of seconds, it was twenty feet away. He'd used up his last bit of strength. He had nothing left. It was no use. The raft was gone.

Desperation and panic started flooding his brain. Stay calm, I must stay calm. He started to tread water again when suddenly he felt something brush his left hand. A bit of yellow rope. Jesus. It's . . . it must be the end of the raft's painter. He grabbed the yellow, floating polypropylene rope and pulled. Dear God, make that it's still connected to the raft. He pulled frantically, and felt the tug of the raft at the other end of the raft's painter. Nothing had ever felt so good. Slowly, one hand at a time, he pulled in the raft, careful not to entangle himself in the painter, treading water between pulls. With the raft finally alongside, he hung there for a moment, his right hand wrapped around the painter, too tired to climb in. After a moment, gathering his strength, he struggled up the two rubber steps and tumbled into the raft. He lay on the bottom exhausted, taking short breaths, and eventually fell into a semi-conscious sleep.

A while later, a barely perceptible tapping sound tore insistently at Gaspard's dazed somnolence, finally awakening him. He leaned on the raft's side and looked about. The fury of the sirocco had passed, replaced by a cool westerly breeze. The seas, although diminished, were still chaotic, a confused maelstrom of large, crisscrossing swells. Gaspard could hear a faint thump, thump, thump coming from somewhere in the distance. Squinting into the sunlight, he saw a human form, waving, or . . . no, someone was striking what looked like a large, wooden box.

Gaspard searched for a paddle inside the raft, but there was none. Only an emergency ration kit and a portable VHF radio transmitter under the life raft's torn cover. He cupped his hands and yelled to the man: 'Hang on!'

Gaspard couldn't make out his faint reply, but noticed that the wind was pushing the life raft closer. 'I'm coming.

Hang on!' he shouted. Gaspard leaned over the edge of the raft and started to paddle with his hands. The raft barely moved. Gaspard looked at the desperate man and saw he couldn't hold onto the wooden object much longer. The man's arm went up in the air and fell limp into the water one more time, and didn't move. The top of his head was now barely visible over the box. He was going under.

Gaspard realized it was now or never. He rose and slumped over the rubber edge of the raft into the cold water. He swam slowly with one hand, trying to conserve what little energy he had left, pulling the life raft with the other. Just as Gaspard reached him, the man tried to grab Gaspard's outstretched arm. He couldn't and, a few feet only from Gaspard, disappeared below the waves. Gaspard took a deep breath, dove and reached down, grabbing the drowning man's arm. He pulled him up, up from the clutches of Poseidon, and alongside the raft. Gaspard climbed aboard, and tried lifting the limp man inside the raft. Something on the man's garment kept getting caught on the raft's towing ring. He was about to slip underwater again when, with his last bit of strength, Gaspard seized both the man's arms and pulled him over the rubber tube.

The man managed an exhausted smile of gratitude, then slumped onto the raft's bottom and fell unconscious.

De Ségur put the small VHF phone to his ear and recognized Antoine's frantic voice: 'It is terrible, terrible. So many, they're gone. Terrible.'

'Calm down, Antoine. What happened?'

'Jean Gaspard reached us on his radio, from the life raft. They were hit by a rogue wave. It was terrible, terrible. The Bellerophon, she went down in minutes.'

'Where is Gaspard?'

'He gave the GPS fix of the life raft. A couple of fishermen here have gone to get him.'

'And the others?'

'I don't know. Gaspard's VHF went dead.'

'How much time to bring him back to port?' asked de Ségur.

'I would say about three hours.'

'Wait for them.'

'Yes sir.'

De Ségur closed his phone and turned somberly to the others: 'The Bellerophon went down in the sirocco. Gaspard is alive. Perhaps others also. We'll know more when he gets back.'

There was a long moment of silence, as the news sank in. Finally, one of the Cathars looked up at de Ségur. 'What do we do now?'

'We proceed as planned.'

CHAPTER 19

The Vatican, Segnatura Room, 8.05 a.m.

During the press conference's tumultuous aftermath, Brentano had seized his opportunity and convened the meeting of the inner Curia. There were hard decisions to be made in light of the dire circumstances. The cardinals entered one by one, their mien somber, and seated themselves once again around the oval, dark walnut table.

I must get this started now, thought Brentano. Before they read the Code. 'Cardinal Signorelli, you must issue the writs of convocation for the Conclave. I assume you can expedite this quickly,' said Brentano.

Before Signorelli could answer, Fouquet interrupted. 'Cardinal, Canon law clearly states there must first be confirmation of the Pope's death by the Camerlengo. As Camerlengo I cannot proceed until—'

'Everyone saw it, cardinal,' said Brentano. 'We may never have the opportunity to see the body.'

'Your Eminences,' interrupted Legnano. 'I cannot believe what I am hearing. We haven't even discussed how we will address the issue of the funeral, even if indeed there is to be one. If not, what form will the symbolic remembrance of Pope Clement's death take? How are we to make arrangements for such an event? I think your discussion of the succession is, if you'll pardon the euphemism, a bit premature.' He looked at Brentano. 'Article 306 B specifies that in the case of the Pope's disappearance, we must wait ninety days before presuming him dead.

'Unless we—'

'Article 306 B applies in case of doubt, cardinal,' interrupted Brentano. 'We all saw it. Pope Clement XXI is dead. Why delay the Conclave unnecessarily? The Church needs a new leader now.'

'With all due respect, monsignor,' said Legnano, his tone rising to Brentano's challenge, 'until all hope is lost and we have confirmation, it is hasty to call the Conclave. We will have plenty of time to do so later. Until then, Cardinal Fouquet, as Camerlengo, you have all papal powers.'

'If the Code is clear, then we must wait,' said Fouquet.

Brentano felt the opportunity slipping away. He looked at Sforza, who hadn't spoken. 'I see. And what say you, Cardinal Sforza?' said Brentano.

'We wait.'

Brentano felt the blood rush to his face. He bit his tongue and walked out. He had urgent calls to make.

The breakfast room of the hotel was remarkably quiet that morning. Having practically inhaled the last of his croissant, Dulac put down the coffee cup he was about to bring to his lips and grabbed his insistent cellphone. He recognized the number: Interpol's forensics section.

'Mr Dulac, it's Gina,' she said, excitement in her voice. 'We have the frame-by-frame analysis of the video. Although the camera blurred just before the moment of impact, we did a computer extrapolation based on the earlier trajectory of the scimitar and compared it to the seating position of the Pope. If we are right, the scimitar comes in contact with the side of the Pope's head.'

'And?' said Dulac, taking a sip of coffee while he waited for her to continue.

'It looks like the blow was a glancing one.'

'What do you mean?' Dulac put the cup down and straightened in his chair.

'I mean it's quite possible that the blow didn't kill him.'

'Jesus to Christ!' Dulac thought quickly. 'Did you get a second opinion?'

'We have MI6's. They agree with us.'

'Agree with what?'

'With the possibility.'

'But he fell forward. His blood was all over the camera's lens.'

'It can happen in the case of a head wound. We checked with pathology at Lyon's Leclerc hospital.'

Dulac reached across the table for his pack of Gitanes. 'Is this information contained?'

'As far as we know, only MI6 knows about this. But they must report it to the P.M.'s office. We haven't checked with other agencies yet.'

'Has anyone advised Legnano?'

'No. Beside Mr Harris, you are the first person—'

'I'm seeing Legnano this morning. He should be made aware of this.'

'Before you do that, there's a slight problem.'

'Hmm . . . There always is.'

'Our colleague, Doctor Guerlan, disagrees with us.'

'Explain.'

'According to Guerlan, with the speed of the blow, it was almost impossible for the scimitar to stop at the side of the head. The scimitar would have continued its trajectory and severed either the regular or the left common carotid artery, or both.'

'Resulting in?'

'Certain death in less than two minutes.'

Dulac paused to light his cigarette. 'And why shouldn't I believe Guerlan's version?'

'Because according to Dr Villandré of Sainte-Ursule hospital, there would have been much more blood. Besides, MI6 and I believe there was a sharp deceleration of the scimitar's movement towards the end of its arc.'

Dulac took a deep drag of his Gitane. 'Great, just pissing great. So we really don't know where we damn well stand. Transfer me to Harris.'

'There's no need to be rude.'

'Sorry, I didn't mean—' Dulac heard a click, and was about to close his cell when he heard the General Secretary's voice.

'Harris.'

'Dulac. I was on the phone with Gina. What do you make of her report?'

'We're cross-checking with the FBI forensics people,' said Harris.

'I'd rather have something more concrete before I go to Legnano with this.'

The young courier handed the package, wrapped in a brown box, to the Swiss Guard at the Sant'Anna entrance of the Vatican, then disappeared into the already dense morning crowd of Via Della Conciliazione.

'It's for Cardinal Fouquet,' said the guard as he stood at the doorway of Fouquet's office, addressing the gray-haired woman seated at her secretary's desk, phone in hand.

She shielded the mouthpiece with her hand. 'Security?'

'We've scanned it. It's clean.'

'Bring it here then,' she ordered, her strong voice belying her frail appearance. 'Leave it on the desk.'

'I have to check when you open it,' said the guard.

'Can't you see I'm busy? I'll open it later.'

'I'll wait.' The young Swiss Guard wasn't backing down. He stood at the desk, his arms crossed over his chest.

'I'll call you back,' she said and put down the phone. She grabbed the package and shook it. Turning towards the guard, she said, 'Another statue of the Virgin Mary? What's your bet?'

The guard wasn't buying into her game, looking impatiently towards the door. 'I have to get back.'

'All right, all right. Hand me the letter-opener over there, will you?' she said, pointing at a table beside her desk and a mug containing an assortment of pens, pencils and a letter-opener.

He reached over and handed her the small-scaled Toledo sword.

'Let's see, I'll bet it's a plaster statuette,' she said, shaking the package again.

'I'll bet it isn't.' The Swiss Guard knew it wasn't. The scanner had confirmed that apart from the plastic disk, the package contained no solids.

She opened the outer wrapping of the box and fumbled with its contents.

'Darn protective material. Now we have to recycle it.' She pulled out the DVD holder. 'All this for a DVD?' She reached in again. 'There's something else . . .'

She removed more insulating material and suddenly her hand drew back quickly. 'It's freezing.' She opened the package more and the transparent gel cold pack slithered onto the desk.

'Oh my God!' She recoiled in horror, her mouth agape, her lips trembling.

The Swiss Guard, seeing she was about to faint, rushed towards the stricken woman.

'Are you all right?' he said, supporting her shoulders.

'Is it . . . ?'

He looked with curiosity at the gel pack on the desk, and said, 'It . . . it looks like an ear.'

The nervous priest intercepted Dulac as he made his way down the marble corridor to the Segnatura room.

'Have you heard the news?'

Before Dulac could ask to what news he was referring, the priest blurted out, 'The Curia received a package containing the Pope's left ear this morning. The Curia and the police are in the Segnatura room now.'

Dulac entered the room, and saw Guadagni, standing amidst the cardinals, immersed in an intense discussion with Legnano and Sforza. They barely seemed to notice him, until Legnano turned to greet him. 'Mr Dulac. You got my message?'

'Which message?'

'I left a message at your hotel for you to come over immediately.'

'I learned about the Pope's ear just now. I was coming to meet you on another subject.'

'Gentlemen, please be seated,' said Legnano. He led Dulac by the arm to a seat next to Cardinal Signorelli, whose corpulence overflowed fluidly on either side of his chair.

Sforza, sitting across from him, his voice heavy with stress, spoke.

'These people, these butchers. Not content to kill him, now they're sending us parts of his body. When will this desecration, this savagery stop?'

'You are sure it's the Pope's?' asked Dulac.

'We're having tests done right now,' said Legnano.

The technician signaled to Legnano that the computer hookup was ready. The room was suddenly silent. The screen came alive with the shape of the same lanky, hooded man.

'De Ségur,' whispered Dulac under his breath.

'Men of little faith, we have kept our bargain. You have paid for a pound of flesh and we have delivered it. The world shall know of your avarice today, at 10.30 a.m.' The screen went blank.

There was a short pause before Legnano spoke. 'That must mean he's still alive. He must be alive.'

Suddenly the cardinals' restraint broke into vociferous exchanges of joy.

Legnano spoke. 'Cardinals, please. Let's not be hasty. This could be trickery. I . . . But Mr Dulac, you were coming here to—'

'Cardinal, have you spoken to Harris about the ear?'

'Not yet.'

Dulac opened his cell, called Harris, and gave him the news. He added: 'Did you get any other corroboration on Gina's theory? I see . . . I agree . . . I'll inform the cardinals.'

The prelates' eyes riveted onto Dulac.

'Your Eminences, there is a chance, and I stress the word chance, that you might be right. The Pope may be alive. Interpol analyzed the trajectory of the scimitar and it corresponds with a side blow to the head. Hence the ear, but—'

'Mio Dio!' exclaimed Sforza.

'Thank God,' said Fouquet.

'You said "chance"?' said Legnano.

'Yes. Because there is also a possibility that the blow severed his carotid, resulting in death.'

The cardinals' exuberance evaporated quickly.

'I see,' said Legnano. 'So we are really no further ahead.'

'We thought it our responsibility to tell you,' said Dulac. 'But I have other news. We have confirmed that the hooded man we saw on that fateful day and here again today is Hugues de Ségur.'

'The man wanted by the French and Italian police in relation to the murders of Archbishops Salvador and Conti?' said Sforza.

'Exactly,' said Dulac. 'He travels under different aliases, one of which is Pierre de Combel. Apparently, that is now his official name within the Cathar sect. Interpol knows he's head of a Cathar right wing group. We don't know their exact purpose, except we have reason to believe it has the financial support of the Cathars.' Dulac paused and turned briefly towards Guadagni, before lighting the dynamite. 'Your Eminences, we also have evidence that Romer, your Swiss Guard, was a Cathar and probably a member of that group.'

Muted exclamations rose from the assembled prelates, as the cardinals looked at each other in a mixture of disbelief and embarrassment. Dulac continued. 'We believe Romer was in on the kidnapping. We—'

'Preposterous. Totally preposterous,' said Sforza. 'The Vatican carefully screens all applicants before they become members of the Swiss Guards.'

'That's what I thought too, your Eminence, before Interpol obtained a voice transcript of a telephone conversation between Romer and de Ségur's lawyer, Claude Pourcelet. In it Romer talks about Aguar's papers, doctored with the help of a certain Umberto Ascari. Both were killed to prevent, we believe, any tracing back to de Ségur. We can send you a copy of the transcript if you wish.'

'That won't be necessary, Mr Dulac,' said Legnano, eyeing Sforza angrily. 'Tell me, how does this de Ségur function?'

'We think his main hideout is in Belize, from which he cannot be extradited. He keeps changing identities. He was seen in Algiers, and recently in Switzerland. The Swiss authorities didn't catch the fakeness of his passport until it was too late. He'd already flown out. He speaks fluent French, English, German, Italian and Arabic.'

'Mr Dulac, I'm confused,' said Legnano. 'Throughout history, Cathars have preached resignation and non-violence to the point of self-sacrifice. Isn't that in contradiction with what you are saying?'

'You're right, Your Eminence. At least partially. That's why Interpol initially thought they were using the Cathar faith as a screen. But there is now a theory within Interpol and other agencies that this Cathar right wing group might be to the Cathars what Hezbollah or Al Qaeda are to Islam, what the Zionists are to the Jewish faith.'

'Violence being acceptable to protect their faiths from desecration by Infidels,' said Legnano.

'Something like that,' said Dulac.

'But what has this got to do with the Pope's kidnapping?' said Sforza.

'We're trying to find out, your Eminence,' said Dulac.

'On another subject, Mr Dulac, what about the $30 million we've paid?' said Brentano. 'Can't you trace that back to him? There must be some sort of trail.'

'There wasn't enough time. By the time we got to Costa Rica, the accounts were closed and the money gone. Even if we had marked it, by the time it got traced, it would've been laundered many, many times. The world at large is using that money as we speak.'

'Mr Dulac, it seems de Ségur is always one step ahead of you,' said Fouquet, smiling. Dulac felt the blood rush to his face, the tips of his ears becoming hot.

'He's been lucky, Monsignor. Mark my words, we will catch him.'

'Ah, yes, you mean like Pablo Escobar?' said Sforza, a sarcastic, smug smile on his face. Dulac felt the blow below the belt and cringed. It was common knowledge that Interpol had let the infamous head of the Medellin drug cartel slip through its hands at least twice. The Colombian army had had to finish the job.

'Monsignori, come,' interrupted Legnano, 'we achieve nothing by casting recrimination on Mr Dulac. May I remind you we have a more pressing issue? Surely the kidnappers will grandstand again this afternoon, and they will want more money. What is the consensus here?'

'Pay,' said Fouquet. 'We have no choice.' The other cardinals nodded in agreement.

'Cardinal Sforza, please prepare the payment arrangements,' said Legnano.

The assembly in the Segnatura room waited silently. 10.30 a.m. passed, as the members of the Curia and the police inspectors sat with growing anxiety before the inert TV monitors. Then 10.45, then 11 a.m. Still nothing.

'They've changed plans,' said Legnano.

'Or they are trying a new method to block the source of the transmission,' said Dulac.

At 11.15, the two monitors flashed on, and the image flickered then focused on the all too familiar scene: hooded figures standing on the platform, above a solitary wooden chair, empty. The monotonous, electronically-altered voice of the lanky man broke the short silence.

'Monsignori, you have learned that we do not negotiate. Unless we receive $600 million American dollars in our accounts today at 2 p.m. Rome time, your Pope will be executed, and delivered to you in small packages. The money shall be hot wire transferred per our instructions in the DVD on its way to you. In case you doubt we can keep our part of the bargain . . .'

The screens flickered again. The man signaled to the two hooded figures and they left the platform. Moments later, they returned, shouldering between them a man dressed in white, his head bandaged.

'It's the Holy Father!' exclaimed Legnano.

Dulac saw the camera focus on the Pope, who held up a copy of the *Herald Tribune*. It was dated the same day.

CHAPTER 20

'$600 million?' said Fouquet. 'That's almost double—'

'Cardinal, de Ségur knows you can't negotiate,' said Dulac. 'He could have asked for the moon and gotten it.'

'What do we do now?' asked Sforza to the cardinals.

'You prepare the payment and await their instructions,' said Dulac.

'What about Interpol?' said Sforza.

'I'm sure we're trying to trace that transmission as we speak. I'll let you know as soon as I have something,' said Dulac.

'We will meet in the Segnatura room at 1 p.m. this afternoon,' said Legnano.

After a speedy gnocchi lunch at Cantabile's, Dulac, in his taxi on the way back to the Vatican, had just gotten off the phone with Harris when his cell rang again. It was Guadagni.

'We have confirmation that the ear's DNA matches the Pope's.'

'Great,' said Dulac, not overly enthused to hear what he already knew.

'Also, de Ségur is starting to slip. We decoded their encryptions and went through their firewalls and have a fix on the transmission: it came from a small town outside of Benghazi.'

'Just a minute.' Dulac got out of the taxi and headed for the Sant'Anna entrance, phone in hand. 'Yes. I've gotten the same info from our Lyon office. I've just finished talking to Harris.'

'So what's the plan?'

'We don't know what de Ségur intends to do. If, of course, the Vatican pays him.'

'They have no choice. What does Harris think?' said Guadagni.

'In anticipation that the Vatican will pay the $600 million before 2 p.m. today and de Ségur delivers his side of the bargain and leaves the Pope and Bruscetti in Libya, Harris has spoken with the French and German foreign affairs ministers. He says we have a problem. If Ali al Kargali gets wind that the Pope is in Libya, you can be sure the crafty Colonel won't just let us walk in and rescue the Pope. That bastard de Ségur knows this.'

'So by going to Benghazi, he's bought himself time and protection.'

'Exactly. That's probably why the second transmission was easy to break into.'

'But what about the French interests there?' said Guadagni.

'Not enough. Nor are the German,' said Dulac.

'Kargali would look like a hero to the Western world if he were to save the Pope.'

'Correct.'

'I don't follow,' said Guadagni.

'I suggest to you that his Muslim friends wouldn't appreciate him going that far. As a serious candidate for the directorship of the Arab League, he won't want to alienate half of Islam. Once Kargali becomes aware that the Pope is sitting in his backyard, he'll have the hottest diplomatic potato under the Arab sun. There is no way of knowing what Kargali will do. He's about as predictable as tomorrow's stock market.'

'We could go in sub rosa, and when—'

'—when we screw up, we'll have a dead pope, de Ségur will be gone and to top it off we'll have a diplomatic row with the Libyans.'

Dulac nodded to the Swiss Guards, standing at the entrance to the Segnatura room.

'Hmm. Any ideas?' Guadagni continued.

'I have to ring off.' Dulac flipped his phone shut.

The prelates were talking excitedly when Dulac entered the Segnatura and sat down. 'Your Eminences, we have their position. They're twenty miles south-east of Benghazi, near a small town called Suluq. The General Secretary is awaiting your instructions.'

'Our instructions?' said Legnano, looking perplexed.

'Harris wants to know if you want to risk alerting the Libyans.'

'Why not?'

'Your Eminences, if we contact the Libyans, consider that the Libyans might move in, the kidnappers could panic and kill the Pope. Or, the Libyans could botch the job and in a skirmish, the Pope gets killed, or the Libyans secure the perimeter and save the Pope. Fine, but now you have to bargain with Kargali for the return of the Pope.'

'I see. And what are the alternatives, Mr Dulac?' asked Legnano, his confidence visibly shaken.

'Better a devil you know than one you don't.'

'What makes you so sure de Ségur isn't, how you say, in bed with Kargali?' asked Legnano.

'De Ségur informing the unpredictable, grandstanding colonel and risk losing control over his precious asset? I doubt it,' said Dulac.

'I see,' said Legnano, shooting occasional glances at the prelates. 'But what guarantees do we have they won't kill him anyway?'

'Other than de Ségur being labeled a stupid, senseless, psychopathic killer, none.'

'Not very reassuring, Mr Dulac,' said Legnano.

'I've been wrong before.' Dulac felt the painful memory resurfacing. He wasn't going to make that mistake twice. No suggestions this time.

At that moment, a prelate dressed in a black cassock rushed in and handed an envelope to Fouquet. He tore open the envelope and read the letter. 'Your Eminences, we have just received their payment instructions.'

'Are the wire transfers ready?' asked Legnano to Sforza.

'Yes. I will give final directions to the Treasury,' said Sforza. 'For those amounts, I need the written confirmation of two members of the Curia. Please sign here, Cardinal Signorelli, Cardinal Legnano.'

'Your Eminences, we are all in agreement to pay?' said Legnano, eyeing the prelates one by one. They nodded.

'Fine.' Legnano and Signorelli approached the table and Sforza offered them a pen. 'Mr Dulac,' said Legnano as he signed the document, 'tell the General Secretary not to inform the Libyans.'

'Yes, your Eminence,' said Dulac. He had a sickening feeling that somehow the Libyans knew already. He rose, walked to the far end of the room and phoned Harris.

'They want us to stay silent. Don't inform the Libyans.'

'They'll have a hell of a mess if Kargali finds out,' said Harris.

'They have one now anyway,' said Dulac.

'How do they think they'll get the Pope out?'

'We haven't discussed that issue yet. Surely the Italian SWAT team needs a bit of exercise,' said Dulac.

'SISMI? Ha! They couldn't rescue a dozing cat off a low-lying tree branch. Anyway, there's nothing more you can do. Get back to Lyon. I want a complete update tomorrow morning,' Harris said, his tone peremptory.

'But we're waiting for word from de Ségur. He's about to receive the money.'

'If that's the case and de Ségur keeps his end of the bargain, you'll have plenty of time for the rest of the investigation.'

'I still have some—'

'Here, Dulac. Tomorrow morning.' The line went dead.

Dulac grabbed a cab back to the hotel and went to the front desk. He had a message from Karen. 'Staying in room 347. Call me if you dare.'

Dulac grabbed the hotel's intercom. 'Bonjour, it's me.'

'Who?'

'All right, I know. I should've called before.'

'Before what? It's been barely a week.'

'I'm sorry. I've been rather busy.'

'And I haven't? You're damn lucky I have an appointment with my doctoral student here tomorrow.'

'How about a drink downstairs?'

'Now?'

'Why not?'

'You don't give a girl much notice.'

Karen preceded Dulac towards the discreet corner table, her square shoulders accentuated by her loose-fitting blue blouse. Dulac walked closely behind her, mesmerized by the alternate swinging of each of her firm, rounded buttocks, separately encased in her custom fitting beige pants. They sat down in the uncomfortable, art-deco chairs.

'So how did the meeting with the cardinals go?' she said.

'Disastrously well,' said Dulac, looking pensive.

'I'm sure they didn't teach you that at Oxford,' she said, replacing the wayward strand of auburn hair behind her right ear.

Dulac looked at his watch. 'That bastard de Ségur is now $600 million richer.'

'So they had no other choice.'

'Not really,' said Dulac.

The waiter came over to their table. 'Dry martini,' said Karen.

'Glenlivet on the rocks,' said Dulac. The waiter left with their order and Dulac eyed Karen. 'I won't go into details, but there's something else about the Pope's past that's related to his kidnapping.'

'Other than the ransom?'

'Yes. I'll have to see Legnano again. I'm sure he knows a lot more than he's telling me.'

'Why would Legnano hide anything?' said Karen, looking perplexed.

'You are blissfully unaware of Vatican politics, my dear. Politics and their sacred code of silence. Getting information from a cardinal is like trying to pry open a safe with a screwdriver.'

Tripoli, 3 p.m., same day

As head of the intelligence section of the People's Security Force in Libya, Ali El Gazzar el Kadaffa rarely had to face any moral dilemmas before making the decisions required by his office. Arguably the most powerful man in Libya after Kargali, Gazzar had worked hard to secure the trust of the wary colonel, and up till now, Gazzar's loyalty to him had been unwavering, unquestionable.

However, that loyalty would now be put to the test: one of his intelligence officers had informed Gazzar that he'd deciphered the codes and broken through the firewalls disguising an astounding video conference. According to the officer, the provenance and content of the video showed that the Pope was being held in Suluq, a small town outside of Benghazi. Any man other than Gazzar would have been ecstatic. Bringing such news to the colonel would result in praise and financial reward.

But Ali El Gazzar had recently acquired a higher allegiance than the one he owed Kargali. Five years prior, Gazzar had married a Catholic woman and six months later had himself secretly converted to Catholicism, something he couldn't afford to broadcast within Libya's predominantly Islamic power structure. Gazzar hid his new religious allegiance meticulously. From all appearances, he was a devout

Muslim, performing his daily incantations at the mosque as required by the Quran, yet all the while praying fervently for the repenting of his sins to his newly found savior, Jesus Christ.

Gazzar had to choose. If he failed to report the Pope's presence in Libya and the colonel found out, Gazzar was a dead man. But if the Pope was whisked out of Libya and escaped before Gazzar had had a reasonable opportunity to determine his presence on Libyan soil, Gazzar would at worst be reprimanded, while saving the Pope from Kargali's unpredictable clutches. Gazzar thought hard and fast. Two conditions were necessary for his plan to work: he had to get the Pope out of Libya within hours, and swear his young intelligence officer to secrecy. In meeting the second condition, he had an inbuilt guarantee. The young officer was his son.

He went to work on the first.

CHAPTER 21

Hotel Dante, 3.10 p.m.

Dulac had just finished ordering their second round of drinks when his encrypted cellphone rang.

'Dulac.'

'Is this inspector Thierry Dulac of Interpol?'

Dulac didn't recognize the voice, or the caller's ID number. 'Who is this?'

'My name is El Gazzar. I'm chief of intelligence of the Libyan People's Security Force.'

Dulac interrupted, angry and surprised. 'Really? And I'm Colonel Gaddaffi—'

'Mr Dulac, don't be upset. How we broke through your encryption is really not important.'

Voice sounds middle-eastern enough, thought Dulac.

The voice continued. 'Do not think of tracing the call to verify its authenticity, Mr Dulac. You'd be wasting time. I will authenticate this call to you later. I have information that you are coordinating the efforts to get a certain package back to the Vatican. Is that correct?'

'Don't know what you're talking about,' said Dulac, getting up from the table and signaling Karen with his upturned right hand of his sudden need for privacy.

'We do not have time for games, Mr Dulac. We know that the recent transmission came from Suluq. I suppose you know this also?'

Dulac was silent as he turned and took a few steps away. He looked around. A few empty tables separated him from the other patrons, busy finishing their meals.

'Mr Dulac, are you there?'

'How do I know you're who you say you are?' Dulac said, feeling a knot form in his stomach. Disclosure of the Pope being held in Libya and its disastrous consequences raced through his mind.

'Listen to me carefully, Mr Dulac. I will be transferring my photo and copy of my security number to your offices at Interpol, so that you can verify my identity. The password to my personal file will be given to Interpol though a secure channel. It will be valid for one entry only. I'm giving you forty-eight hours to get him out of Libya, starting now.' The man's tone was firm, yet not threatening, almost casual. 'In exchange, you will deposit $5 million American dollars into the account given through that channel to the Bank Julius Baer in Zurich. You can check the legitimacy of the account. You have two hours to make the deposit. Do we understand each other, Mr Dulac?'

Dulac stood in utter amazement, too stunned to speak.

'Mr Dulac?'

Dulac gathered his wits. 'If I understand you correctly, you are selling your non-interference in the delivery. That's all. Am I right?'

'Correct.'

'We have no proof the package is even available for delivery.'

'Not my problem. After forty-eight hours, we move in. Is that clear, Mr Dulac?'

Dulac didn't need to answer. He thought he should hang up. Every professional instinct told him that he should not ask the question pressing foremost on his mind, but he couldn't resist. 'I presume the colonel doesn't know?'

The line went dead.

Dulac flipped his cell shut, walked back and whispered to Karen's ear. 'We have to leave. I have a—'

'Can't we finish our drinks?'

'Now.'

'Fine. Fine.'

'We'll go to the room. I have to make some calls.' He straightened and signaled the waiter to close the bill.

'What's this all about?' Karen said as they neared the elevators.

Dulac pressed the button and they waited alone for the lift. 'If this guy is who he says he is, Libyan intelligence knows the Pope is being held near Benghazi. He's saying we have forty-eight hours to get him out, before he informs Kargali.'

'Holy shit!' said Karen.

'My thoughts exactly.'

'But how on earth did he know to contact you?'

'Search me. If he did, maybe others know also.'

'Wow. This could blow sky high,' said Karen as they entered the elevator.

'I have to make a quick check on this guy.' He opened his phone. 'Shit. I can't use this, it's corrupt. I'll have to use yours.'

'And how do you propose to check at this time of night?'

'I happen to have a contact at Julius Baer, the bank where Gazzar wants us to deposit the money. Tonio is an old friend from Montpelier University. I have his home phone number somewhere in my databank.'

'Surely he can't divulge the name of his clients.'

'He owes me. I saved his ass in law school years ago.'

'Wow. What if this Gazzar guy is in with Kargali? And they've set us up?'

'Exactly. If I understand correctly, he'd get the glory and the money. With no risk.'

'I agree, but they'd be asking for a whole lot more money than $5 million.'

'I suppose. Unless . . .'

'What?' said Dulac, a trace of impatience in his voice. 'Unless it's only a down payment.'

Dulac felt his face flush red. As they entered Dulac's room, he said, 'I'll need your cell. I can't use mine until we secure the line.' He sat down at the small desk and called Legnano, then Harris.

'Jesus! Now we have two extortionists to deal with,' Harris exclaimed.

'God knows why, but Gazzar is doing us a favor,' said Dulac. 'The price would be a hundred times that if we were dealing with the colonel.'

'Some favor. We have absolutely no guarantee de Ségur will deliver, nor this Gazzar or whatever his name is. And we don't dare call Kargali. What a fucking, shit-house whore of a mess.'

'I've informed Legnano. He's willing to take the risk with Gazzar, once we've checked out his credentials and the bank,' said Dulac. 'Now that they've paid de Ségur, they want to protect their investment, so to speak.'

'You've informed Legnano? Don't you think that's my responsibility?' Harris's voice was loud enough that Karen heard it. She gave Dulac a compassionate glance.

'Time was pressing. I—'

'Never mind. How did Legnano take it?'

'He's devastated. I think he just realized the mess they're in.'

'Dulac, supposing, just supposing de Ségur and Gazzar keep their word. The only way we can get His Holiness out in time is by a covert 'copter operation. I say covert. Now how the hell do the Italians, the SISMI force, or anybody for that matter, pick up the Pope without a dozen Libyan MIGs shooting down their Hueys when they cross into Libyan air space?'

'Gazzar says he won't interfere if we get him out within forty-eight hours.'

'Why the hell should we believe him?'

'Because he knows that if he double-crosses us, we'll leak to Kargali that his chief intelligence officer knew of the

Pope's presence in Libya, and didn't bother to inform him. As proof, we'll send Kargali a voucher of the bank deposit. Gazzar will be dead within the hour.'

There was silence. 'Good point. But still, those Hueys aren't invisible.' Harris's tone had mellowed somewhat. 'They'll show up on their radars in an instant. Gazzar can't pretend he didn't see the choppers on any of his screens. There are also the Tunisians.'

Dulac took a deep drag on the nicotine stick, exhaled and said, 'Maybe we can help.'

'What do you mean?'

'I happen to know there are three American Army Comanche latest model prototypes, sitting in Stuttgart. It was in the Herald Tribune. The Germans are doing some tests before deciding if they'll buy.'

'I read that too. The ones with stealth technology.'

'Correct.' Another moment of silence, as Dulac sensed Harris's brain digesting the possibilities.

After a moment, Harris said, 'Very interesting. I'll see you in the morning in Lyon.' Dulac closed the phone, pensive. Something in the back of Dulac's mind, or perhaps the bottom of his gut, was telling him he would soon regret his suggestion.

Dulac returned Karen's inquisitive gaze and continued. 'That Comanche is one amazing helicopter. It's got a range of 2000 kilometers, and a top speed of 450 kilometers an hour; that's more than twice the speed of a Huey. It's also practically invisible by radar.'

'For someone who hates flying, you seem to know a lot about it,' said Karen, sitting on the sofa, her arms crossed.

'It was in the Herald Tribune. The article caught my attention.'

Karen kicked off her shoes, rose, and walked to the bathroom. 'I think I'll take a shower.'

'Good idea.'

'Tell me, those Comanches, can't they get shot down by a, what do they call it, a SIM missile?'

'You mean a SAM, a surface-to-air missile.'

'Whatever.' Karen started to brush her hair in front of the mirror over the sink.

'Not if the missile can't see it.'

She stopped brushing and looked at Dulac. 'What do you mean?'

'The Comanche apparently has a 97% stealth rating.'

'All this phallic, anti-phallic weaponry. When will it end? It's beyond me how anyone can still want to invent this stuff.' Karen let her dress slip to the ground and unhooked her bra.

'It's called survival of the fittest,' said Dulac.

She removed her panties and stood naked before the mirror, cupping her taut breasts, and bending a knee slightly, one after the other. 'What do you think?' she said.

'Fabulous.'

She laughed, half-closed the bathroom door and stepped into the shower stall.

Dulac went to the minibar and poured himself a scotch. A short while later, Karen, wrapped in a light blue bathrobe joined him, sitting on the edge of the bed.

'So what's the plan?' Karen said, drying the ends of her hair with a towel.

'Harris will pull the usual strings. The Italians have the equivalent of a SWAT team. It's called SISMI. '*Servizio per le informazioni* . . . something or other. They're surely itching for something like this to redeem themselves.'

'Redeem?'

He put down his glass on the side table and took off his shoes. 'You're probably too young to have heard about the Milano fiasco with the Red Brigades.'

Karen shrugged.

'Gladio? Does that name mean anything to you?'

'Not one bit.'

'Point proven.'

Dulac picked up his glass, leaned back on the bed's headboard, and took a long sip of his scotch, as the dreaded though of seeing Harris the following morning took a firmer hold of his consciousness.

Suluq, Libya, 4.30 p.m.

De Ségur's patience was fighting his eagerness to receive news of the Vatican's payment. He tried to remain calm, knowing that transferring money covertly, untraceably, was an art as delicate as that of diamond cutting: one slip-up and all that work and meticulous planning would be ruined. He reasoned with himself that the only thing he could do for the moment was wait. He'd been informed that if one required an expert in the clandestine world of anonymous bearer shares corporations, their complex layering and quick dissolution, Notario Alfredo Lucino was the man to call in Costa Rica. His fee was steep: three per cent of the funds transferred, automatically deducted upon corporate shutdown.

At 4.45 p.m., de Ségur's satellite phone rang. 'It went like Swiss clockwork,' said Lucino.

'All $600 million?' said de Ségur, as he peered outside at the simmering waves of desert heat off the dunes.

'$600 million. The money has already been wired out of Costa Rica to the intermediary accounts in Belize. I'm shutting down the Costa Rica accounts. The corporations will be liquidated within the hour.'

'Good doing business with you, Lucino.'

'Anytime, Mr. de Ségur. Anytime.'

De Ségur hung up and phoned his agent in Belize.

'Santos.'

'De Ségur. Do you have it?'

'It's already distributed.'

'Excellent.' Santos had just confirmed that de Ségur's numbered accounts in the Fortes Bank of Luxembourg, Pictet Bank of Switzerland, Banque Pasche of Monaco, Bank Frick and Co. AG of Lichtenstein respectively, had increased in total value by $600 million American dollars. It is earning tax-free interest as we speak, thought de Ségur.

'No possibility of a trace?'

'Impossible. The intermediary accounts in Belize, as far as anybody is concerned, never existed. Anyway the source of that money is presumed bona fide and legal.'

'Good work, Santos. One more thing. At 10.30 p.m. tomorrow evening Rome time, I want you to contact Cardinal Legnano's office through the Vatican secretariat. Ask to speak to him personally on my behalf and leave the following message. "Deal closed. Pick up package Suluq, Lat. 31 degrees 40' N, Long. 20 degrees 15' E." But not before tomorrow evening. Understood?'

'Yes sir.'

De Ségur hung up.

'We have it!' said a smiling de Ségur to the Cathars. 'Now it's our turn to deliver.' He turned to one of the Berbers and spoke in Arabic. 'Our guest is well?'

'Yes sir,' replied the swarthy-complexioned man in a dark-blue tunic.

'Good', said de Ségur. Turning to the others, he added, 'We'll take the vans. I've made arrangements for a jet to meet us outside Cairo, at the old military airstrip at Siwa. From there we fly to Belize. Everybody get some rest. Tomorrow will be a tiring day. We leave at 5.15 a.m., sunrise.'

'Mr de Ségur, why can't we leave now?' said one of the Cathars.

'We can't see the dunes. They're like quick-sand. We can't risk getting caught in them.'

Suluq 4.55 a.m., May 28

'We'll travel in tandem,' de Ségur said to one of the drivers. 'Did you find some extra tuareg clothing?'

'Yes, sir.'

'Good. We may need the cover. We'll stop and refuel at Al Jaghbub, near the Egyptian border.'

De Ségur returned inside the house, where the Cathars were busy making last minute preparations for departure, and entered a small dusty room in the back. The man, dressed in a white jellaba, sat passively waiting.

'It is time to bid you adieu, your Holiness,' said de Ségur, bowing slightly.

'So it is.'

'The Berbers will take care of you until your rescuers arrive.'

'I will pray for your soul.'

De Ségur emitted a small guffaw. 'Don't waste your time.' De Ségur turned, and walked outside towards the vans.

Lyon, Interpol offices, 11.05 a.m., 28 May

Dulac made his way down the wide corridor towards Harris's windowed office on the seventh floor of Interpol's headquarters in Lyon, stopping before the office's open doorway. The morning sun, unhampered by the open blinds, was blazing through the full-length windows. Sitting at his desk, wearing a pink shirt and blue bow tie, Harris was engrossed in some voluminous report. Working on Sunday was not unusual for Harris, a man without hobbies — except alcohol. Enveloped by the disc's orange hot rays, Lucifer-like, he seemed oblivious to the heat.

Shielding his eyes, Dulac entered the stifling room and reluctantly shook the general secretary's proffered hand. Close up, Dulac noticed its owner already exuded an odor of gin.

'Well good afternoon. Glad you could drop by,' said Harris.

'The flight was delayed,' said Dulac, unruffled.

'Have a seat,' said Harris, offering Dulac one of the leather chairs as he returned to behind his desk. 'Sun bother you?'

'Yes.'

Harris lowered the venetian blind and sat down. 'You're one lucky sonofabitch, Dulac.'

Dulac disliked the tone of the qualification. 'Oh? Why is that?'

'I've been busy all night and this morning brokering a deal between the Vatican, the Italian Minister of Defense and the US Department of Defense. We muscled the Germans into lending us one of the Comanches.' Harris reclined in his swivel chair and continued. 'A certain commander Klein will go to Paris to pick up Lescop, then on to Rome tonight to refuel and pick you up before going on to Benghazi. They're clearing the flight plan as we speak. He should—'

'Did you say pick me up?'

'Yes, you're going to get the Pope out of Libya. You—'

'You've got to be kidding.'

'Absolutely not. I've discussed this whole matter, and all the options with Legnano and the Italian prime minister. By the way, the $5 million dollars were deposited in Gazzar's Swiss account last night and the clock is ticking. They want to get His Holiness out quickly and discreetly. The usual diplomatic options are out, because everybody's afraid of the possible debacle and Kargali's unpredictability, so they've decided to go in sub rosa, low key, under Kargali's nose. With Gazzar's ultimatum, the only chance we have is going in tonight under the cover of darkness. Besides, the faster we do this, the better chance we have of avoiding a leak. Lescop will back you up.' Harris's voice had that dangerous ring of finality coming from a man who can shift the blame on someone else if things go wrong.

'This is crazy. This—'

'You're going to Benghazi, Dulac. It was your idea in the first place. It's your ballgame. Besides, I cannot think of a better man: your knowledge of Arabic could come in handy on the ground.' Harris swiveled his chair towards the computer and eyed the screen. 'Quite amazing, this Comanche helicopter. It will arrive at 10 p.m. tonight at the Guidonia Air Base. Plenty of time for you to get to Rome.'

Dulac got up, put both fists onto the desk and leaned forward into Harris's face. 'You are sending me, with only Lescop, to get the Pope out of Libya?' he shouted. 'Have you all gone completely fucking mad? This is a job for SISMI, or the US SWATS, not a couple of overweight, middle-aged Interpol agents.'

Harris leaned back in the swivel chair and, his hands in the form of an arch, tapped his fingers together. 'Out of the question. The Italian prime minister can't take the chance they'll screw up again. Also this operation has to appear politically neutral.'

Dulac stood back for a moment, then started pacing back and forth in front of Harris's desk. 'This is absolutely insane, Harris. There is not one shred of evidence that de Ségur will keep his word. I—'

'In that case, we'll have wasted a night flying you and Lescop in and out of Libya and a bit of the Italian's taxpayer's money. They are footing the bill, by the way. End of story.'

'You are completely, utterly mad.'

'Think of it as a diplomatic mission.'

Dulac stopped and glared at Harris. 'I'm no damn diplomat.'

'The Italians believe Interpol best represents the interests of its members, including Italy. You may not know this, Dulac, but they're a big contributor to our budget. It also diffuses the responsibility if things go belly up and—'

'Your confidence in this upcoming fiasco is underwhelming me.'

'I don't have time to argue. We have less than eighteen hours left to get His Holiness out of Libya. You're going to Benghazi, Dulac. Tonight. We both know there's no other option.'

Dulac sat back down, feeling the inevitable hand of destiny squashing his shoulders into his chest. For a moment, both men stared at each other in silence.

'Jesus,' exclaimed Dulac finally.

'I'll take that as a "yes". The Italians will provide air support until the helicopter reaches Libyan air space. After that, you're on your own. By the way, if you get caught, we'll disavow the whole operation, of course.'

'Of course. Just pissing great.'

Harris reached in the desk drawer, took out his pipe, lit it, then reclined in his seat. 'Fine. That's settled. Now for the other item on the agenda. Why don't you give me a rundown of your meetings with the cardinals?'

'Why not? Nothing better to do until I fly into oblivion.'

Dulac wondered why Harris hadn't already broken into his usual demonstration of learned culture. He didn't have long to wait.

'Quid?' said Harris.

Dulac winced at Harris's employment of his high-school Latin. He knew there'd be more to come.

'Et in illo tempore, omnia exeunt,' he replied, knowing Harris would be lost. He paused, while Harris, embarrassed, waited for the translation. Dulac said, 'it means "and then, everybody left". I get the feeling everybody is scrambling for cover, including some cardinals.'

'Explain.'

'I'm convinced de Ségur has high placed allies within the Vatican,' said Dulac. 'Interesting theory.' Harris took a puff from his pipe. 'Give me some meat to nibble on, some dramatis personae.'

'I've found out that Cardinals Brentano and Sforza reviewed Romer's application. They are ultimately responsible for all hiring within the Vatican, which includes Romer and, indirectly, Aguar.'

Harris leaned forward, took the pipe from his mouth, and rattled his left fingers nervously on the tabletop. 'That, Dulac, is a pretty wild suggestion. Even for you.'

'I have more. Romer was definitely in on the kidnapping. That's why he had to dispose of—'

'Woah, hold on a minute,' said Harris, raising his pipe-carrying hand in protest. 'Tell me,' — he pointed the small end of the pipe at Dulac — 'why on earth would Brentano and Sforza have Pope Clement XXI kidnapped?'

'Ambition, for starters.'

'Unproven. Dulac, you're the lawyer, give me some facts.'

'I'm trying to get a meeting with Legnano. My instinct tells me he knows more about the Pope than he's letting on. Question is, will he talk?'

'Dulac, why must you always complicate matters? It's a clear cut case of extortion and ransom. Give us the money and we'll give you back your Pope. End of story.'

Dulac felt for a moment he should tell Harris about the diary. No, that can wait. Besides, I promised Legnano I'd keep it confidential.

'More like Plato's Myth of the Cave,' said Dulac. 'I don't follow.'

'We see only the shadow of the story, mistaking it for reality.'

'Meaning?'

'We have de Ségur, a known Cathar, member of Chimera. We have Romer, a Cathar, who conveniently becomes head of the Swiss Guards. Brentano recommended him. Sforza was responsible for his acceptance as a Swiss Guard and didn't identify his Cathar roots.'

'An oversight.'

'Aguar's credentials and history were known to most police forces across the world.'

'Except Romer? Interpol has a file a mile long on Aguar. Why didn't Romer check with us? It was his job to check before the Vatican hired him. Convenient Aguar slipped through, isn't it?' Dulac smiled at Harris.

'Still but a handful of coincidences. So far, you haven't given me anything that supports any other motive than ransom.'

'If ransom is their motive, why kill Romer? With Aguar dead, Romer wasn't about to get caught.'

'If the cardinals were in on the ransom, what possible gain could they have? It's not as if they could spend it,' said Harris.

'Which supports an ulterior motive.'

'Or their non-involvement.'

Dulac leaned back in his chair, clasped his hands and stretched both arms above and behind his head, 'Go to the head of the class. It's called working both ends of the paradox towards the middle.'

'I don't need your sarcasm, Dulac, I need answers. By the way, since when are you qualified to give advice to the members of Curia on demands of the kidnappers?'

'Since they asked me.'

'Must I remind you that we are, and must be seen as non-political?'

That's it, you gutless wonder. Hide behind your text-book bullshit. 'In the heat of battle, it's not always that easy. The lines get blurred. Anyway, it was their decision. What's the problem?' Dulac said, losing patience.

'The problem, Dulac, is your attitude. You don't seem to give a damn about the rules. Just the other day I received a complaint from one of the members of the Curia. You're interfering—'

'Who could that possibly be?'

'You're missing the point. Who, is not important, it's—'

Dulac felt his fuse about to blow. He leaned forward, putting both hands on the edge of Harris's desk. 'Fine. Pull me off. How about right now? That way I don't get myself killed going to Libya.'

'Don't get your feathers ruffled. I didn't mean—'

'Cut the crap, Harris. We both know you can't pull me off. I'm in this mess too bloody deeply already and you don't have a replacement. Otherwise you would have yanked me eons ago. Plus, the media will be down your throat in a second, asking why.'

Harris pointed his pipe at Dulac again. 'Someday, Dulac, you'll go too far.'

'Right. Until then, I apparently have a Pope to rescue, with or without Brentano's approval.'

'How did you know it was—'

'I didn't. Thanks for confirming it.'

CHAPTER 22

Suluq, 5.15 a.m.

'At 50 km-an-hour average,' said de Ségur, pointing the map to his driver Antoine, 'it will take us six hours to get to Al Jaghbub and two more to get to the Egyptian border. Then we go east. Plenty of time to rendezvous with the jet at 1800 hours.'

Four hours later, as the two van convoy continued to make its way into the undulating vastness of the Great Sand Sea desert, the red disc had risen well above the dunes and was pounding them with increasing intensity. Inside the vans, passengers tried to fan themselves with whatever came to hand. Everyone knew that soon the sun's full power would overwhelm the vans' puny air-conditioners and the heat would become brutal.

By 11 a.m., the water bottles had become disgustingly warm and the thermometer read 41°C. By 2 p.m., the temperature had reached 43°C. De Ségur, sweltering in the oven-on-wheels, looked at the motor's coolant gauge, its needle heavily into the red zone.

'We'll never make it,' said Antoine, conscious of de Ségur's worried gaze. 'The motor is too bloody hot.'

'You'd better make sure we do. It's a long walk for you to Al Jaghbub.' De Ségur picked up his satellite phone and called the driver of the white van ahead.

'We have an overheating motor. What's your status?'

'We're OK.'

'Then stop your van,' de Ségur ordered.

The van ahead stopped and de Ségur ordered Antoine to pull up beside it. 'Get the tuareg clothes,' de Ségur said to Antoine.

Reluctantly, Antoine gathered the clothing on the back seat behind him while de Ségur opened the door and stepped out.

'Come with me,' de Ségur said, pointing to the men in the rear seat of the overheating van.

Leaving Antoine and the remaining passengers in the van, de Ségur and the men walked over and entered the white van. De Ségur sat in front, while the others joined the passengers in the back.

'That way, you'll be lighter,' shouted de Ségur to Antoine through the window. 'It'll help cool your motor.' Turning to his new driver Jean Gaspard, he added, 'Let's go, we've wasted enough time already.'

'Yes sir.'

The convoy started again under the flames of the killer sun. De Ségur mopped his eyes and brow with his already sweat-soaked kerchief, then picked up his bottle and took a swig of piss-hot Evian water. Suddenly, his hand started to shake violently and he dropped the bottle, spilling the contents onto his pants. 'Damn,' said de Ségur. He slowly picked up the bottle from the van's floor, his hand still shaking slightly.

'Are you all right?' said Gaspard.

'I'm fine. Just tired.'

Gaspard threw a glance at his rearview mirror. 'We're losing them,' he said.

De Ségur turned and saw the van slowing, then caught Gaspard's inquiring look. 'We can't wait. Keep going.'

Gaspard pressed on while de Ségur watched the other van gradually disappear into the haze.

De Ségur's satellite phone rang. 'What's going on?' said Antoine, panic in his voice.

'You're holding us up. If we wait for you, both of us won't make the jet. Not much sense in that, is there? If you don't get to Al Jaghbub by 4 p.m., head south. Go to the border at Noma. There's less chance they'll stop you there.'

'But we won't—'

De Ségur turned off his phone.

The sun had started its descent towards the desert's haze-covered dunes when the irregular outline of Al Jaghbub's few palm trees appeared on the horizon. De Ségur looked at his watch again: 5.25 p.m. It's going to be tight.

As they entered the town, Gaspard looked at the fuel gage. 'We'll have to refuel.'

A few moments later, they spotted a half dozen Berbers, sitting beside their 45 gallon gasoline drums. One of them rose, signaling to the van, a wide grin on his face.

'Must be his turn,' said Gaspard. Rolling down his window, he spoke in Arabic: 'How much for 50 liters?'

The scraggly-bearded man came closer, then peeked suspiciously inside the van. 'Hundred liters minimum,' he said.

'How much?' asked Gaspard.

'900 dinars.'

'What? That's—'

'Pay him,' said de Ségur.

A toothless grin formed from the corners of the old Berber's mouth.

'Absolute robbery.' said Gaspard, reaching in his pocket and counting out the 900 dinars.

The Berber took the money, went to the rear of the van, and slowly started to fill the white Isuzu's gas tank with his small rotating hand pump.

De Ségur looked at his watch. 'Get out and help him.' De Ségur's satellite phone rang. He recognized Antoine's edgy voice.

'We're stalled. Our motor just quit. I think it's seized.'

'What is your position?'

'We're about 25 km south of Al Jaghbub.'

'How far to the Egyptian border?'

'About 15 km due east.'

'How much water do you have?'

'About twenty liters.'

De Ségur took a detailed map from a side pocket of the van and unfolded it. 'Head north-east. You'll come to a dirt road leading to Siwa. You're bound to come across a caravan.'

'And then?'

'Once you reach Siwa, there's public transportation to Mersa Matruh, then to Cairo.'

'We're filled up and ready to go,' interrupted Gaspard.

'Good luck.' De Ségur shut off his phone and signaled Gaspard to drive on. The white Isuzu rumbled to life and they exited Al Jaghbub, past the decaying remnants of the Senussi fortress and into the Great Sand Sea desert again. The temperature read 39°C on the van's outside thermometer. De Ségur mopped his brow with his wet kerchief. He turned to Gaspard and said, 'We must get to Siwa before dark.'

'Can't the pilot wait till tomorrow morning?' Gaspard said.

'That plane makes a fat target for US reconnaissance satellites.' De Ségur looked at his watch. 'We must leave tonight.'

'Not a problem,' said Gaspard. 'How are the others in the—'

'They'll be ok.'

Suddenly, the front of the van started to shake and de Ségur shot an anxious glance at Gaspard.

'We've got a flat,' said Gaspard. 'The left front tire has gone.' Gaspard brought the van slowly to a stop.

'Jesus Christ. That's all we need. How far to Siwa?'

'About 90 km.'

De Ségur looked at his watch, then turned to Gaspard. 'What are you waiting for? Get out and fix it.'

Gaspard started out of the van and de Ségur ordered the others to do the same.

After a moment, Gaspard returned from the back of the van looking sheepish. 'Ah . . . we . . . there's no spare.'

De Ségur felt the blood rush to his temples. 'No spare? You mean you didn't check before leaving? This is the god-damn desert, not the Champs-Élysées.' De Ségur grabbed the satellite phone from his pocket and phoned the jet's pilot. 'De Ségur. We're stranded about 90 km from you. We've got a flat.'

'We can't take off after dark. The runway is full of pot-holes and—'

'I know, I know.'

'—and they're hard to see already.'

'We'll make it. Wait for us.'

De Ségur closed the phone and turned towards Gaspard. 'Let's go.'

Gaspard, perplexed, looked at de Ségur. 'But we risk destroying the bearing. The wheel will seize up.'

'What do you suggest? That we sit here and wait for the next Egyptian border patrol to pick us up?'

'We can transfer the flat to the rear and put the good tire on the front. At least we'll have steerage.'

'Then do it.'

'Yes sir.'

As the van started again, the disc started falling into the horizon, fading away in Gaspard's rearview mirror, blinding him. He flipped it into polarized position. 'It'll help if we all sit to the left and keep the weight off the right bare wheel,' said Gaspard.

'Everybody to the left side,' ordered de Ségur. The van tilted slightly.

'At least the motor is getting cooler,' said Gaspard.

They hadn't driven for more than half an hour when suddenly, they heard a loud explosion. 'Christ, not again?' exclaimed de Ségur.

Gaspard nodded silently as he struggled with the steering wheel.

'Two, two bloody flat tires. Unbelievable,' screamed de Ségur, throwing his hands up in frustration. 'Keep going,' he yelled. 'Get this goddamn piece of shit to that plane, understand?'

'Yes sir. I'll try.' Gaspard grabbed the severely shaking steering wheel and pressed on the gas, as the flop-flop-flop of the rapidly deteriorating tire accompanied the hissing sound of the rear wheel's bare rim on the hot sand. Soon, the smoke and smell of burnt rubber invaded the van's interior, surrounding its occupants with nauseous, toxic fumes.

De Ségur rolled down his window and turned towards Gaspard. 'If you value your good health, you'd better make that damn jet.'

The pilot noticed the windsock near the runway changing direction. 'We'll have to take off from the other end,' he said to the co-pilot.

The Bombardier's two Rolls-Royce engines burst into life and the jet started to taxi down the runway.

'Getting pretty dark,' said the co-pilot.

'Just remember any holes you see,' said the pilot as he hit the pedal hard and the jet swerved right, barely missing a large crater.

'Jesus!' said the co-pilot as he looked outside over the pilot's shoulder. 'That would have taken out the whole goddamn landing gear.'

They reached the end of the runway and the pilot pressed full left brake. The Bombardier swung obediently around until its nose pointed down the end of the runway into the darkening dusk. The pilot looked at his Rolex again.

'Call de Ségur on the sat phone,' he said to the co-pilot.

The co-pilot took the Globalstar from its leather holder and dialed de Ségur's number. 'I can't get a signal.' He tried again, to no avail.

'What? How can that be? De Ségur just called us.'

'Don't know. He can probably call us but we can't call him. Don't ask me why.'

'Shit.' The pilot nervously tapped his fingers on one of the throttle levers. 'Five more minutes, then we're outta here.'

As the seconds ticked away, the pilot looked anxiously ahead into the darkening dusk. He glanced at his watch. 'That's it. We can't wait. Get ready for takeoff.'

The co-pilot picked up the clipboard and went through the takeoff checklist. A moment later he said, 'Ready for takeoff.'

The pilot moved the twin throttles all the way forward and the turbines intoned their high-pitched wail. The jet accelerated, shaking slightly as it gathered speed. Halfway down the runway, the pilot bore right to avoid a crater, then straightened his course, hugging the left side.

Suddenly the co-pilot yelled: 'Christ! What the hell—?'

Dead ahead, two lights had swung onto the middle of runway and were bearing down on them on a collision course. The pilot yanked back the throttles and jammed on full brakes. The jet shuddered violently as it veered left, then right, the pilot trying desperately to keep it on the runway. At the last possible instant, the lights swung right, barely missing the plane's left wingtip. As the lights swept past, the pilot caught a glimpse of sparks flying from the rear of a white van. 'Crazy fucking bastards.'

The jet slowly came to a halt, and the pilot's satellite phone rang. 'You weren't really thinking of leaving without us,' said de Ségur.

CHAPTER 23

Guidonia Air Base, 10.25 p.m.

The black, angular shaped, carbon-fiber clad Comanche RAH 66 B surged into view, hovered before Dulac's still unbelieving eyes, and lowered itself quickly onto the tarmac. At least it's not an F-16, he thought. The pilot alighted and walked towards the Guidonia's Air Force base main administrative building. Dulac rose dejectedly from the worn leather seat and walked out to meet him.

'I'm Dulac.'

'*Guten tag*, my name is Gerhard Klein,' said the pilot, offering an immense right hand. 'Sorry to be late.'

Dulac suppressed a smile. The man was well over six feet tall. He was anything but klein. 'Not late enough,' said Dulac.

Klein gave him a quizzical look.

They regained the chopper, and Dulac caught sight of Lescop, dressed in his worn beige gabardine jacket, seated in one of the back seats. Lescop barely acknowledged him.

'You're blaming me for this?' said Dulac as he grabbed the hand hold and boarded the chopper.

'Of course not,' said Lescop, unconvincingly.

'Why can't I stop thinking that your brilliant rescue in the Briand case has something to do with you being here?'

'Flattery I don't need,' said Lescop, a scowl on his unshaven face.

As Dulac settled into the front beside Klein and fastened his safety harness, Lescop poked his bald head between them. 'Is it too late to request a transfer?'

Dulac turned to respond. 'And miss all the fun? Request denied.'

The twin LHTEC T802 motors wailed in protest, the helicopter lifted from the tarmac and, nose down, accelerated into the pale remnants of the evening dusk. Moments later, the dense brightness of Rome's lights disappeared, giving way to the occasional white dots in the Campania countryside. Suddenly two balls of fire burst on either side of the Comanche, streaked headlong in front of the chopper and disappeared into the night.

'What the hell was that?' Dulac asked Klein.

'Our Italian escorts,' replied Klein. 'They kick in the afterburners to show how much faster they are. That just cost the Italian taxpayers about 10,000 Euros.'

'Where are they headed?'

'Probably Tripoli. They'll play games with the Libyan MIG 23s to distract them.'

Dulac could feel his right palm start to sweat over the arm rest. 'How much longer?'

Klein looked at the GPS. 'About two and a half hours. There's 721 km left to Benghazi.' Dulac tried to relax into the uncomfortable seat. Soon, he was being lulled into a dull semi-consciousness by the rhythmic whump, whump of the blades, as random thoughts drifted erratically through his mind. Had de Ségur kept his bargain? Or was the Pope dead? If he was alive, would Gazzar keep his word and not interfere? Had Kargali found out and secured the perimeter? Were they flying into a Libyan trap? The odds were anything but good. More likely would be his nanosecond perception of the explosion when one of the Libyan MIG's missiles would blast him and the intruding helicopter into eternity. I won't feel a damn thing. He nodded off, his head dropping onto his chest.

A soft beeping sound jarred Dulac from his sleep. He looked up, to see the Comanche's GPS blinking in red over the yellow screen map, indicating 'waypoint arrival'.

'We're over our target,' said Klein.

'I don't see anything,' said Dulac, looking out the right window.

'Below, and to the left,' said Klein, pointing downwards from his side window.

Dulac leaned over toward Klein and saw two pinpoints of light barely visible in the sea of darkness. 'That's it?' Dulac said.

'Must be. There's nothing else around.' Dulac felt the hairs of his arms stand erect.

'We're going in. Behind that dune,' said Klein, as he angled the joystick downwards and to the left. The Comanche quickly lost altitude and moments later, settled slowly onto the desert dust. 'You'll have to be quick,' said Klein as Dulac fumbled with the 'copter's door latch. 'We are at the limit of the fuel range and I have to keep it idling.'

'Understood,' said Dulac. Then turning towards the back to Lescop. 'Ready?'

'Ready.'

They stepped out of the helicopter and, feet sinking in the soft sand, climbed their way to the top of the dune. Breathing heavily, Dulac crouched on the still hot sand and signaled Lescop to do the same. A few hundred yards away, they could make out a small, flat roofed one-story house, a soft yellow light coming from its two small windows. Dulac unlatched the safety of his .38 Benelli short-nosed B80S Parabellum pistol, and they guardedly made their way towards the low, earth-brick building. As they neared, the remnants of de Ségur's Alouette helicopter came into view.

'Won't go far with that.' Dulac said, pointing his Benelli at the helicopter. He turned and whispered to Lescop. 'Go to the rear and try and see inside. I'll take a peek through the front. Come back and we'll assess.'

Lescop made a wide arc and disappeared behind the house. Crouching low, Dulac approached the front. Suddenly, he sensed danger, behind him. He half-turned, only to see the dark, turbaned shadow a split second before he felt the blow to his left temple. For a millisecond, all of the stars of the Libyan Desert danced crazily before his eyes, then nothing.

When he awoke, the only thing Dulac could feel was the angry jackhammer pounding relentlessly inside his skull. He was lying down. He opened his eyes. Two rows of gold and yellow teeth were grinning down at him. He tried to get up and a sharp pain shot through his head. 'What . . . ? Where the hell am—?'

'Salaam alaikum. You OK?' said the woman dressed in a dark-blue jellaba.

'Alaikum salaam, I guess so.' Dulac looked at the Berber woman and cautiously felt the large lump on his left temple.

'So sorry. We think you Senussi bandits,' said the woman, looking skeptically at Dulac's lump.

'Where is—'

'Right here,' said Lescop, standing behind Dulac. 'Are you all right?'

'Better than you. And de Ségur?'

'According to her, they left this morning in a couple of trucks,' said Lescop.

'Undoubtedly with the Pope. Damn. And we trusted the bastard,' Dulac said, feeling his lump again carefully.

'Not so,' said Lescop. 'His Holiness is—'

Suddenly, Dulac became aware of the presence of someone in the doorway of the adjoining room. The man, dressed in a white jellaba, his head bandaged, his hands outstretched, started walking towards him.

'Your Holiness!' said Dulac.

'Mr Lescop here has given me the details. Thank God you've come,' he said as he clasped Dulac's hands, then Lescop's. 'Thank God you're here.'

Dulac felt a surge of relief. 'Your Holiness, are you all right?'

'Yes, yes, I'm fine.'

'We've come to take you back, your Holiness. Where is Dr Bruscetti?'

'I haven't seen my dear friend since Sicily. We were taken aboard a boat. Later in the night I remember being caught in a storm. It was terrible, terrible. People were in the water, screaming for help. Many drowned. May God have mercy on their souls. I don't know how I survived. I—'

'We must leave now, your Holiness.' interrupted Dulac. 'We don't have much time. I'll explain later.'

'Yes, yes, of course. I'm ready.' He joined his hands in prayer and bent towards the forever smiling Berber woman. 'Salaam alaikum. God bless you.' Hands still joined, he eyed the other Berber in the room and said, 'Salaam alaikum.'

Led by Lescop, they made their way out of the small house.

As Dulac stepped into the cool of the moonlit night, the slight, sweet smell of Artemisia plants tickled his nostrils briefly. They headed towards the helicopter, its angular shape contrasting with the roundness of the dunes around it.

'Your Holiness, you have to turn sideways to get into the seat of these helicopters,' said Dulac as they reached the door of the chopper.

'Yes, I know.'

'Of course,' said Dulac, feeling embarrassed. 'I forgot. You pilot the papal helicopter.'

'Sometimes. When it's not busy kidnapping me.'

Dulac closed the door and secured the latch. Klein punched the throttle forward, and the Comanche lifted abruptly in a swirl of desert sand. Soon, the lights of the small house disappeared.

Klein turned briefly towards the rear and said, 'Make yourself comfortable, your Holiness. Our trip will last about two and a half hours.'

Fifteen minutes later, Klein drew Dulac's attention to the radar screen. 'We have company.'

'Great,' said Dulac. 'Are they—'

'Libyans. We're still in their airspace. Damn, they're coming in.'

'Jesus, so much for Gazzar's promise.'

Suddenly there was a crackle on the Comanche's VHF radio and some incomprehensible command came through.

'What did he say?' Dulac asked Klein.

Klein grabbed the microphone. 'I didn't copy that. Please repeat, over.'

' . . .Tripoli. You must land Tripoli now,' said the nervous, high-pitched voice. Dulac looked quizzically at Klein.

'Doesn't make sense,' said Klein. 'We're only a few minutes away from leaving their airspace.' He pressed the VHF button again and spoke into the microphone. 'We are leaving Libyan airspace now. Please confirm.'

'Alter course immediately to Tripoli or we shoot,' said the high-strung voice.

'Jesus,' said Dulac, 'they mean business.'

'Bloody Libyans. I know their game,' said Klein. 'They did it last year with a Sudanese reconnaissance plane that had veered off course. They lured him into getting closer to Tripoli then shot him down, claiming he was attacking the Libyan people's capital. Those guys never had a chance.'

'Great. Just pissing great. What do we do?' said Dulac.

'We're close to Benghazi. We'll make a run for it and hope our infrared antimissile system works,' said Klein, as he turned to the rear. 'Everyone get strapped in tight.' Klein steered hard right and the Comanche banked into a 120 degree turn.

'Merde,' said Dulac as his stomach lurched into his throat. Seconds later, he could see a city's lights as Klein punched the stick forward and forced the Comanche into a steep dive. There was a loud pinging sound accompanied by a red flashing light overhead and Dulac's piano-wire nerves wound even tighter. 'Jesus.'

The city's lights were coming up fast when Dulac felt the Comanche shudder. 'They're strafing us,' said Klein.

A Libyan MIG 23 Flogger whooshed past and banked steeply.

'At least they won't fire missiles this close to Benghazi,' said Klein.

'Great,' said Dulac.

Klein glanced at the radar. 'The second one's coming in for the kill,' yelled Klein, as he pulled up steeply and banked 90° to the left. The Comanche shuddered again as 23 mm armor-piercing bullets slammed into the chopper's fuselage, bits of carbon fiber flying about and dust filling the cockpit. Dulac cringed and grabbed the armrests.

'*Sheisse*,' exclaimed Klein.

'What?' said Dulac.

'Nothing.'

Klein took off his helmet and wiped the side of his face with his hand. Dulac saw the damaged helmet. Blood dripped from just above Klein's right eye.

'Holy Christ, you're hit!'

'Just a scratch. I . . . I . . .'

Klein's head fell forward and the chopper started to dive.

'Merde,' exclaimed Dulac. The chopper dove steeper, setting off the alarms again. Dulac shook Klein hard. 'Wake up! Wake up!'

Klein came to, raised his head slowly. Gradually, he pulled back on the stick and steadied the chopper. 'Get the medical kit. It's behind you, to the right,' said Klein.

Dulac unfastened his seat-harness, turned and reached back for the medical kit inside the small compartment. He caught a glimpse of the rear passengers. Both men sat upright, frozen in their seats, speechless. 'Are you OK, your Holiness?'

'I'm all right,' he said, his voice barely audible.

'And you?' said Dulac, eyeing Lescop.

'So far.'

'Get me some gauze and tape,' said Klein.

Dulac faced forward, opened the medical kit, took out a swath of gauze, and tore a piece of tape. He pressed them to Klein's forehead.

'Thanks. If I pass out, throw the autopilot on here,' said Klein, pointing at a toggle on the control panel. 'Then set the heading at 77 degrees,' he said, indicating the knob below the computerized compass.

'Got it,' Dulac replied.

Klein pressed the tape on either side of the wound. 'That should hold me till the next round,' said Klein.

'What do you mean?'

'These bastards aren't through with us yet.' Klein leaned forward and threw a toggle on the control panel.

'Alpha India, Alpha India, this is Unicorn Delta Unicorn, do you copy?' said Klein, his voice calm.

'Who are you calling?' asked Dulac.

'The Italian Air Force. We've got to get these sons of whores off our back.'

'Can't we fire back at them?' asked Dulac.

'With what? Your Benelli?'

'I thought I read this thing has air-to-air missiles and a 20 mm Gatling gun?'

'They took it all off to increase the chopper's range and make it completely undetectable,' said Klein.

'Great. Tell that to the MIG pilots.'

Suddenly, Dulac saw a red light flash on the cockpit display panel indicating 'IML', accompanied by a loud intermittent beeping sound.

'*Sheisse*!' said Klein.

'Does IML stand for what I think it does?' asked Dulac, his voice panicked.

Klein pushed the joystick hard right. 'Those fockers want us dead.'

The Comanche lurched and veered into a banking turn. Dulac, compressed into his seat, winced, expecting the impact of the explosion.

Klein veered hard left. 'Missed, you bastards.'

The red light went out. A few seconds later, it started its ominous flashing again. 'Incoming Missile Lock,' said Klein.

Klein shoved the stick forward and the Comanche dove towards the lights of Benghazi again.

'Jesus, we're going to—' said Dulac, as he saw the top half of a tall building rushing up to meet the Comanche.

Klein banked, and pulled up violently at the last second. The missile swooped past and slammed into the building in a great ball of orange fire.

'Christ, how long can we keep this up?'

'Not long. The only reason we're still alive is the Comanche's infrared suppression system is keeping their heat-seeking missiles from maintaining a lock on us. They're bound to get lucky.'

'Great. Just pissing great.'

Klein looked at his radar, and suddenly the MIGs angled to the right, and headed south. 'They're going. They're breaking off!' Klein's voice was a mixture of astonishment and relief.

'Really?' said Dulac.

'We'll know for sure in a minute.'

Dulac saw the blips on the 'copter's radar head towards the edge of the screen and disappear. Klein took the 'copter up, away from the lights of Benghazi and headed north-east, for the safety of the Mediterranean and its international airspace.

'I love this helicopter,' said Klein.

Ten minutes passed in silence before Dulac, not yet fully convinced they had escaped, asked Klein, 'We were sitting ducks. Why did they break off?'

'No idea. They had every reason to take us down. We're a military helicopter violating their airspace.'

Dulac could only conclude that someone high up had ordered the MIGs to retreat. Was it Gazzar, or Kargali himself?

The Comanche was now host to a high-pitched whistling sound, made by the draft of forced air through the bullet holes in the chopper's tail. Dulac looked back, 'Your Holiness, are you all right?' Dulac said.

'Yes. I, I think so.'

'Lescop?'

'I'm OK.'

Dulac turned towards Klein. 'Will this thing make it?'

'I've seen worse.'

'How far to the Italian Coast?'

'About another hour.'

'Are we within cell range?'

'Maybe.'

Dulac grabbed his encrypted cell from his vest pocket and dialed Legnano's number. He recognized the assistant secretary's voice. 'Dulac. Put me through to His Eminence. It's urgent.'

Moments later Legnano came on the line. 'Mr Dulac. It sounds as—'

'Yes your Eminence. We're still aboard the helicopter. We have His Holiness with us.'

'Mio Dio. This is great news, Mr Dulac. How is His Holiness?'

'Tired. We were . . . Ah, I'll explain later.'

'When will you arrive?'

'We should be in Rome in about an hour and a half.'

'This is great news, Mr Dulac, great news. I'll advise the Curia.'

An hour later Dulac was dozing, dreaming he was in the tranquil comfort of his Paris living room, when from the corner of his eye, he caught a glimpse of Klein, head tilted downwards. 'Hey,' Dulac said, grabbing Klein's arm.

Klein's head snapped back. 'Yes, yes. I'm fine. Just a bit drowsy.'

Dulac pointed to the GPS. 'Where are we now?'

Klein adjusted the scale of the GPS. 'About forty-five minutes to Rome.'

Dulac felt a wave of relief and leaned back in his seat. 'What happened to our Italian friends?' said Dulac.

Klein didn't answer. Suddenly, his head fell fully forward onto his chest, and the chopper started to bank left sharply.

'Jesus. Wake up! Wake up!' yelled Dulac. He shook him. No response. The chopper started to climb. Frantic, Dulac reached for the autopilot toggle, threw it on and turned the knob to 77 degrees on the computerized compass. The chopper leveled slowly and resumed its course.

'Whew,' said Dulac. He looked at Klein, whose face was green. Dulac turned around and looked at Lescop. 'Somebody will have to land this thing. Can you fly a helicopter?'

'Not me,' Lescop answered, shrugging his shoulders in ignorance.

'How about you, your Holiness? You fly the papal helicopter. This can't be much different.'

'No. I cannot. This, this is very different,' he said, palms upward in refusal.

'Can you at least try, your Holiness?' said Dulac.

'Really, I . . . I can't. I'm sorry.'

Dulac turned, faced front and looked into the darkness, feeling helpless and silently praying the autopilot controls of the chopper hadn't been damaged during the attack.

A moment later, Klein came to. 'Where are we?' he said.

'Thank God,' said Dulac. 'You passed out so I put it on autopilot.'

'Good work.' Klein flipped off the autopilot and looked at the GPS. A little red box on the screen was flashing waypoint arrival.

Given the too short amount of time to prepare for the safe and orderly welcoming of the Pope, the members of the Curia had decided to disclose the Pope's rescue and impending arrival to a limited number of Vatican-accredited members of the press.

Braving the chill of the night, a gaggle of reporters and TV crews waited patiently, under the supervision of the Guidonia airbase security forces. Finally, the Comanche's landing lights came into view, piercing the night with their two cone-shaped beams. A murmur ran through the assembled reporters: 'That must be it!' Moments later, the helicopter landed abruptly, and its rotor blades came slowly to a stop.

Behind the reporters, standing beside two papal limousines, Harris, Legnano and Sforza waited in silent expectation. A moment later, the helicopter's door opened. 'It's him. It's His Holiness,' one of the reporters shouted.

Dressed in white, his head bandaged, he waved, climbed carefully down the steps onto the tarmac and kneeled to kiss the ground.

Camera lights burst into a frenzy of flashes. He stood up and waved again. A cheer erupted from the reporters. '*Viva il Papa! Viva, viva il Papa!*'

Eight Swiss Guards suddenly appeared and immediately formed a corridor of protective phalanxes on either side. 'Let the Pope through,' said one of the guards to the onrushing reporters, as they ushered him to one of the limousines.

'Thank God, thank the Lord. Welcome back, your Holiness,' said Cardinal Legnano, standing beside the limousine, his arms open in welcome.

'Thank you, Cardinal. It's good to be back. The Lord is my shepherd and has shown me mercy.'

'How are you feeling, your Holiness?' said Legnano.

'Lucky to be alive. We were attacked by the Libyans.'

'What?' said Legnano.

'We'll deal with that later. Right now, I'm quite tired.'

'Of course, your Holiness. Doctor Mantegna is waiting in the limousine. He'll check your vital signs right away, then we will go to the—'

'No fuss, Legnano. I'll rest at the Papal apartments.'

'Your Holiness, I must insist that we go directly to the hospital. You've been under tremendous stress. And that head wound must be looked at right away.'

'All right, Legnano, all right.'

They entered the limousine and were quickly off, escorted by a gaggle of motorcycle policemen.

Followed by Lescop and Klein, Dulac was making his way through the scribes and TV reporters when he saw Harris wave them over to the other limousine.

'Where did you rescue the pontiff?' a reporter asked Dulac, accidentally jabbing Dulac's left temple with his microphone.

'For Christ's sake,' said Dulac, recoiling in pain. 'Let us through.'

'So where?' insisted the reporter.

'Wait for the Vatican's press conference. You'll get all the information then.'

Undeterred, the reporter shoved the microphone in Lescop's face. 'And you rescued His Holiness—?'

'No comment,' interrupted Lescop.

Klein had taken off his helmet, and the reporters saw his makeshift bandage.

'You've been wounded!' said one of the reporters, signaling to his cameraman to focus on Klein.

'It's nothing,' said the pilot.

'Where did it happen?' continued the reporter.

Klein didn't answer and kept on walking, as other reporters started to gather. 'What is the range of the helicopter?' said another reporter.

The pilot smiled. 'Far.'

'Russia?'

'Why not?'

Harris and Cardinal Sforza, now joined by Dulac, Lescop and Klein stood next to the limousine, surrounded by policemen and the Swiss Guards.

'Well done. Well done, gentlemen,' said Harris as he enthusiastically shook Klein's hand, then Lescop's.

Dulac felt the obvious slight. True to form, asshole.

As Sforza ushered everyone into the limo, Dulac sat next to the door, beside Sforza. After a quick embarrassed look towards Dulac, Sforza said, 'Gentlemen, on behalf of the Christian world, we thank you from the bottom of our hearts. We will not forget you have risked your lives to save His Holiness and bring him back safely.'

Seemingly unimpressed, Harris looked at Sforza, 'Actually, your Eminence, it was essentially a matter of good planning. I—'

'Your Eminence, we had better get Mr Klein to a hospital,' interrupted Dulac.

'I'm all right,' said Klein, sitting next to the chauffeur.

'No you're not,' said Dulac.

'What happened?' said Harris.

'It's a long story,' said Dulac, He turned and eyed Harris. 'Before I forget, according to the Berbers that were keeping the Pope, de Ségur and his goons left yesterday morning by van.'

'I'll bet he's in Benghazi,' said Harris. Dulac shrugged his shoulders.

Sforza leaned forward and spoke to the chauffeur, 'To the Agostino Gemelli Clinic, then to the Vatican.'

'Yes, your Eminence,' said the chauffeur.

Turning to the others, Sforza said, 'We'll meet Inspector Guadagni, Haeflinger and the rest of the Curia.'

'Who is Haeflinger?' said Dulac.

'Colonel Ernst Haeflinger has replaced Romer,' said Sforza. 'Don't worry, we've checked his background.'

'Any news on the cause of Romer's death?' Dulac said.

'Apparently someone poisoned his beer with the same poison that killed Aguar. Inspector Guadagni has started a full investigation.'

A half hour later, they entered the Segnatura room and were greeted by the muted applause of the Cardinals.

'Cardinal Legnano telephoned from the Agostino Gemelli Clinic where His Holiness is undergoing a preliminary examination. Legnano will join us shortly,' said Brentano. 'In the meantime, please be seated.'

Twenty minutes later, as Dulac was still describing the night's events to Harris and the astounded cardinals, Legnano entered the room and all eyes focused on him.

'Gentlemen, the doctors have given me an initial assessment of the Pope's health. His vital signs are good. The Pope is understandably tired, but in good spirits. He will rest for a day or so, and then undergo a comprehensive medical examination.'

The other cardinals nodded their approval.

'What about surgery to save his ear?' asked Fouquet.

'The doctors will do tests at the first opportunity. After so much time, I'm told it looks doubtful,' said Legnano.

'I will prepare the press conference to announce the Pope's return,' said Sforza.

As the early morning dawn broke over Rome, Dulac and Harris took a taxi and headed back to the hotel. Dulac, barely awake, wasn't about to interrupt the long, uncomfortable silence inside the cab when suddenly Harris burst out, 'Let's get this straight between us once and for all, Dulac. If you think you're getting some oohey, goohey gobs of praise from me, a golden star in your little scrap book, you're going to wait a long time. You're sadly mistaken if—'

Dulac exploded. 'For Christ sake, I followed your goddamn scheme, nearly got my butt shot out of the sky while rescuing the Pope out of some hole in Libya, and all I get from you is this shit?'

Harris's tone mellowed. 'All right, all right. So you did well. I'm not questioning that part of the operation, although you could have let us know earlier about de Ségur. We would have—'

'We were a bit busy dodging Libyan missiles, and trying to keep the Comanche in the sky.'

'Yes, yes, I realize that. I don't want to appear ungrateful but we must begin to think ahead.' Harris, his breath smelling of alcohol, turned towards Dulac. 'How long do you think the press will let us off the hook for not catching de Ségur? A week? Two at the most? I hate to have to keep reminding you, Dulac, that until de Ségur is eating lunch behind the bars of La Santé Prison, we've failed, we've—'

'Cut the crap, Harris. You mean I've failed.'

'As you wish. This rescue is only a part of the overall mission. Need I remind you de Ségur has two, no, now three red flag warrants for his arrest?'

'After a good night's sleep, I'll give de Ségur my undivided attention.'

'Get on his tail,' said Harris, his face near Dulac's. 'He's probably lying low in Benghazi. We can still get him while he's in Libya. May I remind you, Dulac, that, as my lawyer friend says, time is of the essence?'

Harris's breath was bearing down on Dulac and he leaned slightly towards the window, away from the offensive odor. 'I doubt he's in Benghazi,' he said. 'He's trying to get the hell out of Libya before Kargali finds out he's been screwed out of the opportunity of a lifetime. If de Ségur is still in Libya when the colonel finds out—'

'If, when, probably . . . I want more than your damn hypotheses and theories, Dulac. I want results.'

'The colonel will throw the dogs after his hide. My bet is he's making a run for it out of Libya. Problem is, we don't know where the bastard is headed with those vans. They—'

'Dulac. Am I getting through?'

'Loud and clear. By the way, when you said that time is of the essence, did you call for a satellite search on the vans?'

'How could I? I had no idea de Ségur was using vans.'

'One might have anticipated the possibility. Of course, by now it's probably too late.' Dulac suppressed a yawn. 'Those satellites would be trying to cover the whole of Northeast Africa.'

'Give it a try,' said Harris. 'One never knows. Have Dieter coordinate it with the French. And call Boning in Tunis. Have him take the next plane to Benghazi.'

Dulac bit his tongue, knowing full well that sending an agent to Benghazi and commencing a satellite recon search was a complete waste of time and money.

'Grab the trail and get on de Ségur's goddamn tail. I want results, Dulac, not excuses.' At that moment, the taxi pulled up before the hotel's entrance. Dulac got out first.

'Thanks for the appreciation,' he said, starting towards the hotel and leaving Harris to pay the cabbie.

CHAPTER 24

Hotel Dante, 11.00 a.m., May 29

After contacting Dieter and Boning, Dulac, his nerves jangled by the confrontation with Harris, retreated to the hotel's lounge and ordered a glass of milk and a ham sandwich. Sitting at the bar, from the corner of his eye, he'd occasionally catch a glimpse of the comings and goings of the hotel's patrons in the lobby. Moments later, Harris's voice at the front desk caught Dulac's attention. He's leaving, finally.

It wasn't until he saw Harris cross the lobby and walk through the rotating doors that Dulac felt a wave of relief. He phoned Karen in Paris.

'Congratulations! The Pope's rescue is all over the news on TV. Tell me all about it. I can't wait to hear how it went,' she said excitedly.

'Later. I'm a bit frazzled right now.'

'Understandably. I thought you'd be asleep.'

'Can't. Too tired.'

'How did it go with Harris?'

'Don't ask. It's getting worse. He can't make it through the morning without a drink, many drinks. It's affecting his judgment,' said Dulac.

'How is that?'

'He's constantly jumping to conclusions. Wrong conclusions. He thinks de Ségur is still in Benghazi. God knows why.'

'Is that so unlikely?'

'Trust me. If you're not an Arab, Libya is a pretty small place. As Westerners, de Ségur and his goons would stick out like red carp in a fish barrel, waiting to be picked off by the Libyan security force. The man might be a psychopath, but he's not stupid. With de Ségur's Cairo contacts, he's probably headed to Egypt.'

'So why aren't you in Egypt?'

'Timing and geography. He left Suluq yesterday. If all went well, he's out of Africa by now, headed to God knows where, probably to his safe haven Belize. If not, and assuming de Ségur plans to leave by air, which is far from certain, we've only got two agents to cover the whole of Egypt. With Boning, three for all of Libya, Tunisia and Sudan. Ever try to hold water with a fish net?'

'Difficult.'

Dulac signaled the bartender. 'Coffee with milk . . .' Then, uncovering the phone's mouthpiece, he continued. 'Sorry. As I was saying, the only way to catch de Ségur is to be one step ahead of him, not chasing behind him all over hell's half acre. Realistically, unless he's still in Africa and we catch him in the desert by satellite tracking in time for the local police to move in, we'll have to wait for new developments. In the meantime, I'm working this side of the investigation.'

'In the Vatican?'

'Correct. I just wanted to say hello. Call you.'

Dulac returned to his room to catch some much needed sleep. He'd just entered some lustful ruminations of his subconscious when the buzzing of his cellphone broke the spell and jolted him awake. He leaned over, grabbed the cell and saw the dreaded Interpol's encrypted number flashing insistently on the LCD. Harris again. Bastard doesn't let up.

‘Have you read Dieter’s preliminary sat recon report?’ said Harris, his tone aggressive.

Asshole is trying to make me feel guilty, thought Dulac. ‘I wasn’t expecting it until later this evening, tomorrow morning even.’

‘It’s on your computer. Read it.’

Naked except for his boxer shorts, Dulac went to the desk and turned on his computer. ‘Got it. Give me a minute.’ He started to read.

May 27th, 12.08 p.m. hours to 5.45 p.m. hours. Extracts from Geostationary satellite DGP-FRA 3ZC log. Initially believed to be closest matches to suspect vehicles. Sat recon unit captured and tracked the following heat imprints, identified and confirmed by local authorities to be vehicles as follows:

1) 1.10 p.m. local time: two vehicles bearing 300 degrees north approached Sudanese border at Kurmuk. Sudanese guards asked to identify occupants. Miscommunication occurred and Sudanese let vehicle through without noting identity of four occupants. Subsequent description of occupants does not fit suspects. Four Japanese tourists believe headed for Khartoum. Result negative.

2) 2.18 p.m. local time: three vehicles near Suluq bearing 270 westerly direction, headed for Tunisia. Intercepted at Ras al-Jedir. Tunisian authorities confirmed identities of twelve occupants: six Dutch nationals, three Swiss, three Americans. No match with suspects. Result negative.

3) 9.08 p.m. local time: immobilized vehicle identified near Siwa Egypt airstrip. Asked Egyptian police to investigate. They found an abandoned

van with two flat tires bearing Tunisian license plates. Checking identity of owner. Result negative.

End of Preliminary Report.'

'Dulac?'

'I'm just finishing reading.'

'Result negative, result negative. That's all I need,' said Harris.

'I warned you yesterday that our chances of finding them with a sat recon—'

'Yes, yes, I know. Any news from Boning?'

'Negative.'

'So basically we're still nowhere.' A moment of silence, and Harris continued. 'You should have gone to Cairo.'

'Didn't I hear someone say recently Benghazi? He's got to be in Benghazi?'

'I don't need your smart-ass sarcasm.'

Another pregnant silence. 'You know, Dulac, I've been thinking. Maybe it's time we got some new blood in the file.' Harris's tone had become conciliatory, dangerously so. 'Besides you've earned a good rest. I'm seriously thinking of giving Lescop a chance to take on more responsibility. I think—'

Dulac felt the axe coming and beat Harris to the swing. 'Piss off, Harris. You're looking for any fucking excuse to dump me. Now that the Pope is safely back in Rome, now that the spotlight has been turned off, I can do what I want with old Dulac. He's expendable. Let's put the old nag out to pasture.'

'I will disregard that comment, in the memory of your deceased father for whom I had the greatest of respect. You will hand over the file to Lescop.'

'That's one hell-fire way of getting it further stalled.'

'One more comment like that and I'll—'

'You'll what, Harris, you'll what. You'll fire me? I'll have my lawyer in your office within minutes.'

'Don't you threaten me, Dulac.'

'Harris, why don't you go and do the anatomically impossible thing.'

Hotel Dante, later that night

Downing his fourth scotch, Dulac extinguished his Gitane on the edge of the glass, got up from the uncomfortable barstool and stumbled his way to the hotel's rotating front door. Outside, the fresh air hit his lungs like the contents of a can of Febreze. He phoned Karen.

'Hi, it's me.'

'Do you know what time it is?' she said drowsily.

'I'm free, free as a goddamn bird. So come fly with me, fly me to the moon, to paradise. I left my love . . . in Costaaa Ricaaa . . .'

'I strongly suggest you keep your day job.'

'Is my shinging that bad?'

'You sound plastered. Any particular reason?'

'No reason, no problem. I've been shus . . . suspended.'

'Again?'

'In and out. Comes with the job. He'll call back and apologize.'

'Really?'

'He needs me. If he thinks Lescop can do a better job in finding de Ségur, he's shadly mistaken.'

'So what's this about Costa Rica?'

'The best diving in the world. Great trekking too.'

'Yeah, sure.'

'See the jaguars, see the jaguars and Dulac, before they're both extinct. Wanna go?'

'Call me when you're sober.' She hung up.

CHAPTER 25

Belize, 7.15 p.m., 29 May

The Bombardier's steep banking onto final approach awoke de Ségur. He looked out the window in time to catch a glimpse of Belmopan's main landing strip before the Bombardier leveled again and the Rolls-Royce engines slowed to a quiet purr. A welcome change from hell, thought de Ségur. The jet landed, taxied to the small terminal building and stopped. Moments later, the steward opened the Bombardier's passenger door and de Ségur stepped down the steep boarding ladder. A lone Customs officer was already waiting at its base, clipboard in hand.

'Good afternoon Mr de Combel. Welcome back,' said the overweight, short man, with a hint of a British accent. 'How was your trip?'

'Fine, Fernando, fine.'

'How many passengers?' he said, eyeing the open doorway of the jet.

'Six, counting myself.'

'Anything to declare?' the Customs officer said perfunctorily. 'No, nothing to declare. How are the wife and children?'

'My young one, Esperanza is in the hospital. She broke her arm playing soccer. And Anna, the older—'

'Kids. They recover quickly.'

'And my wife Isabella, she is trying to make ends meet. It is very hard with the children . . . They eat us right out of the kitchen . . . Ah, but that is not your concern. I'm sorry . . .'

The officer paused, cleared his throat and continued. 'Mr de Combel, as usual I am required to check your passports before you proceed to Customs control at the gate.'

'Yes, yes, of course, Fernando.' De Ségur took the Customs officer by the arm and walked with him towards the other side of the ladder, away from the line of sight of the terminal building. 'You know, Fernando, some of these passengers would rather be discreet about being here in Belize. Depending on who you are, a Belizean stamp on one's passport could be, well, misinterpreted.' De Ségur smiled. 'I'm sure you understand. Plus, some of those passports are a bit past their expiry dates.' De Ségur paused. 'I have a little something here that isn't.' He put his right hand on the Customs officer's shoulder, brought him close and with the other, took out from his vest a thick, white envelope and slipped it into Fernando's pocket.

'Thank you Mr de Combel.' Fernando smiled, quickly stuffing the envelope deeper into his pocket. 'Then you are checked through.' He initialed and handed de Ségur six cards. 'When you are ready, present these at the gate.'

'Actually, Fernando, we would rather be more discreet. Is there a way we can avoid the gate altogether?'

'Is the jet staying here?'

'It will refuel and go on to Costa Rica.'

'Then wait until darkness and go through the guard station at the hangar.' He pointed to the corrugated metal building to the left of the terminal. 'My brother is on guard until midnight. I'll let him know.'

'Excellent.'

'I'll tell the officers at the terminal that the plane is in transit, waiting to refuel.'

Good man, that Fernando, thought de Ségur, as he watched the Customs officer walk back to the terminal building. De Ségur made a cellphone call and climbed up the staircase to the top. Suddenly, he felt dizzy and grabbed the handrail. It's getting worse, he thought, as the dizziness slowly dissipated. He regained the interior of the cabin and addressed the Cathars, sitting anxiously in their seats. 'The van will pick us up at 8.15. In the meantime, everybody relax.'

Back at de Ségur's compound that evening, a general unease permeated the Cathars' dinner conversation, occasionally peppered with banal exchanges on the unusually hot weather. De Ségur's phone rang. He left the table to take the call. After a moment, he returned and addressed the Cathars. 'Gentlemen, I have good news. Antoine and the others made it safely to Cairo. They will return to France in the morning. Now let's go to the salon. We'll be more comfortable there.'

As they sat down in the wicker chairs set about the rustic surroundings, a macaw perched on the feeder outside on the veranda began to crow noisily. De Ségur put down his cognac, went to the window, and closed it. He returned and stood facing the tired and jet-lagged Cathars, moroseness etched onto their faces. 'Gentlemen,' he said, 'I have advised the families of our fallen brothers and sisters about the sinking of the Bellerophon. Their kin are taking it very hard, some of them blaming me for the loss of their loved ones. I assume that responsibility entirely. I will leave for France next week and see each and every family. That is the least I can do.

'In the meantime, you are surely wondering if we should proceed with our mission. I cannot blame you for having your doubts.' He grabbed the back of the wicker chair before him and leaned forward. 'But I ask that you keep your focus on the overall goal. We must continue. Otherwise, the sacrifice of our comrades' lives will have been in vain. The reality is that we will recruit others and rebuild the core. Our ancestors suffered much worse, and they prevailed. We can also. These setbacks will not halt our mission. Our success depends on all of you returning to your dioceses and recruiting new faithful. I ask that you continue to trust me. In turn, I promise you this: the prophecy will be fulfilled. Our time will come.' He paused for a moment, eyeing each of the Cathars one by one. 'Are you with me?'

'Yes,' they answered in unison.

'Good. It's time for Phase Epsilon.'

Paris, 9.10 a.m., ten days later, Saturday 10 June

Karen hadn't heard from Dulac since his drunken phone call ten days earlier. He hadn't returned her many phone messages, and she'd given up repeating the obvious. Although he wasn't the most punctual of message returners, it was uncharacteristic of the man not to give any sign of life whatsoever. Her annoyance had eventually given way to concern, then worry. She decided to drop by his apartment.

Karen hailed a taxi and made her way to the 16 arrondissement, and to the entrance of Dulac's third story flat. The well-worn stone staircase reminded her of their many late evening dashes toward a night of intense lovemaking. She went up, rang and waited. No answer. She rang again. Nothing. She looked down at the bottom of the door and through the space between it and the floor, thought she saw a shadow cross the light. 'Thierry, are you there? It's me Karen.'

The shadow crossed the light again, in the opposite direction. She pounded on the door. 'Thierry, I know you're in there.'

'Go away.'

'What's the matter? Why won't you let me in?' Worry was rapidly changing to resentment.

'Nothing to do with you.' Dulac's voice was hoarse, almost unrecognizable.

'Thierry, I'm not going to stand here talking to you outside your damn door. Either you let me in and we discuss this like grown adults, or I'll leave you to enjoy your childish tantrum. Your choice.'

Karen heard the latch unlock and the door opened. 'My God!' she gasped.

Dressed in an old nightgown, long oily strands of hair hanging limply over his ears, a ten day scraggly beard covering his face, Dulac stood at the door, glass in hand.

'Not quite. Come in.' He shuffled over to the living room amidst the newspapers littering the floor, cleared some of the books strewn on the sofa and offered Karen a small space. 'Been catching up on my Dostoyevsky,' he said as he went over to the bar. 'Drink?'

'No thanks.' Still trying to absorb the shock, she sat down amid the books while he poured himself a drink. 'Why haven't you returned my calls?'

'I've been busy,' he said, not bothering to look at her.

'Doing what? Drinking yourself into oblivion?'

'That too,' he said, seating himself in the recliner across from her.

'Thierry, I know this thing with Harris has been hard on you, but this is not going to solve the problem.'

'What problem?' He took another swig of the scotch.

She got up and walked over, standing and glaring down at him. 'Do you realize what you're doing? You're becoming another Harris. Is that what you want?'

Dulac shot up, standing a few inches from her face. 'That's going too far.'

'Not at all.' She crossed her arms, returning his hate-filled stare.

Dulac backed away. 'I thought I'd get some support. Not criticism.'

'Listen, if you want to drown yourself in alcohol and self-pity, that's your business, but don't look at me for help.' She looked around. 'Just look at this mess. How can you live like this?'

Dulac glanced about at the stacked dishes overflowing in the sink, his shirts and jacket hanging from various kitchen chairs, an old t-shirt strewn onto the dining room table. 'Pretty bad, I must admit.'

'Thierry, you've got to pull yourself together. If you go down this road, you'll go it alone. I had an alcoholic father and I won't—'

'Whoa! I'm not a bloody alky.'

'I'm sure that's what Harris says also.'

'You're pushing your luck, lady.'

'Thierry, you've got some serious decisions to take.'

'Like what? Getting ready for my asshole boss to summon me back? So I can lick his boots again while he cracks the whip?'

'Maybe you should think outside of the box. Look elsewhere. Surely Interpol isn't the only place for a damn good criminal investigator.'

'I suppose.' Dulac looked at her with a vague air of interest. 'Maybe I could sell my story to the press, write a book even.'

'Good idea. In the meantime why don't you shave, take a shower and put some clean clothes on. I'll buy breakfast.'

CHAPTER 26

Papal Library, The Vatican, 9.30 a.m.

The previous evening, Cardinal Signorelli had received word from Castel Gandolfo: the Pope had finished resting and would be returning the following morning to the Vatican to resume his papal duties. Signorelli had convened the members of the inner Curia for a meeting with His Holiness in the papal library, and while they waited for the Pope to enter, the cardinals talked excitedly.

'Must be difficult for His Holiness to come back to the Vatican after only a two week rest,' said Brentano.

'Shouldn't he still be recuperating?' said Sforza to Fouquet.

'He's always been very resilient,' said Brentano.

Legnano spoke. 'He can't be feeling all that—'

'I'm feeling quite well, thank you, Cardinal Legnano,' said the voice in the doorway of the library.

Legnano spun around. 'Your Holiness. I didn't mean—'

'It's quite all right, Cardinal.' Dressed in a white cassock, he walked slowly towards the assembled cardinals and proffered to each of them the papal ring.

'It is good to see you, your Holiness,' said Sforza, kneeling and kissing the ring.

'You are looking well, your Holiness,' said Brentano.

'Enough compliments, Eminences. Please be seated,' he said, as he walked behind the desk and sat down. 'First, as tradition demands, Cardinal Fouquet, you are relieved of your duties as Camerlengo. As of now, I am resuming my functions as Head of State of the Vatican.'

'Yes, of course, your Holiness,' said Fouquet.

'There is apparently a diplomatic issue with Libya?' he eyed Legnano. 'Cardinal?'

'Your Holiness, after the world press found out last week about your rescue from Libya, the Vatican received a diplomatic note protesting a violation and invasion of Libyan airspace. The note mentions that the Vatican planned the whole operation and is responsible for the death of Libyans and destruction of property while Libyan planes tried to extract the intruder from its territory. Gaddaffi wants reparations of $100 million US dollars.'

'Ha! The gall of the man. And what is your opinion?'

'Your Holiness, we believe there was no violation of Libya's territory by the Vatican.'

'How is that, Cardinal?'

'We have legal opinions to the effect that the rescue of a man kept by kidnappers against his will is not an act of aggression against the Libyan state. Furthermore, the helicopter was American, the pilot German.'

'I see. We are treading on rather thin ice, wouldn't you say Cardinal?' he said, smiling wryly.

'That's a matter of interpretation, your Holiness,' said Legnano. 'Obviously the Vatican wants to avoid any diplomatic incident with Libya, if possible.'

'But the helicopter His Holiness was in was attacked by Libyan jets,' Sforza began.

'Cardinal Sforza, we have no proof that they acted under Kargali's orders,' said Brentano. 'They could simply have been defending Libyan airspace, not knowing that His Holiness was aboard.' Turning to the pontiff. 'Of course your Holiness, you were there, you—'

'Enough of your speculations. I will take the matter under consideration. In the meantime, Cardinal Signorelli, schedule my next public appearance in the Hall of Audiences for tomorrow, at 4 p.m. Cardinal Brentano, Cardinal Sforza, I will see you here this afternoon. Monsignor Signorelli will schedule you. Your Eminences, this meeting is over.'

Sitting next to Cardinal Sforza, Cardinal Brentano fidgeted nervously with his red fascia in the antechamber of the papal library. 'Do you have any idea why we've been convened?' he asked Sforza.

'No.'

'Do you think it has to do with—'

At that moment, the door to the papal library opened and Cardinal Signorelli, the Pope's secretary, appeared: 'The Holy Father will see you now, Cardinal Brentano.'

Brentano rose, trying to detect the mood in Signorelli's face as he walked past him. He was inscrutable. Brentano entered and the stern look of the man standing in front of him confirmed his apprehension. This was not a social call.

'Your Holiness,' said Brentano, bending to kiss the proffered papal ring.

'Good day, Cardinal Brentano. Please be seated.' He offered Brentano one of the skinny chairs, went to the other side of the desk and sat down. 'I will go straight to the heart of the matter.'

Brentano felt his pulse quicken.

'After due consideration, I have decided that because of the upcoming changes I will be introducing shortly, Cardinal Gonzalez will be better suited to occupy the position of head of the Congregation For The Doctrine Of The Faith. Gonzalez's nomination will take effect immediately.'

Brentano sat unbelieving, speechless, unable to move, trying to absorb the shock. The implacable look of the man before him did not waver. Finally Brentano spoke. 'But your Holiness, I have served you well up until now.' Brentano heard his voice crack and tried clearing his throat. 'And I will continue to do so in the future, whatever the changes, I assure you.'

'I know this is not easy for you, Cardinal, but try and think of the matter not in personal terms, but in relation of the overall good. You see during these past two weeks, I've had time to further concentrate my thoughts on changes, the essence of which I've been thinking about for a long time. Changes that, as the head of the Congregation, I assure you Brentano, you will disagree with.'

'Your Holiness, could I . . . ? Could you tell me the nature of these changes?'

'In due course, Brentano.'

Brentano couldn't believe what he was hearing. Cardinal Gonzales, a recent arrival from Colombia, knew nothing of the workings of the Vatican. Gonzales was what was commonly referred to in Vatican circles as a 'yes cardinal'. In order to get ahead and through the wall excluding non-Italians, these cardinals tried to please everybody, resulting in pleasing no one. To be replaced by a 'yes cardinal' would add insult to injury. Within hours of the announcement, Brentano would be the laughing stock of the establishment's power brokers.

Brentano's carefully constructed political edifice, skillfully built over the years with the bricks and mortar of his endless maneuvering: all of it was coming crashing down. For a brief moment, while he reeled with the blow, his mind raced, trying to call upon and muster his survival instincts, instincts that had never let him down. He had to fight.

'Perhaps you are prejudging me, your Holiness. I have always been able to conciliate my views with yours. I don't doubt Cardinal Gonzales has many qualities, but he is totally inexperienced in the inner workings of the Vatican. Surely it would be very difficult for him to implement any of your changes.'

'Gonzales will learn, as you did when you first took on the responsibility. I am not judging you, Brentano. I know your character, perhaps even better than you know it yourself.

My decision is final. You will be assigned temporarily to the post of legate for the Conciliation of Interdenominational Faiths.'

Brentano felt desperation settling in and taking over, numbing his brain. He was a drowning man. He clutched for straws. 'But won't that be seen as a demotion, your Holiness?' Brentano regretted the words as soon as they'd passed his lips.

'Brentano, Brentano, always appearances. The days of artifice are over, Brentano. If I have my way, substance will replace form, essence will replace pretense. We have a long, challenging road ahead of us, Cardinal, a road which I invite you to take with me. Now as far as you are concerned, I don't see this as a demotion. I need someone of your experience for this challenging new role. Consider this an opportunity, Cardinal, not a penance.'

Brentano sat stunned. The Pope had made up his mind and there was no higher authority to appeal to. All these years of careful promoting behind the scenes, the trading of favors, the mentoring, the constant networking for support, the sacrifices, the cajoling, all for nothing? No it couldn't be. He had to bide his time. After a moment, Brentano said, 'I suppose I must.'

'Please see to it that the transition goes smoothly.'

'Yes, your Holiness.'

'That will be all, Cardinal.'

Brentano, numb with disbelief, rose slowly and walked out past Signorelli and Sforza without uttering a word.

'Shall I send in Cardinal Sforza, your Holiness?' asked Signorelli.

'Yes, please send him in.'

'Your Holiness,' said Sforza, bowing to kiss the papal ring.

'Please sit down, Cardinal.'

'Thank you.' Sforza looked uneasily at the pontiff, whose intense eyes seemed to bore right through him. 'And how is your health?' ventured Sforza, wishing to break the silence.

'Quite well, considering.'

'I can't begin to imagine the trauma.'

'Cardinal, I survived.'

'Yes, yes, thank the Lord. How about . . . ? I mean, is there any chance they will reattach your ear?'

'I'm told it's too late. Meanwhile I've become accustomed to not being able to hear from the left side. Believe me, Cardinal, that's not always an impediment.'

'Selective hearing. My mother does it all the time.' Sforza laughed, trying to lighten the mood. He thought he saw the beginning of a smile on the otherwise dead serious face. The eyes bored even deeper.

'The reason I have convened you, Cardinal, is to inform you that I have decided to keep you in your present post as head of Investments and Information. I also want to inform you of certain upcoming changes. Because of the nature of these changes, I have decided to replace Cardinal Brentano. He and I wouldn't see eye to eye on many of these. Cardinal Gonzalez will take his place, effective immediately. Some will question my decision, and I am fully aware that Brentano has powerful allies. I'm certain they will ask me to reconsider. I won't. During this process, I require your entire support. Do I have it?'

Sforza, off balance for a moment, quickly regained his composure. 'Yes, yes, of course, your Holiness.'

CHAPTER 27

Belize, somewhere in the Mayan Mountain Range jungle, 3 p.m., Sunday, 11 June

Under de Ségur's planning, the Cathars had left Belize discreetly and returned to their parishes in Southern France. Before their departure, de Ségur had informed them that the nominations of their fallen brethren's replacements would be forthcoming. For the moment, de Ségur could enjoy luxuriating in one of his more personal, intimate passions: listening to classical music.

De Ségur entered the acoustically inert room, went over to his compact disc player and inserted Nikolaus Harnoncourt's rendition of J. S. Bach's Mass in B minor. Having turned the volume up to near-maximum intensity, de Ségur took the baton resting on the mahogany pulpit and stood before the loudspeakers. At the stroke of his baton, the electronic eye switched on the CD player and the Staatskapelle choir burst into the gripping first bars of the 'Kyrie'. De Ségur, every nerve in his body tingling with ecstasy, engulfed himself into the ineffable.

Then it happened.

He was waving the entry of the invisible continuo into the Aria with the baton, when his right hand started to shake uncontrollably and flung the baton away. He stood immobile while the music continued, staring for a moment into space. Soon, tears flooded his eyes. Already? This time there is no mistaking. It's here.

Moments later, the large loudspeakers went silent. He replaced the baton on the pulpit, turned and fell exhausted into the sofa. I don't have much time, he thought. They said six months at the most from the first signs. He picked up the red velvet covered book on the small walnut side table. He still remembered the day when his father had handed him the book titled Pierre de Combel: a Cathar knight's journey.

'It's the story of our famous ancestor,' his father had said in a quivering but solemn voice.

Hugues de Ségur knew Pierre de Combel almost better than he knew himself. His heart would fill with sorrow and pride at the recounting of the trials and tribulations that de Combel had endured, to become one of the mythical figures of southern France. In the besieged town of Minerve, at the head of only five hundred faithful, he'd successfully repulsed the four attacks of Simon de Montfort and his six thousand Catholic knights during some of the fiercest fighting of the Albigensian crusades. After many such bloody defeats at the hands of de Combel, the Inquisition had put a king's ransom on his head. Eventually, through the treachery of de Combel's mistress, five of the Inquisition's monk-knights had caught him, asleep in a small inn near Castelnaudary.

De Ségur read how de Combel had suffered the torture of the rack, in the Inquisition's belief that, as did most of its victims, the knight would eventually renounce his heretic faith. De Combel hadn't. The Inquisition had tortured him for four days, before death had finally delivered him from his tormentors.

Moments later, de Ségur, his eyes watery with anger, put down the book. The ritual was always the same: the ecstasy of the music followed by the agony of history.

De Ségur rose and summoned Gaspard. 'Bring me the list,' he said.

'It's not up to date, sir. Those missing are still on it.'

'Bring it anyway. We can't wait any longer.'

De Ségur looked at the list and sat in silence, lost in thought: eleven Cathars, mostly bishops and deacons, had drowned on the Bellerophon.

'We'll have to contact the bishops in Lombardy, Piedmont, Béziers and Albi,' said Gaspard.

'The new posts must be filled before we get news from Rome. We must take full advantage. Where is the list of new candidates?'

Gaspard brought in a sheet of paper to which was attached the CVs of aspiring Cathar priests. De Ségur reviewed the CVs of the new recruits one more time. He nodded in approval.

'Prepare the nominations. I'll sign them.'

Inside the Vatican, the news of Brentano's demise had spread like locusts on a hot summer night. Nervous, Legnano waited in the antechamber of the papal library, wondering if he'd be next.

'His Holiness will see you now,' said Signorelli to Legnano, as he opened the door to the library and showed Legnano in.

Legnano crossed the room, and then bent over to kiss the proffered papal ring. He straightened and met the holy man's warm smile. He looked more tired than usual.

'Good to see you, Legnano. Please,' he said, pointing to one of the chairs across his desk. 'What is the reaction to Gonzales's nomination?'

Legnano cleared his throat. 'Mainly one of surprise, I'd say, your Holiness.'

'Come, come, Cardinal, we are well used to surprises in the Vatican. Surely you can be a little more explicit.'

'Actually, rumors have already started that there will be more changes. Everybody is a bit nervous, your Holiness.'

'I see. Like at the beginning of, what is the expression, a corporate shake-up?'

'Something to that effect, your Holiness.'

'Don't worry, Cardinal, I'm not about to change your posting.'

Legnano felt a wave of relief. 'I'd be lying if I said the thought never crossed my mind.'

'The reason I've called you, Legnano, is to let you know as senior member of the Curia, that I've decided to convene an ecumenical council.'

Astonished, Legnano fumbled for words. 'A . . . an ecumenical council?'

'Yes. You see, Legnano, during my rest at Castel Gandolfo, I was able to give my undivided attention to some significant changes I have been considering for a long time. I must tell you that I also thought of these changes while I was being held in captivity. They say that there's nothing like a life-threatening danger to focus the mind.'

'Understandably, your Holiness.' Legnano felt a jab of discomfort. He'd lived through the division and discord created by Vatican II's substantial changes in Church doctrine.

'In my prayers, I asked God to protect me, so that I could make these changes. I told myself that if God chose to spare my life, it would be His clear message that I should proceed with these changes. He answered my prayers, and I was reminded only this morning why. You see this file, Legnano?' — he picked up a dark-blue folder on the desk, and waved it at Legnano — 'twenty-seven letters from archbishops mentioning cases of sexual abuses within their dioceses. Probably the tip of the iceberg.' He put it down on the desk and picked up a beige holder. 'I received this from

Signorelli this morning: the Closed Churches file. Did you know that we closed down eighteen churches in the last month alone?'

'I wasn't aware of the exact number, your Holiness.'

'To compound our problems, our financial situation is precarious and getting worse every day.' He crossed his arms and leaned back in his chair. 'Sforza tells me that we've started to sell assets to pay for recurring expenses. One doesn't have to have a doctorate in economics to know where that leads. He says that St. Peter's Pence hasn't been this low since 1929.' He paused, a frown forming on his generous forehead. 'In short, Legnano, we are heading for disaster. The Church, our Church, must change, or die.'

'I, I hadn't thought of it in such drastic terms, your Holiness,' Legnano ventured. 'What would be on the agenda of such an ecumenical council?'

'Everything in due course, Legnano. Don't worry. As Secretary of State, you will be the first to receive my agenda. I simply wanted to advise you. For now, have Cardinal Fouquet draft the writs of convocation to the archbishops. I want this ecumenical council convened as soon as possible, Cardinal.'

'To the archbishops, your Holiness? That would be breaking with tradition. Usually it's the bishops who are—'

'Archbishops only, Cardinal. I have my reasons.'

'I see. Then a four months' notice should be sufficient to give them the opportunity—'

'Six weeks, Legnano. I want it convened in six weeks. They can pass on the invitations to their bishops later.'

'Six weeks, your Holiness, that's—'

'Unusual, I know, but in today's electronic age, quite achievable. I'm making the final corrections to the agenda. You should be receiving it within the next few days, perhaps sooner. In the meantime, that will be all, Cardinal.'

'Yes . . . thank you, your Holiness.' Legnano got up, kissed the papal ring and left the Pope's library hastily. He returned to his office and summoned Fouquet.

'Six weeks?' said Fouquet, his mouth agape.

'The bishops won't be convened directly,' said Legnano, still shaken. 'Highly unorthodox, but there is precedent to that effect.'

'Only when the ecumenical council rubberstamped the already-made decisions of the Pope.'

'Perhaps His Holiness just wants to speed up the convocation process,' said Fouquet.

'Somehow I doubt it. He mentioned wanting to make significant changes, whatever that means.'

'When will I receive the agenda?'

'I'll let you know. In the meantime, start preparing the writs of convocation for His Holiness to sign. I suggest you leave the date out, just in case we can't meet the deadline.'

'Yes of course . . . six weeks . . .' Fouquet mumbled, turned and walked out.

Legnano reached down, opened the main drawer of his walnut desk and pulled out a small, white pack. He lit a cigarette. He hadn't smoked in six months.

Legnano opened the sealed envelope handed to him by the papal secretary's assistant, and slowly read the ecumenical council agenda. He paused, then re-read it. 'Mio Dio,' whispered Legnano, staring at the assistant secretary in disbelief. He dismissed the cleric, walked quickly to his desk and began calling the rest of the Curia members.

'Meet me in my office. It's urgent,' said Legnano to a refractory Sforza. Legnano waited, nervously pacing back and forth in the middle of the room as Signorelli, then Sforza entered, then Gonzales and Fouquet.

Legnano spoke. 'Your Eminences, I apologize for such short notice, but you'll soon understand why I've called this meeting.' He distributed the documents to the cardinals. 'This is the agenda of the ecumenical council. I will read the accompanying translation of the official Latin version.'

Legnano went to his desk, sat down, pushing back his glasses to the top of his aquiline nose. He began reading.

'To the Archbishops

It is our wish, as Pope Clement the 21st, of the Holy Apostolic Roman Catholic Church of Peter, that the following measures, upon being considered by the ecumenical council, be debated and adopted as rules of the Church by said Council, and be confirmed by Ourselves at such time as we deem appropriate.

First: The Credo of the Holy Church, as adopted by the Ecumenical Council of Nicea dated 325 AD, as amended and confirmed by the Ecumenical Council of Nicea of 381 AD, is hereby repealed and replaced by the Credo in Annex 'A', in its existing form or such other form proposed by the Council and confirmed by Ourselves.'

Legnano paused and eyed the silent cardinals, a collective look of astonishment on their faces. 'I don't have a copy of the new credo yet.'

'Most interesting,' said Fouquet.

The cardinals threw glances of feigned interest at each other, trying to hide their rapidly growing discomfort.

Legnano continued.

'Second: The Council shall consider that the principle of the laity of priests, while it has served our Church up till now, be now revisited. A venerable objective per se, it has met with failure and has encouraged hypocrisy, transgression and sometimes criminal behavior.'

Legnano paused, looking up briefly at Sforza, whose usually twinkling eyes were remarkably immobile. Legnano plunged back into his text.

'It has also become a permanent barrier to the successful recruiting of prelates, and the maintaining of a scandal-free Church. It is therefore our wish that the Council review, with the purpose of abolishing it, the principle of laity as a necessary precondition to access to priesthood within the Church.'

Brentano broke in. 'Incredible. Does that mean . . . ?'

'Let me finish, monsignor,' interrupted Legnano, reading on.

'Third: Recent archaeological discoveries, including the discovery of the Gospel of Thomas, have established beyond historical doubt that the Church of our forefathers has encouraged, in the past, the

participation of women in the celebration of the Holy Eucharist. Based on such discoveries, we see no reason, historical, biblical, or otherwise, to prohibit access to the Catholic womanhood of today . . .'

'Women?' exclaimed Signorelli. He is going to allow women . . .'

Legnano slammed his fist onto the desk, 'Monsignori, let me finish.' He read on.

'. . . in the dutiful exercises and offices of the Roman Catholic clergy. The Council shall review and discuss the conditions of implementation of such principle.'

Legnano cleared his throat and looked up from his text. The cardinals sat, staring wide-eyed.

'Astounding,' exclaimed Sforza, looking at Legnano, then at the rest of the prelates.

'Unbelievable. I can't believe what I'm hearing,' said Signorelli.

'Please, cardinals,' said Legnano, his tone now conciliatory.

'Fourth: The current structural organization of the Church has outlived its economic, theological and administrative usefulness, and can no longer be viably sustained. We therefore ask the Council to review and consider the abolition of the role and function of Archbishop, to be replaced on a regional level by a Provincial Bishop. Existing archbishops will be reassigned dioceses or bishoprics by the Holy See, over a period of three years.'

'He's declaring war against the archbishops,' said Sforza. 'He'll never . . .'

'FIFTH!' shouted Legnano, losing patience.

'The Holy See has found it necessary to revisit the following elements of doctrine:

A) Transubstantiation during the Eucharist.
B) The virginal birth of Mary.
C) The physical resurrection of the body of Christ.

We feel the continued affirmation of these elements of doctrine have been increasingly difficult to sustain in the light of historical, ecumenical and biogenetic analysis, and have become a serious threat to the continuation of our Church's primordial beliefs. We feel the non-accentuation of these principles will in no way diminish or violate the essential message of our Lord Jesus Christ. We therefore ask the Council to confirm the non-accentuation of these elements.'

Legnano closed the document. Clasped hands resting on the desk, he leaned forward, eyeing the now mute cardinals one by one, their faces frozen in incredulity. He pushed his glasses atop his nose again, speaking in a quiet but firm voice.

'Now you understand why I've convened you.'

Signorelli spoke. 'This is completely outrageous. This borders on . . . on heresy. Yes, I'll say it, heresy. He'll never get the Council's approval. He'll—'

'Cardinal, may I remind you that he doesn't need the Council's approval. He is the ultimate authority. He is God's interpreter,' said Legnano.

'Doesn't he want to ensure legitimacy?' said Sforza.

'He'll get it by the fact the Council has been convened. That's all he needs to make it legitimate,' answered Legnano.

There was a moment of silence as the cardinals stared at each other. Legnano turned to Gonzales, the newcomer, whose face seemed to irradiate a permanent, beatific grin. 'Monsignor Gonzales, you haven't spoken yet. What do you think of this?'

'I, I would have to analyze the texts more closely,' said Gonzales, seemingly caught by surprise. 'We all know that the Church is in the need of reforms, yes?' He smiled at the cardinals, seeking reassurance. 'Although some of these seem quite drastic, I must admit. On the other hand as you pointed out, Cardinal Legnano, His Holiness is God's interpreter.'

Following the meeting of the Curia the previous day, rumors were flying within the Vatican that the agenda of an upcoming ecumenical council would shake the very foundations of the Catholic Church. Legnano summoned the cardinals to his office, in an attempt to defuse the looming crisis.

Cardinal Jean Fouquet spoke. 'Your Eminences, this is heresy, I say, outright heresy. I cannot send this agenda to the archbishops. They'll revolt and with good reason. Women priests? Abolition of the Holy Credo? These attack the very core of our beliefs. These alone are sufficient grounds for deposing him.'

'What are you saying?' said Sforza, his eyes twinkling with astonishment.

'I'm saying we depose Clement XXI as of unsound mind,' said Fouquet, his tone peremptory.

The cardinals looked at Fouquet in disbelief. 'You cannot be serious,' said Signorelli.

'I'm dead serious, Cardinal,' continued Fouquet, glaring down at the expansive Signorelli. 'Pope Clement's kidnapping has obviously affected his judgment to the point of insanity. Heresy and insanity. Both are grounds for deposition under Canon law,' said Fouquet.

'Monsignor,' said Sforza. 'Even if we were to agree to this, this extraordinary procedure, from what I remember in my seminary days, it is long and sometimes inconclusive. Also, I remind you that Pope Benedict IX held the papacy three times, even if deposed.'

'Your Eminences, we don't have the luxury to wait,' said Fouquet. 'Once he issues the writs of convocation for the Council, we cannot start the deposition procedure. I say we act now.'

'Your Eminences, please, a bit of calm,' said Legnano. 'Before we even think of such a move, consider its effect on the Church. The deposition proceedings will wreak absolute havoc. There will be a fight for power. It will turn into an ugly legal battle before the courts of the Vatican. Do we really want this? Don't forget once the procedure is started, it can't be stopped. Who knows what this may lead to? Another schism? Do we want to trigger another Avignon? Come now, surely we don't have to go that far.'

'Why not let the ecumenical council judge him?' said the cherubic Signorelli. 'That way, he will see the error of his ways or if he persists, we'll have the solid support of the Church to depose him.'

Gonzales, who had remained markedly silent, spoke. 'Monsignori, let me be the devil's advocate for a brief moment.'

'Of course,' said Sforza.

'What if the Council accepts the Pope's proposed changes?'

The cardinals didn't have long to think of a response, before Cardinal Legnano spoke again. 'Your Eminences, we have another urgent problem to discuss.'

The cardinals looked at Legnano, then at each other, perplexed.

Legnano took a piece of paper from underneath his agenda and waved it at the cardinals. 'I received this, earlier this morning. It's from de Ségur. It's about the diary.'

Upon receiving Legnano's pressing call about the letter, Dulac had caught the mid-morning flight to Rome and taken a taxi to the Vatican. He entered Legnano's office.

'Thank you for coming on such short notice, inspector,' said Legnano, clasping Dulac's hand warmly.

'De Ségur rings my bell every time, Your Eminence.'

'I'm not sure what you mean.'

'Gets my attention, if you prefer.'

'By the way, inspector, I've heard that you've been suspended. Is that information correct?' Legnano asked, a look of sympathy on his rugged face.

'Good news travels fast.'

'Actually, this might be better . . .'

'I'm not sure I follow.'

'Never mind, I'll explain later. Please, inspector.' Legnano showed him to the sofa in the center, and handed Dulac de Ségur's letter. 'We received this yesterday.'

Dulac sat down and read.

'To Cardinal Guiseppe Legnano, Secretary of State, the Vatican.

Your Eminence,

This letter constitutes an offer to sell to the Vatican the extracts of the document entitled 'My Diary', by Oberleuitnant Hans-Georg

Weber, third Army, 42nd division, more particularly chapters 11 to 15, covering the period in 1943 during which the Oberleuitnant was stationed in Naples. To the best of our knowledge, we possess the only version of the diary. We find it is becoming increasingly difficult to assure its confidentiality. You will undoubtedly agree that it would be safer in the Vatican's archives, which offer better protection against loss and/or eventual dissemination to the press. The price is €10 million, to be deposited by hot wire transfer, at a bank account we will disclose in due course. Upon receipt of the funds, the extracts of the diary will be deposited at a trustee of your choosing.

Your acceptance must be confirmed by the following announcement before the beginning of the Pope's Angelus tomorrow on Radio Vatican: 'Prata florescent quotidie magis.'

Time is of the essence. Hugues de Ségur.'

'The man doesn't let up,' said Dulac. 'If I remember my Latin, he's saying "the meadows will bloom, day by day."'

'Very good Mr Dulac,' Legnano said.

'Has His Holiness seen it?'

'There's no need to implicate and embarrass His Holiness any further. We've discussed it within the Curia, Mr Dulac, and concluded that even if we pay de Ségur, he'll make copies and continue his blackmail.'

'I see,' said Dulac, starting to feel ill at ease.

'Mr Dulac, I won't beat around the bush.' Legnano, his hands clasped on his lap, shifted slightly to face Dulac. 'The Vatican is facing an internal crisis of major proportions. We really didn't need this additional bit of aggravation. The Curia discussed the impact this diary would have on the papacy if made public and we decided this threat must be eliminated.'

Dulac sat in silence, his jaw agape. 'I, I think I misunderstood.'

'You heard correctly, Mr Dulac.'

'Why, why are you telling me this, your Eminence?'

'Because we think you can best execute the mandate.'

Dulac sat upright on the edge of the sofa, 'I'm, I'm sorry. I'm at a loss here. You want me to eliminate de Ségur?'

'I didn't say that, Mr Dulac. We want you to eliminate the threat.'

'Pretty thin distinction. Anyways, I've been suspended. I don't—'

'Actually it's all the better for us. You can give this, this mandate your complete attention. Consider it a private matter, Mr Dulac. Nothing to do with Interpol. You will be paid accordingly.' Legnano took back the letter from Dulac's quivering hands.

'Monsignor, just out of interest, what would be the terms of this . . . mandate?'

'Before we discuss the details, we wish to determine your level of commitment. Should you refuse, Mr Dulac, this conversation never occurred. Are we clear on that?'

'I'm still having trouble digesting all this, your Eminence.'

'Of course. But as the letter states, we don't have much time. Tell me, as a matter of professional interest, Mr Dulac, if you were to accept, I presume you would call on some . . . I believe you have some contacts?'

'I'm not sure what you mean by contacts.'

'I mean, in your capacity as Interpol agent, you may have come across persons that could—'

'None that come to mind, off hand. But I'm still curious. Why me, your Eminence?'

'Because we trust you, Mr Dulac. Because this file is highly sensitive. Because you are the only one, apart from ourselves and de Ségur, who knows about the diary. Besides we thought it would seem natural that you would be motivated to "close the file", so to speak.'

Dulac shifted uncomfortably in the sofa. 'Thanks for the vote of confidence, your Eminence, but you still haven't answered my question. How am I supposed to eliminate the threat without eliminating the person behind it?'

'I leave that entirely up to you, Mr Dulac. It's the result that counts.'

'If I were to even consider this, just the logistics for this kind of operation would be expensive. Very expensive.'

'Mr Dulac, I haven't made myself clear. Price is not a meaningful consideration.'

'And you want my answer yesterday.'

Legnano nodded.

CHAPTER 28

Dulac endured the bumpy flight back to Paris, resisting the temptation of the usual dose of Glenlivet, and instead invited Karen for dinner at Montet's. After a mundane meal, they skipped dessert, rushed to Karen's flat and replaced the dessert with a session of vigorous sex.

As Karen lay naked in bed beside him, perspiring and replete, Dulac could feel her heavy breathing warming his right shoulder. She moved up and kissed his neck softly.

'So you stick this beautiful neck out and lose your head if it doesn't work. Is that it?' she said.

'Metaphorically and physically.' He reached over to the night table and grabbed the package of Gitanes.

'So apart from the money, why would you even consider the Curia's mandate?'

Dulac sat up on the edge of the bed and lit a cigarette. 'That bastard de Ségur is long overdue for some prison time. When he got away last year with the French president's help, I swore to myself I was going to make that happen. Here is the perfect opportunity for me to keep that promise.'

'And if it works, Interpol gets the credit, just like when you rescued the Pope?'

Dulac took a long drag, 'Thanks. I really didn't need that comment.'

'I'm sorry. That was uncalled for. It's just that whatever you do, you can't seem to win.'

Dulac stood up and walked to the window. The evening's last rays of soft gold light shone on the leaves of the small oak trees below. After a moment he turned, watching her as she lay lounging in the residual warmth of his side of the bed. 'I'm still puzzled as to why Legnano chose me. Why not a professional firm?'

'Like the Mafia?' she said, her left elbow propped on a pillow.

'He doesn't have to go down that route. I'm sure there are other ways.' Dulac blew a puff of smoke onto the window pane. 'I must admit it would give me the greatest of pleasures to trump that prick Harris.'

'Careful. Aren't you letting a bit of vengeance cloud your judgment?'

'I've thought of that. Not really.'

'What if things go wrong? What about your career?'

'What career? Weren't you the one to say "time to think out of the box, Thierry?"'

'This isn't exactly what I had in mind.'

'When opportunity knocks, *Carpe diem*. Seize the day.'

'I suppose.'

'Besides, with the Vatican's deep pocket . . .' Thoughtful, Dulac started back towards the bed. 'Come to think of it, many years ago I knew the son of the Venezuelan Ambassador to Belize. A certain Juan Garcia. I wonder what happened to him.' Dulac donned his boxer shorts. He returned to the living room, opened his laptop, and typed in Interpol's people search databank. 'Code invalid,' read the computer screen. Damn. Harris again, that asshole. He called Gina, at forensics.

'Gina Marino.'

'Dulac. Listen Gina, I need a small favor.'

The following morning, Dulac discovered a brown envelope under his door as he entered his apartment. Good girl, that Gina. As Dulac went through the file, he could see that Juan Garcia's reputation had gone from dubious to bad. Descendant of a wealthy sugar cane Venezuelan family, he'd inherited the right business at the wrong time: worldwide antitrust law enforcement coupled with increasing union demands and the rising strength of the American sugar barons had made for decreased profit margins in his once protected segment of the industry. Juan had become a minor player, an untenable position for a man of his expensive appetite: one Ferrari 360, one Aston Martin Virage, one Donzi 35 R speedboat. A sailboat in Douarnenez. Christ, I'll bet he still has that old Dragon class sailboat. Memories of prior, happier times came flooding back. Dulac took out the photographs. They showed Garcia in various sexual positions with a well-endowed, middle-aged blonde. He looked at the back of the photographs: 'Cartel leader Vic Baldoni's wife Michèlle & Juan Garcia.'

The report went on, mentioning that many of the South American sugar barons had noticed the similarity between the harvesting, refining and distribution of sugar and that of cocaine. Although the allegations were still unproven, Garcia's flamboyant lifestyle seemed to give credence to the supposition. A recent investigation by the Venezuelan Department of Justice had fizzled out, for lack of live witnesses. Men and women whom Garcia came into contact with had the disturbing propensity of winding up missing, or dead.

Dulac knew that under normal circumstances, it would be impossible for anyone not in Garcia's immediate entourage to reach a man like Juan Garcia. However Dulac had a trump card, his father Paul. Ex-French ambassador to Venezuela, Paul Dulac knew Juan's father. A few calls later to the right people in the French and Venezuelan diplomatic corps, and Dulac had Juan Garcia's private telephone number.

'Is this Juan Garcia?' said Dulac.

'Who is speaking?'

Dulac immediately recognized the voice. 'Thierry Dulac, you might—'

'How did you get this number?'

'Through the Venezuelan embassy. You might remember that my father Paul and your father sailed together in France about twenty years ago? The Thalassa Cup?' Dulac waited for a reply.

'You have the wrong number.'

'Hold on a second. Just hold on. Surely you remember that day I couldn't let go the mainsheet and that we nearly rammed the breakwater off Douarnenez. I think the name of your father's boat was . . . Aphrodite, yes Aphrodite.'

Another pause. 'But of course I remember. Just checking.' The voice became friendlier. 'How are you? What have you been up to these past . . . Has it been twenty years already?' said Garcia in a curious mix of Oxford and Spanish accent.

'Something like that.'

'To what do I owe the pleasure?'

'I'm calling you because I have some business I'd like to discuss with you. An interesting opportunity, I think.'

'What kind of opportunity?'

'Sorry, it's rather confidential. Not the sort of thing for eager ears.'

'I understand. Where are you, my friend?'

'In Paris. And you?'

'I'm in Florence till tomorrow afternoon,' said Garcia.

'Would you have some free time for me? An hour will be plenty.'

'What is this about?'

'I'd rather tell you privately,' said Dulac.

'I see. We could have lunch at 12.30 at The Trattoria Stromboli. Do you know it?'

'In Piazza Della Signoria, I think.'

'That's right. What kind of business did you say you were in my friend?'

'See you then.'

CHAPTER 29

Florence, Piazza Della Signoria, 12.15 p.m., Thursday, 15 June

Sitting a bread roll's throw away from the imitation of the statue of David in the city plaza, Dulac recognized the heavyset man who in his prime had often been mistaken for Antonio Banderas. The Venezuelan crossed the Piazza Della Signoria and approached the small café and restaurant. Put on a bit of weight, have we Juan?

Dulac couldn't help notice two men with oversized necks and undersized heads walking not so discreetly behind Garcia. Drawing closer to Dulac's table, Garcia recognized the Frenchman and smiled. The bodyguards continued on as Garcia stopped and sat down.

'So what brings you to Florence?' Dulac said, trying to jumpstart the conversation.

'I'm picking up a drawing by Piero di Cosimo. I'm still awaiting the last of the authentication certificates. In this business, you can't be too careful. Too many crooks,' Juan said, leaning over towards Dulac in feigned confidence. 'So tell me my friend, what's this business you can't talk to me about over the phone?'

The waiter came to the table and hovered, pen and pad in hand. 'Double espresso,' said Garcia.

'Same,' said Dulac.

Dulac waited for the waiter to leave before answering.

'Well, it goes like this. A certain party wishes to have abducted an important fugitive from French justice.'

Garcia's eyes narrowed into slits. 'So?'

'I thought you might—'

'Might what? I'm in the sugar business.'

'I don't have time for games, Juan.'

Garcia's face hardened. 'I don't like your tone of voice, my friend. What do you mean "games"?'

'I mean I did my homework. Interpol has a half meter long file on your personal protection alone. Don't get me wrong, Juan. I'm not here to—'

'Santa Maria! So you're with Interpol?' Garcia looked nervously at Dulac, then turned and discreetly shot a quick glance at his bodyguards sitting behind him.

'Let's just say I have access to certain privileged information.'

'Every rich man in Venezuela is a kidnap target. Protection is not an option.'

'Precisely. And I'm sure you've hired the best.'

'I'm still alive.' Juan smiled, showing two front teeth separated by a singularly wide gap.

Dulac tried to be reassuring, 'Juan, I swear this has nothing to do with you. I want some names, that's all.'

'Sure. Names. Of course. Why didn't I think of it? Russian, Italian or Jewish mafia? Which do you want?'

'Not funny.'

'Interpol! Who would have thought? Anyway this target of yours, I presume your party can't get him out the legal way because of the lack of an extradition treaty?'

'Dead-on.'

'And who is this French fugitive of justice?'

'Let's just say he's wanted in at least two jurisdictions for extortion, kidnapping and murder.'

'Sounds like pretty big game.'

'The biggest, and out of season.'

'Let me get this straight, Dulac. If I understand correctly, you, an Interpol agent, are asking me to furnish you with, with mercenaries?' Garcia smiled derisively.

'Absolutely not.'

Garcia blew a long whistle through his gapped teeth then laughed. 'I didn't come here to get insulted.'

'Relax, relax, my friend.' Garcia put up a hand in protest. 'Don't be offended. Like Dylan said: "Times, they are a-changing".'

Garcia turned towards his men and gave them a short palm down signal of his right hand. Facing Dulac again, he continued. 'Even if I had such contacts, it would be very, very expensive, my friend.'

'Money is no object. Including your finder's fee.'

'I was getting to that. But tell me, my friend, why isn't Interpol taking care of this? Or for that matter, the French Sureté? They've done some extra-curricular work like this before.'

'It's a complicated story, but my party chooses not to use the official routes.'

'I know someone at Mossad.'

'Out of the question.'

Garcia looked suspiciously at Dulac. 'This is not some religious, Islamic thing, is it?'

'Not exactly.'

'Not exactly?'

'I can only tell you that my principal's motives are personal, not religious.'

'The last thing I need is a fatwa on my head.'

'No chance.'

Garcia leaned back in his chair and stretched his arms over his head. 'This game you're playing is very dangerous, my friend. I don't want to think of what happens if you miss.'

Before leaving, Garcia had given Dulac a name: Eric Roquebrun. 'He's good, but he's a handful to control,' warned Garcia.

'Tell me more.'

'He's a great tactician, but in the heat of battle, he'll do everything to get the job done.'

'Isn't that good?'

'He's got some collateral damage to his credit.'

'Don't you have someone else?'

'Sure, but he's temporarily unavailable.'

'How temporary?'

'Could be a while. Ahmed is doing life in Beirut on three charges of rape and four counts of murder.'

Back in his apartment, Dulac phoned Gina.

'Again? But Mr Dulac, you're still suspended. I can't access . . . If they find out I gave you access—'

'Gina, they need you more than they need me.'

'I don't know, I . . .'

It had cost Dulac a massage and pedicure at Lyon's upscale body shop, Chez Chloe, to get Gina to do another summary Interpol database search.

'Eric Roquebrun, 46 years old, ex CRS, ex "Force Tactique", fired for sexual harassment of a 26-year-old woman recruit and the brutalizing of two members of his unit. Last known address: Casier Postal 4800, Marseilles. Box closed for non-payment on renewal. Current whereabouts and employment unknown.'

Just the kind of man you'd want your sister to marry, Dulac thought.

CHAPTER 30

Paris, Restaurant Chez Aurélie, 12.40 p.m.

After his futile search for Roquebrun's whereabouts, Dulac phoned Garcia and convinced him to have Roquebrun contact him. Roquebrun agreed to meet Dulac at Chez Aurélie, one of the seizième arrondissement's more discreet and intimate cafés. As he sipped his glass of chilled rosé, Dulac kept reminding himself that behind the mercenary's mustachioed smile, sad droopy eyelids and wire-framed spectacles, resided not a benign university professor about to admonish his student, but a battle-hardened killer out for the pleasure of the hunt and the spilling of human blood.

'You must understand that de Ségur is to stand trial in France. He's no good to me dead, otherwise the deal is off. Is that clear?' Dulac said.

'If he's hiding out in Belize, he's got a lot of locals on his payroll. There's bound to be collateral damage,' said Roquebrun.

'That's your problem. Alive or no deal.'

Roquebrun twisted one of the ends of his mustache for a moment, as if to think more clearly. 'I can manage that. Any satellite photos?'

'Yes. We've identified four buildings, smack in the middle of the Mayan Mountain Range: one main and three smaller houses, the whole thing surrounded by a barbed-wire fence, probably electrified. He's got a generator plant supplying the power. He has a helicopter at the north-east end of the compound.'

'He lives well.'

'That's a matter of perspective. Self-imprisonment has never held any great appeal to me.'

'He's undoubtedly bought a lot of tolerance from public officials and a lot of protection.' Roquebrun looked squarely at Dulac. 'For this operation to be successful, Mr Dulac, we need two things: the non-interference of the Belizean police and the element of surprise.'

Dulac bit into the cold and overcooked bavette steak. He put down his knife and fork and summoned the waiter. 'Garcon, you dare call this steak? Take this, this rhinoceros hide back and get me something edible, a salmon filet or something. Surely you can't overcook that?'

'Yes sir, I mean no sir,' said the contrite waiter.

Dulac turned to Roquebrun. 'What about men? You have your, your—'

'Mercenaries, Mr Dulac, mercenaries. That's what we are. I need two days' notice to round up my team. They're enjoying a bit of R and R, after we hammered the piss out of those Colombian buggers.'

'Anything to do with the Ines Botalla rescue?'

Roquebrun looked around warily at the rest of the café's patrons. 'Officially, no. Unofficially, yes,' he whispered, taking Dulac into his confidence.

'I'm impressed.'

'That cost the French government $20 million US, including the payments to the Colombian government. Your clients' pockets better be deep.'

'How deep?'

Roquebrun paused, stared at Dulac, and twisted the other end of his mustache. 'We're talking say, $22 million US here.'

'Rather steep.'

'Inflation, you know.'

'I'll need confirmation from my principal. Shall we say a couple of million down payment, and the rest when you deliver de Ségur to the French police?'

Roquebrun burst into the hard laughter of the humorless man. 'You've got to be joking. In this kind of business, it's 50 per cent down, or no deal. We've got a lot of up-front expenses: reconnaissance work, coordination and field equipment, payments to facilitators.'

'$11 million is a lot of expenses.'

'It's my ass that will be fired at, Mr Dulac. Not yours. Take it or leave it.'

'I'll see what I can do.' Dulac got up to leave.

'À bientôt,' said the mercenary, giving Dulac a surprisingly soft, almost effeminate handshake. 'Call me.' He handed Dulac a small piece of folded paper.

Dulac walked away quickly and soon melted into the hectic flow of Parisian pedestrians.

Back at his apartment, Dulac phoned Legnano.

'Timely that you called, Mr Dulac. We have just received payment instructions from de Ségur. Payment is due in three hours, but that is not your problem. You calling me means that you have found someone, Mr Dulac? That you accept?'

'Yes.' I must be insane, Dulac thought. 'A certain Eric Roquebrun.'

'And you have checked him out, so to speak?'

'He's been referred by an acquaintance. We don't have time to—'

'Of course. I understand.'

'And what is his . . . fee?'

'$22 million US. $11 million now and the rest upon delivery of the goods.'

'What? That's unacceptable. We must pay de Ségur and now this? And without any guarantees?'

'Monsignor, believe me. These people don't negotiate. Or give any guarantees.'

‘But what proof do we have that he can deliver?’

‘You mean other than his sordid reputation?’

‘I see.’ Legnano paused for a moment.

‘And how exactly will this Roquefort—’

‘Roquebrun, your Eminence.’

‘—Roquebrun eliminate the threat?’

‘The plan is he and his men will capture and abduct de Ségur and bring him to France. When de Ségur is in custody, the Vatican can negotiate with the French authorities for a lesser sentence in exchange for his keeping quiet. You’ll have the cards, this time, your Eminence.’

‘We, Mr Dulac, we are to negotiate?’

‘I suspect you have a little more clout with the French Minister of Justice than I do.’

‘That’s a high price for only part of the bargain. We want the threat eliminated, Mr Dulac, not postponed.’

‘Your Eminence, I may be suspended, but I’m still an officer of the law. That’s the best I can offer.’

There was a pause, and Dulac almost hoped Legnano would refuse. ‘I’ll get back to you, Mr Dulac.’

CHAPTER 31

The Vatican, 3 p.m., 17 June

'His Holiness will see you now,' said the assistant secretary to Cardinal Gonzales.

Gonzales entered the papal library and walked to the far end of the room.

'My dear Gonzales, you are looking well. How are you?' he said as he rose to greet the cardinal.

'I'm getting acclimatized to the rarefied atmosphere of the inner Curia.'

'I warned you: acceptance takes time. How did the transfer from Cardinal Brentano go?'

'I, well, there are still many files that I'm not—'

'It's not going smoothly?'

'I would have liked more help. He says he's too busy with his new functions.'

'I'll have a word with him. And the other Curia members?'

'Just courteous.'

'Normal. They don't know you. How was their reaction to my agenda?'

'Not good. They're talking about deposing you, on grounds of heresy and insanity,' said Gonzales.

There was a moment of silence. 'So rumor has it. I'm not entirely surprised. Who exactly?'

'Sforza and Fouquet,' said Gonzales.

'From Fouquet, to be expected. Sforza is disappointing. I thought he would support at least some of the changes. What were the others' reactions?'

'Legnano was neutral. And Signorelli would let you proceed and have the ecumenical council overrule you. He thinks that you'll have to bend to its wishes, or risk being deposed.'

'Ah, Legnano. He's smart. He'll wait to see which way the wind blows before taking sides.' He paused for a moment, seemingly lost in thought. 'So they want to depose me? What small minds surround us, Gonzales. But I have a surprise for them.'

'A surprise?'

'Monsignor, when one embarks on such a bold venture, one needs the help of destiny. But you see, sometimes even destiny needs a little push, a little nudge.' He blinked a knowing eye towards the Colombian. 'Let's see what we can do to help it.'

Gonzales continued. 'There's another matter.'

'Yes?'

'With the Curia's approval, Legnano has given a mandate to inspector Dulac to have de Ségur captured and brought to justice. Legnano wants to eliminate the threat permanently.'

Fouquet, his brown hair disheveled, his complexion flushed with anger, swept into Legnano's office. 'I won't send them. Not with what we know.'

'You haven't sent them yet? Monsignor, you must send out the writs of convocation as instructed. You have no choice,' said Legnano.

'But if we depose him . . .'

'You can't hold up the convocation waiting for the results of any removal procedure. Canon law is clear. If you refuse to send them, I must act in your place.'

'I see,' said Fouquet. 'Then will you begin the procedure to depose?'

'You know better than to ask that, Cardinal. I am still the Secretary of State. I am, until otherwise legally and properly advised, the executor of his wishes. I am bound.'

'I interpret that as a negative.'

'This discussion is closed, your Eminence,' said Legnano. He was about to escort Fouquet to the door when the phone on his desk rang. He hesitated.

'I'll see my way out,' said Fouquet.

'Yes, your Holiness, I'll come immediately,' said Legnano. As he made his way to the papal library, Legnano felt the wheels of destiny starting to move and gather speed. The incline was getting steeper and the momentum, if not checked, would be soon unstoppable. The opposing camps were starting to form. The division he had predicted was already there, could already be felt. The conservatives and the progressives were drawing clear battle lines, something they had, in recent times, never been forced to do. An ominous, open conflict within the Church seemed inevitable. If anyone in the Vatican understood the Church, with all of its faults and human frailties, it was he. His beloved Church was under attack, and if necessary, he would defend it to the death. Upon becoming a cardinal, a Prince of the Church, he had vowed to do so.

'You wish to see me, your Holiness?' said the cardinal, as he entered the papal library and walked towards the prelate, sitting at his desk. Legnano stared for a moment at Perugino's painting of the Resurrection of Christ looming — perhaps prophetically — overhead.

'Yes, Legnano. Please be seated.'

Legnano pulled up one of the spindly-legged uncomfortable chairs.

'I've heard some rumblings about a movement to depose me. You are aware of this, Cardinal?'

'Your Holiness, I . . . Yes, I am aware that . . .' Legnano fidgeted nervously with his rosary.

'There is no need to be evasive Legnano. I know Sforza's and Fouquet's position.'

I'm sure you do. Gonzales must have run into your office right after the meeting, thought Legnano. 'Your Holiness, I must say I did find the agenda, how should I say—'

'Heretical?'

'No, I wouldn't go that far. But it is quite drastic. Some would even say, revolutionary.'

'Drastic times require drastic measures, Legnano. These changes are long overdue.'

For a man under personal attack, with the threat of deposition hanging over his head, the Pope seemed remarkably calm, thought Legnano.

'Actually, I've called you on another issue. Apparently, you've given a mandate to someone concerning the diary?'

Legnano fumbled for words, 'Ah, you see your Holiness, I—'

'Shouldn't I have been consulted first on this delicate matter?'

Legnano felt his face reddening. 'We, we didn't want to implicate you.'

'I see. And what exactly is the nature of this mandate, Eminence?'

'I'm about to give the mandate to Inspector Dulac, your Holiness. A mandate to remove de Ségur. Unless we eliminate the threat, he will continue to blackmail us forever. We have no other choice.'

'So our role in this is precisely what?'

'We are providing additional financial support to Interpol's agent, Dulac.' Not really a lie, Legnano told himself, just looking at the truth from a slightly different perspective. 'He in turn will organize de Ségur's capture. Since Interpol has a warrant for his arrest, we can always argue that it's Interpol's exclusive responsibility.'

'Sounds extremely risky, Cardinal. What if this goes wrong and someone traces the mandate back to you?'

'Impossible, your Holiness. We've taken every precaution against that possibility.'

'Tread very carefully with this, Legnano.'

CHAPTER 32

Paris, late afternoon, 17 June

Dulac awaited the fateful phone call from the Vatican as he sat drinking the last of his Glenlivet, listening to Maurizio Pollini's rendition of Chopin's Prelude No. 14 in E flat minor. The phone rang.

'We accept, Mr Dulac,' said Legnano, his voice barely audible over the loud, dizzying arpeggios.

'Just a second, I'll lower the volume. There, that's better. So you're going ahead?'

'We have no choice.'

'So I can call Roque—?'

'No details, Mr Dulac. Just get the job done. Oh, and by the way, you will receive one million dollars for your troubles, Mr Dulac, upon delivery of the goods. It will be credited to a trust account here at the Vatican bank. If you agree, of course.'

Dulac sat in stunned disbelief. 'Mr Dulac?'

'Yes?'

'Is that acceptable?'

Dulac hesitated, his mind reeling at the offer, yet fighting within the innermost depths of his professional conscience to hold onto the remnants of his fundamental values.

After a moment, he said, 'Your Eminence, your offer is most generous, but I cannot accept it. I'm still an Interpol agent, an officer of the law. By taking the money I'd be putting a definite end to my career.'

'I see,' said the cardinal, resignation in his voice.

'I am not prepared to do that.'

'I understand, Mr Dulac. Most commendable. Does that mean you refuse the mandate?'

'Monsignor, I still want to see de Ségur behind bars.'

'Good.'

The line went dead.

Dulac flipped his phone shut and turned off the CD player. I must be absolutely insane. I've just committed the crime of conspiracy to kidnap, even if this doesn't get off the ground. With a bloody cardinal no less. And to top it off, I've just refused more money than I will ever see for the rest of my life!

Dulac went to the bar, poured himself another scotch then returned to the sofa and sat down. After a long swig, he deposited the glass on the small table beside the sofa. On the opposite wall, his mother, her reproachful stern stare frozen in a mix of pastel and charcoal, stared back at him as if to admonish him. Well, Mother, now what should I do? Suddenly a gust of wind swooshed through the open window and sent the paper score off the Steinway's music support fluttering to the floor. He rose, put the Polonaise piece back onto the support, went to the window and closed it. Below in the courtyard, children were scurrying about, gathering their toys before the impending storm. Dulac went back to the sofa, sat down and took another gulp. He felt in every bone of his body the fatefulness of his next decision.

Then the images of de Ségur's victims flew briefly before his eyes: Romer, the rosy-complexioned, taciturn Swiss Guard; Aguar.

He put down his glass on the table, picked up the phone and dialed Roquebrun's number. 'Dulac. My principal agrees. When can we discuss planning?'

'I'll meet you at 7 p.m. in the lobby of the Hotel Durocher. I'll give you the deposit instructions.'

Dulac hung up, put a hand to his chest and felt palpitations through his shirt.

An hour later, the Glenlivet having mellowed his mood, or numbed his brain, he didn't care to know which, Dulac hailed a cab and rode through the evening smog to the hotel.

'I reserved a suite, so we can spread out,' said Roquebrun in the lobby, as he led Dulac towards the elevators.

'Spread out?'

'I knew your client would accept. I have a map of the area, plus a preliminary report on de Ségur's habits, ins and outs, location of guards, etc.'

'You don't waste time.'

They took the elevator and Dulac felt his palpitations start again. This seemed wrong, definitely wrong. His instincts were telling him to turn and run. He didn't listen to them and followed the mercenary down the corridor into the room. Roquebrun took off his worn, brown leather jacket and threw it onto the sofa. He put on his glasses, opened an attaché case and unfolded a map on the table.

'It's a 1:32,0000 topographical map of the Mayan Mountain Range in Belize. De Ségur is probably near here,' Roquebrun said, pointing to a mountain. 'It corresponds to the satellite latitude-longitude you gave me. I know that area. Mount Margaret is the most remote, difficult part of the jungle to access.' He pointed to a section of the map. 'If you look closely, there is a small road there. It's the only way in.'

'What's your plan?' said Dulac, feeling inextricably drawn in.

'We know that they allow a fuel truck in past the guard house, for the bimonthly delivery of diesel fuel. They're due for a delivery in two days.'

'I think I know where you're going with this.'

'We'll have to hijack the truck. Once we secure the target, we'll pick him up with a rented chopper. You'll be there. You'll be in the helicopter that picks us up.

'Me, pick you up? In a helicopter? No way. I've had just about enough of helicopters, thank you very much.'

'That's the deal. You're my safety net. I don't want to be shot at by the Belizean army once we secure de Ségur and we're flying him out of Belize.'

'So you're asking me to secure the Belizean government's support?'

'Only their non-interference.'

'But I have no contacts with the Belizeans.'

'Actually you do.'

Dulac looked quizzically at Roquebrun.

'Juan Garcia. Juan is enjoying some snorkeling there as we speak.'

'I see,' said Dulac.

'So. Do we have a deal, Mr Dulac?'

Dulac felt his unease and distaste about contacting Garcia mounting. 'Well, in for a penny . . .'

'Good. I'll notify Garcia. Oh, and before you go see the government officials, get yourself some kind of cover. De Ségur probably has his men watching all over the place.'

'Cover?'

'You're on vacation. Don't you have a girlfriend who wants to do some snorkeling? It's the best in the world after Sharm-El-Sheikh.'

'I have good news and not-so-good news,' said Dulac over the phone to Karen.

'I'll bite,' she said.

'Remember I offered to take you on a trip to Costa Rica?'

'Thierry, that was two weeks ago. You were dead drunk. I won't hold you to it. I'm surprised you even remembered.'

'First the good. I have two tickets to Belize, instead of Costa Rica. Is that OK?'

'Beggars can't be choosers. And the not-so-good?'

'We leave tomorrow.'

The Airbus 360 landed smoothly and Dulac felt the loosening of his grip on the arm rest of the business class seat. He mopped the perspiration off his brow with the airline's perfumed face cloth he'd held, up till now, tightly clutched in his fist. Beside him Karen, relaxed, returned the travel brochure to the seat-back in front of her.

'Ladies and gentlemen, welcome to Belize,' said the Air France, long-legged stewardess. 'We apologize for the delay. Please have your passport ready before proceeding to clear Customs at the main terminal.'

'We'll be picked up by Juan Garcia,' said Dulac, turning to Karen.

'The same guy you went to see in Florence?'

'Yes. His father is the Venezuelan ambassador to Belize. Juan spends a fair bit of time snorkeling here, that is when he's not racing his Dragon in Douarnenez or getting his adrenaline fix in one of his Ferraris,' said Dulac, as he rose and felt the sharp tingle in his numb legs.

'Sounds promising.' Karen smiled warmly, gently squeezing Dulac's arm, her face aglow with anticipation.

As Dulac and Karen started towards the entrance of the airport, Dulac noticed a black limo to his left, a few dozen yards way. Suddenly a chauffeur wearing a tan-colored suit erupted from the limo's front door and intercepted them.

'Mr Dulac?'

'Yes?'

'Please come this way. Let me put the luggage inside the car.'

'But we haven't passed Customs,' said Karen.

'That won't be necessary. Mr Garcia's diplomatic immunity extends to members of his family and their guests.'

As the chauffeur, Karen and Dulac approached the limo, the rear door opened and a sun-glassed man in a pink open shirt and beige slacks stepped out.

'Thierry my friend, how was your trip?' said Garcia, with a smile as wide as the Rio Orinoco.

'Terrible, thank you. Juan Garcia, meet Karen Dawson.'

'Delighted, Madame. Please.' As Garcia bowed slightly, he gave her a lecherous smile and ushered them into the limo's backseat.

The threesome exchanged banalities on the weather, Belizean beaches and the tribulations of flying, while the Mercedes glided silently along the sparsely travelled road through the sub-tropical countryside, the turquoise ocean to the right, the jungle's dense green to the left. Fifteen minutes later, the imitation ante-bellum, gray stucco columns of the Hotel Mirador's presumptuous facade surged into view.

After check-in, Garcia led them through the lobby into the adjacent, pink walled lounge. 'Did you receive my email?' asked Dulac, as they settled into the brown wicker chairs.

Garcia waived the waiter over. Turning to Dulac, 'I've looked into it. It will be difficult. The people I'm thinking of are expensive.'

'My client understands.'

The waiter, a white-haired man in his seventies, wearing a worn black suit and a morose scowl, ambled over. 'Yes?'

'Miss Dawson?' said Garcia.

'Perrier, no ice.'

'Thierry, my friend?'

'Scotch on the rocks.'

'And I'll have a Campari soda,' said Garcia. The waiter shuffled away towards the bar.

Turning to Dulac, Garcia said, 'If you insist, I can arrange a meeting.'

'I do. But I'm a bit worried,' said Dulac, leaning towards Garcia.

'What about?'

'How can I be sure they won't double-cross me and warn him?' Dulac could feel Karen's increasing discomfort, as he continued to ignore her and concentrated on Garcia.

'Trust me. They won't,' Garcia said.

'Why not?'

'Because the ones I'm thinking of work for my father.'

'Then do it.' Dulac could hardly believe the sound of his own voice, and that he was getting in so deep, so quickly.

'Not so fast. Remember, we are in Belize. You'll have to be patient. Don't look for the wind. The wind will come to you, as we say in the sailboat racing game,' said Garcia.

'I have until tomorrow,' said Dulac.

Karen leaned forward and glared at Dulac. 'Hey, am I supposed to just disappear, or do you mind telling me what this is all about?'

Garcia looked at Dulac in unease.

'No, I didn't brief her,' replied Dulac, timidly returning Karen's angry stare.

'Brief me? Brief me about what? This is a vacation, isn't it?' Karen bent forward again, eyes ablaze. 'Well?'

'Sort of,' said Dulac meekly.

'Sort of? This takes the goddamn cake.'

'Calm down, will you.' Dulac looked around as guests at other tables started to stare. 'Of course it's a vacation. Just a little side business, that's all.'

'I'm sorry, Ms Dawson I didn't mean to ruin your—' said Garcia.

'Mr Garcia, you're not ruining anything. He's doing the ruining all by himself,' she said, pointing an angry finger at Dulac. 'I've obviously been led down the garden path, thinking I could spend a relaxing vacation with your friend here.'

'I, ah, I really don't know what to say,' said Garcia, fumbling with his napkin and wiping the perspiration from his brow.

'I'm waiting,' Karen said, her stare still locked onto Dulac, her arms crossed over her pale-blue blouse.

'Groundwork. Call it preliminary groundwork,' said Dulac.

Karen rose abruptly from her chair. 'Do all the groundwork you want. I'm going snorkeling.' She rushed towards the exit.

'I'm terribly sorry. I thought you had told her,' said Garcia.

'About it all being a front? No.'

'Lots of character,' said Garcia. 'You're a lucky man.'

An afternoon in the warm, cobalt waters off the Belize Barrier Reef and swimming amidst schools of blue tang, yellow parrotfish, angelfish, lazy groupers, and large loggerhead turtles had managed to dull the edge off Karen's wrath. After Dulac's purchase of two bottles of Veuve Clicquot, the most expensive Hermes scarf in all of Belize City and a scorching night of reconciliatory sex, Karen had absolved Dulac of his sins of omission. The following morning, Dulac's meeting with the Belizean government officials had been cordial, expensive, but fruitful: the promise of a $5.2 million US dollars anonymous donation to the Belizean Horticultural Development Corporation had secured their non-interference in Dulac's plans to abduct de Ségur from Belizean soil. His mission accomplished, Dulac had had to apologize to Karen, yet again. He had to return to Paris on urgent business. 'Suit yourself. I'm staying here,' had been her reply to his query as to what her plans were. He'd taken the afternoon flight back to Paris.

The next morning Dulac, tired and jet lagged, was finishing the last of his bowl of café au lait and croissant and about to call Roquebrun when the France 2 announcer attracted his attention on TV:

'There's been another leak at the Vatican. We have been told that Pope Clement XXI is about to make history. His Holiness has convened an ecumenical council to make major changes in dogma. According to our well-informed source, the changes would allow women access to the priesthood. Also, in an effort to streamline the Church's heavy bureaucracy and antiquated structure, the Holy See plans to abolish the function of Archbishop, and at a later date that of cardinal. We tried to interview the Camerlengo, Cardinal Fouquet, who won't officially confirm or deny.'

Really? Dulac thought. Dulac always preferred the written word to the sensational, truncated news on TV. He turned off the monitor, dressed quickly, walked to the newsstand on the corner of the street, and was soon standing in a tumultuous line-up, people jostling about for the few remaining copies of *Le Monde*.

'Sorry, no more,' said the harassed looking vendor to the clients, as Dulac saw a young boy buy the last copy.

Dulac approached the lad. 'I'll give you five Euros.'

'Ten.'

'Thief. Here.'

Dulac grabbed the newspaper, walked briskly home and as he hurried up the stairs to his flat, he tripped, just managing to hang on to the railing before falling. Good God, he thought. Continuing to read below the bold headlines, he felt a strange mixture of curiosity, exhilaration, and fear.

CHAPTER 33

The Vatican, 8.30 a.m., 20 June

'It's me, Cardinal,' said Sforza, anger in his voice as he knocked on Fouquet's office door. The door opened and Sforza rushed in, newspaper in hand, shaking it at Fouquet. 'Have you read this?'

'What could I do?' said Fouquet. 'I couldn't deny it, could I?'

'A bit more vagueness wouldn't have hurt.'

'I reacted as best I could.'

'The Pope planted this. He leaked the information to the press. Now the truth comes out. He plans to eliminate cardinals as well,' said Sforza, still shaking the newspaper at Fouquet. 'He's trying to pre-empt any deposition procedure on our part. This is a declaration of war. War to the finish.'

'What do you have in mind?' said Fouquet.

'First we have to find out who our allies are. Who we can count on. We must draw up a list of all the conservative archbishops, cardinals, bishops, everybody. We must call them before it's too late.'

'I agree.'

'I won't allow him to take the Church down the path of heresy,' said Sforza. 'Catholic dogma is not to be determined by a popularity contest.'

'What can I do?'

'You can gather the complete Canon law legislation and jurisprudence on the procedure to depose the Pope. There's no time to waste.'

The Vatican, later the same day

The Vatican's telephone lines were swamped. Calls were flooding in from everywhere. Calls of congratulations, calls of support, threats and expressions of joy, anger, disbelief and admonition: atheists, agnostics, priests, bishops, archbishops from Uruguay to Greenland, all wanted to be heard.

The following morning, fueled by the news of the upcoming reforms, St. Peter's Square was filled to capacity, as word spread that the Pope would make a loggia appearance. Situated over the main doors of the Basilica and overseeing the Square, the loggia — or balcony — was reserved for the Pope's special announcements, such as the beatification of a recent candidate for sainthood, or the official papal reaction to a world event.

At 10.30 a.m., Cardinal Legnano, standing next to the French doors which gave access to the balcony, pushed aside the drapes, and peered discreetly outside. He looked at his watch. At that moment, Gonzales rushed in. 'Sorry your Holiness, your Eminence. I was delayed.'

'Never mind, Cardinal. Where are the others?' said Legnano.

'They should be joining us any minute,' said Gonzales.

Through the space of the slightly ajar doors, Legnano could hear the dull murmur of the crowd's anxiousness and impatience.

'We can't wait much longer, your Holiness,' said Legnano, looking out the window.

'You're right, Cardinal. The people have waited long enough.'

Legnano opened the large, glass paneled doors, and the three most influential men of the Catholic world walked outside onto the balcony. At the sight of the prelates, suddenly the crowd broke into a thunderous cheer, rising into a crescendo of joy. 'Viva il Papa. Vi-va, Vi-va, Vi-va!'

The words became a rhythmic incantation of 100,000 voices chanting in unison.

'You have certainly won their hearts, your Holiness,' said Legnano as he responded to the cheering crowd by waving discreetly.

At the western extremity of the Square, a scuffle had broken out between a handful of dissenters and some of the faithful. Members of the Vigilanza, the Vatican's security forces, were already intervening.

'You can't please all of them, your Holiness,' said Gonzales.

'I know. Not even all of the Curia.' He threw a critical glance at Legnano.

Directly below, fervent followers waved hastily-made placards bearing *Finalmente*, and *Papa te amo*, in bold, handwritten letters.

'It's time you joined them, your Holiness,' said Gonzales. 'I've had the popemobile prepared.'

'Yes, I should,' he said, waving to the crowd.

Gonzales walked to the entrance of the papal chamber and talked briefly to one of the Swiss Guards standing in the doorway.

Moments later, the threesome walked downstairs to the entrance of the Basilica. As the popemobile pulled up and stopped in front of it, Gonzales signaled the driver over.

'Your Holiness, your Eminences,' said the driver as he bowed. 'Your Holiness wishes to have the top up, or down?'

'Down. I want to shake hands with members of my flock.'

Moments later, the white customized Mercedes started its slow tour of St Peter's square, to the tumultuous applause of the crowd. Cries of joy erupted from well-wishers, who would rush out, sometimes briefly clutching his offered hand, sometimes prostrating themselves in front of the car. 'God bless His Holiness. We support you. We love you.' The crowd would not let the popemobile return to the steps of the Basilica, so the driver started another slow tour of St Peter's Square, stopping now and then before overenthusiastic worshippers standing in front of the Mercedes and blowing kisses. The crowd chanted louder still: '*Viva il Papa. Vi-va. Vi-va.*'

After the triumphant tour, the popemobile slowed and came to a stop at the entrance. Still the well-wishers grabbed his hands, touched his cassock, and prostrated themselves before him.

Cardinal Gonzales walked up, embraced him, and whispered in his ear. 'Congratulations. You have won. They won't dare depose you now.'

CHAPTER 34

Paris, 10.45 a.m., 22 June

As Dulac walked down the corridor and neared Roquebrun's suite in the Hotel Durocher, his palpitations started again. I don't believe it. I'm participating, no, instigating the very crime we're arresting de Ségur for. How the hell did I get into this? I should tell Roquebrun to take a hike, phone Legnano, and call the whole thing off.

The door at room 237 opened.

'Come in, Dulac, come in. Meet my assistant Fernando. Good news. I've just received the deposit money and the team is a go.'

'Great,' said Dulac apathetically, barely acknowledging the short heavy set man with a scar running down his left cheek.

'We've just chartered a helicopter in Belize. Fernando and I were going through the logistics of the oil truck hijacking. Care for a drink?'

You're bloody right I'd care for a drink. 'Scotch, no ice. On second thought, make it a double.'

Later that afternoon, Dulac returned to his flat and sat in front of the Steinway, trying to park his conscience in a faraway place. He attacked the fortissimo first chords of Chopin's Polonaise in A flat major and rushed the piece at double the normal tempo. Two mazurkas later, his hands cramped and useless, Dulac repaired to the kitchen to toss a frozen macaroni into the microwave. After drowning the tasteless pasta with a half-bottle of Julienas red, he retired to the study and went to his bookshelf. He glanced at his collection of assorted, often read books on French history, and something undefined, subconscious drew him to his copy of Zoe Ogdebourg's The Cathars and their beliefs: Massacre at Montségur. He couldn't remember the last time he'd read it, but some vague pulsation buried deep in his subconscious resurfaced, summoning him to read it anew.

A few hours, Gitanes and scotches later, his book having fallen beside his recliner chair, Dulac fell into a deep, sonorous sleep.

The following morning, Dulac's conscience had returned, somewhat mollified by the previous night's workings of his subconscious. He could justify the hiring of Roquebrun. After all, had anyone criticized the Mossad's methods when they'd abducted Eichmann from Brazil? On the contrary, they'd earned the world's admiration and praise. Surely, there would be no reproach if de Ségur was brought before the French courts. It was the 'if' that bothered him. A thousand things could go wrong, any one of which would turn his plan into a well-publicized fiasco: Interpol plot to illegally abduct French citizen backfires, would read the headlines of Le Monde. His fragile tenure at Interpol would come to an abrupt end.

But that could wait. Something else bothered him: the curious similarity between the papal announcements and what he had just finished reading the previous night about Catharism and its basic tenets. The coincidence started to foster an intuition, and the strange, bizarre insight hatched in his mind, took hold, and grew. He went to the bathroom and started to shave.

No, impossible, he thought. It couldn't be. Just a bit too wild, even for you. And the helicopter incident.

'Jesus,' he exclaimed. 'Of course!' He phoned Karen. 'Still mad at me?' he said.

'Who is this?'

'All right, so it was wrong to bring you to Belize.'

'Not at all. The rest of my vacation, if I can call it that, was fabulous. I—'

'Listen, you've seen the news about the Pope.'

'So? It's about time they let the other half of the world into their private club.'

'Never mind the details. I've got to see you this morning.'

It was the urgency in his voice that made her accept.

An hour later, they sat at Dulac's favorite morning hangout, the Café Montfort, waiting for their croissants and espressos.

'Why the sudden interest in Catharism?' Karen said.

'I studied Catharism in my law courses at Montpellier University. Everybody in the south does.'

'You mean the French south.'

'Certainly not the American,' said Dulac, as the waiter deposited their breakfast on the table.

'It's just an expression.'

'You Americans are so damn ethnocentric.'

'Touché.'

Dulac took a bite of his coffee-dipped croissant and continued. 'Know anything about the Cathars' beliefs?'

'If I remember from my mythology courses, it's a sort of dualistic religion, with a greater and a lesser God. But it's been a while since I've delved into the subject.'

'I'll give you a quick summary. They recognize the Pope, but have only one layer beneath him: bishops. No archbishops, no cardinals, just bishops. They have women priests, they have a credo that has nothing to do with the Catholic one. They do not believe in the physical resurrection of Christ or the virginal birth. They—'

'And what does Cathar doctrine have to do with my otherwise enjoyable breakfast with you?'

'It may be just a coincidence, but the reforms proposed by the Pope . . .'

'Surely other religions have the same beliefs. Take my friend Anna Singer. She's an Episcopalian minister in Montana. Women pastors are becoming common in the Anglican Church. It's about time Catholicism finally caught up to the 21st century.'

'I suppose you're right. But let me tell you something that I can't explain, but that has been troubling me since . . .' Dulac's gaze trailed off into the distance.

'Since?'

'I can't pinpoint it exactly. Karen, I have this, this strange feeling about the Pope.'

'So do a lot of people. They're saying he's bitten off more than he can chew. Then there's the disturbing parallel with Jean-Paul I and his sudden death after he proposed to revamp the Church. Every newspaper has brought this story back to life. Crass reporting at its worst, but it sure sells newspapers.'

'It's not that really. Well, yes that too partially, but it's the coincidence.'

'So you're saying the Pope, just because he's finally introducing changes, is being influenced by Catharism?'

'Maybe.'

Karen stiffened in her chair and crossed her arms. 'That's preposterous.'

'At the risk of sounding crazy, I'll go one step further. What if the Pope isn't really the Pope?'

Karen looked at Dulac, then suddenly burst out laughing. 'If it weren't this early in the morning and I didn't know you better, Thierry, I'd say you were—'

'I'm dead serious.'

Karen stopped giggling and stared at Dulac's somber, dispassionate eyes. 'I'm beginning to think you are serious.

You're beginning to freak me out. What the hell do you mean?'

'I'm saying the man, the man I rescued from Libya, the man who waved at the balcony last week, is an impostor.'

Karen sat speechless, mouth agape. After a moment, she spoke. 'That's the wildest, most unbelievable thing I've ever heard. Surely someone, you, anybody in his immediate staff, the rest of the world would've noticed before now. You were sitting next to him in the helicopter.'

'I was in pretty bad shape during that helicopter ride. His head was heavily bandaged. Speaking of the helicopter, there's something that happened during our return from Libya that supports my theory.'

'I'm dying to hear it,' Karen said, a supercilious smirk across her lips.

'Stop being so damn facetious for a second. When we were attacked by Libyan jets, Klein was hurt and passed out. The 'copter went into a dive and I asked the Pope if he could take over. He flatly refused, without even trying. Actually, he panicked, saying this helicopter was totally different from the papal helicopter, which by the way, he routinely pilots.'

'Sounds plausible.'

'Except that the principles of flying any helicopter are the same: pedals, joystick, throttle. Believe me, I've been in enough of them recently to have observed that.'

'What about his immediate staff? Surely they would have recognized an impostor?'

'With today's techniques in microsurgery and plastic surgery, not necessarily. And, I'm told he's started to replace key members of his staff, including members of the Curia.'

'Wait a second, you said they checked the blood type when they received the ear, and that it matched the Pope's.'

'Yes. That was before we rescued the, the impostor. The switch was made in Libya.'

'OK, so assuming for a moment I go along with your theory. Who would want to do this?'

'Hugues de Ségur, for one.'

'Jesus,' Karen said, her shoulders hunched, her forearms leaning on the table, her hands crossed as she started to listen intently. 'Why him?'

'Suppose you have a Cathar whose only real motivations are revenge and control. By kidnapping the Pope, the ransom money serves as a front, a false flag. A useful one at that. This would be the sweetest revenge of all. Payback for the Catholics' murderous crusades against the Cathars, and a chance to control the Catholic world, the majority of whose members merely pay lip service to antiquated, irrelevant dogma. They are ripe for drastic changes. His timing is perfect. Think of it: 1.2 billion Catholics will follow his puppet, cloaked in the persona of the Pope, while believing in his infallibility. It's as ironic as it is brilliant.'

'Thierry, this is absolutely insane. Surely someone, someone would have noticed and tried to remove your impostor from office.'

'To answer your question as to why I, or anybody else for that matter, didn't notice, let me remind you of Saddam Hussein's doubles. Two have been confirmed only recently. Interpol and MI6 suspect they impersonated the dictator for years. The CIA has proven beyond doubt that President Clinton negotiated the release of the American hostages held in Pyongyang with one of Dictator Kim Jong's three doubles. That's only the ones we know about. It took the CIA years to find out. There are other cases of impersonations by—'

'I get your point. So what now?'

Dulac took another sip of his espresso. 'I was afraid you'd ask that.'

'You have no real, tangible evidence, nothing concrete.'

'Worse. I don't know whose agenda I'd be playing into.'

'What do you mean?'

'I'll bet my bonus de Ségur is behind this. Apart from Romer, he had to have someone inside the Vatican. Someone higher up.'

Karen's eyes widened yet again. 'You're suggesting there's a conspiracy at the Vatican to remove the Pope and replace him by a Cathar impostor?'

'Why not? Between prelates who want changes at any cost, and can't afford to wait for reforms that may, or may never occur. It's perfect. An alliance between the Cathars and some avant-garde prelates in the Vatican. Not all that far-fetched, if you look at the Church's history of murderous alliances and conspiracies.'

'This is absolutely mind-blowing, Thierry. But how can you prove any of this?'

'I've got to call Gina.'

CHAPTER 35

The Vatican, 8.10 a.m., Friday 23 June

'Cardinal Sforza will see you now, Cardinal Brentano,' said the elderly nun with the hooked, witch-like chin.

Seated behind his plain walnut desk, Sforza tried to appear somber, trying to disguise his contentment as Brentano walked in. With Brentano's removal from the Curia, a large power vacuum had been created, a vacuum Sforza intended to fill personally.

Brentano looked as if he hadn't slept all week. His usually piercing eyes, now encircled by red rims, had dulled to a viscous green. Sforza couldn't help noticing that the furrows on either side of Brentano's mouth had deepened noticeably. He looked ten years older than his 65 years. Now ousted from the Curia, Brentano's authority had all but evaporated. Both knew it and the relationship of former equals had changed forever. Yet Brentano still wielded a significant amount of influence. It was said that he managed to exert that influence by dubious means. Stories were rampant that he kept personal, secret files on everyone of influence. Even on the Pope. Sforza knew that to underestimate such a man would be a grave mistake.

'How are you?' said Sforza in a mechanical tone, not really wishing to know the state of his former adversary's health.

'Tired. I will not hide from you that these past few days have been extremely stressful.'

'I understand.' Sforza had to be compassionate, but not overly so. To show too much sympathy would appear hypocritical.

'Let me get to the point,' said Brentano. 'There are rumors circulating about a movement to depose the Pope.'

'I've heard of it.' Sforza felt no need to inform Brentano of the extent of his involvement.

'Am I wrong in thinking that you support this view?'

'The matter is under serious consideration by the Curia.'

'Come, come Cardinal, I've heard that you're one of the instigators,' said Brentano, his tone caustic.

'Cardinal, you surely didn't come here to tell me what you already know,' said Sforza. 'You have surely considered that you will need support from inside and outside the Vatican for such a procedure to succeed.'

Ah. Here it comes. The offer of his support in exchange for mine later, in his bid for the papacy, thought Sforza. 'Yes I have.'

There was a brief moment of silence, as Sforza waited for Brentano's pitch.

'You are undoubtedly also aware that once the procedure is started, it will paralyze the Vatican for the duration of the proceedings?'

'Perhaps, although unlikely.'

Another moment of uneasy silence. Like gladiators before the fight, each man wanted to know where the other stood before compromising his own position.

Brentano yielded first. 'The papacy can't stand to be paralyzed for six months, maybe more. We are at a crossroads. If you are part of this, I ask that you reconsider. I will not support any movement to depose Clement XXI. As a matter of fact, I will oppose it.'

'Really?' Sforza sat astounded, as Brentano stood impassive, staring down at him.

'I thought this might surprise you,' said Brentano. 'But you fail to see that the papacy itself is at stake here, Cardinal. It goes beyond differing views on dogma. If you undertake this, it will take years to come to any kind of resolution. The Church is already weak enough. It can't take yet another schism within its ranks. That will kill it as surely as I stand here before you. I ask you to reconsider, Cardinal, in the name of the papacy, in the name of the Church. Let the ecumenical council take a decision on this matter. I always find that it is easy to let things take their natural course, down the path of least resistance, rather than force the issue. Do you agree?'

Sforza sat silent, his mouth agape. Here was a man who had recently suffered the humiliation of being removed from the Curia by the Pope and that would have given him every reason to embrace the movement to depose him. Brentano was the last person, Sforza thought, to oppose the Pope's removal. 'The movement has gathered a lot of momentum already. I don't think it can be stopped,' said Sforza, now knowing what he wanted to know. He looked at his watch. 'I'm afraid I must cut our meeting short, Cardinal Brentano, I have a Curia meeting in ten minutes.'

As Brentano walked down the corridor outside Sforza's office, a warm feeling of deep satisfaction invaded his being. The opening gambit had worked: Sforza had taken the bait and had appeared genuinely shaken. Moments later, Brentano entered his new, minuscule office, went straight to his desk and picked up the phone.

Dulac waited on the line while at the other end, the phone kept ringing. After a moment, he heard Gina's familiar voice came online.

'Good morning, Gina. How are things?'

'Fine, Mr Dulac.'

'Any news on de Ségur?'

'What do you mean?'

'How is Lescop doing?'

'I'm really not the one to ask. Why don't you contact him directly?' She didn't sound the least bit sympathetic.

'Just wondering if you'd heard anything. I have a question for you, Gina. Suppose you wanted to find out if someone is being impersonated by another, and you didn't have fingerprints or DNA samples to compare. What would you use?'

'Well, we'd probably do a morphological analysis of the body and the head. Then, we'd do an iris recognition scan. It's more trustworthy than fingerprints.'

'Interesting. How close would the scanner have to be from the persons you'd be comparing?'

'With the new OnSight scanner, about two meters.'

'Not possible. What else?'

'Mr Dulac, I really don't have time to—'

'What else?'

'There's the good old voice analyzer.'

'Gina, let me buy you lunch.'

'Today?'

'I can be in Lyon before 2 p.m.'

'Well, I don't know. I—'

'Thanks, Gina. You're terrific.'

After making reservations at the St Amable, Dulac had taken the 11.54 am TGV train to Lyon. Sitting with Gina, sipping their glasses of rosé, Dulac waited for the waiter to leave before dropping the bomb.

'What? The Pope an impostor?' exclaimed Gina, her dark eyes sparkling with disbelief and indignation. 'You've taken me away from my full workload to tell me that?'

'I know it sounds a bit crazy, but just bear with me a moment.'

'You really need a rest, Mr Dulac.'

'Just listen to me for a moment, Gina. There are too many inconsistencies, too many coincidences. I just need a bit of tangible evidence.'

'Even if I were to agree, I can't do a voice analyzer test without proper authorization. Besides, use of the equipment must be logged. I can just imagine Mr Schwarz's reaction if—'

'But you could get access to the voice files.'

'Even if I could, there's no guarantee the recordings would be of good enough quality to make a reliable comparison. There are so many variables and factors.' She paused, then continued. 'This is completely off the wall, Mr Dulac, even for you.'

'You're probably right. But what have we got to lose? If the voice samples all match, end of story. You'll have spent a couple of hours—'

'More like a couple of days on a wild, crazy goose chase. I'd have to dig out recordings of His Holiness's past speeches, compare them with his recent ones, get at least three different sources of each of the samples.' She crossed her arms. 'No, definitely not. I don't have that kind of spare time when my schedule is quiet, never mind now. Besides, the voice analyzer isn't a universally accepted detection tool.'

'I don't need bulletproof evidence, Gina. I just need something to work with. Something I can sink my teeth into. By the way, the Pope or whoever he is will be giving a special address tomorrow in St Peter's Square. You could get a fresh sample.'

'You're really hung up on this. What other evidence do you have?'

'None. You're my only hope, Gina.'

CHAPTER 36

The hot air was stifling, the sun beating mercilessly on the tens of thousands of faithful, packed tightly in St. Peter's Square for the Pope's Special Audience. The Vatican secretariat had announced that the Pope's address would be given on the steps of the Basilica. A white canvas canopy, supported by four columns, had been erected to protect His Holiness and his entourage from the midday sun. Rumors were flying that the Pope would announce more dogma changes.

'*In nomine patris, et filii et spiritus sancti . . .*' he began, slowly making the sign of the cross.

The tens of thousands of faithful listened, riveted to his every word.

'Dear brothers and sisters, I wish to thank you for your overwhelming and enthusiastic support concerning the changes I have proposed recently.'

A loud cheer rose from the crowd.

'Today, I will not go into the details of such changes. That will be left to the ecumenical council.' He stopped and took a sip of the water glass beside him, then continued. 'I assure you that the Holy Spirit has guided me in seeing the light of the Eternal. His wishes for change will be my trusted mission.' He took another sip of water, and mopped his brow with a small kerchief. The heat had become brutal. 'Upon me rests the great responsibility to implement God's vision for our Holy, Apostolic Church, the Church of the Nazarene, and making sure that it—'

Suddenly, a guard collapsed from the row of Swiss Guards standing between the assembled prelates and the crowd. Two of his colleagues immediately bent down to help the stricken man. Moments later, a medical team rushed to his side.

Legnano whispered. 'Perhaps we should adjourn, your Holiness, before we all faint.'

'I agree, Cardinal. This is too much. We will resume in the Great Hall.'

Cardinal Legnano stepped up to the microphone and announced that the papal address had been postponed for an hour and would resume at the Great Hall of Audiences. Murmurs of disappointment ran through the crowd. The Great Hall could contain only a small proportion of the faithful, and many would have to follow the Pope's address on the large video screens on either side of St Peter's Square.

The prelates started their way across the stage towards the doors of St. Peter's Basilica. Legnano, slightly ahead, walked up the last few stairs and reached the entrance to the Basilica, when suddenly a small commotion broke out behind him.

'Someone get a doctor, quick,' said Sforza. 'It's the Pope. He's collapsed.'

A hum rose from the huge crowd as the news spread quickly. Something had happened to the Pope. 'Has he been shot?' asked some of the faithful. The assassination attempt on Pope John Paul II of May 13, 1981 couldn't help but resurface in the collective memory. The Swiss Guards reacted quickly, rushing to the scene, trying to fend off the overly curious.

'Please, let the doctor through,' said one of the guards.

Moments later, a doctor arrived, quickly putting on his stethoscope and kneeling down. The look of anxiety on the doctor's narrow, thin-featured face did nothing to ease everyone's apprehension. 'Call the ambulance. We must get His Holiness to the hospital,' the doctor said.

'How serious is it?' asked one of the reporters.

'No comment,' replied the doctor, still trying to get a pulse reading.

'Did he faint? Is it a stroke? A heart attack?'

The doctor didn't answer.

In the distance, the ambulance siren could be heard above the human tumult, as it made its way slowly through the crowd.

'Please. Stay back. Give His Holiness room,' said the doctor as two attendants bearing a stretcher made their way through the crowd.

'We will issue a statement in due course,' said Signorelli to the hustling reporters busy snapping pictures as the attendants lifted the burdened stretcher into the ambulance.

Dulac, from the comfort of his well-worn leather couch, looked distractedly at the France 2 brunette anchorwoman, as she impassively described the fuel shortage in Kosovo and its effect on the population. Suddenly, images of the Vatican and St. Peter's Square filled the screen and she was handed a written report.

'We have just learned that His Holiness Pope Clement XXI has had a malaise on the steps of the Basilica, during the Special Audience at St. Peter's Square. He has been taken to Rome's Agostino Gemelli Clinic and initial reports indicate his condition is serious, but stable. We will keep you informed of further developments.'

Dulac's phone rang. It was Karen. 'I'm looking at it too,' he said.

'This is unbelievable. This can't be just a coincidence,' said Karen.

'Maybe.'

'I'm beginning to get this, this ugly feeling of déjà-vu.'

The other members of the inner Curia were waiting in the papal library for Cardinal Legnano to join then. The cardinal entered, accompanied by a middle-aged woman wearing a white smock.

'Your Eminences, this is Dr Cavallo, from the trauma department of the Agostino Gemelli Clinic,' said Legnano.

The continuous twitching of her left eyelid did nothing to dispel their collective anxiety. 'She will give us her preliminary report. Dr Cavallo,' said Legnano.

'He's had a massive stroke,' said the doctor as she sat down, resting her hands on the conference table. 'It's impossible to assess the amount of brain damage, but the preliminary diagnostic indicates his left side is more affected than the right, which means motor skills will be impaired.'

'Is his life in danger?' asked Fouquet.

'His vital signs are steady, but you must make a decision.'

'What do you mean?' asked Cardinal Gonzales.

'He must be put into an induced coma, to reduce the swelling of the brain. If not, the brain risks being flooded by the oversupply of blood; that could kill him.

'What decision is there, then?' said Sforza.

'There is an alternative, your Eminence,' said the doctor.

'Which is?'

'That we try to operate now to relieve the cranial pressure. I don't recommend it, in his present state. The operation is very stressful and could also prove fatal.'

'What are the risks with the induced coma?'

'Although the patient's brain slowly heals itself, so to speak, there is severe risk of infection due to the slowing of his metabolism and weakening of his immune system. Pneumonia is a distinct possibility.'

'*Mio Dio*,' said Legnano.

'The more we wait, the more the flooding and damage. There are risks in both options, and my role is to inform you. The final decision however is yours.'

The cardinals looked at each other uneasily, waiting for someone to take the initiative. 'I must warn you that even if he survives the induced coma, he could come out of this completely paralyzed. On the other hand, there have been cases of miraculous recovery,' she said.

Legnano spoke. 'Monsignori, we must hope that the Holy Father has the necessary strength and stamina to heal. I favor the induced coma. What do you say, Cardinal Gonzales?'

Before the cardinal could answer, Fouquet interjected. 'I think we should wait until we have more information; we can't decide intelligently without more facts.'

'Perhaps I haven't made myself clear, Monsignor,' said the doctor, looking at Fouquet. 'You don't have the luxury to wait. I must leave this room with your decision.'

The first ring from Dulac's phone jolted him from his light sleep. He recognized Gina's number.

'What is it, Gina?'

'Sorry I woke you, Mr Dulac. I couldn't wait. I just finished the diphthong and rhythm pattern analysis,' she said breathlessly. 'Plus the overlapping wave amplitudes are completely out of synch and—'

'Gina, slow down. Speak to me in plain English.'

'It's a 95.4 per cent to 98.6 per cent mismatch with any of the samples I was able to get.'

Dulac sprang up from his bed. 'I knew it! Gina, If you were here I'd kiss you. You're the greatest.'

'Now don't jump to conclusions. As I told you, these voice analyzer tests—'

'Gina, send me an encrypted copy by email then lock your file on this. You must keep this confidential. Understood?'

'Pretty hot stuff, eh?'

'That's the understatement of the decade.'

'Cardinal Legnano is extremely busy, Mr Dulac. Under the circumstances, I doubt he has time to see you,' said Legnano's assistant over the phone.

'Have you any news on the Pope?' said Dulac.

'His condition is stable.'

'Is the cardinal in his office now?'

'Mr Dulac, Cardinal Legnano is very busy.'

'Thanks.' Dulac hung up. He'd scheduled a meeting with Roquebrun, but following the events of the previous day, he'd called and canceled it. There were more pressing issues to be resolved. He dialed Legnano's number again, using his cellphone this time.

'At least let me speak to him. I promise I'll be brief.'

'Just a minute, I'll see if he'll talk to you,' said the assistant.

'Yes Mr Dulac,' said the cardinal, his voice a mixture of annoyance and impatience.

'Your Eminence, I must see you. It's urgent.'

'Mr Dulac, the Pope went into an induced coma last night and we are on vigil. He may not make it. If it's about the diary and de Ségur—'

'I've canceled my meeting with Roquebrun.'

'Who is Roquebrun?'

'The man we hired for . . . your mandate.'

'Yes, under the circumstances, that was the best thing to do.'

'I must talk to you about something else. Believe me, I wouldn't be phoning if it wasn't vitally important.'

'I see. What is this about?'

'I can be in Rome by early afternoon.'

'You'll have to take your chances, Mr Dulac. If the Pope's health deteriorates, I won't be reachable.'

'I'll be at your office at two o'clock.'

Dulac's flight arrived late and the traffic from the airport was in gridlock. The cacophony of Rome's impatient drivers leaning on their cars' horns had nothing melodic to offer Dulac's ears, those of a classically trained musician. Carrying his computer, he hurried through the Sant'Anna entrance to the Vatican, flashing his pass to the Swiss Guards. He rushed along the dark corridors and into the reception room of Legnano's office. Dulac stood at the doorway, trying to catch his breath. The bespectacled assistant secretary looked up from his desk, acknowledged Dulac's presence and gestured him to one of the empty chairs.

'Please wait while I inform His Eminence.'

A half hour passed, and there was still no sign of Legnano. Dulac's patience was wearing beyond thin. He stared at the young priest, who seemed to consciously ignore him, busying himself in his correspondence.

'Any chance of seeing him now?' Dulac said.

The prelate shook his head. Another fifteen minutes passed in oppressive silence. Suddenly, Dulac stood up and bolted towards the cardinal's office door.

'You can't! You can't go in!' said the bewildered priest. Dulac paid no heed and opened the door.

Legnano looked up, surprised. 'What is the meaning of this, Mr Dulac?'

'I'm sorry, your Eminence, but this can't wait.'

Dulac sat down in front of the cardinal, put his computer satchel onto the cardinal's desk and opened it. Turning it on, he scrolled down to 'voice comparison analysis', and double-clicked on the icon.

'Mr Dulac, the Pope's condition is deteriorating and I don't have time—'

'Your Eminence, I think you should see this. It's a digital wave analysis and comparison of the voice of the man who gave the speech yesterday in St. Peters Square, and previous speeches given by Pope Clement XXI.'

'Get to the point, Mr Dulac.'

'It's not the same voice.'

'What do you mean?'

'I've had a voice analyzer test done. It's not the same voice.'

The cardinal slowly removed his glasses and put them on the table. A frown started to form on Legnano's wide brow.

Dulac continued. 'Every speech pattern is picked up: inflections, pauses, word choices, articulation, density of the consonants, pitch of the vowels, highs and lows. Nothing matches.'

'The Holy Father has been under severe stress. Surely a person's voice can change in such circumstances—'

'That's taken into consideration and factored in, Your Eminence.'

Cardinal Legnano reclined in his chair. 'Come, Mr Dulac, surely you are a little tired.'

'Please, your Eminence. At least look at the wave patterns.'

The cardinal put his glasses back on his thick, aquiline nose and peered warily at the computer.

Dulac pointed to the open pages in front of the Cardinal. 'These are yesterday's speech wave patterns on the left. Now look at the wave patterns on the right page.'

'They're quite different.'

'My point exactly.'

'I've heard His Holiness speak many times, and I didn't see any difference yesterday, or for that matter last week.'

'The human ear can be easily tricked by good acting and possibly a larynx operation. Not so with the voice analyzer.'

'What are you getting at, Mr Dulac?'

'The man who spoke at St Peter's yesterday is an impostor.'

There was an uneasy silence, while Dulac waited for Legnano's reaction of shock, negation, or confrontation. To Dulac's amazement, Legnano remained impassive.

'Where did you get this, this voice analyzer information, Mr Dulac?'

'I became suspicious when I read about the leak in Le Monde, so on a hunch, I ordered a voice analysis comparison between his recent speech and earlier ones. The wave pattern analysis is fresh from our lab in Lyon. It's 98 per cent reliable. Yesterday's pattern is a 92 per cent mismatch with the earlier patterns, and—'

'So you're convinced that the man who is in a coma is not the Pope?'

'We need a DNA analysis to confirm it, of course. That's why I—'

'For the moment, that won't be necessary, Mr Dulac.'

'I beg your pardon?'

'You see, Mr Dulac, I already know the man in a coma is not the Pope.'

Dulac felt his lower jaw drop to his chest. He sat forward on the edge of his chair, staring at the cardinal in bewilderment.

'You've just confirmed what I already suspected. Yesterday, after the meeting of the Curia with Dr Cavallo, the doctor pulled me aside and we spoke privately. She's new to the hospital and she wanted some information concerning the Pope's medical records. She assured me there was no breach of confidentiality, but that she was simply curious. She asked me if I knew why the plastic surgery operations on the Pope's face had not been recorded in his medical history.'

'Good God!'

'Who knows about this voice analyzer test, Mr Dulac?'

'To my knowledge, besides ourselves, only Gina Marino at Interpol forensics.'

Legnano rose, walked slowly to the window, hands clasped behind his back and looked outside. 'Do you realize the scandal this will create if this information were to be made public?'

'I'm beginning to.'

Still at the window, Legnano turned and faced Dulac. 'For the moment, I must ask you to keep this information completely confidential, Mr Dulac.'

'It's bound to leak out.'

'Perhaps, but not through us. You may not be aware of the seriousness of the crisis within the Curia. The recent announcements by the — let's call him the Pope for the moment — have wreaked havoc within the Curia. It's a complex situation. I must deal with this in the best interests of the Church. For the moment I need you and Miss Marino's complete discretion.'

'I understand. Yes, of course, your Eminence.'

'Are you planning to stay in Rome?'

'I hadn't given it much thought.'

'I would prefer it if you did. I'll schedule a meeting with the Curia tomorrow. I'll need you to corroborate this, this information.'

'They know, I'm telling you, they know,' said the panic-stricken voice over the phone.

'Who, they?'

'Dulac. He's just advised Legnano. And someone else from Interpol knows. A Gina somebody at their forensics section. They did a voice analyzer test. If they go public, we're finished—'

'Calm down. They won't go public with only a voice analyzer test. They'll need more than that.'

'Dulac said it was 98 per cent accurate. A mismatch of 92 per cent.'

'Damn that Dulac. He's becoming a major pain.'

'They are going to trace this back to me!'

'Don't panic.'

'So what do I do?'

'You stay calm and keep your ear glued to that bug. I want you to keep me informed of Legnano's every move. That's what you're going to do.'

'Yes but if they give those test results to—'

'I'll take care of it. What hotel is Dulac staying at?'

'As far as I know, he stays at the Hotel Dante.'

'Then you have nothing to worry about.'

'That's easy for you to say. You're not here in the Vatican. If—'

'I said I'll take care of it.'

Leaving Legnano's office, Dulac felt uneasy. Legnano's decision to wait till the morning to advise the rest of the Curia did not sit well with his conscience. With such stupendous news, why hadn't Legnano called an emergency meeting of the Curia?

He grabbed a cab back to the hotel. Inside the taxi, he called Gina.

'Gina Marino.'

'It's me, Dulac. How many copies of the voice analyzer test do you usually keep?'

'Well, normally I keep two copies on CDs. One for the file and one for myself. But since I didn't log the use of the analyzer I've only kept one CD for myself.'

'I'm going to ask that you keep that CD under wraps. Don't let anybody see it, not even your cat.'

Back at the hotel, Dulac grabbed a copy of the Corriere Della Sera from the front desk, crossed the lobby and sat himself down in one of the plump sofas. The headline read: Pope Clement XXI's condition serious but stable. He went to the arts section and the striking face of Renée Fleming adorned the page reserved for concerts and recitals. *La Traviata* was playing at the Teatro dell'Opera.

Dulac though for a moment. He needed to clear his mind, unload if only for a moment the oppressive burden weighing down his conscience. Nothing I can do tonight. I'll see tomorrow how Legnano wants to play this. Dulac rose, went to the main desk and summoned the manager.

'I want you to get me a ticket to this performance. Tonight.' He pointed at the newspaper.

'But sir, that's impossible. That concert has been sold out for weeks,' said the tall man with thick swept back hair, looking at Dulac with an air of reproach.

'Do you have an envelope?'

'Yes, of course.' The manager handed Dulac an envelope bearing the hotel's logo. Dulac took out his wallet, counted four hundred euros, and put them inside the envelope.

'Put the envelope in my inbox. I'm sure a seat can be found at that price. Do we understand each other?' Dulac smiled.

'I'll, I'll see what I can do.' The manager's expression softened slightly.

'Fine. I'll be in the dining room.'

Dulac was finishing his scotch when the waiter came over with a small silver tray bearing a white envelope in the center. 'With the compliments of the manager, Mr Dulac. Have an enjoyable concert.'

As his taxi headed for the Teatro dell'Opera, Dulac's brain broiled with conflicting thoughts. Gina said it was a 92 per cent mismatch. What about the eight per cent? What if I'm wrong? No, the microsurgery. And the helicopter incident. And the monumental changes. There were too many coincidences. He had to be right. He could feel the burden of a secret growing, becoming heavier by the minute, till he thought it would burst, that he couldn't contain it. He had to share it with someone. He thought of phoning Karen. After all, she knew his theory. Yet she didn't know it had been confirmed. No, he promised Legnano to keep it secret. He had to wait.

'Sir, we've arrived,' said the perplexed cabbie as Dulac sat immobile in the back seat of the stopped taxi.

'Yes, yes of course. How much?'

'Thirty-five euros.'

Dulac paid and got out. Inside the opera house, the rich golden rococo ornamentation of one of the world's most acoustically perfect opera houses enveloped him, as he made his way to his seat under the soft light of the Louis XV style chandeliers.

Dulac sat down and perused the program. Verdi's *La Traviata*. After an ill-received first performance in 1853 in Naples, it had taken many years before the public and critics recognized this opera as Verdi's ultimate masterpiece. Dulac leaned back and let the opening chords of the orchestra engulf him in a world of ineffable delight.

Back at the hotel, Dulac went to the front desk. 'Any messages for room 3416?' he asked.

'Yes. Well actually, no,' said the clerk. 'A gentleman was here earlier and left a message in your inbox.'

Dulac eyed the empty mailbox quizzically.

'A few minutes later, he came back and retrieved his message,' said the clerk. 'He said he will contact you personally tomorrow morning.'

'Really? What time was he here?'

'Around 10, 10.15 p.m. or so.'

'Did he leave his name?'

'No.'

'Can you describe him?'

'A short man, rather heavy set, dark hair, mid-forties I'd guess.'

'Did he leave his name?'

'No. I asked him and he didn't answer.'

'So he just left?'

'As a matter of fact I remember him asking where the washroom was. I pointed to the ones near the elevator, over there.'

'After, did you see him leave?'

'Sorry sir, I didn't notice. I was busy with the—'

'All right,' interrupted Dulac.

Dulac took the elevator to the third floor, turned right down the dimly-lit corridor and stopped beside his room's door. He pulled out his short-nosed .38 Benelli from his leg holster and cocked it. His heart began pounding and he felt a mist of sweat form under his arms. Dulac inserted the electronic card into the slot and the light turned green. He kneeled beside the door, turned the door handle gently, then flung the door open as hard as he could. The inside door knob struck the wall with a resounding crash. Dulac, two hands on his pistol in front of him, panned from left to right in the darkness. Nothing. He waited a full minute, then turned on the light. He swept the room, his right eye peering down the Benelli's gun sight. Clean. He cautiously approached the bathroom. He turned on the light, pointing the gun at the shower stall. Empty. He returned to the bedroom. It looked undisturbed: his bathrobe was on the chair where he'd left it, the courtesy slippers at the foot of the bed. He went around towards the desk. Shit, the computer. It's on!

'Drop the gun.'

Dulac felt the unmistakably large, round shape of a silencer on the back of his head. He dropped the Benelli onto the carpet. He started to turn around. The gun pressed harder on his head.

'Don't move.' The voice was low, powerful.

Dulac stood, hands in the air. 'What do you want?'

'Your password.'

'What do you mean?'

The gun pressed harder still against his head. 'Don't fuck with me. Your password.'

'Has this got to do with the voice analyzer?'

'Your password or you're dead.'

'Easy. Easy. OK, it's THD 8507.' Dulac thought fast. When he finds out the password is fake, I'm dead. If I unlock the computer, I'm also dead. 'Actually, it has a triple password.'

'Sit down and type it in.'

Dulac started towards the desk and for a split second, felt no pressure on the back of his head. Instantly he twisted, and swung with his right fist. He heard a muffled crack of the silencer as the bullet bit into his right forearm. He grabbed the man's gun arm with both hands, swung the gun upwards as two more bullets flew above his head. He hit the man in the groin with his right knee. The man gasped and recoiled slightly, both of them still hanging on desperately to the gun. They fell to the floor, and Dulac swung the gun downwards between them. They stared at each other wildly, Dulac struggling to twist the gun away from his gut. The muffled sound of two more bullets erupted and Dulac cringed, waiting for the pain.

Dulac felt the hands around the gun go limp. They weren't his hands. Dulac looked down and saw a dark spot starting to form on the man's white shirt. He could feel the pumping of a heart, but he wasn't sure if it was his. He could hear his own lungs screaming for more air.

Curiously, the man beside him, his eyes glazed over, had himself stopped breathing. Dulac rose slowly, and went to the bathroom. He started retching into the sink. After a moment he looked up and aspersed his face with cold water. Blood was dripping from his shirt-sleeve. He looked into the mirror and saw a deathly ghoul staring back, shaking slightly. Soon, his whole body was convulsing, letting out the stress. He breathed deeply, and after a moment the shaking decreased slightly. He raised his right sleeve and inspected the wound. The bullet had gashed the skin across his inner forearm. I am one lucky bastard, Dulac thought as he grabbed a small towel and wrapped it around. He returned to the bedroom, picked up the phone awkwardly, and pressed the Questura Centrale's number.

'Get me Inspector Guadagni.'

'Who's calling?'

'Tell him it's Dulac.' He breathed in and out forcibly, progressively regaining control of his frayed nerves. Finally, the shaking stopped. He tried but couldn't stop looking at the bloody corpse sprawled grotesquely on the carpet.

'Guadagni.'

'It's me, Dulac.' He cleared his throat. 'I have a problem.'

'What is it?'

'There's a man lying on my hotel-room carpet. He's dead.'

'How?' said Guadagni, as a policewoman started taking photographs of the corpse, the man's gun and Dulac's Benelli.

'I'll give you the short version. He came up behind me, put a gun to my head. I dropped my gun. We had a scuffle, I went for his gun. We struggled, fell and the shots went off.'

'And the long version?'

'You'll get that when you find out who this asshole was.'

'I don't suppose you have any idea?' said Guadagni, scratching his wiry gray mane and looking warily at Dulac.

'Probably some small-time hotel thief.'

'We'll see what we have on him. In the meantime, better have someone take a look at that arm.'

Dulac turned to the hotel manager, who had accompanied the police to his room. 'Your man on duty at the desk. Was he on duty an hour ago?'

'Yes, why?'

'Get him up here.'

'There is no need to publicize this . . . this unfortunate incident.'

'Now,' growled Dulac.

'Yes sir.' The manager flipped open his cellphone and called the desk clerk.

'*Mio Dio!*' exclaimed the clerk as he looked at the inert body.

'Is this the man who gave you the message for my inbox?' said Dulac.

'Yes that's him.'

Dulac turned to Guadagni. 'Oldest trick in the book. He gave the clerk a fake message, saw him put it in my inbox. He got my room number, waited a few minutes, then claimed the message back.'

'And here is his door-card. We found it in his pocket,' said a policeman, as he approached Guadagni.

'Recognize it?' said Guadagni as he showed the card to the hotel manager.

'It's not one of ours.'

'Probably a Chinese multi-key job,' said Guadagni. 'They're flooding the market these days.' He turned towards Dulac. 'I'll need you to drop by the Questura Centrale to sign a deposition. In the meantime, I'll have my man drop you off at the hospital.'

'Much appreciated,' said Dulac.

'We'll have your things transferred to another room, Mr Dulac,' said the manager. 'That's the least we can do.' He turned and eyed the clerk. 'Bring Mr Dulac's suitcase and computer to the presidential suite.'

'Not the computer. It stays with me,' said Dulac.

CHAPTER 37

Dulac, his arm in a makeshift sling one of Guadagni's men had improvised, waited in the emergency room of the Agostino Gemelli Clinic for the doctor to return. Suddenly the thought jolted him upright. Christ, Gina. He grabbed his cellphone and scrolled down the list of telephone numbers. He called her home. The line was busy. Busy? At this time of night? He tried again. Busy. He called her cell. No answer. He waited three minutes and called her home again. Still busy.

Something has happened to her, he thought. He called the Lyon operator. 'I'm Inspector Thierry Dulac, Interpol. ID number 537-5672. I want to know if this number is really busy, or defective.'

'I'm sorry sir, I—'

'For God's sake, this is an emergency. Someone's life is at stake.'

'Yes sir. One moment.'

After a seemingly interminable wait, the operator returned. 'There seems to be something wrong with the line, sir. I am having—'

Dulac hung up and dialed Lescop's number. After the fourth ring a drowsy voice answered.

'Hello?'

'Lescop, it's me, Dulac.'

'What . . . what time is it?'

'Never mind. It's Gina. I think she's in trouble. Get some backup and get over to her place right away.'

'What?'

'Just do as I say. Her life may be in danger. There's no time to explain. Call me when you get there.'

'All right. All right. I'm going.' Dulac hung up and called Harris.

'Harris.' His voice sounded as if he was already awake, almost as if he were expecting the call.

'Thierry Dulac. I have an emergency.' There was a pause.

'Do you realize what time it is?'

'Gina Marino is in trouble. I've sent Lescop and a backup over to her house.'

'What the hell is this about?'

'It's a long story. I'll fill you in when I get back to Lyon.'

'This had better be good, Dulac.' Harris hung up.

Dulac could feel the local anesthetic the nurse had shot in his arm spreading to his fingers. He heard the insistent ring of his phone in his pocket.

'Cellphones are not allowed in the hospital,' said the buxom red-headed nurse.

'It's an emergency.' Dulac flipped open his cell with his good hand.

'Lescop. We've entered the house. There's no sign of Gina. Somebody has definitely been here.'

'What do you mean?'

'They've turned the place upside down. The house is trashed. I don't think they found what they were looking for. Any idea what?'

'Call the police. Have them send all-points on Gina. Call me when you get news.' Dulac flipped his phone shut and slowly put it back in his pocket. Who the hell is behind this? Jesus. No. It can't be. Legnano? How could that possibly be?

Yet he's the only other person who knows about the voice analyzer results.

Dulac sat waiting in the antechamber of Legnano's office, trying to keep a grip on his temper. Legnano's secretary was busy opening the morning mail, when Dulac's cell rang.

'Lescop. We've found Gina. Or rather, she found us.'

'What do you mean?'

'She's fine. She walked in the office this morning. Apparently her sister had her fortieth birthday last night and Gina spent the night there.'

Dulac drew a deep breath. 'Thank God she's OK.'

'Well, temporarily, yes.'

'Explain.'

'She hasn't seen her house yet. Or what's left of it.' At that moment, Cardinal Legnano walked in.

'Call you later.' Dulac hung up.

'Mr Dulac. What are you doing here?' said Legnano.

Dulac jumped up and stood inches from the cardinal, blocking his way. 'Surprised to see me, your Eminence?'

Legnano backed away. 'Well, yes. But I'm glad—'

'Let's cut the crap, Cardinal, shall we?'

'I beg your pardon?'

'Enough of your bullshit.'

The cardinal frowned and looked at Dulac's bandaged arm.

'That's right. Your guy missed. He's dead.'

Legnano, his look a mix of incomprehension and irritation, took another step back. 'Mr Dulac, what in heaven's name are you talking about?'

'Apart from Gina and myself, you were the only person to know about the voice analyzer results. Last night, your man broke into my hotel room, tried to hack my computer, then tried to kill me.'

'Mr Dulac, you're talking complete nonsense. I swear to you on my cardinal's oath that I have nothing to do with any theft, or attack on you or for that matter anybody else.'

'Then who, Cardinal?' Dulac thrust his face closer to the cardinal's.

'I am, I mean, I have no idea Mr Dulac.' Legnano stepped back again.

'And why should I believe you?'

'Mr Dulac, I swear on my oath as a cardinal that I had nothing to do with this.'

Dulac and the cardinal stared at each other for a moment. Although the cardinal seemed truthful, Dulac reserved final judgment. 'If what you are saying is true,' Dulac continued, 'then someone else must have overheard our conversation. Your secretary perhaps?'

'Monsignor Patuelli? Impossible. He's been with me for fifteen years. I have complete faith in his discretion.'

'At the Vatican, I'm beginning to think nothing is impossible.' Dulac pointed at different areas of the room. 'Your office. Has it been swept clean?'

'You mean for listening devices?' said Legnano with an air of surprise.

'It's never been bugged before?'

Legnano became thoughtful. 'Actually, yes. About seven years ago, before a synod of bishops. I'll, I'll have Haeflinger check again. In any case, Mr Dulac, I was going to call you. I've convened the Curia to inform them about this, this—'

'Impostor, Cardinal. Impostor.'

'Astounding,' exclaimed Sforza, his bird-like eyes twinkling.

'That's preposterous, unbelievable,' said Fouquet, staring at Dulac stiffly. 'I'm sure someone would have noticed. The doctors gave him a complete medical examination when they checked the Pope's state of health upon his return from Libya.'

'I asked that very question to Dr Cavallo,' said Legnano. 'She said that unless you were a plastic surgeon, you wouldn't notice.'

'That would explain why he was not interested in the reattachment of his ear,' said Sforza.

'That would explain a lot of things, your Eminence,' said Dulac.

'If Mr Dulac and the doctor are right, de Ségur has given us quite a ride for our money, as they say in America,' said Legnano.

'It's all crystal clear, your Eminence,' said Dulac. 'De Ségur has substituted a Cathar 'pope' to effect changes within the Church and control the agenda. His puppet would progressively install Cathar doctrine, abolish archbishops, cardinals even.' Dulac paused and looked at the members of the Curia. 'De Ségur must have had collaborators inside the Vatican. I'm talking at the highest level. At the level of—'

Suddenly Dulac's, then everyone else's gaze turned towards where Cardinal Gonzales had sat. The chair was empty.

Legnano stood up and rushed to the Swiss Guards, on station at the room's entrance. 'Get Cardinal Gonzales and bring him here. He must not leave the Vatican.' Legnano returned to the table and rejoined the bewildered prelates.

For a long moment, no one dared break the agonizing silence that had befallen them, a somber assembly of Christ's most respected representatives.

Sitting calmly behind his desk, Legnano looked at the cardinals one by one and said, 'Does anyone have any suggestions as to what we do next?'

The cardinals eyed each other timidly, blank expressions on their sullen faces.

Suddenly Fouquet blurted out, 'We must simply tell the truth. The truth will carry us through. It always has.'

Legnano rose from his chair, went around to the front of his desk and leaned back slightly with his hands on the edge of the desk. 'Cardinal, that is the most inane, absurd, ridiculous remark I have heard in a long time.' Staring at Fouquet, Legnano stood away from the desk and crossed his arms on his chest. 'So according to you, we should tell the public that we have paid kidnappers $600 million in exchange for the Pope, that we didn't check his identity before paying them the money, that an impostor has been sitting here in his place, making changes, and we have only now found out we've been duped. And to top it off, this false pope has announced major reforms, which to our surprise and embarrassment,' — he looked about the room — 'yes embarrassment, your Eminences, these reforms have been overwhelmingly approved by our faithful.'

Legnano started across the room towards the window, all the while talking. 'Truth be told though, we have a slight problem. Our Pope, sorry, our impostor, is a Cathar, not even a Catholic priest. Shall I go on, Cardinals?' He paused briefly, taking in the effect. 'And we don't know where the real Pope is, or even if he is alive for that matter.' He stopped beside the window and looked outside, hands clasped behind his back.

Slowly, Legnano turned and eyed the cardinals one by one, leaving Fouquet until last. 'Is this the truth you are suggesting we tell our 1.2 billion faithful and the rest of the world?'

Fouquet's face had become the red color of his cassock's fascia. 'I only suggested we should eventually—'

'Enough, Cardinal, enough. Anyone have a better idea?' said Legnano.

At that moment, Haeflinger and two of his men burst into the room, escorting Cardinal Gonzales between them.

'What is the meaning of this?' said Gonzales, freeing his arm from the Swiss Guard.

'You left the room rather precipitously, your Eminence.'

'What do you mean?'

'We think you may have something to do with this, this false pope,' said Legnano.

'Absolutely ridiculous. I merely went outside to make a private call.'

'And may we ask to whom?'

'To the hospital. I was simply inquiring about the Pope's health.'

'You mean the impostor's health,' said Fouquet.

'As far as I'm concerned, that still hasn't been proven,' said Gonzales.

Suddenly, the insistent ring of the telephone on the small desk broke the tension. Legnano reached for it. 'Sì . . . sì . . . Call me when you have news. Thank you, doctor.' He turned to the assembly. 'We won't get a confession soon. Dr Cavallo warns that his coma has deepened.'

'Well, at least we won't have to depose him,' said Sforza.

'Cardinal, your cynicism is a little out of place, don't you think?' said Legnano. 'That man, whoever he is, is fighting for his life.'

'You're right,' said Sforza, a look of apology on his face. He turned to the rest of the cardinals. 'But in the name of God, what are we going to do?'

Dulac had felt more and more uncomfortable during the raucous squabbling of cardinals over a solution to their 'problem'. Sforza wanted to set in motion the Conclave of cardinals, to elect a successor to the illegitimate Pope. As interim successor to the real Pope, the Camerlengo, Cardinal Fouquet asserted he had de facto full powers to act immediately. Legnano retorted that until it was proven beyond all reasonable doubt that the stricken man was an impostor, the man in the coma was still the Pope.

At around 10 a.m. Dulac left the discordant assembly and took a taxi back to the hotel. 'Message for you, Mr Dulac,' said the young raven-haired woman at the front desk. Dulac grabbed the envelope and started towards the elevator. As he reached it, he opened the envelope and read the short message. 'Jesus,' he whispered, and hit the up button. He re-read the message which was addressed to Inspector Thierry Dulac, Interpol, Hotel Dante.

Dulac
Call me urgent on hard-line, number 501-2 256 458,
Belize City. Repeat urgent.
Hugues de Ségur

Dulac rushed out of the elevator, down the corridor. He fumbled with his room card and tried to open the door. 'Damn. Can't they get this low-tech junk to work?' he mumbled. At the second try, the light turned green. He went to his desk, dialed the number and heard the distinctive buzz tone of a North American exchange.

'Mr Dulac undoubtedly,' said the voice after the fifth ring.

Dulac recognized the nasal, clipped accent of his compatriot. In an instant, Dulac felt all of the frustration and bottled-up anger he'd accumulated over the three years of chasing down his enemy, his nemesis, come to the surface. Dulac sat down on the edge of the bed, and reached for his pack of Gitanes on the night table.

'Yes?'

'I'm quite surprised you returned the call. I wasn't expecting such courtesy from the man trying to get rid of me.'

'You've got it ass-backwards, de Ségur. It was your man who tried to kill me last night.'

'Wrong again. I'm talking about Roquebrun. Did you really think that I wouldn't find out about your silly plan to—'

'What the hell is this about then?'

'Dulac, your polemics won't get us anywhere. Just so you know where I'm coming from, I have the latest news concerning the state of health of the Pope.'

'You mean your impostor from Benghazi.'

'As you wish. According to my informant, he won't make it. That is why I decided to call you.' There was a moment of silence. 'It was going so well, until . . .' De Ségur started to cough uncontrollably. 'Sorry. I—'

'Until your plan to control 1.6 billion Catholics went sour?'

'As always you oversimplify, Dulac. But as much as I hate to admit it, I'll give you credit for the voice analyzer. We thought the larynx operation had gone perfectly.'

'It doesn't take an Einstein to figure out what you're up to with this impostor.'

'We checked his medical records, but we hadn't foreseen a stroke. Always risky, the business of impersonation. Everything was going according to plan, until then.'

Dulac lit a cigarette and took a deep drag. 'For how long did you think you could get away with this? A couple of months? A year? Someone else was bound to find out. The Vatican would surely—'

'Attack his reforms? On what grounds? Merely because they would eventually doubt the Pope's legitimacy? Look at it even now. The Curia doesn't know what to do. They don't dare reveal the truth.'

'You seem well informed on the Curia. Gonzales?'

'Of course.'

'Beside Gonzales and Romer, who were the conspirators on the inside?' said Dulac.

'That's irrelevant now. No, I called, much to my dismay and distaste, believe me, to meet you and to quote the hackneyed expression, "make you an offer you can't refuse".'

'What offer could I possibly refuse from a kidnapper and a murderer?'

'Ah, sarcasm, the easiest form of humor and the trait of an ordinary mind. Your predictability never ceases to amuse me, Dulac. Classifications aside, I've arranged for us to meet in Belize City, tomorrow evening. I've reserved a ticket in your name for the morning flight to New York. The connecting flight to Belize City gets in at 4 p.m.'

'Why in hell's name would I go anywhere to meet you?'

'Because I have something here that you want.'

'If you're talking about the diary—'

'Dulac, trust me. I guarantee you will accept my offer. Oh, and don't bother calling Roquebrun. I'm told he's enjoying the Vatican's money in a five star brothel in Kuala Lumpur.'

'Bastard. Out of curiosity, who ratted? Garcia?'

'Must be, although that's also irrelevant now.'

'Not to me. If you didn't, Garcia must have ordered the contract to whack me.'

'Why don't you ask him? By the way, I booked your room at the Hotel Mirador and I've deposited $10,000 USD in your Paris bank account, for incidentals. You're probably thinking you'll need company. Shall we meet in the hotel restaurant, say at 7 p.m.? Oh, and Dulac, time is pressing. Don't disappoint me.'

The line went dead.

'Go for it,' said Karen over the phone. 'What have you got to lose?'

'Try two miserable days flying half way round the planet on a quack call from a murdering psychopath.'

'Like it or not, in one way or another, he's always kept his promise.'

'That's a strange way of looking at it,' said Dulac. 'At first, I thought he wanted to sell me the diary, but why go through all that trouble? He can send it directly to the Vatican. There's something else, but why me?'

'Bizarre as it may seem, you're probably the only one he can trust.'

'I've checked the reservations and they're confirmed and paid for. And I received ten grand in my account. I suppose if he wanted me dead, he would just hire another hit man.' Dulac took a drag from his Gitane. First, I've got to call Gina again. Then I have some unfinished business in Belize.'

'If you don't mind, this time I won't go with you. But do be careful, Thierry.'

'Don't worry, I'll have professional backup.'

CHAPTER 38

André Jourdan, the retired French Bureau operative working as a freelance bodyguard, had agreed to cover Dulac in Belize. At 6 p.m., they entered the Hotel Mirador's lobby and went to the front desk.

'Yes, Mr de Ségur has a reservation for four at 7 p.m.,' said the clerk.

Dulac and Jourdan went to their rooms, and Dulac called Garcia. 'Hello Juan.'

'Thierry? Thierry, my friend.' Garcia's millisecond hesitation confirmed to Dulac he had his man. 'How are you? You sound local.'

'I am.'

'You are proceeding with . . . ?'

'We have unfinished business, Juan. Meet me at the Mirador in the lobby in an hour.'

'Why so rushed, my friend? Why don't we have lunch tomorrow?'

'Always "my friend" eh? Cut the crap, Juan. In an hour. In the lobby. I guarantee it's in your best interest to be there.'

'If you insist.'

Dulac flipped his phone shut. He took the envelope on his desk and went to Jourdan's room.

'Stay in the lobby, in the background until I signal you to join. I don't want to tip my hand early.'

'Understood.'

Four scotches later, Dulac and Jourdan stood beside the elevators, hiding behind a large tropical plant but with a clear view of the lobby. Dulac fidgeted nervously with the legal-size brown envelope.

A few moments later, Dulac saw Garcia walk in. 'That's him,' he whispered to Jourdan. Garcia looked about, spotted the seated busty blonde busy powdering her nose, and sat down in the sofa facing her. When she confronted his stare, he gave her that lecherous, tooth-gaped smile of his. She turned away icily, and she resumed pampering her delicate appendage.

Garcia glanced about the lobby, then continued staring at the girl. She seemed oblivious to his very existence. Dulac recognized the bodyguards in Florence as two men walked in, nodded to Garcia, and looked furtively about.

Dulac waited for them to sit down then walked over to Garcia, breaking Garcia's one-way connection to the blonde magnet. 'Let's go to the lounge,' said Dulac, ignoring Garcia's offered hand. Dulac glanced over in Jourdan's direction and nodded almost imperceptibly.

'Suit yourself.' Garcia looked back at the men in the chairs, and they rose in unison, following Dulac and Garcia into the lounge.

Dulac and Garcia sat down in the wicker chairs and ordered drinks. As Dulac deposited the envelope next to him on the small table, from the corner of his eye, he saw Jourdan sit down discreetly behind Garcia's men and reach inside his vest.

'So, Juan, surprised to see me?' said Dulac.

'Yes, to see you in Belize so soon,' said Garcia, looking unfazed.

'Let's stop the charade, Juan. In case you haven't heard, your hit man is dead.'

'I don't understand what you're talking about.'

'And your mother gave virginal birth to an angel, right Juan?'

'Keep this—'

'But first, let's talk about your asshole Roquebrun.' Dulac stared at Garcia for any hint of reaction at the mention of the name.

'Sure. You contacted him?'

'You know goddamn well I contacted him. The Vatican paid him $11 million up front. That bastard has run to Kuala Lumpur with it and probably another couple of million from de Ségur.'

'I just gave you his name, that's all. I didn't have any dealings with him.'

'Bullshit. You got a nice fat payback from Roquebrun and that's fine. That's the price of doing business. But for you to sell me out to de Ségur, to try and have me whacked, that I take offence to.'

'I, I don't know what you're talking about.'

'You'd better do better than that, Juan. Way better.' Dulac reached forward and took the envelope on the table. He saw Garcia's men instinctively reach inside their vests. 'I'll tell you what I'm going to do. I'm going to postpone leaking out to the other members of your sugar cartel the fact you have been screwing the head man Vic Baldoni's wife Michèlle, for the last six months. Here.' Dulac reached in the envelope and threw the lurid photographs on the table beside the drinks. 'These are for you. The best-ever shots of your Latin ass in action.'

Garcia looked down. His face went white. 'Jesus Christ.'

'And in exchange, you're going to deposit 11.1 million USD into a trust account of Hayes and Smith, lawyers in London before the end of the week. $11 million USD to the benefit of the Vatican, care of Cardinal Andrea Sforza, and $100,000 to my benefit, for personal damages.'

Garcia's expression had lost all of its smugness and joviality. 'You wouldn't.'

'You bet your sweating Latin balls I would. And you're going to tell me about my meeting with de Ségur.'

'You're meeting de Ségur?' Garcia looked genuinely surprised.

'At seven. He insisted that I have dinner with him. He says it's urgent.'

'Give me two weeks for the money. I don't know anything about a meeting with de Ségur, I swear.'

'Allow me to doubt that too, Juan. Two commissions are better than one.'

'On my mother's grave, I don't know why de Ségur called you.'

'I'm about to find out, and if you lied Garcia, your sweet sugar friends, I don't want to even think of how they'll kill you.'

'Please, my wife, I have two children, please, for our fathers' friendship sake.'

'You should have thought of that before. Remember, Juan, one week.'

The nurse sat drowsily ensconced in her chair, reading, when suddenly the strident cry of an alarm at the console and the blinking red light pulled her out of her Danielle Steel dream, into urgent reality. In a split second, she was on the intercom. 'Life assist in room 1047. Life assist, room 1047.'

Seconds later, two doctors hurried past her, followed by an assistant pulling a cart with a defibrillator and an oxygen tank. As they rushed past the Swiss Guard posted at the papal room and entered, what they saw confirmed their fears. The white pulse line on the gray backdrop of the monitor showed that he was on the verge of death.

The young doctor with the crew cut put the Schiller defibrillator's paddles on the patient's chest. 'Contact,' he ordered.

The torso heaved, with the spasm of 1,700 volts violently repulsing the doctor's paddles. 'Contact.' The doctor looked at the monitor. 'Contact. Again.'

All eyes focused intently on the dormant monitor. Nothing. Then suddenly, a small blip, then a second, then a third, interrupted the line. Soon, the vital signs became stronger and a look of collective relief appeared on the faces of the two doctors and the assistant.

'Get the anesthetist,' said the young doctor with the crew cut. 'We have to pull him out of the coma or we'll lose him.'

'If he comes out of the coma, the intracranial hypertension will destroy the rest of his brain,' said the short, red-headed female anesthetist, looking at the young doctor. 'There's a strong chance he'll be a vegetable.'

The doctor opened his cellphone and called Cardinal Legnano. 'We have to decide now, your Eminence. He won't survive another attack.'

'What do you recommend?' said Legnano.

'It's not my call.'

'I'll convene the Curia.'

'That's your decision.'

'Keep him in the coma', said Sforza. 'If he happens to—'

'He could survive the operation,' said Legnano.

'And be a walking dead man,' said Fouquet.

'Your Eminences, why do I have the impression your decision is more influenced by political expediency than by his chances of survival?' said Legnano.

'That's unfair, Cardinal,' said Sforza.

'You seem to forget,' said Fouquet, 'that some of the doctors already suspect the man in room 1047 is not the Pope. That suspicion will grow.'

'If he stays a vegetable, we still have a problem,' said Sforza. 'The whole ugly story will eventually come out.'

'On top of it, he is living proof of the—'

'I don't believe what I'm hearing,' said Legnano, banging his fist on the desk. 'The man will live if I can help it. Who are we to play God?' He dialed the hospital's number. 'Doctor, Cardinal Legnano. We've decided. Pull His Holiness out of the coma and proceed with the operation.'

Belize City, Hotel Mirador, Château Caribbean Restaurant, 7.05 p.m.

Dulac and Jourdan sat at the elegantly set table in the discreet room, to the side of the main dining room. In front of them, the sun's rays caressed the shores of the outlying islands with their soft, diffuse light.

Suddenly, Dulac's reverie was interrupted as three men in bad suits entered the room, opening an invisible path for the man behind them, dressed in a blue blazer and mauve shirt and smoking an expensive looking cigar.

'Welcome to Belize, Dulac,' said Hugues de Ségur. 'And this is?'

'André Jourdan,' said the ex-French Bureau operative, his face expressionless.

De Ségur nodded.

Dulac thought de Ségur appeared considerably thinner than when he last saw him, at the opera in Paris three years prior. He glanced at the bad suits, as two of them posted themselves on either side of the door, the third at the other end of the room. Dulac turned to de Ségur. 'I thought this was a friendly meeting.'

'Even in Belize, one can't be too careful; you never know what silly moves Interpol might try. I hear you've been suspended.'

'You heard right. What's the offer?'

'Always in such a hurry, Dulac. Take off your Interpol straitjacket for a while and enjoy the view.' He took a puff from his cigar and blew away and to the side. De Ségur then took the wine list from the waiter standing beside him. 'I'm afraid the selection here is rather limited. No good Bordeaux to speak of. How about a Penfold's Shiraz?'

Dulac nodded in acquiescence. 'Anything before? Dry martini?'

'Scotch on the rocks,' said Dulac.

'And you?' said de Ségur to Jourdan.

'Mineral water.'

'Two Glenlivets,' said de Ségur to the waiter, who bowed and left the room.

'By the way, I'm curious. Who is this, this impostor of yours?' said Dulac.

'You mean my Pope?' said de Ségur, blowing a lungful of smoke away from the table. 'A little respect please, at least for the function. I'm surprised your people at Interpol haven't found out yet. Anyway, that's all moot now. He's an unemployed Israeli actor by the name of David Silverman, who had the good fortune for us to be the Pope's lookalike, well, almost, and to owe a substantial amount of money to the Tel-Aviv Mafia. They were going to collect, rather permanently, so we had no trouble convincing Silverman that instead, it would only cost him a small replaceable part of his anatomy. In exchange, we erased his debt to the Mafia.'

'And all this for?'

'I don't have time to go through with you the years of planning, organizing and recruiting for this operation. We were so close to succeeding. So very close . . .' De Ségur's eyes became wistful, looking past Dulac into empty space. 'The world would be a different place if—'

'So we have, for the moment, a Jewish Pope?'

'With a Cathar agenda,' said de Ségur with obvious pride.

'What happened to the real Pope?'

'Most unfortunate. He became lost when the Bellerophon sank, outside of Benghazi. Shall we order?'

Dulac began to look at the menu when suddenly he saw de Ségur's head start twitching uncontrollably, jerking de Ségur back in his chair, which began tilting backwards dangerously. One of the suits lunged towards the chair and caught it just as de Ségur was about to fall over backwards.

Clutching his throat with his right hand, de Ségur gasped. 'Water, water.'

The guard grabbed the water glass and brought it to de Ségur's lips and shaking head. Finally, the attack subsided, and de Ségur took careful sips. His head twitched again and sent half the contents of the glass down the front of his blazer and shirt.

'Damn. At least it's not the scotch.'

Dulac twisted slightly in his chair and looked uncomfortably at de Ségur, who had regained his composure.

'Creutzfeldt-Jacob disease, Dulac, commonly known as mad cow. Inoperable, incurable and deadly. It seems I inherited the defective gene from my late father. I had a twenty per cent chance of getting the prion mutation.' De Ségur took another puff from his cigar. 'Until recently, I thought I'd beaten the odds.'

They both sat in uneasy silence for a moment, as Dulac digested the information. 'Sorry to hear that.'

'You don't have to be. Soon all your problems with me will be over, Dulac.'

'How long do you have?'

'Between two and four months, if these quacks don't kill me first with their bloody drugs.'

The waiter brought the cabaret with the drinks and set it on the table.

'Give both scotches to him,' said de Ségur, pointing to Dulac. The waiter did as ordered and left. 'Besides my men and my doctors, you're the first to know about my condition.'

'Surely you didn't—'

'Yes, you're right, Dulac. I didn't fly you all the way to Belize to discuss with you my declining health and premature death. What I want, Dulac, is to die in France, in my native village of Montferrier. To die honorably in the presence of my Cathar friends and their families, and especially my grandchildren. Is that not a fair request, Dulac?'

Dulac looked at de Ségur askance. 'Fair? Fairness is something I have difficulty associating with you. Where was fairness when you had archbishops Conti and Salvador murdered for what they were about to reveal on Chimera? Where was fairness when you had Olga Fedova killed by your hit man, leaving her four children destitute orphans in Moscow?' Dulac's voice heated up. 'Where was your fairness when Chimera, headed by you, planted false flags all over Europe and murdered innocents by the hundreds? Shall I go on? Where was fairness when you had Romer, Aguar and Ascari killed, to cover your tracks in the kidnapping of Pope Clement XXI? No, fairness is really not part of my vocabulary with you.'

De Ségur put down his cigar and slowly drank another glass of water.

'Dulac, I'm probably wasting my breath, but when will you see the bigger picture? Can't you, for a moment, stop thinking like a robot they've trained you to be, at the Army school at Lyon they call Interpol, and think for yourself? Did you think I enjoyed the inevitable collateral damage? Do you think British soldiers in Iraq enjoy killing innocent bystanders when fighting the insurgents? Did you ever think it was for the greater good? Did you ever for one moment think that a better world might emerge, if the archaic, stifling rules by which a billion Catholics live today, were chucked and replaced by a set of more credible beliefs?' De Ségur took another sip of water and continued. 'How many Africans die of AIDS every year because your Pope Clement XXI still prohibits the use of contraceptives? Look around you. How many of these so-called Catholics actually practice their faith? One in a thousand? How many continue to pretend they believe in something they know, in the bottom of their hearts, to be unbelievable, unreasonable and ridiculous?'

'So your strange, self-glorified messianic view supposedly justifies the means?' said Dulac, reaching for his pack of Gitanes.

'Spare me your obsolete, watered down, oversimplified rules of ethics, will you. Besides, isn't that what Catholics have done all along? Isn't that what they did against the Cathars, the Saracens, the Muslims and any religion that dared oppose them? I'm playing by their rules, Dulac. They invented collateral damage, not me.'

'Times were different then. In case you haven't noticed, the world has changed since.' Dulac lit a cigarette and inhaled deeply.

'Not enough. Not nearly enough.' De Ségur signaled the waiter for more water.

'I didn't come here to discuss theology with a meandering megalomaniac. What . . . ?'

'You're right. Enough waste of my breath.' De Ségur coughed heavily. 'Damn these drugs. They'll kill me before the disease does.'

'So why did you send for me?'

'I want you to negotiate on my behalf. I want—'

'Just a damn minute. Why in the hell should I help you get anything?'

'Because Dulac, I have something you want. Something the Curia wants desperately.'

'If it's the diary . . .'

'It's not the diary.'

'No? What then?'

'First, let's get back to what I want in this deal.'

'I'm dying to hear it.'

'Your sarcasm again, Dulac.'

'Sorry, I didn't mean—'

'You get me a postponement of my trial for just six months, that's all I ask. Look at it this way: it'll be saving the French taxpayer time and money. I won't live long enough to go to trial. That way, my name is less muddied. My three grandchildren, Dulac. They're Cathars. That's all that matters to me now.'

'Speaking of which, I want the names of your collaborators.'

'Forget it, Dulac. You'll have to find them yourself.'

'And what, pray tell, do I get in return? What's the quid pro quo for my alleged support?'

'This is your quid pro quo, Dulac.' De Ségur put his cellphone on speaker and dialed. 'Albert?'

'Yes, Mr de Ségur.'

'Go to the room. Put him facing the computer's minicam web camera.'

'Yes sir.'

Moments later, Albert called back. 'He's on now. Can you see him?'

'Yes.' De Ségur handed Dulac his cellphone.

'Jesus. It's the Pope.'

'Yes, the real one this time.'

Dulac sat thunderstruck. 'I thought you said he was lost in the Bay of Benghazi?'

'Correction. I said he became lost in the Bay of Benghazi. The stress of the amputation plus his near drowning when the Bellerophon sank were too much for him. He's suffering from, what do they call it? "Severe post-traumatic stress". I think that's the proper medical term. Pope Clement XXI is, to put it kindly, "lost".'

CHAPTER 39

His calls from Dulac and to the French Minister of Justice concluded, Cardinal Legnano went to the Segnatura room and broke the news to the cardinals.

'He's alive?' asked Sforza.

'Alive, but apparently mentally ill,' said Legnano. 'From what Dulac tells us, His Holiness is suffering from extensive post-traumatic stress.'

Signorelli spoke. 'I've had Haeflinger check the encrypted cellphone they found in Cardinal Gonzales's room. During the past two weeks he's been calling Belize almost daily, and there are a number of calls to the same number from various telephones in the Vatican.'

'My God,' said Sforza.

'What de Ségur is offering in exchange for the postponement of his trial is that we get the real Pope back to the Vatican here quickly, before the impostor dies, and we substitute him,' said Legnano. 'I've spoken with the French Minister of Justice and he agrees in principle. They would hold de Ségur in what they call '*garde à vue*'. Basically hold him under heavy surveillance, without charging him formally. They are willing to do so for four months only.'

'*Mio Dio*, it's beautiful. That way, the world will never know,' said Sforza, the illuminated expression on his face bordering on the beatific.

'Beautiful no, but ironic, definitely,' said Fouquet smiling.

'Ironic?' queried Legnano.

'Don't you find it ironic that the real pope has a fake heart attack and survives, and the false pope has a real stroke and will most probably die?'

The prelates sat in silence. All understood the implications of de Ségur's offer, and a sense of profound relief and satisfaction permeated the room. Words were superfluous.

Finally, Sforza broke the silence. 'Tell Dulac to inform de Ségur that we agree.'

'I already have, your Eminence,' said Legnano. 'De Ségur is waiting for a fax letter from the French Minister of Justice, whom I've called an hour ago. Minister George Berilet has scheduled an emergency meeting of the French Cabinet, and in principle has agreed to postpone de Ségur's trial. They fully realize the urgency of the situation. As part of the agreement, de Ségur will hire a private jet to fly Dulac and His Holiness directly to the Guidonia Air base. The plane will arrive here late tomorrow morning. Haeflinger and his men will be there to receive His Holiness, and bring him to the clinic. If all goes well, His Holiness will arrive before, well . . . before anything happens at the clinic.'

'What about the diary? De Ségur has our money,' said Sforza.

'Dulac tried to get hold of it. Apparently de Ségur wouldn't back down,' said Legnano. 'De Ségur insists he needs it as an insurance policy against the French government changing its mind and prosecuting early. He's left a special provision in his will: the diary is to be auctioned off shortly after his death.'

After a long moment, Signorelli, Fouquet, Sforza, and Legnano got up one by one and left the Segnatura room.

Led by Legnano, they walked, not hurriedly, in the direction of the Basilica. A general feeling of well-being permeated their beings. They had hoped and prayed for a miracle and it had happened. The papacy had come to a hair's breadth of collapsing, but in the end, stronger than the will of mere mortals, fate (some will say God) had intervened and decided for them. In a most strange way order, if not truth, had triumphed. At least for the moment.

The cardinals entered the Basilica, made their way to the gigantic, black marble Bernini altar and one by one, knelt down before it. For once in a very, very long time, they prayed together and gave thanks to the Lord.

EPILOGUE

On June 29, a Bombardier jet coming from Belize landed at Guidonia Air Force Base briefly, before resuming its flight to Paris. During the brief interval, a man with a heavily bandaged face was taken off the plane in a wheelchair, into a van carrying him to the Agostino Gemelli Clinic. He was admitted there under the name of David Silverman, an Israeli whose occupation was listed as actor, suffering from a stroke. Three days after being admitted, the hospital records show that said David Silverman died of a second stroke. No relatives could be found to claim the body, so according to Jewish law, it was cremated two days after his death.

The Vatican, 'L'Osservatore Romano,' July 2
Page 1
'After a fight for his life, the Pope was taken out of his coma, and underwent surgery to relieve pressure on his brain. The doctors classified his recovery as 'miraculous', under the circumstances. They have prescribed an undetermined period of rest for the pontiff: it appears that the stress of the operation on his brain has caused the pontiff to suffer from disorientation and cognitive difficulties. Cardinal Fouquet announced today that the ecumenical council, summoned by Pope Clement the

21st shortly before his stroke, has been postponed indefinitely. As Camerlengo, Cardinal Fouquet has taken over the pontiff's duties until His Holiness is able to return to office.'

Page 2
'Cardinal Estevan Gonzales, recently nominated head of the Congregation for the Promulgation of the Faith, has resigned yesterday for health reasons. His predecessor Cardinal Eugenio Brentano has temporarily taken over his previous functions, while awaiting a decision from the Pope.'

Paris, Sotheby's, October 27
At a recent auction for certain items belonging to the estate of the late Hugues de Ségur, a book entitled 'My Diary,' written by Hans-Georg Weber, ex-Nazi SS officer stationed in Naples during WWII, fetched 75,000 Euros, thereby setting a new record for a war officer's diary. Sotheby's representative indicated that the buyer wished to remain anonymous.

Lyon, Le Progrès, December 18, page 4
'During the annual General Assembly meeting of Interpol held today at Interpol's headquarters, General Secretary Richard Harris's four year mandate was not renewed. Instead, Jean Martignet, a twenty year veteran of the French Sureté, was elected in his place. Among staff members interviewed about the nomination, there was a general feeling of acceptance, as Martignet has promised to modernize the organization and lead it into the 21st century. One of his first projects will be to incorporate anew the function of Director of Crimes against Persons, previously abolished by his predecessor. According to well-informed sources, recently reinstated Interpol agent Thierry Dulac is the front-runner candidate for the post.'

Sarah Lawrence College, Bronxville, New York, December 20 'The Hard Way' college newspaper, page 4

'Dean Joanna Tooms of the Anthropology and Mythology Faculty is pleased to announce the return of Doctor Karen

Dawson to the faculty. After spending four years teaching at La Sorbonne, Professor Dawson has accepted a post teaching at the pre-doctoral level, in replacement of Professor Li Yung Sun who has returned to Seoul.'

THE END

Thank you for reading this book.

If you enjoyed it please leave feedback on Amazon or Goodreads, and if there is anything we missed or you have a question about, then please get in touch. We appreciate you choosing our book.

Founded in 2014 in Shoreditch, London, we at Joffe Books pride ourselves on our history of innovative publishing. We were thrilled to be shortlisted for Independent Publisher of the Year at the British Book Awards.

www.joffebooks.com

We're very grateful to eagle-eyed readers who take the time to contact us. Please send any errors you find to corrections@joffebooks.com. We'll get them fixed ASAP.

Printed in Great Britain
by Amazon

82613349R00181